# A Vindication of the Rights of Woman

# MARY WOLLSTONECRAFT

# A VINDICATION OF THE RIGHTS OF WOMAN

## WITH STRICTURES ON POLITICAL AND MORAL SUBJECTS

*Introduction by Katha Pollitt*

*Notes by Katherine Lee, University of Missouri*

THE MODERN LIBRARY

NEW YORK

# MARY WOLLSTONECRAFT

Mary Wollstonecraft, the pioneering feminist and Enlightenment thinker, who counted herself among "those who are bold enough to advance before the age they live in," was born in London on April 27, 1759. She was the second of seven children of Edward John Wollstonecraft, a would-be gentleman-farmer, and Elizabeth Dickson Wollstonecraft, an Irish woman from County Donegal. Wollstonecraft's lifelong crusade for independence and female equality was deeply rooted in a traumatic childhood. Her father was a violent alcoholic, who abused his wife and frequently relocated the family while squandering a substantial inheritance. What little formal education she received was at a day school for girls in the market town of Beverley, Yorkshire, where the Wollstonecrafts lived for six years. A close friendship with a cultivated young woman named Fanny Blood expanded her horizons and became the most formative experience of her adolescence.

Wollstonecraft left home at the age of nineteen. Determined to achieve financial independence, she secured employment as a companion to a wealthy widow in Bath. Three years later, however, she was called back to nurse her dying mother and subsequently assumed responsibility for the welfare of her younger sisters. Wollstonecraft came of age intellectually at the London community Newington Green, where she established a private school and associated with a circle of rational Dissenters, led by Dr. Richard Price, a moral philosopher and minister. Forced to close her school in 1786, she wrote *Thoughts on the Education of Daughters* (1787), a pedagogical treatise, and reluctantly accepted the demeaning position of governess to the daughters of Lord and Lady Kingsborough of County Cork, Ireland, only to be dismissed after nine months of service.

"I am going to be the first of a new genus," vowed Wollstonecraft when she returned to London in 1787 to embark on a career as a professional writer. With the help of eminent publisher Joseph Johnson, she issued *Mary, A Fiction* (1788), a semiautobiographical novel, and *Original Stories from Real Life* (1788), a children's book, illustrated by William Blake. While employed as a translator and reviewer on Johnson's liberal journal, the newly founded *Analytical Review*, she consorted with a group of radical intellectuals that included Swiss painter Henry Fuseli, political philosopher William Godwin, theologian Joseph Priestly, and veteran activist Thomas Paine. Wollstonecraft gained instant notoriety in 1790 with the publication of *A Vindication of the Rights of Men*, an angry response to Edmund Burke's *Reflections on the Revolution in France* (1790), a conservative attack on the French Revolution. Meanwhile, Wollstonecraft's controversial attack on Burke provoked hostile public reaction, and Horace Walpole later called her "a hyena in petticoats."

*A Vindication of the Rights of Woman*, Wollstonecraft's most famous and influential work, was published in 1792. A sustained argument for female emancipation that extended the Enlightenment credo of inalienable human rights to women, it is widely regarded as a landmark of feminist thought. "*A Vindication of the Rights of Woman* speaks as much to the problems of women at the turn of the twenty-first century as it did to those of the contemporaries of Mary Wollstonecraft," reflected critic and scholar Miriam Brody. And her biographer Eleanor Flexnor noted: "What is so astonishing about the *Vindication* is not that Wollstonecraft wrote it, but that she was alone in raising the issues that she did, in a period of social change first signaled by the rebellion of the American colonies against British rule and then by the tremendous upheaval of the French Revolution. Hers was the only audible voice raised to assert that women, as well as men, had an inalienable right to freedom, that they too were human beings."

Wollstonecraft journeyed to Paris in December 1792 to witness the French Revolution firsthand. Though horrified by the Reign of Terror, she wrote *An Historical and Moral View of the Origin and Progress of the*

*French Revolution, and the Effect It Has Produced in Europe* (1794), which explains the excesses of the revolution as a reaction to the despotism of the ancien régime and foresees an improved society emerging from the conflict. Wollstonecraft's ill-fated love affair with Gilbert Imlay, a dashing American businessman living in Paris, produced an illegitimate daughter, Fanny Imlay, and led her to two failed attempts at suicide. An interlude in Scandinavia inspired *Letters Written During a Short Residence in Sweden, Norway, and Denmark* (1796), a travelogue filled with sharp social commentary.

Mary Wollstonecraft returned to England in 1795 and soon became involved with William Godwin, whom she married on March 29, 1797. She died of blood poisoning on September 10, 1797, eleven days after giving birth to a daughter. This child, Mary Wollstonecraft Godwin, would later marry the poet Percy Bysshe Shelley and write the gothic novel *Frankenstein* (1818). In 1798 William Godwin published his candid *Memoirs of the Author of A Vindication of the Rights of Woman*, which scandalized the public, and edited Wollstonecraft's *Posthumous Works,* a four-volume opus that included *The Wrongs of Woman; or Maria,* an unfinished novel exposing the injustices inflicted on women by the English legal system.

"Mary Wollstonecraft's life had been an experiment from the start, an attempt to make human conventions conform more closely to human needs," observed Virginia Woolf. "The outbreak of revolution in France expressed some of her deepest theories and convictions, and she dashed off in the heat of that extraordinary moment those two eloquent and daring books—[*A Vindication of the Rights of Men*] and *A Vindication of the Rights of Woman,* which are so true that they seem now to contain nothing new in them—their originality has become our commonplace. . . . We hear her voice and trace her influence even now among the living."

"*A Vindication of the Rights of Woman* establishes Wollstonecraft as the greatest of polemical feminists," remarked Ellen Moers in *The New York Review of Books.* "She wished to teach her whole sex not to grovel. From the observation of her own life, and that of her sisters, friends, pupils, and employers; from wide reading in the works of the *philosophes,* to whose company she aspired, Wollstonecraft came to understand the social conditions governing the lives of all women and to denounce their institutionalized repression—a social fact that she was the first to grasp in its entirety, and that her writings did most to change."

# Contents

# INTRODUCTION

## Katha Pollitt

*A Vindication of the Rights of Woman* was published in 1792, the same year the French National Convention abolished the monarchy, Tom Paine brought out *The Rights of Man,* and a mass petition campaign in Britain called for the abolition of slavery. Written at white heat—in six weeks by one account, three months by another—it was an instant success, much read and more discussed, and it made its thirty-three-year-old author a minor celebrity. Only a few years before, Mary Wollstonecraft had been working her way through the very short list of occupations open to genteel women forced to earn their own living: She had been a lady's companion, a seamstress, a schoolteacher, and a lonely governess in rural Ireland to the daughters of Lady Kingsborough, whom she detested as a tyrant and a fool and who returned the compliment by firing her. For most women of her day and class, marriage would have been the only way of escaping from looming disaster, but Wollstonecraft had seen marriage close up. As a child, she had slept outside her mother's door to keep her brutal father away; as a young woman, she had arranged a precipitous escape for her sister Eliza, whose postpartum derangement Mary attributed to marital abuse; a year later she had rushed to Portugal only to find her beloved newlywed friend Fanny Blood dying in childbirth. Wollstonecraft resolved to make her way as a writer. It was a bold move, especially for a woman—but then Wollstonecraft was nothing if not daring: On the boat back from Portugal, she had single-handedly argued the captain into taking on board the crew of a foundering French vessel; they would otherwise have drowned. Wollstonecraft found her way to Joseph Johnson, the publisher, and was welcomed into his brilliant circle of radicals and Dissenters—Tom Paine, William Blake, the Swiss-born painter Henry Fuseli, Joseph Priestley, Dr. Richard Price. In their discussions and debates, they addressed and referred to her as Wollstonecraft, as if she were a man like themselves. Blake illustrated her children's book, *Original Stories from Real Life*; his poem "Mary" is probably about her:

> And thine is a Face of sweet Love in despair,
> And thine is a Face of mild sorrow & care,
> And thine is a Face of wild terror & fear
> That shall never be quiet till laid on its bier.

Contrary to myth, *Vindication*'s early reception was largely favorable. Conservative publications mostly ignored it. Liberal reviewers overlooked or dismissed its radical implications and welcomed it as a treatise on the importance of education and moral reform for women, a not unpopular cause. That aristocratic women and the increasing numbers of middle-class women who imitated them were ignorant, frivolous, coquettish, and idle was, after all, a widespread sentiment, albeit one expressed with particular vigor by Wollstonecraft; nor was she alone in claiming that education, that Enlightenment panacea, would make women more serious, useful, industrious, chaste, interesting, and content—better wives, better mothers, better neighbors, better candidates for heaven.

The image of Wollstonecraft as a harpy, a loose woman, and a general threat to king and country, hearth and home, mostly came later. First, the Jacobin Terror demoralized many who had welcomed the French Revolution and drove British opinion rightward. Then, after Wollstonecraft's death—at thirty-seven, following the birth of her daughter Mary—her husband, the anarchist philosopher William Godwin, published a candid memoir, which, as is so often the case with memoirs, did lasting damage to its ostensible honoree. Godwin revealed that Mary had been madly in love with Henry Fuseli and had begged to live with him and his wife; that she had never been married to Gilbert Imlay, the American adventurer-businessman who was the father of her daughter Fanny; that she had twice attempted suicide over Imlay's growing coldness, and, to cap it off, had been pregnant when she married Godwin. Is this what those fine phrases about women as reasonable beings came down to? her critics now demanded. Overthrowing governments and having babies outside marriage? Throwing yourself at men and into rivers? In an instant, *Vindication* went from progressive tract to radical feminist manifesto, and its author endured a posthumous stoning that has endured to our day. In a caricature for *The New York Review of Books* in 1972, at the very crest of the reborn women's movement, David Levine gave Wollstonecraft a disapproving scowl (her portraits by John Opie show a pensive, beautiful woman who radiates intelligence). Reviewing Claire Tomalin's 1974 biography in the *Times Literary Supplement,* Richard Cobb called her "always silly," "almost always egotistical," and "generally envious, rancorous, and meddlesome." Reviewing Janet Todd's 2000 biography in the *London Review of Books,* Susan Eilenberg castigated Wollstonecraft for "arrogance, self-pity, hypocrisy, histrionics and hypochondria," as well as "rancor" and "narcissism." A writer, self-centered! Imagine. At the same time, women as different as George Eliot and Emma Goldman have been drawn to Wollstonecraft, in whose life eighteenth-century rationalism and nineteenth-century romanticism seem so curiously mingled and who in her accomplishment and her struggles stands as an emblematic figure of female genius and rebellion. One isn't surprised, somehow, that of her two daughters, Fanny committed suicide and Mary eloped with the poet Shelley and, while still in her teens, wrote *Frankenstein.*

Modern readers may scorn or thrill to Wollstonecraft's dramatic life and intense personality—she was definitely a diva—but *A Vindication of the Rights of Woman* is as hard to get clearly into our sights in 2001 as it was in the 1790s. In her brief biographical sketch of Wollstonecraft, Virginia Woolf, who admired the author's improvised, passionate dash through life, thought history had rendered *Vindication* and its predecessor, *A Vindication of the Rights of Men,* obsolete: "They are so true that they seem now to contain nothing new in them—their originality has become our commonplace." Nothing new? Commonplace? When that essay was published, in 1929, British women under thirty had just won the vote and wives had had the right to divorce their adulterous husbands for six years. Legal, economic, and social sex discrimination was a ubiquitous feature of daily life. The best schools and the best universities—as Woolf herself observed in *A Room of One's Own* and *Three Guineas*—were still overwhelmingly reserved for men—men of privilege, that is. *A Vindication of the Rights of Men,* Woll-stonecraft's call for egalitarian democracy, had fared no better. In 1929, after all, Britain still possessed a monarch, a hereditary aristocracy, a House of Lords, an established church, and a colonial empire of black and brown people kept in subjection by armed force. Indeed, except for the empire, those institutions persist in Britain today. Perhaps there is something in Wollstonecraft's writings that is not so dated after all.

Or, rather, perhaps *Vindication* seems uncontroversial not because its arguments have become common wisdom but because the implications of those arguments go further than we may care to look. To re-gard women as fully possessed of reason and to extend to women the "rights of man" may not be so simple as it seems. It is worth noting that the bourgeois revolutions of the eighteenth century, for all the homage they paid to reason and rights and liberty and equality, did lit-tle or nothing to improve the legal, economic, or social standing of women. Abigail Adams's plaintive, playful direction to her hus-band John Adams, then engaged in the Continental Congress— "Remember the ladies"—did not prevent him or his fellow Founding Fathers from ignoring the ladies entirely. In France, women played a crucial role in the revolution, as agitators and streetfighters, intellec-tuals, political hostesses, and influential wives and mistresses of male politicians; women had their own political clubs, and Olympe de Gouges and Théroigne de Méricourt wrote feminist polemics even more daring than Wollstonecraft's. These efforts gained women noth-ing: de Gouges was guillotined, Théroigne was confined to a mental hospital, and the Napoleonic code that emerged from the turmoil of the revolution was arguably even more oppressive to women than the laws of the ancien régime.

It is customary to speak of the American and French revolutions as based on the ideology of bourgeois individualism, but this is not quite right: The married male citizen was not just an individual but the head of a household. His home was his castle—not also the castle of his wife. As a husband, he represented his wife at the polls and controlled her money and property; his domicile was her legal residence, to which she could be forcibly returned should she leave him; he was legally responsible should she fall into debt or be charged with a crime committed with his knowledge. Vestiges of this old system still exist: Think of all those official forms that ask for "head of household," not to mention the still prevalent custom of women's taking their hus-band's last name upon marriage.

Mary Wollstonecraft was not the first writer to call for women to receive a real, challenging education that would equip them for adult life, not just a few years of haphazard schooling plus a smattering of "accomplishments"—French, piano, watercolors—intended to increase their value on the marriage market. But she was the first to connect the education of women to the transformation of women's social position, of relations between the sexes, and even of society itself. She was the first to argue that women's intellectual equality would—and should—have actual consequences. The winds of change sweep through her pages: "Let not men then in the pride of power, use the same arguments that tyrannic kings and venal ministers have used, and fallaciously assert that woman ought to be subjected because she has always been so.—But, when man, governed by reasonable laws, enjoys his natural freedom, let him despise woman, if she do not share it with him; and, till that glorious period arrives, in descanting on the folly of the sex, let him not overlook his own."

In the eighteenth century, "the sex" was a synonym for "women," as "men" meant both males and people—and that, in a nutshell, was the problem Wollstonecraft confronted: He is rational, she is sensual; he is culture, she is nature; he exists for himself, she exists in relation to his desires; he is a whole human being, only sometimes defined as male, but she is always a partial being, always at every moment female. It was not only men who saw gender in this light—women did too: "This desire of being always women is the very consciousness which degrades the sex." But how could women—"the sex"—escape the constraints of femininity without sacrificing their sexuality? At times, Wollstonecraft writes as if women could be equal to men only to the extent that they cut themselves off from love, passion, desire—the very thing she herself was unable to do.

Wollstonecraft is sometimes criticized for her harsh and sweeping attack on women. Whatever its biographical and psychological origins, it was a brilliant rhetorical strategy: Having conceded the veracity of the misogynist portrait of her sex, she turns the tables. Women are what society and men have made them: "taught from their infancy that beauty is woman's sceptre, the mind shapes itself to the body, and roaming around its gilt cage, only seeks to adorn its prison."

Men have no right to complain if they find themselves saddled with a useless child-wife prone to vapors and infidelity. This is what raising women for nothing but marriage and man-pleasing has produced: Denied other forms of power, women will tyrannize through sex and cunning and weakness. Very well, but what if men's complaints were not so sincere? What if they actually preferred the silly, manipulative, servile, dependent child-women? Rousseau, after all, is a particular target of Wollstonecraft's sarcasm, precisely because in *Emile*, his novel of education, he designs for young Sophie an upbringing calculated to turn her into a docile featherhead. Burke, her other major foe, had declared that weakness and imperfection were part of the very definition of beauty, the female principle, as strength and power belonged to the male principle, the sublime.

Wollstonecraft was that rare combination, a sublime woman. She wasted little time trying to persuade men that they should prefer women who were their equals—too bad for you if you don't, was more her line. Women had to be educated for the same reasons as men: to develop their capacities and talents, to withstand the vicissitudes of life, to be able to earn a living if they had to, to be moral mothers who would raise moral children and to be worthy of God. She did not argue for the worth of a distinctive women's culture or set of values or innate nature: She would have little sympathy for, say, Carol Gilligan's claim that women are empathic as opposed to rational, follow a distinct path to moral maturity, and have different educational needs than their male classmates.

The voice of *Vindication* is like no other woman writer's voice before and like few since: sarcastic, energetic, unapologetic, passionate, prickly, proud. Wollstonecraft does not defer. She does not try to be charming or clever or deft. She does not try to make the reader like her. Admire her, yes, and justly so: For a young, self-educated woman to present herself as the intellectual equal of Rousseau on the left and Burke on the right took remarkable courage. Wollstonecraft not only challenged these celebrated thinkers on their own philosophical grounds, she pursued them, she trapped them, she trampled them, and, for the coup de grâce, she lumped them together with conventional mediocrities like Dr. Fordyce and Dr. Gregory, authors of popular advice books for young girls.

Read as a treatise on education, *Vindication* has been completely, well, vindicated. Today, girls and women study every subject under the sun (including botany, as Wollstonecraft suggested they do, to the horror of one critic for whom pistils and stamens meant only one thing) and engage with distinction in every field. With the notable exception of sex education, which is still controversial, even her most advanced pedagogical notions have come to be the norm: public schools (complete with socially stratified academic and vocational tracks, unfortunately), coeducation, athletic training for girls, child-centered "progressive"education—even home schooling!

And yet, read carefully, *Vindication* bristles with live issues and questions both unsettled and unsettling. Wollstonecraft herself suggested that raising girls to be full human beings would lead to unpredictable places—maybe someday women would be physicians; maybe they would vote; who knows but that with proper training they could be as strong as men. Yet, like feminists today, she struggled with the interconnected issues of motherhood, self-development, work, romance, and equality in the home. You can see the strain of combining these not easily compatible things in her claim that tepid or even unhappy marriages were best for child rearing, and in her curious attraction to the situation of the widow with children. She wanted women to be independent, to develop their gifts, to take part in the world, to be equal partners in marriage—but she also took for granted that mothers, and not fathers, would be the primary parents and that domestic responsibilities and high achievement were incompatible.

In some ways, Wollstonecraft was ahead not only of her time but of our own. She was an early proponent of the view that the mind has no sexual character and that gender differences and male dominance are socially constructed, created by the way men and women are treated from the moment of birth—as by, for example, giving dolls to little girls and letting boys run wild outdoors. This idea has come under continuous attack—from religious authorities, who see women's subordination as divinely ordained; from Freudians, for whom "anatomy is destiny"; and most recently from evolutionary psychologists, who believe that natural selection has shaped the sexes to be the coy flirts and hell-raising soldiers Wollstonecraft despised. At the popular level, we may pay lip service to the notion of the equality of the sexes, but someone is buying all those copies of *Men Are from Mars, Women Are from Venus* and choosing Barbie for daughters and GI Joe for sons. The man-trapping manipulative cunning that Wollstonecraft deplored in young women was on full display in *The Rules;* the wifely submission she deemed an affront to God is the recently affirmed official doctrine of the Southern Baptist church, the largest Protestant denomination in America, which has also, for good measure, banned women from the ministry.

Like Simone de Beauvoir, who took a similar caustic view of her sex, Wollstonecraft wrote as a solitary female venturing into an overwhelmingly masculine intellectual world. She had no women's movement to back her up or contest her views from within a feminist context—to remind her, say, that not all women were fashion plates and flibbertigibbets. (Interestingly, *Vindication* is not even addressed to women, who are always referred to as "they," never "we." Its intended audience is the mostly male liberal intelligentsia.) It is easy, but anachronistic, for modern readers to criticize her for lacking a sense of female solidarity or sisterhood, for underestimating female sexuality, for equating the masculine with the human, and for accepting at face value concepts such as "reason" and "rights." Nobody thought like a late-twentieth-century feminist in 1792. It was hard enough to be an eighteenth-century feminist.

Wollstonecraft grasped intuitively what many other feminists, and many other leftists, have not: that the condition of women was part and parcel of society as a whole. Changing the position of women would require immense economic and social changes—and would spark still more. It is not an accident that *Vindication*, the first modern feminist text, was written by a supporter of the French Revolution: The rights of men and the rights of women would be vindicated together. True, Wollstonecraft primarily addressed the situation of women who were middle-class or higher—in her unfinished novel *Maria, Or the Wrongs of Woman*, she would take up the issues of class in greater depth—but no one who was concerned only with them could have written her books, or lived her life. She has been called a liberal feminist, but if by liberal we mean someone who wishes to ameliorate but not fundamentally to alter society, Wollstonecraft was no liberal; she was a revolutionary. It was of prostitutes, after all—those females middle-class women were not supposed to mention, much less champion—that Wollstonecraft wrote indelibly, "It is not charity but justice that is wanting in the world."

Circumstances change and customs alter, but as long as those words ring true, Mary Wollstonecraft will be a living writer.

———

KATHA POLLITT is a poet and columnist for *The Nation*. She is the author, most recently, of *Subject to Debate: Sense and Dissents on Women, Politics, and Culture*. She lives in New York City.

# Author's Introduction

After considering the historic page, and viewing the living world with anxious solicitude, the most melancholy emotions of sorrowful indignation have depressed my spirits, and I have sighed when obliged to confess that either Nature has made a great difference between man and man, or that the civilization which has hitherto taken place in the world has been very partial. I have turned over various books written on the subject of education, and patiently observed the conduct of parents and the management of schools; but what has been the result?—a profound conviction that the neglected education of my fellow-creatures is the grand source of the misery I deplore, and that women, in particular, are rendered weak and wretched by a variety of concurring causes, originating from one hasty conclusion. The conduct and manners of women, in fact, evidently prove that their minds are not in a healthy state; for, like the flowers which are planted in too rich a soil, strength and usefulness are sacrificed to beauty; and the flaunting leaves, after having pleased a fastidious eye, fade, disregarded on the stalk, long before the season when they ought to have arrived at maturity. One cause of this barren blooming I attribute to a false system of education, gathered from the books written on this subject by men who, considering females rather as women than human creatures, have been more anxious to make them alluring mistresses than affectionate wives and rational mothers; and the understanding of the sex has been so bubbled by this specious homage, that the civilized women of the present century, with a few exceptions, are only anxious to inspire love, when they ought to cherish a nobler ambition, and by their abilities and virtues exact respect.

In a treatise, therefore, on female rights and manners, the works which have been particularly written for their improvement must not be overlooked, especially when it is asserted, in direct terms, that the minds of women are enfeebled by false refinement; that the books of instruction, written by men of genius, have had the same tendency as more frivolous productions; and that, in the true style of Mahometanism,[1] they are treated as a kind of subordinate beings, and not as a part of the human species, when improvable reason is allowed to be the dignified distinction which raises men above the brute creation, and puts a natural sceptre in a feeble hand.

Yet, because I am a woman, I would not lead my readers to suppose that I mean violently to agitate the contested question respecting the quality or inferiority of the sex; but as the subject lies in my way, and I cannot pass it over without subjecting the main tendency of my reasoning to misconstruction, I shall stop a moment to deliver, in a few words, my opinion. In the government of the physical world it is observable that the female in point of strength is, in general, inferior to the male. This is the law of Nature; and it does not appear to be suspended or abrogated in favour of woman. A degree of physical superiority cannot, therefore, be denied, and it is a noble prerogative! But not content with this natural pre-eminence, men endeavour to sink us still lower, merely to render us alluring objects for a moment; and women, intoxicated by the adoration which men, under the influence of their senses, pay them, do not seek to obtain a durable interest in their hearts, or to become the friends of the fellow-creatures who find amusement in their society.

I am aware of an obvious inference. From every quarter have I heard exclamations against masculine women, but where are they to be found? If by this appellation men mean to inveigh against their ardour in hunting, shooting, and gaming, I shall most cordially join in the cry; but if it be against the imitation of manly virtues, or, more properly speaking, the attainment of those talents and virtues, the exercise of which ennobles the human character, and which raises females in the scale of animal being, when they are comprehensively termed mankind, all those who view them with a philosophic eye must, I should think, wish with me, that they may every day grow more and more masculine.

This discussion naturally divides the subject. I shall first consider women in the grand light of human creatures, who, in common with men, are placed on this earth to unfold their faculties; and afterwards I shall more particularly point out their peculiar designation.

I wish also to steer clear of an error which many respectable writers have fallen into; for the instruction which has hitherto been addressed to women, has rather been applicable to *ladies*, if the little indirect advice that is scattered through "Sandford and Merton"[2] be excepted; but, addressing my sex in a firmer tone, I pay particular attention to those in the middle class, because they appear to be in the most natural state. Perhaps the seeds of false refinement, immorality, and vanity, have ever been shed by the great. Weak, artificial beings, raised above the common wants and affections of their race, in a premature unnatural manner, undermine the very foundation of virtue, and spread corruption through the whole mass of society! As a class of mankind they have the strongest claim to pity; the education of the rich tends to render them vain and helpless, and the unfolding mind is not strengthened by the practice of those duties which dignify the human character. They only live to amuse themselves, and by the same law which in Nature invariably produces certain effects, they soon only afford barren amusement.

But as I purpose taking a separate view of the different ranks of society, and of the moral character of women in each, this hint is for the present sufficient; and I have only alluded to the subject because it appears to me to be the very essence of an introduction to give a cursory account of the contents of the work it introduces.

My own sex, I hope, will excuse me, if I treat them like rational creatures, instead of flattering their *fascinating* graces, and viewing them as if they were in a state of perpetual childhood, unable to stand alone. I earnestly wish to point out in what true dignity and human happiness consists. I wish to persuade women to endeavour to acquire strength, both of mind and body, and to convince them that the soft phrases, susceptibility of heart, delicacy of sentiment, and refinement of taste, are almost synonymous with epithets of weakness, and that those beings who are only the objects of pity, and that kind of love which has been termed its sister, will soon become objects of contempt.

Dismissing, then, those pretty feminine phrases, which the men condescendingly use to soften our slavish dependence, and despising that weak elegancy of mind, exquisite sensibility, and sweet docility of manners, supposed to be the sexual characteristics of the weaker vessel, I wish to show that elegance is inferior to virtue, that the first object of laudable ambition is to obtain a character as a human being, regardless of the distinction of sex, and that secondary views should be brought to this simple touchstone.

This is a rough sketch of my plan; and should I express my conviction with the energetic emotions that I feel whenever I think of the subject, the dictates of experience and reflection will be felt by some of my readers. Animated by this important object, I shall disdain to cull my phrases or polish my style. I aim at being useful, and sincerity will render me unaffected; for wishing rather to persuade by the force of my arguments than dazzle by the elegance of my language, I shall not waste my time in rounding periods, or in fabricating the turgid bombast of artificial feelings, which, coming from the head, never reach the heart. I shall be employed about things, not words! and, anxious to render my sex more respectable members of society, I shall try to avoid that flowery diction which has slided from essays into novels, and from novels into familiar letters and conversations.

These pretty superlatives, dropping glibly from the tongue, vitiate the taste, and create a kind of sickly delicacy that turns away from simple unadorned truth; and a deluge of false sentiments and over-stretched feelings, stifling the natural emotions of the heart, render the domestic pleasures insipid, that ought to sweeten the exercise of those severe duties, which educate a rational and immortal being for a nobler field of action.

The education of women has of late been more attended to than formerly; yet they are still reckoned a frivolous sex, and ridiculed or pitied by the writers who endeavour by satire or instruction to improve them. It is acknowledged that they spend many of the first years of their lives in acquiring a smattering of accomplishments; meanwhile strength of body and mind are sacrificed to libertine notions of beauty, to the desire of establishing themselves—the only way women can rise in the world—by marriage. And this desire making mere animals of them, when they marry they act as such children may be expected to act—they dress, they paint, and nickname God's creatures. Surely these weak beings are only fit for a seraglio! Can they be expected to govern a family with judgement, or take care of the poor babes whom they bring into the world?

If, then, it can be fairly deduced from the present conduct of the sex, from the prevalent fondness for pleasure which takes place of ambition and those nobler passions that open and enlarge the soul, that the instruction which women have hitherto received has only tended, with the constitution of civil society, to render them insignificant objects of desire—mere propagators of fools!—if it can be proved that in aiming to accomplish them, without cultivating their understandings, they are taken out of their sphere of duties, and made ridiculous and useless when the short-lived bloom of beauty is over,* I presume that *rational* men will excuse me for endeavouring to persuade them to become more masculine and respectable.

Indeed the word masculine is only a bugbear; there is little reason to fear that women will acquire too much courage or fortitude, for their apparent inferiority with respect to bodily strength must render them in some degree dependent on men in the various relations of life; but why should it be increased by prejudices that give a sex to virtue, and confound simple truths with sensual reveries?

Women are, in fact, so much degraded by mistaken notions of female excellence, that I do not mean to add a paradox when I assert that this artificial weakness produces a propensity to tyrannize, and gives birth to cunning, the natural opponent of strength, which leads them to play off those contemptible infantine airs that undermine esteem even whilst they excite desire. Let men become more chaste and modest, and if women do not grow wiser in the same ratio it will be clear that they have weaker understandings. It seems scarcely necessary to say that I now speak of the sex in general. Many individuals have more sense than their male relatives; and, as nothing preponderates where there is a constant struggle for an equilibrium without it has naturally more gravity, some women govern their husbands without degrading themselves, because intellect will always govern.

---

*A lively writer (I cannot recollect his name) asks what business women turned of forty have to do in the world?

TO

# M. TALLEYRAND-PÉRIGORD

### *Late Bishop of Autun*[1]

Sir,—Having read with great pleasure a pamphlet[2] which you have lately published, I dedicate this volume to you—the first dedication that I have ever written, to induce you to read it with attention; and, because I think that you will understand me, which I do not suppose many pert witlings will, who may ridicule the arguments they are unable to answer. But, sir, I carry my respect for your understanding still farther; so far that I am confident you will not throw my work aside, and hastily conclude that I am in the wrong, because you did not view the subject in the same light yourself. And, pardon my frankness, but I must observe, that you treated it in too cursory a manner, contented to consider it as it had been considered formerly, when the rights of man, not to advert to woman, were trampled on as chimerical—I call upon you, therefore, now to weigh what I have advanced respecting the rights of woman and national education; and I call with the firm tone of humanity, for my arguments, sir, are dictated by a disinterested spirit—I plead for my sex, not for myself. Independence I have long considered as the grand blessing of life, the basis of every virtue; and independence I will ever secure by contracting my wants, though I were to live on a barren heath.

It is then an affection for the whole human race that makes my pen dart rapidly along to support what I believe to be the cause of virtue; and the same motive leads me earnestly to wish to see woman placed in a station in which she would advance, instead of retarding, the progress of those glorious principles that give a substance to morality. My opinion, indeed, respecting the rights and duties of woman seems to flow so naturally from these simple principles, that I think it scarcely possible but that some of the enlarged minds who formed your admirable constitution will coincide with me.

In France there is undoubtedly a more general diffusion of knowledge than in any part of the European world, and I attribute it, in a great measure, to the social intercourse which has long subsisted between the sexes. It is true—I utter my sentiments with freedom—that in France the very essence of sensuality has been extracted to regale the voluptuary, and a kind of sentimental lust has prevailed, which, together with the system of duplicity that the whole tenor of their political and civil government taught, have given a sinister sort of sagacity to the French character, properly termed *finesse*, from which naturally flow a polish of manners that injures the substance by hunting sincerity out of society. And modesty, the fairest garb of virtue! has been more grossly insulted in France than even in England, till their women have treated as *prudish* that attention to decency which brutes instinctively observe.

Manners and morals are so nearly allied that they have often been confounded; but, although the former should only be the natural reflection of the latter, yet, when various causes have produced factitious and corrupt manners, which are very early caught, morality becomes an empty name. The personal reserve, and sacred respect for cleanliness and delicacy in domestic life, which French women almost despise, are the graceful pillars of modesty; but, far from despising them, if the pure flame of patriotism have reached their bosoms, they should labour to improve the morals of their fellow-citizens, by teaching men, not only to respect modesty in women, but to acquire it themselves, as the only way to merit their esteem.

· Contending for the rights of woman, my main argument is built on this simple principle, that if she be not prepared by education to become the companion of man, she will stop the progress of knowledge and virtue; for truth must be common to all, or it will be inefficacious with respect to its influence on general practice. And how can woman be expected to co-operate unless she knows why she ought to be virtuous? unless freedom strengthens her reason till she comprehends her duty, and see in what manner it is connected with her real good. If children are to be educated to understand the true principle of patriotism, their mother must be a patriot; and the love of mankind, from which an orderly train of virtues spring, can only be produced by considering the moral and civil interest of mankind; but the education and situation of woman at present shuts her out from such investigations.

In this work I have produced many arguments, which to me were conclusive, to prove that the prevailing notion respecting a sexual character was subversive of morality, and I have contended, that to render the human body and mind more perfect, chastity must more universally prevail, and that chastity will never be respected in the male world till the person of a woman is not, as it were, idolized, when little virtue or sense embellish it with the grand traces of mental beauty, or the interesting simplicity of affection.

Consider, sir, dispassionately these observations, for a glimpse of this truth seemed to open before you when you observed, "that to see one-half of the human race excluded by the other from all participation of government was a political phenomenon that, according to abstract principles, it was impossible to explain."[3] If so, on what does your constitution rest? If the abstract rights of man will bear discussion and explanation, those of woman, by a parity of reasoning, will not shrink from the same test; though a different opinion prevails in this country, built on the very arguments which you use to justify the oppression of woman—prescription.

Consider—I address you as a legislator—whether, when men contend for their freedom, and to be allowed to judge for themselves respecting their own happiness, it be not inconsistent and unjust to subjugate women, even though you firmly believe that you are acting in the manner best calculated to promote their happiness? Who made man the exclusive judge, if woman partake with him of the gift of reason?

In this style argue tyrants of every denomination, from the weak king to the weak father of a family; they are all eager to crush reason, yet always assert that they usurp its throne only to be useful. Do you not act a similar part when you *force* all women, by denying them civil and political rights, to remain immured in their families groping in the dark? for surely, sir, you will not assert that a duty can be binding which is not founded on reason? If, indeed, this be their destination, arguments may be drawn from reason; and thus augustly supported, the more understanding women acquire, the more they will be attached to their duty—comprehending it—for unless they comprehend it, unless their morals be fixed on the same immutable principle as those of man, no authority can make them discharge it in a virtuous manner. They may be convenient slaves, but slavery will have its constant effect, degrading the master and the abject dependent.

But if women are to be excluded, without having a voice, from a participation of the natural rights of mankind, prove first, to ward off the charge of injustice and inconsistency, that they want reason, else this flaw in your NEW CONSTITUTION[4] will ever show that man must, in some shape, act like a tyrant, and tyranny, in whatever part of society it rears its brazen front, will ever undermine morality.

I have repeatedly asserted, and produced what appeared to me irrefragable arguments drawn from matters of fact to prove my assertion, that women cannot by force be confined to domestic concerns; for they will, however ignorant, intermeddle with more weighty affairs, neglecting private duties only to disturb, by cunning tricks, the orderly plans of reason which rise above their comprehension.

Besides, whilst they are only made to acquire personal accomplishments, men will seek for pleasure in variety, and faithless husbands will make faithless wives; such ignorant beings, indeed, will be very excusable when, not taught to respect public good, nor allowed any civil rights, they attempt to do themselves justice by retaliation.

The box of mischief thus opened in society, what is to preserve private virtue, the only security of public freedom and universal happiness?

Let there be then no coercion *established* in society, and the common law of gravity prevailing, the sexes will fall into their proper places. And now that more equitable laws are forming your citizens, marriage may become more sacred; your young men may choose wives from motives of affection, and your maidens allow love to root out vanity.

The father of a family will not then weaken his constitution and debase his sentiments by visiting the harlot, nor forget, in obeying the call of appetite, the purpose for which it was implanted. And the mother will not neglect her children to practise the arts of coquetry, when sense and modesty secure her the friendship of her husband.

But, till men become attentive to the duty of a father, it is vain to expect women to spend that time in their nursery which they, "wise in their generation," choose to spend at their glass; for this exertion of cunning is only an instinct of nature to enable them to obtain indirectly a little of that power of which they are unjustly denied a share; for, if women are not permitted to enjoy legitimate rights, they will render both men and themselves vicious to obtain illicit privileges.

I wish, sir, to set some investigations of this kind afloat in France; and should they lead to a confirmation of my principles when your constitution is revised, the Rights of Woman may be respected, if it be fully proved that reason calls for this respect, and loudly demands JUSTICE for one-half of the human race.

I am, Sir,
Yours respectfully,
M.W.

# NOTE

When I began to write this work, I divided it into three parts, supposing that one volume would contain a full discussion of the arguments
which seemed to me to rise naturally from a few simple principles; but
fresh illustrations occurring as I advanced, I now present only the first
part to the public.

Many subjects, however, which I have cursorily alluded to, call for
particular investigation, especially the laws relative to women, and the
consideration of their peculiar duties. These will furnish ample matter for a second volume,[1] which in due time will be published, to elucidate some of the sentiments, and complete many of the sketches
begun in the first.

# A Vindication of the
# Rights of Woman

# CHAPTER I

# The Rights and Involved Duties of Mankind Considered

In the present state of society it appears necessary to go back to first principles in search of the most simple truths, and to dispute with some prevailing prejudice every inch of ground. To clear my way, I must be allowed to ask some plain questions, and the answers will probably appear as unequivocal as the axioms on which reasoning is built; though, when entangled with various motives of action, they are formally contradicted, either by the words or conduct of men.

In what does man's pre-eminence over the brute creation consist? The answer is as clear as that a half is less than the whole, in Reason.

What acquirement exalts one being above another? Virtue, we spontaneously reply.

For what purpose were the passions implanted? That man by struggling with them might attain a degree of knowledge denied to the brutes, whispers Experience.

Consequently the perfection of our nature and capability of happiness must be estimated by the degree of reason, virtue, and knowledge, that distinguish the individual, and direct the laws which bind society: and that from the exercise of reason, knowledge and virtue naturally flow, is equally undeniable, if mankind be viewed collectively.

The rights and duties of man thus simplified, it seems almost impertinent to attempt to illustrate truths that appear so incontrovertible; yet such deeply rooted prejudices have clouded reason, and such spurious qualities have assumed the name of virtues, that it is necessary to pursue the course of reason as it has been perplexed and involved in error, by various adventitious circumstances, comparing the simple axiom with casual deviations.

Men, in general, seem to employ their reason to justify prejudices, which they have imbibed, they can scarcely trace how, rather than to root them out. The mind must be strong that resolutely forms its own principles; for a kind of intellectual cowardice prevails which makes many men shrink from the task, or only do it by halves. Yet the imperfect conclusions thus drawn, are frequently very plausible, because they are built on partial experience, on just, though narrow, views.

Going back to first principles, vice skulks, with all its native deformity, from close investigation; but a set of shallow reasoners are always exclaiming that these arguments prove too much, and that a measure rotten at the core may be expedient. Thus expediency is continually contrasted with simple principles, till truth is lost in a mist of words, virtue, in forms, and knowledge rendered a sounding nothing, by the specious prejudices that assume its name.

That the society is formed in the wisest manner, whose constitution is founded on the nature of man, strikes, in the abstract, every thinking being so forcibly, that it looks like presumption to endeavour to bring forward proofs; though proof must be brought, or the strong hold of prescription will never be forced by reason; yet to urge prescription as an argument to justify the depriving men (or women) of their natural rights, is one of the absurd sophisms which daily insult common sense.

The civilization of the bulk of the people of Europe is very partial; nay, it may be made a question, whether they have acquired any virtues in exchange for innocence, equivalent to the misery produced by the vices that have been plastered over unsightly ignorance, and the freedom which has been bartered for splendid slavery. The desire of dazzling by riches, the most certain pre-eminence that man can obtain, the pleasure of commanding flattering sycophants, and many other complicated low calculations of doting self-love, have all contributed to overwhelm the mass of mankind, and make liberty a convenient handle for mock patriotism. For whilst rank and titles are held of the utmost importance, before which Genius "must hide its diminished head,"[1] it is, with a few exceptions, very unfortunate for a nation when a man of abilities, without rank or property, pushes himself forward to notice. Alas! what unheard-of misery have thousands suffered to purchase a cardinal's hat for an intriguing obscure adventurer, who longed to be ranked with princes, or lord it over them by seizing the triple crown!

Such, indeed, has been the wretchedness that has flowed from hereditary honours, riches, and monarchy, that men of lively sensibility have almost uttered blasphemy in order to justify the dispensations of Providence. Man has been held out as independent of His power who made him, or as a lawless planet darting from its orbit to steal the celestial fire of reason; and the vengeance of Heaven, lurking in the subtile flame, like Pandora's pent-up mischiefs, sufficiently punished his temerity, by introducing evil into the world.

Impressed by this view of the misery and disorder which pervaded society, and fatigued with jostling against artificial fools, Rousseau[2] became enamoured of solitude, and, being at the same time an optimist, he labours with uncommon eloquence to prove that man was naturally a solitary animal. Misled by his respect for the goodness of God, who certainly—for what man of sense and feeling can doubt it!—gave life only to communicate happiness, he considers evil as positive, and the work of man; not aware that he was exalting one attribute at the expense of another, equally necessary to divine perfection.

Reared on a false hypothesis, his arguments in favour of a state of nature are plausible, but unsound. I say unsound; for to assert that a state of nature is preferable to civilization, in all its possible perfection, is, in other words, to arraign supreme wisdom; and the paradoxical exclamation, that God had made all things right, and that error has been introduced by the creature, whom He formed, knowing what He formed, is as unphilosophical as impious.

When that wise Being who created us and placed us here, saw the fair idea, He willed, by allowing it to be so, that the passions should unfold our reason, because He could see that present evil would produce future good. Could the helpless creature whom He called from nothing break loose from his providence, and boldly learn to know good by practising evil, without His permission? No. How could that energetic advocate for immortality argue so inconsistently? Had mankind remained for ever in the brutal state of nature, which even his magic pen cannot paint as a state in which a single virtue took root, it would have been clear, though not to the sensitive unreflecting wanderer, that man was born to run the circle of life and death, and adorn

God's garden for some purpose which could not easily be reconciled with His attributes.

But if, to crown the whole, there were to be rational creatures produced, allowed to rise in excellence by the exercise of powers implanted for that purpose; if benignity itself thought fit to call into existence a creature above the brutes,* who could think and improve himself, why should that inestimable gift, for a gift it was, if man was so created, as to have a capacity to rise above the state in which sensation produced brutal ease, be called, in direct terms, a curse? A curse it might be reckoned, if the whole of our existence were bounded by our continuance in this world; for why should the gracious fountain of life give us passions, the power of reflecting, only to imbitter our days and inspire us with mistaken notions of dignity? Why should He lead us from love of ourselves to the sublime emotions which the discovery of His wisdom and goodness excites, if these feelings were not set in motion to improve our nature, of which they make a part, ** and render us capable of enjoying a more godlike portion of happiness? Firmly persuaded that no evil exists in the world that God did not design to take place, I build my belief on the perfection of God.

Rousseau exerts himself to prove that all *was* right originally: a crowd of authors that all *is* now right: and I, that all will *be* right.

But, true to his first position, next to a state of nature, Rousseau celebrates barbarism, and apostrophising the shade of Fabricius,³ he forgets that, in conquering the world, the Romans never dreamed of establishing their own liberty on a firm basis, or of extending the reign of virtue. Eager to support his system, he stigmatizes, as vicious, every effort of genius; and, uttering the apotheosis of savage virtues, he exalts those to demi-gods, who were scarcely human—the brutal Spartans who, in defiance of justice and gratitude, sacrificed, in cold blood,

---

*Contrary to the opinion of anatomists, who argue by analogy from the formation of the teeth, stomach, and intestines, Rousseau will not allow a man to be a carnivorous animal. And, carried away from nature by a love of system, he disputes whether man be a gregarious animal, though the long and helpless state of infancy seems to point him out as particularly impelled to pair, the first step towards herding.

**What would you say to a mechanic whom you had desired to make a watch to point out the hour of the day, if, to show his ingenuity, he added wheels to make it a repeater, etc., that perplexed the simple mechanism; should he urge—to excuse himself—had you not touched a certain spring you would have known nothing of the matter, and that he should have amused himself by making *an experiment* without doing you any harm, would you not retort fairly upon him, by insisting that if he had not added those needless wheels and springs, the accident could not have happened?

the slaves who had shown themselves heroes to rescue their oppressors.

Disgusted with artificial manners and virtues, the citizen of Geneva, instead of properly sifting the subject, threw away the wheat with the chaff, without waiting to inquire whether the evils which his ardent soul turned from indignantly, were the consequence of civilization or the vestiges of barbarism. He saw vice trampling on virtue, and the semblance of goodness taking the place of the reality; he saw talents bent by power to sinister purposes, and never thought of tracing the gigantic mischief up to arbitrary power, up to the hereditary distinctions that clash with the mental superiority that naturally raises a man above his fellows. He did not perceive that regal power, in a few generations, introduces idiotism into the noble stem, and holds out baits to render thousands idle and vicious.

Nothing can set the regal character in a more contemptible point of view, than the various crimes that have elevated men to the supreme dignity. Vile intrigues, unnatural crimes, and every vice that degrades our nature, have been the steps to this distinguished eminence; yet millions of men have supinely allowed the nerveless limbs of the posterity of such rapacious prowlers to rest quietly on their ensanguined thrones.*

What but a pestilential vapour can hover over society when its chief director is only instructed in the invention of crimes, or the stupid routine of childish ceremonies? Will men never be wise?—will they never cease to expect corn from tares, and figs from thistles?

It is impossible for any man, when the most favourable circumstances concur, to acquire sufficient knowledge and strength of mind to discharge the duties of a king, entrusted with uncontrolled power; how then must they be violated when his very elevation is an insuperable bar to the attainment of either wisdom or virtue, when all the feelings of a man are stifled by flattery, and reflection shut out by pleasure! Sure it is madness to make the fate of thousands depend on the caprice of a weak fellow-creature, whose very station sinks him *necessarily* below the meanest of his subjects! But one power should not be thrown down to exalt another—for all power inebriates weak man; and its abuse proves that the more equality there is established among men, the more virtue and happiness will reign in society. But this and

---

*Could there be a greater insult offered to the rights of man than the beds of justice in France, when an infant was made the organ of the detestable Dubois?[4]

any similar maxim deduced from simple reason, raises an outcry—the Church or the State is in danger, if faith in the wisdom of antiquity is not implicit; and they who, roused by the sigh of human calamity, dare to attack human authority, are reviled as despisers of God, and enemies of man. These are bitter calumnies, yet they reached one of the best of men,* whose ashes still preach peace, and whose memory demands a respectful pause, when subjects are discussed that lay so near his heart.

After attacking the sacred majesty of kings, I shall scarcely excite surprise by adding my firm persuasion that every profession, in which great subordination of rank constitutes its power, is highly injurious to morality.

A standing army, for instance, is incompatible with freedom; because subordination and rigour are the very sinews of military discipline; and despotism is necessary to give vigour to enterprises that one will directs. A spirit inspired by romantic notions of honour, a kind of morality founded on the fashion of the age, can only be felt by a few officers, whilst the main body must be moved by command, like the waves of the sea; for the strong wind of authority pushes the crowd of subalterns forward, they scarcely know or care why, with headlong fury.

Besides, nothing can be so prejudicial to the morals of the inhabitants of country towns as the occasional residence of a set of idle superficial young men, whose only occupation is gallantry, and whose polished manners render vice more dangerous, by concealing its deformity under gay ornamental drapery. An air of fashion, which is but a badge of slavery, and proves that the soul has not a strong individual character, awes simple country people into an imitation of the vices, when they cannot catch the slippery graces, of politeness. Every corps is a chain of despots, who, submitting and tyrannising without exercising their reason, become deadweights of vice and folly on the community. A man of rank or fortune, sure of rising by interest, has nothing to do but to pursue some extravagant freak; whilst the needy *gentleman*, who is to rise, as the phrase turns, by his merit, becomes a servile parasite or vile pander.

Sailors, the naval gentlemen, come under the same description, only their vices assume a different and a grosser cast. They are more positively indolent, when not discharging the ceremonials of their sta-

*Dr. Price.[5]

tion; whilst the insignificant fluttering of soldiers may be termed active idleness. More confined to the society of men, the former acquire a fondness for humour and mischievous tricks; whilst the latter, mixing frequently with well-bred women, catch a sentimental cant. But mind is equally out of the question, whether they indulge the horse-laugh, or polite simper.

May I be allowed to extend the comparison to a profession where more mind is certainly to be found—for the clergy have superior opportunities of improvement, though subordination almost equally cramps their faculties? The blind submission imposed at college to forms of belief serves as a novitiate to the curate, who must obsequiously respect the opinion of his rector or patron, if he mean to rise in his profession. Perhaps there cannot be a more forcible contrast than between the servile dependent gait of a poor curate and the courtly mien of a bishop. And the respect and contempt they inspire, render the discharge of their separate functions equally useless.

It is of great importance to observe that the character of every man is, in some degree, formed by his profession. A man of sense may only have a cast of countenance that wears off as you trace his individuality, whilst the weak, common man has scarcely ever any character, but what belongs to the body; at least, all his opinions have been so steeped in the vat consecrated by authority, that the faint spirit which the grape of his own vine yields, cannot be distinguished.

Society, therefore, as it becomes more enlightened, should be very careful not to establish bodies of men who must necessarily be made foolish or vicious by the very constitution of their profession.

In the infancy of society, when men were just emerging out of barbarism, chiefs and priests, touching the most powerful springs of savage conduct, hope and fear, must have had unbounded sway. An aristocracy, of course, is naturally the first form of government. But, clashing interests soon losing their equipoise, a monarchy and hierarchy break out of the confusion of ambitious struggles, and the foundation of both is secured by feudal tenures. This appears to be the origin of monarchical and priestly powers, and the dawn of civilization. But such combustible materials cannot long be pent up; and, getting vent in foreign wars and intestine insurrections, the people acquire some power in the tumult, which obliges their rulers to gloss over their oppression with a show of right. Thus, as wars, agriculture, commerce, and literature, expand the mind, despots are compelled to make covert corruption hold fast the power which was formerly snatched by open force.* And this baneful lurking gangrene is most quickly spread by luxury and superstition, the sure dregs of ambition. The indolent puppet of a court first becomes a luxurious monster, or fastidious sensualist, and then makes the contagion which his unnatural state spread, the instrument of tyranny.

It is the pestiferous purple[6] which renders the progress of civilization a curse, and warps the understanding, till men of sensibility doubt whether the expansion of intellect produces a greater portion of happiness or misery. But the nature of the poison points out the antidote; and had Rousseau mounted one step higher in his investigation, or could his eye have pierced through the foggy atmosphere, which he almost disdained to breathe, his active mind would have darted forward to contemplate the perfection of man in the establishment of true civilization, instead of taking his ferocious flight back to the night of sensual ignorance.

---

*Men of abilities scatter seeds that grow up and have a great influence on the forming opinion; and when once the public opinion preponderates, through the exertion of reason, the overthrow of arbitrary power is not very distant.

# CHAPTER II

# THE PREVAILING OPINION OF A SEXUAL
# CHARACTER DISCUSSED

To account for, and excuse the tyranny of man, many ingenious arguments have been brought forward to prove, that the two sexes, in the acquirement of virtue, ought to aim at attaining a very different character; or, to speak explicitly, women are not allowed to have sufficient strength of mind to acquire what really deserves the name of virtue. Yet it should seem, allowing them to have souls, that there is but one way appointed by Providence to lead *mankind* to either virtue or happiness.

If then women are not a swarm of ephemeron triflers, why should they be kept in ignorance under the specious name of innocence? Men complain, and with reason, of the follies and caprices of our sex, when they do not keenly satirise our headstrong passions and grovelling vices. Behold, I should answer, the natural effect of ignorance! The mind will ever be unstable that has only prejudices to rest on, and the current will run with destructive fury when there are no barriers to break its force. Women are told from their infancy, and taught by the example of their mothers, that a little knowledge of human weakness, justly termed cunning, softness of temper, *outward* obedience, and a scrupulous attention to a puerile kind of propriety, will obtain for them the protection of man; and should they be beautiful, everything else is needless, for at least twenty years of their lives.

Thus Milton describes our first frail mother[1]; though when he tells us that women are formed for softness and sweet attractive grace, I cannot comprehend his meaning, unless, in the true Mahometan strain, he meant to deprive us of souls, and insinuate that we were beings only designed by sweet attractive grace, and docile blind obedience, to gratify the senses of man when he can no longer soar on the wing of contemplation.

How grossly do they insult us who thus advise us only to render ourselves gentle, domestic brutes! For instance, the winning softness so warmly and frequently recommended, that governs by obeying. What childish expressions, and how insignificant is the being—can it be an immortal one?—who will condescend to govern by such sinister methods? "Certainly," says Lord Bacon, "man is of kin to the beasts by his body; and if he be not of kin to God by his spirit, he is a base and ignoble creature!"² Men, indeed, appear to me to act in a very unphilosophical manner, when they try to secure the good conduct of women by attempting to keep them always in a state of childhood. Rousseau was more consistent when he wished to stop the progress of reason in both sexes, for if men eat of the tree of knowledge, women will come in for a taste; but, from the imperfect cultivation which their understandings now receive, they only attain a knowledge of evil.

Children, I grant, should be innocent; but when the epithet is applied to men, or women, it is but a civil term for weakness. For if it be allowed that women were destined by Providence to acquire human virtues, and, by the exercise of their understandings, that stability of character which is the firmest ground to rest our future hopes upon, they must be permitted to turn to the fountain of light, and not forced to shape their course by the twinkling of a mere satellite. Milton, I grant, was of a very different opinion; for he only bends to the indefeasible right of beauty, though it would be difficult to render two passages which I now mean to contrast, consistent. But into similar inconsistencies are great men often led by their senses:

> To whom thus Eve with *perfect beauty* adorn'd.
> My author and disposer, what thou bid'st
> *Unargued* I obey; so God ordains;
> God is *thy law, thou mine:* to know no more
> Is woman's *happiest* knowledge and her *praise.*³

These are exactly the arguments that I have used to children; but I have added, your reason is now gaining strength, and, till it arrives at some degree of maturity, you must look up to me for advice,—then you ought to *think*, and only rely on God.

Yet in the following lines Milton seems to coincide with me, when he makes Adam thus expostulate with his Maker:

> Hast Thou not made me here Thy substitute,
> And these inferior far beneath me set?
> Among *unequals* what society
> Can sort, what harmony or true delight?
> Which must be mutual, in proportion due
> Given and received; but in *disparity*
> The one intense, the other still remiss
> Cannot well suit with either, but soon prove
> Tedious alike; of *fellowship* I speak
> Such as I seek, fit to participate
> All rational delight—[4]

In treating therefore of the manners of women, let us, disregarding sensual arguments, trace what we should endeavour to make them in order to co-operate, if the expression be not too bold, with the Supreme Being.

By individual education, I mean, for the sense of the word is not precisely defined, such an attention to a child as will slowly sharpen the senses, form the temper, regulate the passions as they begin to ferment, and set the understanding to work before the body arrives at maturity; so that the man may only have to proceed, not to begin, the important task of learning to think and reason.

To prevent any misconstruction, I must add, that I do not believe that a private education can work the wonders which some sanguine writers have attributed to it. Men and women must be educated, in a great degree, by the opinions and manners of the society they live in. In every age there has been a stream of popular opinion that has carried all before it, and given a family character, as it were, to the century. It may then fairly be inferred, that, till society be differently constituted, much cannot be expected from education. It is, however, sufficient for my present purpose to assert that, whatever effect circumstances have on the abilities, every being may become virtuous by the exercise of its own reason; for if but one being was created with vicious inclinations, that is positively bad, what can save us from atheism? or if we worship a God, is not that God a devil?

Consequently, the most perfect education, in my opinion, is such an exercise of the understanding as is best calculated to strengthen the body and form the heart. Or, in other words, to enable the individual to attain such habits of virtue as will render it independent. In fact, it is a farce to call any being virtuous whose virtues do not result from the exercise of its own reason. This was Rousseau's opinion respecting men; I extend it to women, and confidently assert that they have been drawn out of their sphere by false refinement, and not by an endeavour to acquire masculine qualities. Still the regal homage which they receive is so intoxicating, that until the manners of the times are changed, and formed on more reasonable principles, it may be impossible to convince them that the illegitimate power which they obtain by degrading themselves is a curse, and that they must return to nature and equality if they wish to secure the placid satisfaction that unsophisticated affections impart. But for this epoch we must wait—wait perhaps till kings and nobles, enlightened by reason, and, preferring the real dignity of man to childish state, throw off their gaudy hereditary trappings; and if then women do not resign the arbitrary power of beauty—they will prove that they have *less* mind than man.

I may be accused of arrogance; still I must declare what I firmly believe, that all the writers who have written on the subject of female education and manners, from Rousseau to Dr. Gregory,[5] have contributed to render women more artificial, weak characters, than they would otherwise have been; and consequently, more useless members of society. I might have expressed this conviction in a lower key, but I am afraid it would have been the whine of affectation, and not the faithful expression of my feelings, of the clear result which experience and reflection have led me to draw. When I come to that division of the subject, I shall advert to the passages that I more particularly disapprove of, in the works of the authors I have just alluded to; but it is first necessary to observe that my objection extends to the whole purport of those books, which tend, in my opinion, to degrade one-half of the human species, and render women pleasing at the expense of every solid virtue.

Though, to reason on Rousseau's ground, if man did attain a degree of perfection of mind when his body arrived at maturity, it might be proper, in order to make a man and his wife *one*, that she should rely entirely on his understanding; and the graceful ivy, clasping the oak that supported it, would form a whole in which strength and beauty would be equally conspicuous. But, alas! husbands, as well as their helpmates, are often only overgrown children,—nay, thanks to early debauchery, scarcely men in their outward form,—and if the blind lead the blind, one need not come from heaven to tell us the consequence.

Many are the causes that, in the present corrupt state of society, contribute to enslave women by cramping their understandings and sharpening their senses. One, perhaps, that silently does more mischief than all the rest, is their disregard of order.

To do everything in an orderly manner is a most important precept, which women, who, generally speaking, receive only a disorderly kind of education, seldom attend to with that degree of exactness that men, who from their infancy are broken into method, observe. This negligent kind of guesswork—for what other epithet can be used to point out the random exertions of a sort of instinctive common sense never brought to the test of reason?—prevents their generalizing matters of fact; so they do today what they did yesterday, merely because they did it yesterday.

This contempt of the understanding in early life has more baneful consequences than is commonly supposed; for the little knowledge which women of strong minds attain is, from various circumstances, of a more desultory kind than the knowledge of men, and it is acquired more by sheer observations on real life than from comparing what has been individually observed with the results of experience generalized by speculation. Led by their dependent situation and domestic employments more into society, what they learn is rather by snatches; and as learning is with them in general only a secondary thing, they do not pursue any one branch with that persevering ardour necessary to give vigour to the faculties and clearness to the judgement. In the present state of society a little learning is required to support the character of a gentleman, and boys are obliged to submit to a few years of discipline. But in the education of women, the cultivation of the understanding is always subordinate to the acquirement of some corporeal accomplishment. Even when enervated by confinement and false notions of modesty, the body is prevented from attaining that grace and beauty which relaxed half-formed limbs never exhibit. Besides, in youth, their faculties are not brought forward by emulation; and having no serious scientific study, if they have natural sagacity, it is turned too soon on life and manners. They dwell on effects and modifications, without tracing them back to causes; and complicated rules to adjust behaviour are a weak substitute for simple principles.

As a proof that education gives this appearance of weakness to females, we may instance the example of military men, who are, like them, sent into the world before their minds have been stored with knowledge, or fortified by principles. The consequences are similar; soldiers acquire a little superficial knowledge, snatched from the muddy current of conversation, and from continually mixing with society, they gain what is termed a knowledge of the world; and this acquaintance with manners and customs has frequently been confounded with a knowledge of the human heart. But can the crude fruit of casual observation, never brought to the test of judgement, formed by comparing speculation and experience, deserve such a distinction? Soldiers, as well as women, practise the minor virtues with punctilious politeness. Where is then the sexual difference, when the education has been the same? All the difference that I can discern arises from the superior advantage of liberty which enables the former to see more of life.

It is wandering from my present subject, perhaps, to make a political remark; but as it was produced naturally by the train of my reflections, I shall not pass it silently over.

Standing armies can never consist of resolute robust men; they may be well-disciplined machines, but they will seldom contain men under the influence of strong passions, or with very vigorous faculties; and as for any depth of understanding, I will venture to affirm that it is as rarely to be found in the army as amongst women. And the cause, I maintain, is the same. It may be further observed that officers are also particularly attentive to their persons, fond of dancing, crowded rooms, adventures, and ridicule.* Like the *fair* sex, the business of their lives is gallantry; they were taught to please, and they only live to please. Yet they do not lose their rank in the distinction of sexes, for they are still reckoned superior to women, though in what their superiority consists, beyond what I have just mentioned, it is difficult to discover.

The great misfortune is this, that they both acquire manners before morals, and a knowledge of life before they have from reflection any acquaintance with the grand ideal outline of human nature. The consequence is natural. Satisfied with common nature, they become a prey

---

*Why should women be censured with petulant acrimony because they seem to have a passion for a scarlet coat? Has not education placed them more on a level with soldiers than any other class of men?

to prejudices, and taking all their opinions on credit, they blindly submit to authority. So that if they have any sense, it is a kind of instinctive glance that catches proportions, and decides with respect to manners, but fails when arguments are to be pursued below the surface, or opinions analysed.

May not the same remark be applied to women? Nay, the argument may be carried still further, for they are both thrown out of a useful station by the unnatural distinctions established in civilized life. Riches and hereditary honours have made cyphers of women to give consequence to the numerical figure; and idleness has produced a mixture of gallantry and despotism into society, which leads the very men who are the slaves of their mistresses to tyrannize over their sisters, wives, and daughters. This is only keeping them in rank and file, it is true. Strengthen the female mind by enlarging it, and there will be an end to blind obedience; but as blind obedience is ever sought for by power, tyrants and sensualists are in the right when they endeavour to keep woman in the dark, because the former only want slaves, and the latter a plaything. The sensualist, indeed, has been the most dangerous of tyrants, and women have been duped by their lovers, as princes by their ministers, whilst dreaming that they reigned over them.

I now principally allude to Rousseau, for his character of Sophia[6] is undoubtedly a captivating one, though it appears to me grossly unnatural. However, it is not the superstructure, but the foundation of her character, the principles on which her education was built, that I mean to attack; nay, warmly as I admire the genius of that able writer, whose opinions I shall often have occasion to cite, indignation always takes place of admiration, and the rigid frown of insulted virtue effaces the smile of complacency which his eloquent periods are wont to raise when I read his voluptuous reveries. Is this the man who, in his ardour for virtue, would banish all the soft arts of peace, and almost carry us back to Spartan discipline? Is this the man who delights to paint the useful struggles of passion, the triumphs of good dispositions, and the heroic flights which carry the glowing soul out of itself? How are these mighty sentiments lowered when he describes the pretty foot and enticing airs of his little favourite! But for the present I waive the subject, and instead of severely reprehending the transient effusions of overweening sensibility, I shall only observe that whoever has cast a benevolent eye on society must often have been gratified by the sight of humble mutual love not dignified by sentiment, or strengthened by a union in intellectual pursuits. The domestic trifles of the day have afforded matters for cheerful converse, and innocent caresses have softened toils which did not require great exercise of mind or stretch of thought; yet has not the sight of this moderate felicity excited more tenderness than respect?—an emotion similar to what we feel when children are playing or animals sporting;* whilst the contemplation of the noble struggles of suffering merit has raised admiration, and carried our thoughts to that world where sensation will give place to reason.

Women are therefore to be considered either as moral beings, or so weak that they must be entirely subjected to the superior faculties of men.

Let us examine this question. Rousseau declares that a woman should never for a moment feel herself independent, that she should be governed by fear to exercise her *natural* cunning, and made a coquettish slave in order to render her a more alluring object of desire, a *sweeter* companion to man, whenever he chose to relax himself. He carries the arguments, which he pretends to draw from the indications of nature, still further, and insinuates that truth and fortitude, the cornerstones of all human virtue, should be cultivated with certain restrictions, because, with respect to the female character, obedience is the grand lesson which ought to be impressed with unrelenting rigour.

What nonsense! When will a great man arise with sufficient strength of mind to puff away the fumes which pride and sensuality have thus spread over the subject? If women are by nature inferior to men, their virtues must be the same in quality, if not in degree, or virtue is a relative idea; consequently their conduct should be founded on the same principles, and have the same aim.

Connected with man as daughters, wives, and mothers, their moral character may be estimated by their manner of fulfilling those simple duties; but the end, the grand end, of their exertions should be to unfold their own faculties, and acquire the dignity of conscious virtue. They may try to render their road pleasant; but ought never to forget,

---

*Similar feelings has Milton's pleasing picture of paradisiacal happiness ever raised in my mind; yet, instead of envying the lovely pair, I have with conscious dignity or satanic pride turned to hell for sublimer objects. In the same style, when viewing some noble monument of human art, I have traced the emanation of the Deity in the order I admired, till, descending from that giddy height, I have caught myself contemplating the grandest of all human sights; for fancy quickly placed in some solitary recess an outcast of fortune, rising superior to passion and discontent.

in common with man, that life yields not the felicity which can satisfy an immortal soul. I do not mean to insinuate that either sex should be so lost in abstract reflections or distant views as to forget the affections and duties that lie before them, and are, in truth, the means appointed to produce the fruit of life; on the contrary, I would warmly recommend them, even while I assert that they afford most satisfaction when they are considered in their true sober light.

Probably the prevailing opinion that woman was created for man, may have taken its rise from Moses' poetical story[7]; yet as very few, it is presumed, who have bestowed any serious thought on the subject ever supposed that Eve was, literally speaking, one of Adam's ribs, the deduction must be allowed to fall to the ground, or only be so far admitted as it proves that man, from the remotest antiquity, found it convenient to exert his strength to subjugate his companion, and his invention to show that she ought to have her neck bent under the yoke, because the whole creation was only created for his convenience or pleasure.

Let it not be concluded that I wish to invert the order of things. I have already granted that, from the constitution of their bodies, men seemed to be designed by Providence to attain a greater degree of virtue. I speak collectively of the whole sex; but I see not the shadow of a reason to conclude that their virtues should differ in respect to their nature. In fact, how can they, if virtue has only one eternal standard? I must therefore, if I reason consequentially, as strenuously maintain that they have the same simple direction as that there is a God.

It follows then that cunning should not be opposed to wisdom, little cares to great exertions, or insipid softness, varnished over with the name of gentleness, to that fortitude which grand views alone can inspire.

I shall be told that woman would then lose many of her peculiar graces, and the opinion of a well-known poet might be quoted to refute my unqualified assertion. For Pope has said, in the name of the whole male sex:

> Yet ne'er so sure our passion to create,
> As when she touch'd the brink of all we hate.[8]

In what light this sally places men and women I shall leave to the judicious to determine. Meanwhile, I shall content myself with observing, that I cannot discover why, unless they are mortal, females should always be degraded by being made subservient to love or lust.

To speak disrespectfully of love is, I know, high treason against sentiment and fine feelings; but I wish to speak the simple language of truth, and rather to address the head than the heart. To endeavour to reason love out of the world would be to out-Quixote Cervantes, and equally offend against common sense; but an endeavour to restrain this tumultuous passion, and to prove that it should not be allowed to dethrone superior powers, or to usurp the sceptre which the understanding should ever coolly wield, appears less wild.

Youth is the season for love in both sexes; but in those days of thoughtless enjoyment provision should be made for the more important years of life, when reflection takes place of sensation. But Rousseau, and most of the male writers who have followed his steps, have warmly indicated that the whole tendency of female education ought to be directed to one point—to render them pleasing.

Let me reason with the supporters of this opinion who have any knowledge of human nature. Do they imagine that marriage can eradicate the habitude of life? The woman who has only been taught to please will soon find that her charms are oblique sunbeams, and that they cannot have much effect on her husband's heart when they are seen every day, when the summer is passed and gone. Will she then have sufficient native energy to look into herself for comfort, and cultivate her dormant faculties? or is it not more rational to expect that she will try to please other men, and, in the emotions raised by the experience of new conquests, endeavour to forget the mortification her love or pride has received? When the husband ceases to be a lover, and the time will inevitably come, her desire of pleasing will then grow languid, or become a spring of bitterness; and love, perhaps, the most evanescent of all passions, gives place to jealousy or vanity.

I now speak of women who are restrained by principle or prejudice. Such women, though they would shrink from an intrigue with real abhorrence, yet, nevertheless, wish to be convinced by the homage of gallantry that they are cruelly neglected by their husbands; or, days and weeks are spent in dreaming of the happiness enjoyed by congenial souls, till their health is undermined and their spirits broken by discontent. How then can the great art of pleasing be such a necessary study? it is only useful to a mistress. The chaste wife and serious mother should only consider her power to please as the polish of her virtues, and the affection of her husband as one of the comforts that render her task less difficult, and her life happier. But, whether she be loved or neglected, her first wish should be to make herself respectable, and not to rely for all her happiness on a being subject to like infirmities with herself.

The worthy Dr. Gregory fell into a similar error. I respect his heart, but entirely disapprove of his celebrated *Legacy to his Daughters.*

He advises them to cultivate a fondness for dress, because a fondness for dress, he asserts, is natural to them. I am unable to comprehend what either he or Rousseau mean when they frequently use this indefinite term. If they told us that in a pre-existent state the soul was fond of dress, and brought this inclination with it into a new body, I should listen to them with a half-smile, as I often do when I hear a rant about innate elegance. But if he only meant to say that the exercise of the faculties will produce this fondness, I deny it. It is not natural; but arises, like false ambition in men, from a love of power.

Dr. Gregory goes much further; he actually recommends dissimulation, and advises an innocent girl to give the lie to her feelings, and not dance with spirit, when gaiety of heart would make her feet eloquent without making her gestures immodest. In the name of truth and common sense, why should not one woman acknowledge that she can take more exercise than another? or, in other words, that she has a sound constitution; and why, to damp innocent vivacity, is she darkly to be told that men will draw conclusions which she little thinks of? Let the libertine draw what inference he pleases; but, I hope, that no sensible mother will restrain the natural frankness of youth by instilling such indecent cautions. Out of the abundance of the heart the mouth speaketh; and a wiser than Solomon hath said that the heart should be made clean, and not trivial ceremonies observed, which it is not very difficult to fulfil with scrupulous exactness when vice reigns in the heart.

Women ought to endeavour to purify their hearts; but can they do so when their uncultivated understandings make them entirely dependent on their senses for employment and amusement, when no noble pursuits set them above the little vanities of the day, or enable them to curb the wild emotions that agitate a reed, over which every passing breeze has power? To gain the affections of a virtuous man, is affectation necessary? Nature has given woman a weaker frame than man; but, to ensure her husband's affections, must a wife, who, by the exercise of her mind and body whilst she was discharging the duties of a daughter, wife, and mother, has allowed her constitution to retain its natural strength, and her nerves a healthy tone,—is she, I say, to condescend to use art, and feign a sickly delicacy, in order to secure her husband's affection? Weakness may excite tenderness, and gratify the arrogant pride of man; but the lordly caresses of a protector will not gratify a noble mind that pants for and deserves to be respected. Fondness is a poor substitute for friendship!

In a seraglio, I grant, that all these arts are necessary; the epicure must have his palate tickled, or he will sink into apathy; but have women so little ambition as to be satisfied with such a condition? Can they supinely dream life away in the lap of pleasure, or the languor of weariness, rather than assert their claim to pursue reasonable pleasures, and render themselves conspicuous by practising the virtues which dignify mankind? Surely she has not an immortal soul who can loiter life away merely employed to adorn her person, that she may amuse the languid hours, and soften the cares of a fellow-creature who is willing to be enlivened by her smiles and tricks, when the serious business of life is over.

Besides, the woman who strengthens her body and exercises her mind will, by managing her family and practising various virtues, become the friend, and not the humble dependent of her husband; and if she, by possessing such substantial qualities, merit his regard, she will not find it necessary to conceal her affection, nor to pretend to an unnatural coldness of constitution to excite her husband's passions. In fact, if we revert to history, we shall find that the women who have distinguished themselves have neither been the most beautiful nor the most gentle of their sex.

Nature, or, to speak with strict propriety, God, has made all things right; but man has sought him out many inventions to mar the work. I now allude to that part of Dr. Gregory's treatise, where he advises a wife never to let her husband know the extent of her sensibility or affection. Voluptuous precaution, and as ineffectual as absurd. Love, from its very nature, must be transitory. To seek for a secret that would render it constant, would be as wild a search as for the philosopher's stone, or the grand panacea; and the discovery would be equally useless, or rather pernicious, to mankind. The most holy band of society is friendship. It has been well said, by a shrewd satirist, "that rare as true love is, true friendship is still rarer."

This is an obvious truth, and, the cause not lying deep, will not elude a slight glance of inquiry.

Love, the common passion, in which chance and sensation take place of choice and reason, is, in some degree, felt by the mass of mankind; for it is not necessary to speak, at present, of the emotions that rise above or sink below love. This passion, naturally increased by suspense and difficulties, draws the mind out of its accustomed state, and exalts the affections; but the security of marriage, allowing the fever of love to subside, a healthy temperature is thought insipid only by those who have not sufficient intellect to substitute the calm tenderness of friendship, the confidence of respect, instead of blind admiration, and the sensual emotions of fondness.

This is, must be, the course of nature. Friendship or indifference inevitably succeeds love. And this constitution seems perfectly to harmonize with the system of government which prevails in the moral world. Passions are spurs to action, and open the mind; but they sink into mere appetites, become a personal and momentary gratification when the object is gained, and the satisfied mind rests in enjoyment. The man who had some virtue whilst he was struggling for a crown often becomes a voluptuous tyrant when it graces his brow; and, when the lover is not lost in the husband, the dotard, a prey to childish caprices and fond jealousies, neglects the serious duties of life, and the caresses which should excite confidence in his children are lavished on the overgrown child, his wife.

In order to fulfil the duties of life, and to be able to pursue with vigour the various employments which form the moral character, a master and mistress of a family ought not to continue to love each other with passion. I mean to say that they ought not to indulge those emotions which disturb the order of society, and engross the thoughts that should be otherwise employed. The mind that has never been engrossed by one object wants vigour,—if it can long be so, it is weak.

A mistaken education, a narrow uncultivated mind, and many sexual prejudices, tend to make women more constant than men; but, for the present, I shall not touch on this branch of the subject. I will go still further, and advance, without dreaming of a paradox, that an unhappy marriage is often very advantageous to a family, and that the neglected wife is, in general, the best mother. And this would almost always be the consequence if the female mind were more enlarged; for, it seems to be the common dispensation of Providence, that what we gain in present enjoyment should be deducted from the treasure of life, experience; and that when we are gathering the flowers of the day, and revelling in pleasure, the solid fruit of toil and wisdom should not be caught at the same time. The way lies before us, we must turn to the right or left; and he who will pass life away in bounding from one pleasure to another, must not complain if he acquire neither wisdom nor respectability of character.

Supposing, for a moment, that the soul is not immortal, and that man was only created for the present scene,—I think we should have reason to complain that love, infantine fondness, ever grew insipid and palled upon the sense. Let us eat, drink, and love, for tomorrow we die, would be, in fact, the language of reason, the morality of life; and who but a fool would part with a reality for a fleeting shadow? But, if awed by observing the improbable powers of the mind, we disdain to confine our wishes or thoughts to such a comparatively mean field of action, that only appears grand and important, as it is connected with a boundless prospect and sublime hopes, what necessity is there for falsehood in conduct, and why must the sacred majesty of truth be violated to detain a deceitful good that saps the very foundation of virtue? Why must the female mind be tainted by coquettish arts to gratify the sensualist, and prevent love from subsiding into friendship, or compassionate tenderness, when there are not qualities on which friendship can be built? Let the honest heart show itself, and *reason* teach passion to submit to necessity; or, let the dignified pursuit of virtue and knowledge raise the mind above those emotions which rather embitter than sweeten the cup of life, when they are not restrained within due bounds.

I do not mean to allude to the romantic passion, which is the concomitant of genius. Who can clip its wing? But that grand passion not proportioned to the puny enjoyments of life, is only true to the sentiment, and feeds on itself. The passions which have been celebrated for their durability have always been unfortunate. They have acquired strength by absence and constitutional melancholy. The fancy has hovered round a form of beauty dimly seen; but familiarity might have turned admiration into disgust, or, at least, into indifference, and allowed the imagination leisure to start fresh game. With perfect propriety, according to this view of things, does Rousseau make the mistress of his soul, Eloisa, love St. Preux,[10] when life was fading before her; but this is no proof of the immortality of the passion.

Of the same complexion is Dr. Gregory's advice respecting delicacy of sentiment, which he advises a woman not to acquire, if she have determined to marry. This determination, however, perfectly consistent with his former advice, he calls *indelicate*, and earnestly persuades his daughters to conceal it, though it may govern their conduct, as if it were indelicate to have the common appetites of human nature.

Noble morality! and consistent with the cautious prudence of a little soul that cannot extend its views beyond the present minute division of existence. If all the faculties of woman's mind are only to be cultivated as they respect her dependence on man; if, when a husband be obtained, she have arrived at her goal, and meanly proud, rests satisfied with such a paltry crown, let her grovel contentedly, scarcely raised by her employments above the animal kingdom; but, if struggling for the prize of her high calling, she look beyond the present scene, let her cultivate her understanding without stopping to consider what character the husband may have whom she is destined to marry. Let her only determine, without being too anxious about present happiness, to acquire the qualities that ennoble a rational being, and a rough inelegant husband may shock her taste without destroying her peace of mind. She will not model her soul to suit the frailties of her companion, but to bear with them; his character may be a trial, but not an impediment to virtue.

If Dr. Gregory confined his remark to romantic expectations of constant love and congenial feelings, he should have recollected that experience will banish what advice can never make us cease to wish for, when the imagination is kept alive at the expense of reason.

I own it frequently happens, that women who have fostered a romantic unnatural delicacy of feeling, waste their* lives in *imagining* how happy they should have been with a husband who could love them with a fervid increasing affection every day, and all day. But they might as well pine married as single, and would not be a jot more unhappy with a bad husband than longing for a good one. That a proper education, or, to speak with more precision, a well-stored mind, would enable a woman to support a single life with dignity, I grant; but that she should avoid cultivating her taste, lest her husband should occasionally shock it, is quitting a substance for a shadow. To say the truth, I do not know of what use is an improved taste, if the individual be not rendered more independent of the casualties of life; if new sources of enjoyment, only dependent on the solitary operations of the mind, are not opened. People of taste, married or single, without distinction, will ever be disgusted by various things that touch not less observing minds. On this conclusion the argument must not be allowed to

*For example, the herd of Novelists.

hinge: but in the whole sum of enjoyment is taste to be denominated a blessing?

The question is, whether it procures most pain or pleasure? The answer will decide the propriety of Dr. Gregory's advice, and show how absurd and tyrannic it is thus to lay down a system of slavery, or to attempt to educate moral beings by any other rules than those deduced from pure reason, which apply to the whole species.

Gentleness of manners, forbearance and long suffering, are such amiable Godlike qualities, that in sublime poetic strains the Deity has been invested with them; and, perhaps, no representation of His goodness so strongly fastens on the human affections as those that represent Him abundant in mercy and willing to pardon. Gentleness, considered in this point of view, bears on its front all the characteristics of grandeur, combined with the winning graces of condescension; but what a different aspect it assumes when it is the submissive demeanour of dependence, the support of weakness that loves, because it wants protection; and is forbearing, because it must silently endure injuries; smiling under the lash at which it dare not snarl. Abject as this picture appears, it is the portrait of an accomplished woman, according to the received opinion of female excellence, separated by specious reasoners from human excellence. Or, they* kindly restore the rib, and make one moral being of a man and woman; not forgetting to give her all the "submissive charms."

How women are to exist in that state where there is neither to be marrying nor giving in marriage, we are not told. For though moralists have agreed that the tenor of life seems to prove that *man* is prepared by various circumstances for a future state, they constantly concur in advising *woman* only to provide for the present. Gentleness, docility, and a spaniel-like affection are, on this ground, consistently recommended as the cardinal virtues of the sex; and, disregarding the arbitrary economy of nature, one writer has declared that it is masculine for a woman to be melancholy. She was created to be the toy of man, his rattle, and it must jingle in his ears whenever, dismissing reason, he chooses to be amused.

To recommend gentleness, indeed, on a broad basis is strictly philosophical. A frail being should labour to be gentle. But when forbearance confounds right and wrong, it ceases to be a virtue; and, however convenient it may be found in a companion—that companion will

* *Vide* Rousseau and Swedenborg.[11]

ever be considered as an inferior, and only inspire a vapid tenderness, which easily degenerates into contempt. Still, if advice could really make a being gentle, whose natural disposition admitted not of such a fine polish, something towards the advancement of order would be attained; but if, as might quickly be demonstrated, only affection be produced by this indiscriminate counsel, which throws a stumbling-block in the way of gradual improvement, and true melioration of temper, the sex is not much benefited by sacrificing solid virtues to the attainment of superficial graces, though for a few years they may procure the individuals regal sway.

As a philosopher, I read with indignation the plausible epithets which men use to soften their insults; and, as a moralist, I ask what is meant by such heterogeneous associations, as fair defects, amiable weaknesses, etc.? If there be but one criterion of morals, but one archetype for man, women appear to be suspended by destiny, according to the vulgar tale of Mahomet's coffin; they have neither the unerring instinct of brutes, nor are allowed to fix the eye of reason on a perfect model. They were made to be loved, and must not aim at respect, lest they should be hunted out of society as masculine.

But to view the subject in another point of view. Do passive indolent women make the best wives? Confining our discussion to the present moment of existence, let us see how such weak creatures perform their part? Do the women who, by the attainment of a few superficial accomplishments, have strengthened the prevailing prejudice, merely contribute to the happiness of their husbands? Do they display their charms merely to amuse them? And have women who have early imbibed notions of passive obedience, sufficient character to manage a family or educate children? So far from it, that, after surveying the history of woman, I cannot help agreeing with the severest satirist, considering the sex as the weakest as well as the most oppressed half of the species. What does history disclose but marks of inferiority, and how few women have emancipated themselves from the galling yoke of sovereign man? So few that the exceptions remind me of an ingenious conjecture respecting Newton—that he was probably a being of superior order accidentally caged in a human body. Following the same train of thinking, I have been led to imagine that the few extraordinary women who have rushed in eccentrical directions out of the orbit prescribed to their sex, were *male* spirits, confined by mistake in female frames. But if it be not philosophical to think of sex when the soul is mentioned, the inferiority must depend on the organs; or the heavenly fire, which is to ferment the clay, is not given in equal portions.

But avoiding, as I have hitherto done, any direct comparison of the two sexes collectively, or frankly acknowledging the inferiority of woman, according to the present appearance of things, I shall only insist that men have increased that inferiority till women are almost sunk below the standard of rational creatures. Let their faculties have room to unfold, and their virtues to gain strength, and then determine where the whole sex must stand in the intellectual scale. Yet let it be remembered that for a small number of distinguished women I do not ask a place.

It is difficult for us purblind mortals to say to what height human discoveries and improvements may arrive, when the gloom of despotism subsides, which makes us stumble at every step; but, when morality shall be settled on a more solid basis, then, without being gifted with a prophetic spirit, I will venture to predict that woman will be either the friend or slave of man. We shall not, as at present, doubt whether she is a moral agent, or the link which unites man with brutes. But should it then appear that like the brutes they were principally created for the use of man, he will let them patiently bite the bridle, and not mock them with empty praise; or, should their rationality be proved, he will not impede their improvement merely to gratify his sensual appetites. He will not, with all the graces of rhetoric, advise them to submit implicitly their understanding to the guidance of man. He will not, when he treats of the education of women, assert that they ought never to have the free use of reason, nor would he recommend cunning and dissimulation to beings who are acquiring, in like manner as himself, the virtues of humanity.

Surely there can be but one rule of right, if morality has an eternal foundation, and whoever sacrifices virtue, strictly so called, to present convenience, or whose *duty* it is to act in such a manner, lives only for the passing day, and cannot be an accountable creature.

The poet then should have dropped his sneer when he says:

> If weak women go astray,
> The stars are more in fault than they.[12]

For that they are bound by the adamantine chain of destiny is most certain, if it be proved that they are never to exercise their own reason, never to be independent, never to rise above opinion, or to feel the dignity of a rational will that only bows to God, and often forgets that the universe contains any being but itself and the model of perfection to which its ardent gaze is turned, to adore attributes that, softened into virtues, may be imitated in kind, though the degree overwhelms the enraptured mind.

If, I say, for I would not impress by declamation when Reason offers her sober light, if they be really capable of acting like rational creatures, let them not be treated like slaves; or, like the brutes who are dependent on the reason of man, when they associate with him; but cultivate their minds, give them the salutary sublime curb of principle, and let them attain conscious dignity by feeling themselves only dependent on God. Teach them, in common with man, to submit to necessity, instead of giving, to render them more pleasing, a sex to morals.

Further, should experience prove that they cannot attain the same degree of strength of mind, perseverance, and fortitude, let their virtues be the same in kind, though they may vainly struggle for the same degree; and the superiority of man will be equally clear, if not clearer; and truth, as it is a simple principle, which admits of no modification, would be common to both. Nay the order of society, as it is at present regulated, would not be inverted, for woman would then only have the rank that reason assigned her, and arts could not be practised to bring the balance even, much less to turn it.

These may be termed Utopian dreams. Thanks to that Being who impressed them on my soul, and gave me sufficient strength of mind to dare to exert my own reason, till, becoming dependent only on Him for the support of my virtue, I view, with indignation, the mistaken notions that enslave my sex.

I love man as my fellow; but his sceptre, real or usurped, extends not to me, unless the reason of an individual demands my homage; and even then the submission is to reason, and not to man. In fact, the conduct of an accountable being must be regulated by the operations of its own reason; or on what foundation rests the throne of God?

It appears to me necessary to dwell on these obvious truths, because females have been insulated, as it were; and while they have been stripped of the virtues that should clothe humanity, they have been decked with artificial graces that enable them to exercise a short-lived tyranny. Love, in their bosoms, taking place of every nobler passion, their sole ambition is to be fair, to raise emotion instead of inspiring respect; and this ignoble desire, like the servility in absolute monarchies, destroys all strength of character. Liberty is the mother of virtue, and if women be, by their very constitution, slaves, and not allowed to breathe the sharp invigorating air of freedom, they must ever languish like exotics, and be reckoned beautiful flaws in nature. Let it also be remembered, that they are the only flaw.

As to the argument respecting the subjection in which the sex has ever been held, it retorts on man. The many have always been enthralled by the few; and monsters, who scarcely have shown any discernment of human excellence, have tyrannized over thousands of their fellow-creatures. Why have men of superior endowments submitted to such degredation? For, is it not universally acknowledged that kings, viewed collectively, have ever been inferior, in abilities and virtue, to the same number of men taken from the common mass of mankind—yet have they not, and are they not still treated with a degree of reverence that is an insult to reason? China is not the only country where a living man has been made a God. *Men* have submitted to superior strength to enjoy with impunity the pleasure of the moment; *women* have only done the same, and therefore till it is proved that the courtier, who servilely resigns the birthright of a man, is not a moral agent, it cannot be demonstrated that woman is essentially inferior to man because she has always been subjugated.

Brutal force has hitherto governed the world, and that the science of politics is in its infancy, is evident from philosophers scrupling to give the knowledge most useful to man that determinate distinction.

I shall not pursue this argument any further than to establish an obvious inference, that as sound politics diffuse liberty, mankind, including woman, will become more wise and virtuous.

# CHAPTER III

# THE SAME SUBJECT CONTINUED

Bodily strength from being the distinction of heroes is now sunk into such unmerited contempt that men, as well as women, seem to think it unnecessary; the latter, as it takes from their feminine graces, and from that lovely weakness, the source of their undue power; and the former, because it appears inimical to the character of a gentleman.

That they have both, by departing from one extreme run into another, may easily be proved; but first it may be proper to observe that a vulgar error has obtained a degree of credit, which has given force to a false conclusion, in which an effect has been mistaken for a cause.

People of genius have very frequently impaired their constitutions by study or careless inattention to their health, and the violence of their passions bearing a proportion to the vigour of their intellects, the sword's destroying the scabbard has become almost proverbial, and superficial observers have inferred from thence that men of genius have commonly weak, or, to use a more fashionable phrase, delicate constitutions. Yet the contrary, I believe, will appear to be the fact; for, on diligent inquiry, I find that strength of mind has in most cases been accompanied by superior strength of body,—natural soundness of constitution,—not that robust tone of nerves and vigour of muscles, which arise from bodily labour, when the mind is quiescent, or only directs the hands.

Dr. Priestley[1] has remarked, in the preface to his biographical chart, that the majority of great men have lived beyond forty-five. And considering the thoughtless manner in which they have lavished their strength when investigating a favourite science, they have wasted the lamp of life, forgetful of the midnight hour; or, when lost in poetic dreams, fancy has peopled the scene, and the soul has been disturbed, till it shook the constitution by the passions that meditation has raised,—whose objects, the baseless fabric of a vision, faded before the exhausted eye,—they must have had iron frames. Shakespeare never grasped the airy dagger with a nerveless hand, nor did Milton tremble when he led Satan far from the confines of his dreary prison. These were not the ravings of imbecility, the sickly effusions of distempered brains, but the exuberance of fancy, that "in a fine frenzy" wandering, was not continually reminded of its material shackles.

I am aware that this argument would carry me further than it may be supposed I wish to go; but I follow truth, and still adhering to my first position, I will allow that bodily strength seems to give man a natural superiority over woman; and this is the only solid basis on which the superiority of the sex can be built. But I still insist that not only the virtue but the *knowledge* of the two sexes should be the same in nature, if not in degree, and that women, considered not only as moral but rational creatures, ought to endeavour to acquire human virtues (or perfections) by the *same* means as men, instead of being educated like a fanciful kind of *half* being—one of Rousseau's wild chimeras.*

*"Researches into abstract and speculative truths, the principles and axioms of sciences—in short, everything which tends to generalize our ideas—is not the proper province of women; their studies should be relative to points of practice; it belongs to them to apply those principles which men have discovered; and it is their part to make observations which direct men to the establishment of general principles. All the ideas of women, which have not the immediate tendency to points of duty, should be directed to the study of men, and to the attainment of those agreeable accomplishments which have taste for their object; for as to works of genius, they are beyond their capacity; neither have they sufficient precision or power of attention to succeed in sciences which require accuracy; and as to physical knowledge, it belongs to those only who are most active, most inquisitive, who comprehend the greatest variety of objects; in short, it belongs to those who have the strongest powers, and who exercise them most, to judge of the relations between sensible beings and the laws of nature. A woman who is naturally weak, and does not carry her ideas to any great extent, knows how to judge and make a proper estimate of those movements which she sets to work, in order to aid her weakness; and these movements are the passions of men. The mechanism she employs is much more powerful than ours, for all her levers move the human heart. She must have the skill to incline us to do everything which her sex will not enable her to do herself, and which is necessary or agreeable to her; therefore she ought to study the mind of

But if strength of body be with some show of reason the boast of men, why are women so infatuated as to be proud of a defect? Rousseau has furnished them with a plausible excuse, which could only have occurred to a man whose imagination had been allowed to run wild, and refine on the impressions made by exquisite senses; that they might forsooth have a pretext for yielding to a natural appetite without violating a romantic species of modesty, which gratifies the pride and libertinism of man.

Women, deluded by these sentiments, sometimes boast of their weakness, cunningly obtaining power by playing on the *weakness* of men; and they may well glory in their illicit sway, for, like Turkish bashaws,[2] they have more real power than their masters; but virtue is sacrificed to temporary gratifications, and the respectability of life to the triumph of an hour.

Women, as well as despots, have now perhaps more power than they would have if the world, divided and subdivided into kingdoms and families, were governed by laws deduced from the exercise of reason; but in obtaining it, to carry on the comparison, their character is degraded, and licentiousness spread through the whole aggregate of society. The many become pedestal to the few. I, therefore, will venture to assert that till women are more rationally educated, the progress of human virtue and improvement in knowledge must receive continual checks. And if it be granted that woman was not created merely to gratify the appetite of man, or to be the upper servant, who provides his meals and takes care of his linen, it must follow that the first care of

---

man thoroughly, not the mind of man in general, abstractedly, but the dispositions of those men to whom she is subject either by the laws of her country or by the force of opinion. She should learn to penetrate into the real sentiments from their conversation, their actions, their looks and gestures. She should also have the art, by her own conversation, actions, looks, and gestures, to communicate those sentiments which are agreeable to them, without seeming to intend it. Men will argue more philosophically about the human heart; but women will read the heart of men better than they. It belongs to women—if I may be allowed the expression—to form an experimental morality, and to reduce the study of man to a system. Women have most wit, men have most genius; women observe, men reason. From the concurrence of both we derive the clearest light and the most perfect knowledge which the human mind is of itself capable of attaining. In one word, from hence we acquire the most intimate acquaintance, both with ourselves and others, of which our nature is capable; and it is thus that art has a constant tendency to perfect those endowments which nature has bestowed. The world is the book of women."—ROUSSEAU's *Emilius*.

I hope my readers still remember the comparison which I have brought forward between women and officers.

those mothers or fathers who really attend to the education of females should be, if not to strengthen the body, at least not to destroy the constitution by mistaken notions of beauty and female excellence; nor should girls ever be allowed to imbibe the pernicious notion that a defect can, by any chemical process of reasoning, become an excellence. In this respect I am happy to find that the author of one of the most instructive books that our country has produced for children, coincides with me in opinion. I shall quote his pertinent remarks to give the force of his respectable authority to reason.*

But should it be proved that woman is naturally weaker than man, whence does it follow that it is natural for her to labour to become still weaker than nature intended her to be? Arguments of this cast are an insult to common sense, and savour of passion. The *divine right* of husbands, like the divine right of kings, may, it is to be hoped, in this enlightened age, be contested without danger; and though conviction may not silence many boisterous disputants, yet, when any prevailing prejudice is attacked, the wise will consider, and leave the narrow-minded to rail with thoughtless vehemence at innovation.

*"A respectable old man gives the following sensible account of the method he pursued when educating his daughter: 'I endeavoured to give both to her mind and body a degree of vigour which is seldom found in the female sex. As soon as she was sufficiently advanced in strength to be capable of the lighter labours of husbandry and gardening, I employed her as my constant companion. Selene—for that was her name—soon acquired a dexterity in all these rustic employments which I considered with equal pleasure and admiration. If women are in general feeble both in body and mind, it arises less from nature than from education. We encourage a vicious indolence and inactivity, which we falsely call delicacy. Instead of hardening their minds by the severer principles of reason and philosophy, we breed them to useless arts, which terminate in vanity and sensuality. In most of the countries which I had visited they are taught nothing of an higher nature than a few modulations of the voice, or useless postures of the body; their time is consumed in sloth or trifles, and trifles become the only pursuits capable of interesting them. We seem to forget that it is upon the qualities of the female sex that our own domestic comforts and the education of our children must depend. And what are the comforts or the education which a race of beings, corrupted from their infancy, and unacquainted with all the duties of life, are fitted to bestow? To touch a musical instrument with useless skill, to exhibit their natural or affected graces to the eyes of indolent and debauched young men, to dissipate their husband's patrimony in riotous and unnecessary expenses, these are the only arts cultivated by women in most of the polished nations I had seen. And the consequences are uniformly such as may be expected to proceed from such polluted sources—private misery and public servitude.

" 'But Selene's education was regulated by different views, and conducted upon severer principles—if that can be called severity which opens the mind to a sense of moral and religious duties, and most effectually arms it against the inevitable evils of life.' "—MR DAY'S *Sandford and Merton*, vol. iii.

The mother who wishes to give true dignity of character to her daughter must, regardless of the sneers of ignorance, proceed on a plan diametrically opposite to that which Rousseau has recommended with all the deluding charms of eloquence and philosophic sophistry, for his eloquence renders absurdities plausible, and his dogmatic conclusions puzzle, without convincing, those who have not ability to refute them.

Throughout the whole animal kingdom every young creature requires almost continual exercise, and the infancy of children, conformable to this intimation, should be passed in harmless gambols that exercise the feet and hands, without requiring very minute direction from the head, or the constant attention of a nurse. In fact, the care necessary for self-preservation is the first natural exercise of the understanding as little inventions to amuse the present moment unfold the imagination. But these wise designs of nature are counteracted by mistaken fondness or blind zeal. The child is not left a moment to its own direction—particularly a girl—and thus rendered dependent. Dependence is called natural.

To preserve personal beauty—woman's glory—the limbs and faculties are cramped with worse than Chinese bands,[3] and the sedentary life which they are condemned to live, whilst boys frolic in the open air, weakens the muscles and relaxes the nerves. As for Rousseau's remarks, which have since been echoed by several writers, that they have naturally, that is, from their birth, independent of education, a fondness for dolls, dressing, and talking, they are so puerile as not to merit a serious refutation. That a girl, condemned to sit for hours together listening to the idle chat of weak nurses, or to attend at her mother's toilet, will endeavour to join the conversation, is, indeed, very natural; and that she will imitate her mother or aunts, and amuse herself by adorning her lifeless doll, as they do in dressing her, poor innocent babe! is undoubtedly a most natural consequence. For men of the greatest abilities have seldom had sufficient strength to rise above the surrounding atmosphere; and if the pages of genius have always been blurred by the prejudices of the age, some allowance should be made for a sex, who, like kings, always see things through a false medium.

In this manner, may the fondness for dress, conspicuous in woman, be easily accounted for, without supposing it the result of a desire to please the sex on which they are dependent. The absurdity, in short, of supposing that a girl is naturally a coquette, and that a desire connected with the impulse of nature to propagate the species, should appear even before an improper education has, by heating the imagination, called it forth prematurely, is so unphilosophical, that such a sagacious observer as Rousseau would not have adopted it, if he had not been accustomed to make reason give way to his desire of singularity, and truth to a favourite paradox.

Yet thus to give a sex to mind was not very consistent with the principles of a man who argued so warmly, and so well, for the immortality of the soul. But what a weak barrier is truth when it stands in the way of an hypothesis! Rousseau respected—almost adored virtue—and yet he allowed himself to love with sensual fondness. His imagination constantly prepared inflammable fuel for his inflammable senses; but, in order to reconcile his respect for self-denial, fortitude, and those heroic virtues, which a mind like his could not coolly admire, he labours to invert a law of nature, and broaches a doctrine pregnant with mischief, and derogatory to the character of supreme wisdom.

His ridiculous stories, which tend to prove that girls are *naturally* attentive to their persons, without laying any stress on daily example, are below contempt. And that a little miss should have such a correct taste as to neglect the pleasing amusement of making O's, merely because she perceived that it was an ungraceful attitude, should be selected with the anecdotes of the learned pig.*

I have, probably, had an opportunity of observing more girls in their infancy than J. J. Rousseau. I can recollect my own feelings, and I have looked steadily around me; yet, so far from coinciding with him in opinion respecting the first dawn of the female character, I will venture to affirm, that a girl, whose spirits have not been damped by inactivity, or innocence tainted by false shame, will always be a romp, and the doll will never excite attention unless confinement allows her no alternative. Girls and boys, in short, would play harmlessly together, if the distinction of sex was not inculcated long before nature makes any

---

*"I once knew a young person who learned to write before she learned to read, and began to write with her needle before she could use a pen. At first, indeed, she took it into her head to make no letter than the O: this letter she was constantly making of all sizes, and always the wrong way. Unluckily, one day, as she was intent of this employment, she happened to see herself in the looking-glass; when, taking a dislike to the constrained attitude in which she sat while writing, she threw away her pen, like another Pallas, and determined against making the O any more. Her brother was also equally averse to writing; it was the confinement, however, and not the constrained attitude, that most disgusted him."—ROUSSEAU's *Emilius*.

difference. I will go further, and affirm, as an indisputable fact, that most of the women, in the circle of my observation, who have acted like rational creatures, or shown any vigour of intellect, have accidentally been allowed to run wild, as some of the elegant formers of the fair sex would insinuate.

The baneful consequences which flow from inattention to health during infancy and youth, extend further than is supposed—dependence of body naturally produces dependence of mind; and how can she be a good wife or mother, the greater part of whose time is employed to guard against or endure sickness? Nor can it be expected that a woman will resolutely endeavour to strengthen her constitution and abstain from enervating indulgences, if artificial notions of beauty, and false descriptions of sensibility, have been early entangled with her motives of action. Most men are sometimes obliged to bear with bodily inconveniences, and to endure, occasionally, the inclemency of the elements; but genteel women are, literally speaking, slaves to their bodies, and glory in their subjection.

I once knew a weak woman of fashion, who was more than commonly proud of her delicacy and sensibility. She thought a distinguishing taste and puny appetite the height of all human perfection, and acted accordingly. I have seen this weak sophisticated being neglect all the duties of life, yet recline with self-complacency on a sofa, and boast of her want of appetite as a proof of delicacy that extended to, or, perhaps, arose from, her exquisite sensibility; for it is difficult to render intelligible such ridiculous jargon. Yet, at the moment, I have seen her insult a worthy old gentlewoman, whom unexpected misfortunes had made dependent on her ostentatious bounty, and who, in better days, had claims on her gratitude. Is it possible that a human creature could have become such a weak and depraved being, if, like the Sybarites, dissolved in luxury, everything like virtue had not been worn away, or never impressed by precept, a poor substitute, it is true, for cultivation of mind, though it serves as a fence against vice?

Such a woman is not a more irrational monster than some of the Roman emperors, who were depraved by lawless power. Yet, since kings have been more under the restraint of law, and the curb, however weak, of honour, the records of history are not filled with such unnatural instances of folly and cruelty, nor does the despotism that kills virtue and genius in the bud, hover over Europe with that destructive blast which desolates Turkey, and renders the men, as well as the soil, unfruitful.

Women are everywhere, in this deplorable state; for, in order to preserve their innocence, as ignorance is courteously termed, truth is hidden from them, and they are made to assume an artificial character before their faculties have acquired any strength. Taught from their infancy that beauty is woman's sceptre, the mind shapes itself to the body, and roaming round its gilt cage, only seeks to adore its prison. Men have various employments and pursuits which engage their attention, and give a character to the opening mind; but women, confined to one, and having their thoughts constantly directed to the most insignificant part of themselves, seldom extend their views beyond the triumph of the hour. But were their understanding once emancipated from the slavery to which the pride and sensuality of man and their short-sighted desire, like that of dominion in tyrants, of present sway, has subjected them, we should probably read of their weaknesses with surprise. I must be allowed to pursue the argument a little further.

Perhaps, if the existence of an evil being were allowed, who, in the allegorical language of Scripture, went about seeking whom he should devour, he could not more effectually degrade the human character, than by giving a man absolute power.

This argument branches into various ramifications. Birth, riches, and every extrinsic advantage that exalt a man above his fellows, without any mental exertion, sink him in reality below them. In proportion to this weakness, he is played upon by designing men, till the bloated monster has lost all traces of humanity. And that tribes of men, like flocks of sheep, should quietly follow such a leader, is a solecism that only a desire of present enjoyment and narrowness of understanding can solve. Educated in slavish dependence, and enervated by luxury and sloth, where shall we find men who will stand forth to assert the rights of man, or claim the privilege of moral beings, who should have but one road to excellence? Slavery to monarchs and ministers, which the world will be long in freeing itself from, and whose deadly grasp stops the progress of the human mind, is not yet abolished.

Let not men then in the pride of power, use the same arguments that tyrannic kings and venal ministers have used, and fallaciously assert that woman ought to be subjected because she has always been so. But, when man, governed by reasonable laws, enjoys his natural freedom, let him despise woman, if she do not share it with him; and, till that glorious period arrives, in descanting on the folly of the sex, let him not overlook his own.

Women, it is true, obtaining power by unjust means, by practising or fostering vice, evidently lose the rank which reason would assign them, and they become either abject slaves or capricious tyrants. They lose all simplicity, all dignity of mind, in acquiring power, and act as men are observed to act when they have been exalted by the same means.

It is time to effect a revolution in female manners—time to restore to them their lost dignity—and make them, as a part of the human species, labour by reforming themselves to reform the world. It is time to separate unchangeable morals from local manners. If men be demi-gods, why let us serve them! And if the dignity of the female soul be as disputable as that of animals—if their reason does not afford sufficient light to direct their conduct whilst unerring instinct is denied—they are surely of all creatures the most miserable! and, bent beneath the iron hand of destiny, must submit to be a *fair defect* in creation. But to justify the ways of Providence respecting them, by pointing out some irrefragable reason for thus making such a large portion of mankind accountable and not accountable, would puzzle the subtilest casuist.

The only solid foundation for morality appears to be the character of the Supreme Being; the harmony of which arises from a balance of attributes;—and, to speak with reverence, one attribute seems to imply the *necessity* of another. He must be just, because He is wise; He must be good, because He is omnipotent. For to exalt one attribute at the expense of another equally noble and necessary, bears the stamp of the warped reason of man—the homage of passion. Man, accustomed to bow down to power in his savage state, can seldom divest himself of this barbarous prejudice, even when civilization determines how much superior mental is to bodily strength; and his reason is clouded by these crude opinions, even when he thinks of the Deity. His omnipotence is made to swallow up, or preside over His other attributes, and those mortals are supposed to limit His power irreverently, who think that it must be regulated by His wisdom.

I disclaim that specious humility which, after investigating nature, stops at the Author. The High and Lofty One, who inhabiteth eternity, doubtless possesses many attributes of which we can form no conception; but Reason tells me that they cannot clash with those I adore—and I am compelled to listen to her voice.

It seems natural for man to search for excellence, and either to trace it in the object that he worships, or blindly to invest it with perfection, as a garment. But what good effect can the latter mode of worship have on the moral conduct of a rational being? He bends to power; he adores a dark cloud, which may open a bright prospect to him, to burst in angry, lawless fury, on his devoted head—he knows not why. And, supposing that the Deity acts from the vague impulse of an undirected will, man must also follow his own, or act according to rules, deduced from principles which he disclaims as irreverent. Into this dilemma have both enthusiasts and cooler thinkers fallen, when they laboured to free men from the wholesome restraints which a just conception of the character of God imposes.

It is not impious thus to scan the attributes of the Almighty: in fact, who can avoid it that exercises his faculties? For to love God as the fountain of wisdom, goodness, and power, appears to be the only worship useful to a being who wishes to acquire either virtue or knowledge. A blind unsettled affection may, like human passions, occupy the mind and warm the heart, whilst, to do justice, love mercy, and walk humbly with our God, is forgotten. I shall pursue this subject still further, when I consider religion in a light opposite to that recommended by Dr. Gregory, who treats it as a matter of sentiment or taste.

To return from this apparent digression. It were to be wished that women would cherish an affection for their husbands, founded on the same principle that devotion ought to rest upon. No other firm base is there under heaven—for let them beware of the fallacious light of sentiment; too often used as a softer phrase for sensuality. It follows then, I think, that from their infancy women should either be shut up like Eastern princes, or educated in such a manner as to be able to think and act for themselves.

Why do men halt between two opinions, and expect impossibilities? Why do they expect virtue from a slave, from a being whom the constitution of civil society has rendered weak, if not vicious?

Still I know that it will require a considerable length of time to eradicate the firmly rooted prejudices which sensualists have planted; it will also require some time to convince women that they act contrary to their real interest on an enlarged scale, when they cherish or affect weakness under the name of delicacy, and to convince the world that the poisoned source of female vices and follies, if it be necessary, in compliance with custom, to use synonymous terms in a lax sense, has been the sensual homage paid to beauty:—to beauty of features; for it has been shrewdly observed by a German writer, that a pretty woman, as an object of desire, is generally allowed to be so by men of all descriptions; whilst a fine woman, who inspires more sublime emotions by displaying intellectual beauty, may be overlooked or observed with indifference, by those men who find their happiness in the gratification of their appetites. I foresee an obvious retort—whilst man remains such an imperfect being as he appears hitherto to have been, he will, more or less, be the slave of his appetites; and those women obtaining most power who gratify a predominant one, the sex is degraded by a physical, if not by a moral necessity.

This objection has, I grant, some force; but while such a sublime precept exists, as, "Be pure as your heavenly Father is pure"; it would seem that the virtues of man are not limited by the Being who alone could limit them; and that he may press forward without considering whether he steps out of his sphere by indulging such a noble ambition. To the wild billows it has been said, "Thus far shalt thou go, and no farther; and here shall thy proud waves be stayed." Vainly then do they beat and foam, restrained by the power that confines the struggling planets in their orbits, matter yields to the great governing Spirit. But an immortal soul, not restrained by mechanical laws and struggling to free itself from the shackles of matter, contributes to, instead of disturbing, the order of creation, when, co-operating with the Father of spirits, it tries to govern itself by the invariable rule that, in a degree, before which our imagination faints, the universe is regulated.

Besides, if woman be educated for dependence, that is, to act according to the will of another fallible being, and submit, right or wrong, to power, where are we to stop? Are they to be considered as viceregents allowed to reign over a small domain, and answerable for their conduct to a higher tribunal, liable to error?

It will not be difficult to prove that such delegates will act like men subjected by fear, and make their children and servants endure their tyrannical oppression. As they submit without reason, they will, having no fixed rules to square their conduct by, be kind, or cruel, just as the whim of the moment directs; and we ought not to wonder if sometimes, galled by their heavy yoke, they take a malignant pleasure in resting it on weaker shoulders.

But, supposing a woman, trained up to obedience, be married to a sensible man, who directs her judgement without making her feel the servility of her subjection, to act with as much propriety by this reflected light as can be expected when reason is taken at secondhand, yet she cannot ensure the life of her protector; he may die and leave her with a large family.

A double duty devolves on her; to educate them in the character of both father and mother; to form their principles and secure their property. But, alas! she has never thought, much less acted for herself. She has only learned to please* men, to depend gracefully on them; yet, encumbered with children, how is she to obtain another protector—a husband to supply the place of reason? A rational man, for we are not treading on romantic ground, though he may think her a pleasing docile creature, will not choose to marry a *family* for love, when the world contains many more pretty creatures. What is then to become of her? She either falls an easy prey to some mean fortune-hunter, who defrauds her children of their paternal inheritance, and renders her miserable; or becomes the victim of discontent and blind indulgence. Unable to educate her sons, or impress them with respect,—for it is not a play on words to assert, that people are never respected, though filling an important station, who are not respectable,—she pines under the anguish of unavailing impotent regret. The serpent's tooth enters into her very soul, and the vices of licentious youth bring her with sorrow, if not with poverty also, to the grave.

This is not an overcharged picture; on the contrary, it is a very possible case, and something similar must have fallen under every attentive eye.

---

*"In the union of the sexes, both pursue one common object, but not in the same manner. From their diversity in this particular, arises the first determinate difference between the moral relations of each. The one should be active and strong, the other passive and weak; it is necessary the one should have both the power and the will, and that the other should make little resistance.

"This principle being established, it follows that woman is expressly formed to please the man: if the obligation be reciprocal also, and the man ought to please in his turn, it is not so immediately necessary: his great merit is in his power, and he pleases merely because he is strong. This, I must confess, is not one of the refined maxims of love; it is, however, one of the laws of nature, prior to love itself.

"If woman be formed to please and be subjected to man, it is her place, doubtless, to render herself agreeable to him, instead of challenging his passion. The violence of his desires depends on her charms; it is by means of these she should urge him to the exertion of those powers which nature hath given him. The most successful method of exciting them, is, to render such exertion necessary by resistance; as, in that case, self-love is added to desire, and the one triumphs in the victory which the other is obliged to acquire. Hence arise the various modes of attack and defence between the sexes; the boldness of one sex and the timidity of the other; and, in a word, that bashfulness and modesty with which nature hath armed the weak in order to subdue the strong."—ROUSSEAU'S *Emilius*.

I shall make no other comment on this ingenious passage than just to observe, that it is the philosophy of lasciviousness.

I have, however, taken it for granted, that she was well disposed, though experience shows, that the blind may as easily be led into a ditch as along the beaten road. But supposing, no very improbable conjecture, that a being only taught to please must still find her happiness in pleasing; what an example of folly, not to say vice, will she be to her innocent daughters! The mother will be lost in the coquette, and, instead of making friends of her daughters, view them with eyes askance, for they are rivals—rivals more cruel than any other, because they invite a comparison, and drive her from the throne of beauty, who has never thought of a seat on the bench of reason.

It does not require a lively pencil, or the discriminating outline of a caricature, to sketch the domestic miseries and petty vices which such a mistress of a family diffuses. Still she only acts as a woman ought to act, brought up according to Rousseau's system. She can never be reproached for being masculine, or turning out of her sphere; nay, she may observe another of his grand rules, and, cautiously preserving her reputation free from spot, be reckoned a good kind of woman. Yet in what respect can she be termed good? She abstains, it is true, without any great struggle, from committing gross crimes; but how does she fulfil her duties? Duties! in truth she has enough to think of to adorn her body and nurse a weak constitution.

With respect to religion, she never presumed to judge for herself; but conformed, as a dependent creature should, to the ceremonies of the Church which she was brought up in, piously believing that wiser heads than her own have settled that business; and not to doubt is her point of perfection. She therefore pays her tithe of mint and cumin— and thanks her God that she is not as other women are. These are the blessed effects of a good education! These are the virtues of man's helpmate!*

I must relieve myself by drawing a different picture.

Let fancy now present a woman with a tolerable understanding, for I do not wish to leave the line of mediocrity, whose constitution, strengthened by exercise, has allowed her body to acquire its full

*"O how lovely," exclaims Rousseau, speaking of Sophia, "is her ignorance! Happy is he who is destined to instruct her! She will never pretend to be the tutor of her husband, but will be content to be his pupil. Far from attempting to subject him to her taste, she will accommodate herself to his. She will be more estimable to him, than if she was learned, he will have a pleasure in instructing her."—Rousseau's *Emilius.*

I shall content myself with simply asking, how friendship can subsist when love expires, between the master and his pupil.

vigour; her mind, at the same time, gradually expanding itself to comprehend the moral duties of life, and in what human virtue and dignity consist.

Formed thus by the discharge of the relative duties of her station, she marries from affection, without losing sight of prudence, and looking beyond matrimonial felicity, she secures her husband's respect before it is necessary to exert mean arts to please him and feed a dying flame, which nature doomed to expire when the object became familiar, when friendship and forbearance take place of a more ardent affection. This is the natural death of love, and domestic peace is not destroyed by struggles to prevent its extinction. I also suppose the husband to be virtuous; or she is still more in want of independent principles.

Fate, however, breaks this tie. She is left a widow, perhaps, without a sufficient provision; but she is not desolate! The pang of nature is felt; but after time has softened sorrow into melancholy resignation, her heart turns to her children with redoubled fondness, and anxious to provide for them, affection gives a sacred heroic cast to her maternal duties. She thinks that not only the eye sees her virtuous efforts from whom all her comfort now must flow, and whose approbation is life; but her imagination, a little abstracted and exalted by grief, dwells on the fond hope that the eyes which her trembling hand closed, may still see how she subdues every wayward passion to fulfil the double duty of being the father as well as the mother of her children. Raised to heroism by misfortunes, she represses the first faint dawning of a natural inclination, before it ripens into love, and in the bloom of life forgets her sex—forgets the pleasure of an awakening passion, which might again have been inspired and returned. She no longer thinks of pleasing, and conscious dignity prevents her from priding herself on account of the praise which her conduct demands. Her children have her love, and her brightest hopes are beyond the grave, where her imagination often strays.

I think I see her surrounded by her children, reaping the reward of her care. The intelligent eye meets hers, whilst health and innocence smile on their chubby cheeks, and as they grow up the cares of life are lessened by their grateful attention. She lives to see the virtues which she endeavoured to plant on principles, fixed into habits, to see her children attain a strength of character sufficient to enable them to endure adversity without forgetting their mother's example.

The task of life thus fulfilled, she calmly waits for the sleep of death, and rising from the grave, may say—"Behold, Thou gavest me a talent, and here are five talents."

I wish to sum up what I have said in a few words, for I here throw down my gauntlet, and deny the existence of sexual virtues, not excepting modesty. For man and woman, truth, if I understand the meaning of the word, must be the same; yet the fanciful female character, so prettily drawn by poets and novelists, demanding the sacrifice of truth and sincerity, virtue becomes a relative idea, having no other foundation than utility, and of that utility men pretend arbitrarily to judge, shaping it to their own convenience.

Women, I allow, may have different duties to fulfil; but they are *human* duties, and the principles that should regulate the discharge of them, I sturdily maintain, must be the same.

To become respectable, the exercise of their understanding is necessary, there is no other foundation for independence of character; I mean explicitly to say that they must only bow to the authority of reason, instead of being the *modest* slaves of opinion.

In the superior ranks of life how seldom do we meet with a man of superior abilities, or even common acquirements? The reason appears to me clear, the state they are born in was an unnatural one. The human character has ever been formed by the employments the individual, or class, pursues; and if the faculties are not sharpened by necessity, they must remain obtuse. The argument may fairly be extended to women; for, seldom occupied by serious business, the pursuit of pleasure gives that insignificancy to their character which renders the society of the *great* so insipid. The same want of firmness, produced by a similar cause, forces them both to fly from themselves to noisy pleasures, and artificial passions, till vanity takes place of every social affection, and the characteristics of humanity can scarcely be discerned. Such are the blessings of civil governments, as they are at present organized, that wealth and female softness equally tend to debase mankind, and are produced by the same cause; but allowing women to be rational creatures, they should be incited to acquire virtues which they may call their own, for how can a rational being be ennobled by anything that is not obtained by its *own* exertions?

# CHAPTER IV

# OBSERVATIONS ON THE STATE OF
# DEGRADATION TO WHICH WOMAN IS REDUCED
# BY VARIOUS CAUSES

That woman is naturally weak, or degraded by a concurrence of circumstances, is, I think, clear. But this position I shall simply contrast with a conclusion, which I have frequently heard fall from sensible men in favour of an aristocracy: that the mass of mankind cannot be anything, or the obsequious slaves, who patiently allow themselves to be driven forward, would feel their own consequence, and spurn their chains. Men, they further observe, submit everywhere to oppression, when they have only to lift up their heads to throw off the yoke; yet, instead of asserting their birthright, they quietly lick the dust, and say, "Let us eat and drink, for tomorrow we die."[1] Women, I argue from analogy, are degraded by the same propensity to enjoy the present moment, and at last despise the freedom which they have not sufficient virtue to struggle to attain. But I must be more explicit.

With respect to the culture of the heart, it is unanimously allowed that sex is out of the question; but the line of subordination in the mental powers is never to be passed over.* Only "absolute in loveli-

---

*Into what inconsistencies do men fall when they argue without the compass of principles. Women, weak women, are compared with angels; yet, a superior order of beings should be supposed to possess more intellect than man; or, in what does their superiority consist? In the same strain, to drop the sneer, they are allowed to possess more goodness of heart; piety, and benevolence. I doubt the fact, though it be courteously brought forward, unless ignoness," the portion of rationality granted to woman is, indeed, very scanty; for denying her genius and judgement, it is scarcely possible to divine what remains to characterize intellect.

The stamen of immortality, if I may be allowed the phrase, is the perfectibility of human reason; for, were man created perfect, or did a flood of knowledge break in upon him, when he arrived at maturity, that precluded error, I should doubt whether his existence would be continued after the dissolution of the body. But, in the present state of things, every difficulty in morals that escapes from human discussion, and equally baffles the investigation of profound thinking, and the lightning glance of genius, is an argument on which I build my belief of the immortality of the soul. Reason is, consequentially, the simple power of improvement; or, more properly speaking, of discerning truth. Every individual is in this respect a world in itself. More or less may be conspicuous in one being than another; but the nature of reason must be the same in all, if it be an emanation of divinity, the tie that connects the creature with the Creator; for, can that soul be stamped with the heavenly image, that is not perfected by the exercise of its own reason?* Yet outwardly ornamented with elaborate care, and so adorned to delight man, "that with honour he may love,"** the soul of woman is not allowed to have this distinction, and man, ever placed between her and reason, she is always represented as only created to see through a gross medium, and to take things on trust. But dismissing these fanciful theories, and considering woman as a whole, let it be what it will, instead of a part of man, the inquiry is whether she have reason or not. If she have, which, for a moment, I will take for granted, she was not created merely to be the solace of man, and the sexual should not destroy the human character.

Into this error men have, probably, been led by viewing education in a false light; not considering it as the first step to form a being advancing gradually towards perfection;*** but only as a preparation for life. On this sensual error, for I must call it so, has the false system of female manners been reared, which robs the whole sex of its dignity,

---

rance be allowed to be the mother of devotion; for I am firmly persuaded that, on an average, the proportion between virtue and knowledge, is more upon a par than is commonly granted.

*"The brutes," says Lord Monboddo,[2] "remain in the state in which nature has placed them, except in so far as their natural instinct is improved by the culture *we* bestow upon them."

** *Vide* Milton.

***This word is not strictly just, but I cannot find a better.

and classes the brown and fair with the smiling flowers that only adorn the land. This has ever been the language of men, and the fear of departing from a supposed sexual character, has made even women of superior sense adopt the same sentiments.* Thus understanding, strictly speaking, has been denied to woman; and instinct, sublimated into wit and cunning, for the purposes of life, has been substituted in its stead.

The power of generalizing ideas, of drawing comprehensive conclusions from individual observations, is the only acquirement, for an immortal being, that really deserves the name of knowledge. Merely to observe, without endeavouring to account for anything, may (in a very incomplete manner) serve as the common sense of life; but where is the store laid up that is to clothe the soul when it leaves the body?

This power has not only been denied to women; but writers have insisted that it is inconsistent, with a few exceptions, with their sexual

---

*"Pleasure's the portion of th' *inferior* kind;
But glory, virtue, Heaven for *man* designed."

After writing these lines, how could Mrs. Barbauld³ write the following ignoble comparison?

### "TO A LADY WITH SOME PAINTED FLOWERS

"Flowers to the fair: to you these flowers I bring,
And strive to greet you with an earlier spring.
*Flowers,* SWEET, *and gay, and* DELICATE LIKE YOU;
*Emblems of innocence, and beauty too.*
With flowers the Graces bind their yellow hair
And flowery wreaths consenting lovers wear.
*Flowers the sole luxury which Nature knew,*
In Eden's pure and guiltless garden grew.
To loftier forms are rougher tasks assign'd;
The sheltering oak resists the stormy wind,
The tougher yew repels invading foes,
And the tall pine for future navies grows;

But this soft family, to cares unknown,
Were born for pleasure and delights ALONE.
Gay without toil, and lovely without art,
They spring to CHEER the sense, and GLAD the heart.
Nor blush, my fair, to own you copy these;
*Your* BEST, *your* SWEETEST *empire is*—to PLEASE."

So the men tell us; but virtue, says reason, must be acquired by *rough* toils, and useful struggles with worldly *cares.*

character. Let men prove this, and I shall grant that woman only exists for man. I must, however, previously remark, that the power of generalizing ideas, to any great extent, is not very common amongst men or women. But this exercise is the true cultivation of the understanding; and everything conspires to render the cultivation of the understanding more difficult in the female than the male world.

I am naturally led by this assertion to the main subject of the present chapter, and shall now attempt to point out some of the causes that degrade the sex, and prevent women from generalizing their observations.

I shall not go back to the remote annals of antiquity to trace the history of woman; it is sufficient to allow that she has always been either a slave or a despot, and to remark that each of these situations equally retards the progress of reason. The grand source of female folly and vice has ever appeared to me to arise from narrowness of mind; and the very constitution of civil governments has put almost insuperable obstacles in the way to prevent the cultivation of the female understanding; yet virtue can be built on no other foundation. The same obstacles are thrown in the way of the rich, and the same consequences ensue.

Necessity has been proverbially termed the mother of invention; the aphorism may be extended to virtue. It is an acquirement, and an acquirement to which pleasure must be sacrificed; and who sacrifices pleasure when it is within the grasp, whose mind has not been opened and strengthened by adversity, or the pursuit of knowledge goaded on by necessity? Happy is it when people have the cares of life to struggle with, for these struggles prevent their becoming a prey to enervating vices, merely from idleness. But if from their birth men and women be placed in a torrid zone, with the meridian sun of pleasure darting directly upon them, how can they sufficiently brace their minds to discharge the duties of life, or even to relish the affections that carry them out of themselves?

Pleasure is the business of woman's life, according to the present modification of society; and while it continues to be so, little can be expected from such weak beings. Inheriting in a lineal descent from the first fair defect in nature—the sovereignty of beauty—they have, to maintain their power, resigned the natural rights which the exercise of reason might have procured them, and chosen rather to be short-lived queens than labour to obtain the sober pleasures that arise from equality. Exalted by their inferiority (this sounds like a contradiction), they constantly demand homage as women, though experience should teach them that the men who pride themselves upon paying this arbitrary insolent respect to the sex, with the most scrupulous exactness, are most inclined to tyrannize over, and despise the very weakness they cherish. Often do they repeat Mr. Hume's[4] sentiments, when, comparing the French and Athenian character, he alludes to women,— "But what is more singular in this whimsical nation, say I to the Athenians, is, that a frolic of yours during the saturnalia, when the slaves are served by their masters, is seriously continued by them through the whole year, and through the whole course of their lives, accompanied, too, with some circumstances, which still further augment the absurdity and ridicule. Your sport only elevates for a few days those whom fortune has thrown down, and whom she too, in sport, may really elevate for ever above you. But this nation gravely exalts those whom nature has subjected to them, and whose inferiority and infirmities are absolutely incurable. The women, though without virtue, are their masters and sovereigns."

Ah! why do women—I write with affectionate solicitude— condescend to receive a degree of attention and respect from strangers different from that reciprocation of civility which the dictates of humanity and the politeness of civilization authorize between man and man? And why do they not discover, when "in the noon of beauty's power," that they are treated like queens only to be deluded by hollow respect, till they are led to resign, or not assume, their natural prerogatives? Confined, then, in cages like the feathered race, they have nothing to do but to plume themselves, and stalk with mock majesty from perch to perch. It is true they are provided with food and raiment, for which they neither toil nor spin; but health, liberty, and virtue are given in exchange. But where, amongst mankind, has been found sufficient strength of mind to enable a being to resign these adventitious prerogatives—one who, rising with the calm dignity of reason above opinion, dared to be proud of the privileges inherent in man? And it is vain to expect it whilst hereditary power chokes the affections, and nips reason in the bud.

The passions of men have thus placed women on thrones, and till mankind become more reasonable, it is to be feared that women will avail themselves of the power which they attain with the least exertion, and which is the most indisputable. They will smile—yes, they will smile, though told that:

> In beauty's empire is no mean,
> And woman, either slave or queen,
> Is quickly scorned when not adored.[5]

But the adoration comes first, and the scorn is not anticipated.

Louis XIV, in particular, spread factitious manners, and caught, in a specious way, the whole nation in his toils; for, establishing an artful chain of despotism, he made it the interest of the people at large individually to respect his station, and support his power. And women, whom he flattered by a puerile attention to the whole sex, obtained in his reign that prince-like distinction so fatal to reason and virtue.

A king is always a king, and a woman always a woman.* His authority and her sex ever stand between them and rational converse. With a lover, I grant, she should be so, and her sensibility will naturally lead her to endeavour to excite emotion, not to gratify her vanity, but her heart. This I do not allow to be coquetry; it is the artless impulse of nature. I only exclaim against the sexual desire of conquest when the heart is out of the question.

This desire is not confined to women. "I have endeavoured," says Lord Chesterfield,[6] "to gain the hearts of twenty women, whose persons I would not have given a fig for." The libertine who, in a gust of passion, takes advantage of unsuspecting tenderness, is a saint when compared with this cold-hearted rascal—for I like to use significant words. Yet only taught to please, women are always on the watch to please, and with true heroic ardour endeavour to gain hearts merely to resign or spurn them when the victory is decided and conspicuous.

I must descend to the minutiae of the subject.

I lament that women are systematically degraded by receiving the trivial attentions which men think it manly to pay to the sex, when in fact, they are insultingly supporting their own superiority. It is not condescension to bow to an inferior. So ludicrous, in fact, do these ceremonies appear to me that I scarcely am able to govern my muscles when I see a man start with eager and serious solicitude to lift a handkerchief or shut a door, when the *lady* could have done it herself, had she only moved a pace or two.

A wild wish has just flown from my heart to my head, and I will not

---

*And a wit always a wit, might be added, for the vain fooleries of wits and beauties to obtain attention, and make conquests, are much upon a par.

stifle it, though it may excite a horse-laugh. I do earnestly wish to see the distinction of sex confounded in society, unless where love animates the behaviour. For this distinction is, I am firmly persuaded, the foundation of the weakness of character ascribed to woman; is the cause why the understanding is neglected, whilst accomplishments are acquired with sedulous care; and the same cause accounts for their preferring the graceful before the heroic virtues.

Mankind, including every description, wish to be loved and respected by *something,* and the common herd will always take the nearest road to the completion of their wishes. The respect paid to wealth and beauty is the most certain and unequivocal, and, of course, will always attract the vulgar eye of common minds. Abilities and virtues are absolutely necessary to raise men from the middle rank of life into notice, and the natural consequence is notorious—the middle rank contains most virtue and abilities. Men have thus, in one station at least, an opportunity of exerting themselves with dignity, and of rising by the exertions which really improve a rational creature; but the whole female sex are, till their character is formed, in the same condition as the rich, for they are born—I now speak of a state of civilization—with certain sexual privileges; and whilst they are gratuitously granted them, few will ever think of works of supererogation to obtain the esteem of a small number of superior people.

When do we hear of women who, starting out of obscurity, boldly claim respect on account of their great abilities or daring virtues? Where are they to be found? "To be observed, to be attended to, to be taken notice of with sympathy, complacency, and approbation, are all the advantages which they seek." True! my male readers will probably exclaim; but let them, before they draw any conclusion, recollect that this was not written originally as descriptive of women, but of the rich. In Dr. Smith's[7] *Theory of Moral Sentiments* I have found a general character of people of rank and fortune, that, in my opinion, might with the greatest propriety be applied to the female sex. I refer the sagacious reader to the whole comparison, but must be allowed to quote a passage to enforce an argument that I mean to insist on, as the one most conclusive against a sexual character. For if, excepting warriors, no great men of any denomination have ever appeared amongst the nobility, may it not be fairly inferred that their local situation swallowed up the man, and produced a character similar to that of women, who are *localized*—if I may be allowed the word— by the rank they are placed in by *courtesy?* Women, commonly called ladies, are not to be contradicted, in company, are not allowed to exert any manual strength; and from them the negative virtues only are expected, when any virtues are expected—patience, docility, good humour, and flexibility—virtues incompatible with any vigorous exertion of intellect. Besides, by living more with each other, and being seldom absolutely alone, they are more under the influence of sentiments than passions. Solitude and reflection are necessary to give to wishes the force of passions, and to enable the imagination to enlarge the object, and make it the most desirable. The same may be said of the rich; they do not sufficiently deal in general ideas, collected by impassioned thinking or calm investigation, to acquire that strength of character on which great resolves are built. But hear what an acute observer says of the great:

"Do the great seem insensible of the easy price at which they may acquire the public admiration; or do they seem to imagine that to them, as to other men, it must be the purchase either of sweat or of blood? By what important accomplishments is the young nobleman instructed to support the dignity of his rank, and to render himself worthy of that superiority over his fellow-citizens, to which the virtue of his ancestors had raised them? Is it by knowledge, by industry, by patience, by self-denial, or by virtue of any kind. As all his words, as all his motions are attended to, he learns an habitual regard to every circumstance of ordinary behaviour, and studies to perform all those small duties with the most exact propriety. As he is conscious how much he is observed, and how much mankind are disposed to favour all his inclinations, he acts, upon the most indifferent occasions, with that freedom and elevation which the thought of this naturally inspires. His air, his manner, his deportment, all mark that elegant and graceful sense of his own superiority, which those who are born to inferior station can hardly ever arrive at. These are the arts by which he proposes to make mankind more easily submit to his authority, and to govern their inclinations according to his own pleasure; and in this he is seldom disappointed. These arts, supported by rank and preeminence, are, upon ordinary occasions, sufficient to govern the world. Louis XIV, during the greater part of his reign, was regarded, not only in France, but all over Europe, as the most perfect model of a great prince. But what were the talents and virtues by which he acquired this great reputation? Was it by the scrupulous and inflexible justice of all his undertakings, by the immense dangers and difficulties with which they were attended, or by the unwearied and unrelenting application with which he pursued them? Was it by his extensive knowledge, by his exquisite judgement, or by his heroic valour? It was by none of these qualities. But he was, first of all, the most powerful prince in Europe, and consequently held the highest rank among kings; and then, says his historian, 'he surpassed all his courtiers in the gracefulness of his shape, and the majestic beauty of his features. The sound of his voice, noble and affecting, gained those hearts which his presence intimidated. He had a step and a deportment which could suit only him and his rank, and which would have been ridiculous in any other person. The embarrassment which he occasioned to those who spoke to him, flattered that secret satisfaction with which he felt his own superiority.' These frivolous accomplishments, supported by his rank, and, no doubt too, by a degree of other talents and virtues, which seems, however, not to have been much above mediocrity, established this prince in the esteem of his own age, and have drawn, even from posterity, a good deal of respect for his memory. Compared with these, in his own times, and in his own presence, no other virtue, it seems, appeared to have any merit. Knowledge, industry, valour, and beneficence trembled, were abashed, and lost all dignity before them."

Woman also thus "in herself complete," by possessing all these *frivolous* accomplishments, so changes the nature of things:

> That what she wills to do or say
> Seems wisest, virtuousest, discreetest, best;
> All higher knowledge in *her presence* falls
> Degraded. Wisdom in discourse with her
> Loses discountenanced, and, like folly shows;
> Authority and reason on her wait.[8]

And all this is built on her loveliness!

In the middle rank of life, to continue the comparison, men, in their youth, are prepared for professions, and marriage is not considered as the grand feature in their lives; whilst women, on the contrary, have no other scheme to sharpen their faculties. It is not business, extensive plans, or any of the excursive flights of ambition, that engross their attention; no, their thoughts are not employed in rearing such noble structures. To rise in the world, and have the liberty of running from pleasure to pleasure, they must marry advantageously, and to this object their time is sacrificed, and their persons often legally prostituted. A man when he enters any profession has his eye steadily fixed on some future advantage (and the mind gains great strength by having all its efforts directed to one point), and, full of his business, pleasure is considered as mere relaxation; whilst women seek for pleasure as the main purpose of existence. In fact, from the education, which they receive from society, the love of pleasure may be said to govern them all; but does this prove that there is a sex in souls? It would be just as rational to declare that the courtiers in France, when a destructive system of despotism had formed their character, were not men, because liberty, virtue, and humanity, were sacrificed to pleasure and vanity. Fatal passions, which have ever domineered over the *whole* race!

The same love of pleasure, fostered by the whole tendency of their education, gives a trifling turn to the conduct of women in most circumstances; for instance, they are ever anxious about secondary things; and on the watch for adventures instead of being occupied by duties.

A man, when he undertakes a journey, has, in general, the end in view; a woman thinks more of the incidental occurrences, the strange things that may possibly occur on the road; the impression that she may make on her fellow-travellers; and, above all, she is anxiously intent on the care of the finery that she carries with her, which is more than ever a part of herself, when going to figure on a new scene; when, to use an apt French turn of expression, she is going to produce a sensation. Can dignity of mind exist with such trivial cares?

In short, women, in general, as well as the rich of both sexes, have acquired all the follies and vices of civilization, and missed the useful fruit. It is not necessary for me always to premise, that I speak of the condition of the whole sex, leaving exceptions out of the question. Their senses are inflamed, and their understandings neglected, consequently they become the prey of their senses, delicately termed sensibility, and are blown about by every momentary gust of feeling. Civilized women are, therefore, so weakened by false refinement, that, respecting morals, their condition is much below what it would be were they left in a state nearer to nature. Ever restless and anxious, their over-exercised sensibility not only renders them uncomfortable themselves, but troublesome, to use a soft phrase, to others. All their thoughts turn on things calculated to excite emotion and feeling, when they should reason, their conduct is unstable, and their opinions are wavering—not the wavering produced by deliberation or progressive views, but by contradictory emotions. By fits and starts, they are warm in many pursuits; yet this warmth, never concentrated into perseverance, soon exhausts itself; exhaled by its own heat, or meeting with some other fleeting passion, to which reason has never given any specific gravity, neutrality ensues. Miserable, indeed, must be that being whose cultivation of mind has only tended to inflame its passions! A distinction should be made between inflaming and strengthening them. The passions thus pampered, whilst the judgement is left unformed, what can be expected to ensue? Undoubtedly, a mixture of madness and folly!

This observation should not be confined to the *fair* sex; however, at present, I only mean to apply it to them.

Novels, music, poetry, and gallantry, all tend to make women the creatures of sensation, and their character is thus formed in the mould of folly during the time they are acquiring accomplishments, the only improvement they are excited, by their station in society, to acquire. This overstretched sensibility naturally relaxes the other powers of the mind, and prevents intellect from attaining that sovereignty which it ought to attain to render a rational creature useful to others, and content with its own station; for the exercise of the understanding, as life advances, is the only method pointed out by nature to calm the passions.

Satiety has a very different effect, and I have often been forcibly struck by an emphatical description of damnation; when the spirit is represented as continually hovering with abortive eagerness round the defiled body, unable to enjoy anything without the organs of sense. Yet, to their senses, are women made slaves, because it is by their sensibility that they obtain present power.

And will moralists pretend to assert that this is the condition in which one-half of the human race should be encouraged to remain with listless inactivity and stupid acquiescence? Kind instructors! what were we created for? To remain, it may be said, innocent; they mean in a state of childhood. We might as well never have been born, unless it were necessary that we should be created to enable man to acquire the noble privilege of reason, the power of discerning good from evil, whilst we lie down in the dust from whence we were taken, never to rise again.

It would be an endless task to trace the variety of meannesses, cares, and sorrows, into which women are plunged by the prevailing opinion, that they were created rather to feel than reason, and that all the power they obtain must be obtained by their charms and weakness:

Fine by defect, and amiably weak!⁹

And, made by this amiable weakness entirely dependent, excepting what they gain by illicit sway, on man, not only for protection, but advice, is it surprising that, neglecting the duties that reason alone points out, and shrinking from trials calculated to strengthen their minds, they only exert themselves to give their defects a graceful covering, which may serve to heighten their charms in the eye of the voluptuary, though it sink them below the scale of moral excellence.

Fragile in every sense of the word, they are obliged to look up to man for every comfort. In the most trifling danger they cling to their support, with parasitical tenacity, piteously demanding succour; and their *natural* protector extends his arm, or lifts up his voice, to guard the lovely trembler—from what? Perhaps the frown of an old cow, or the jump of a mouse; a rat would be a serious danger. In the name of reason, and even common sense, what can save such beings from contempt; even though they be soft and fair.

These fears, when not affected, may produce some pretty attitudes; but they show a degree of imbecility which degrades a rational creature in a way women are not aware of—for love and esteem are very distinct things.

I am fully persuaded that we should hear of none of these infantine airs, if girls were allowed to take sufficient exercise, and not confined in close rooms till their muscles are relaxed, and their powers of digestion destroyed. To carry the remark still further, if fear in girls, instead of being cherished, perhaps, created, were treated in the same manner as cowardice in boys, we should quickly see women with more dignified aspects. It is true, they could not then with equal propriety be termed the sweet flowers that smile in the walk of man; but they would be more respectable members of society, and discharge the important duties of life by the light of their own reason. "Educate women like men," says Rousseau, "and the more they resemble our sex the less power they will have over us." This is the very point I aim at. I do not wish them to have power over men; but over themselves.

In the same strain have I heard men argue against instructing the poor; for many are the forms that aristocracy assumes. "Teach them to read and write," say they, "and you take them out of the station assigned them by nature." An eloquent Frenchman has answered them, I will borrow his sentiments. "But they know not, when they make man a brute, that they may expect every instant to see him transformed into a ferocious beast. Without knowledge there can be no morality."

Ignorance is a frail base for virtue! Yet, that it is the condition for which woman was organized, has been insisted upon by the writers who have most vehemently argued in favour of the superiority of man; a superiority not in degree, but offence; though, to soften the argument, they have laboured to prove, with chivalrous generosity, that the sexes ought not to be compared; man was made to reason, woman to feel: and that together, flesh and spirit, they make the most perfect whole, by blending happily reason and sensibility into one character.

And what is sensibility? "Quickness of sensation, quickness of perception, delicacy." Thus is it defined by Dr. Johnson;[10] and the definition gives me no other idea than of the most exquisitely polished instinct. I discern not a trace of the image of God in either sensation or matter. Refined seventy times seven they are still material; intellect dwells not there; nor will fire ever make lead gold!

I come round to my old argument: if woman be allowed to have an immortal soul, she must have, as the employment of life, an understanding to improve. And when, to render the present state more complete, though everything proves it to be but a fraction of a mighty sum, she is incited by present gratification to forget her grand destination, nature is counteracted, or she was born only to procreate and rot. Or, granting brutes of every description a soul, though not a reasonable one, the exercise of instinct and sensibility may be the step which they are to take, in this life, towards the attainment of reason in the next; so that through all eternity they will lag behind man, who, why we cannot tell, had the power given him of attaining reason in his first mode of existence.

When I treat of the peculiar duties of women, as I should treat of the peculiar duties of a citizen or father, it will be found that I do not mean to insinuate that they should be taken out of their families, speaking of the majority. "He that hath wife and children," says Lord Bacon, "hath given hostages to fortune; for they are impediments to great enterprises, either of virtue or mischief. Certainly the best works, and of greatest merit for the public, have proceeded from the unmarried or childless men."[11] I say the same of women. But the welfare of society is not built on extraordinary exertions; and were it more reasonably organized, there would be still less need of great abilities, or heroic virtues.

In the regulation of a family, in the education of children, understanding, in an unsophisticated sense, is particularly required—strength both of body and mind; yet the men who, by their writings, have most earnestly laboured to domesticate women, have endeavoured, by arguments dictated by a gross appetite, which satiety had rendered fastidious, to weaken their bodies and cramp their minds. But, if even by these sinister methods they really *persuaded* women, by working on their feelings, to stay at home, and fulfil the duties of a mother and mistress of a family, I should cautiously oppose opinions that led women to right conduct, by prevailing on them to make the discharge of such important duties the main business of life, though reason were insulted. Yet, and I appeal to experience, if by neglecting the understanding they be as much, nay, more detached from these domestic employments, than they could be by the most serious intellectual pursuit, though it may be observed, that the mass of mankind will never vigorously pursue an intellectual object,* I may be allowed to infer that reason is absolutely necessary to enable a woman to perform any duty properly, and I must again repeat, that sensibility is not reason.

The comparison with the rich still occurs to me; for, when men neglect the duties of humanity, women will follow their example; a common stream hurries them both along with thoughtless celerity. Riches and honours prevent a man from enlarging his understanding, and enervate all his powers by reversing the order of nature, which has ever made true pleasure the reward of labour. Pleasure—enervating pleasure—is, likewise, within women's reach without earning it. But, till hereditary possessions are spread abroad, how can we expect men to be proud of virtue? And, till they are, women will govern them by the most direct means, neglecting their dull domestic duties to catch the pleasure that sits lightly on the wing of time.

"The power of the woman," says some author, "is her sensibility"; and men, not aware of the consequence, do all they can to make this power swallow up every other. Those who constantly employ their

---

*The mass of mankind are rather the slaves of their appetites than of their passions.

sensibility will have most; for example, poets, painters, and composers.* Yet, when the sensibility is thus increased at the expense of reason, and even the imagination, why do philosophical men complain of their fickleness? The sexual attention of man particularly acts on female sensibility, and this sympathy has been exercised from their youth up. A husband cannot long pay those attentions with the passion necessary to excite lively emotions, and the heart, accustomed to lively emotions, turns to a new lover, or pines in secret, the prey of virtue or prudence. I mean when the heart has really been rendered susceptible, and the taste formed; for I am apt to conclude, from what I have seen in this fashionable life, that vanity is oftener fostered than sensibility by the mode of education, and the intercourse between the sexes, which I have reprobated; and that coquetry more frequently proceeds from vanity than from that inconstancy which overstrained sensibility naturally produces.

Another argument that has had great weight with me must, I think, have some force with every considerate benevolent heart. Girls who have been thus weakly educated are often cruelly left by their parents without any provision, and, of course, are dependent on not only the reason, but the bounty of their brothers. These brothers are, to view the fairest side of the question, good sort of men, and give as a favour what children of the same parents had an equal right to. In this equivocal humiliating situation a docile female may remain some time with a tolerable degree of comfort. But when the brother marries—a probable circumstance—from being considered as the mistress of the family, she is viewed with averted looks as an intruder, an unnecessary burden on the benevolence of the master of the house and his new partner.

Who can recount the misery which many unfortunate beings, whose minds and bodies are equally weak, suffer in such situations—unable to work, and ashamed to beg? The wife, a cold-hearted, narrow-minded woman—and this is not an unfair supposition, for the present mode of education does not tend to enlarge the heart any more than the understanding—is jealous of the little kindness which her husband shows to his relations; and her sensibility not rising to humanity, she is

*Men of these descriptions pour sensibility into the compositions, to amalgamate the gross materials; and, moulding them with passion, give to the inert body a soul; but, in woman's imagination, love alone concentrates these ethereal beams.

displeased at seeing the property of *her* children lavished on an helpless sister.

These are matters of fact, which have come under my eye again and again. The consequence is obvious; the wife has recourse to cunning to undermine the habitual affection which she is afraid openly to oppose; and neither tears nor caresses are spared till the spy is worked out of her home, and thrown on the world, unprepared for its difficulties; or sent, as a great effort of generosity, or from some regard to propriety, with a small stipend, and an uncultivated mind, into joyless solitude.

These two women may be much upon a par with respect to reason and humanity, and, changing situations, might have acted just the same selfish part; but had they been differently educated, the case would also have been very different. The wife would not have had that sensibility, of which self is the centre, and reason might have taught her not to expect, and not even to be flattered by, the affection of her husband, if it led him to violate prior duties. She would wish not to love him merely because he loved her, but on account of his virtues; and the sister might have been able to struggle for herself instead of eating the bitter bread of dependence.

I am, indeed, persuaded that the heart, as well as the understanding, is opened by cultivation, and by—which may not appear so clear—strengthening the organs. I am not now talking of momentary flashes of sensibility, but of affections. And, perhaps, in the education of both sexes, the most difficult task is so to adjust instruction as not to narrow the understanding, whilst the heart is warmed by the generous juices of spring, just raised by the electric fermentation of the season; nor to dry up the feelings by employing the mind in investigations remote from life.

With respect to women, when they receive a careful education, they are either made fine ladies, brimful of sensibility, and teeming with capricious fancies, or mere notable women. The latter are often friendly, honest creatures, and have a shrewd kind of good sense, joined with worldly prudence, that often render them more useful members of society than the fine sentimental lady, though they possess neither greatness of mind nor taste. The intellectual world is shut against them. Take them out of their family or neighbourhood, and they stand still; the mind finding no employment, for literature affords a fund of amusement which they have never sought to relish, but frequently to despise. The sentiments and taste of more cultivated minds appear ridiculous, even in those whom chance and family connections have led them to love; but in mere acquaintance they think it all affectation.

A man of sense can only love such a woman on account of her sex, and respect her because she is a trusty servant. He lets her, to preserve his own peace, scold the servants, and go to church in clothes made of the very best materials. A man of her own size of understanding would probably not agree so well with her, for he might wish to encroach on her prerogative, and manage some domestic concerns himself; yet women, whose minds are not enlarged by cultivation, or the natural selfishness of sensibility by reflection, are very unfit to manage a family, for, by an undue stretch of power, they are always tyrannizing to support a superiority that only rests on the arbitrary distinction of fortune. The evil is sometimes more serious, and domestics are deprived of innocent indulgences, and made to work beyond their strength, in order to enable the notable woman to keep a better table, and outshine her neighbours in finery and parade. If she attend to her children, it is in general to dress them in a costly manner; and whether this attention arise from vanity or fondness, it is equally pernicious.

Besides, how many women of this description pass their days, or at least their evenings, discontentedly. Their husbands acknowledge that they are good managers and chaste wives, but leave home to seek for more agreeable—may I be allowed to use a significant French word— *piquant* society; and the patient drudge, who fulfils her task like a blind horse in a mill, is defrauded of her just reward, for the wages due to her are the caresses of her husband; and women who have so few resources in themselves, do not very patiently bear this privation of a natural right.

A fine lady, on the contrary, has been taught to look down with contempt on the vulgar employments of life, though she had only been incited to acquire accomplishments that rise a degree above sense; for even corporeal accomplishments cannot be acquired with any degree of precision unless the understanding has been strengthened by exercise. Without a foundation of principles taste is superficial; grace must arise from something deeper than imitation. The imagination, however, is heated, and the feelings rendered fastidious, if not sophisticated, or a counter poise of judgement is not acquired when the heart still remains artless, though it becomes too tender.

These women are often amiable, and their hearts are really more sensible to general benevolence, more alive to the sentiments that civilize life, than the square-elbowed family drudge; but, wanting a due proportion of reflection and self-government, they only inspire love, and are the mistresses of their husbands, whilst they have any hold on their affections, and the Platonic friends of his male acquaintance. These are the fair defects in Nature; the women who appear to be created not to enjoy the fellowship of man, but to save him from sinking into absolute brutality, by rubbing off the rough angles of his character, and by playful dalliance to give some dignity to the appetite that draws him to them. Gracious Creator of the whole human race! hast Thou created such a being as woman, who can trace Thy wisdom in Thy works, and feel that Thou alone art by Thy nature exalted above her, for no better purpose? Can she believe that she was only made to submit to man, her equal—a being, who, like her, was sent into the world to acquire virtue? Can she consent to be occupied merely to please him—merely to adorn the earth—when her soul is capable of rising to Thee? And can she rest supinely dependent on man for reason, when she ought to mount with him the arduous steeps of knowledge?

Yet if love be the supreme good, let woman be only educated to inspire it, and let every charm be polished to intoxicate the senses; but if they be moral beings, let them have a chance to become intelligent; and let love to man be only a part of that glowing flame of universal love, which, after encircling humanity, mounts in grateful incense to God.

To fulfil domestic duties much resolution is necessary, and a serious kind of perseverance that requires a more firm support than emotions, however lively and true to nature. To give an example of order, the soul of virtue, some austerity of behaviour must be adopted, scarcely to be expected from a being who, from its infancy, has been made the weathercock of its own sensations. Whoever rationally means to be useful must have a plan of conduct; and in the discharge of the simplest duty, we are often obliged to act contrary to the present impulse of tenderness or compassion. Severity is frequently the most certain as well as the most sublime proof of affection; and the want of this power over the feelings, and of that lofty, dignified affection which makes a person prefer the future good of the beloved object to a present gratification is the reason why so many fond mothers spoil their children, and has made it questionable whether negligence or indulgence be most hurtful; but I am inclined to think that the latter has done most harm.

Mankind seem to agree that children should be left under the management of women during their childhood. Now, from all the observation that I have been able to make, women of sensibility are the most unfit for this task, because they will infallibly, carried away by their feelings, spoil a child's temper. The management of the temper, the first, and most important branch of education, requires the sober steady eye of reason; a plan of conduct equally distant from tyranny and indulgence: yet these are the extremes that people of sensibility alternately fall into; always shooting beyond the mark. I have followed this train of reasoning much further, till I have concluded, that a person of genius is the most improper person to be employed in education, public or private. Minds of this rare species see things too much in masses, and seldom, if ever, have a good temper. That habitual cheerfulness, termed good humour, is, perhaps, as seldom united with great mental powers, as with strong feelings. And those people who follow, with interest and admiration, the flights of genius; or, with cooler approbation suck in the instruction which has been elaborately prepared for them by the profound thinker, ought not to be disgusted, if they find the former choleric, and the latter morose; because liveliness of fancy, and a tenacious comprehension of mind, are scarcely compatible with that pliant urbanity which leads a man, at least, to bend to the opinions and prejudices of others, instead of roughly confronting them.

But, treating of education, or manners, minds of a superior class are not to be considered, they may be left to chance; it is the multitude, with moderate abilities, who call for instruction, and catch the colour of the atmosphere they breathe. This respectable concourse, I contend, men and women, should not have their sensations heightened in the hot-bed of luxurious indolence, at the expense of their understanding; for, unless there be a ballast of understanding, they will never become either virtuous or free: an aristocracy, founded on property or sterling talents, will ever sweep before it the alternately timid and ferocious slaves of feeling.

Numberless are the arguments, to take another view of the subject, brought forward with a show of reason, because supposed to be deduced from nature, that men have used morally and physically, to degrade the sex. I must notice a few.

The female understanding has often been spoken of with contempt, as arriving sooner at maturity than the male. I shall not answer this argument by alluding to the early proofs of reason, as well as genius, in

Cowley,[12] Milton, and Pope,* but only appeal to experience to decide whether young men, who are early introduced into company (and examples now abound), do not acquire the same precocity. So notorious is this fact, that the bare mentioning of it must bring before people, who at all mix in the world, the idea of a number of swaggering apes of men, whose understandings are narrowed by being brought into the society of men when they ought to have been spinning a top or twirling a hoop.

It has also been asserted, by some naturalists, that men do not attain their full growth and strength till thirty; but that women arrive at maturity by twenty. I apprehend that they reason on false ground, led astray by the male prejudice, which deems beauty the perfection of woman—mere beauty of features and complexion, the vulgar acceptation of the word, whilst male beauty is allowed to have some connection with the mind. Strength of body and that character of countenance which the French term a *physionomie,* women do not acquire before thirty, any more than men. The little artless tricks of children, it is true, are particularly pleasing and attractive; yet, when the pretty freshness of youth is worn off, these artless graces become studied airs, and disgust every person of taste. In the countenance of girls we only look for vivacity and bashful modesty; but, the springtide of life over, we look for soberer sense in the face, and for traces of passion, instead of the dimples of animal spirits; expecting to see individuality of character, the only fastener of the affections.** We then wish to converse, not to fondle; to give scope to our imaginations as well as to the sensations of our hearts.

At twenty the beauty of both sexes is equal; but the libertinism of man leads him to make the distinction, and superannuated coquettes are commonly of the same opinion; for when they can no longer inspire love, they pay for the vigour and vivacity of youth. The French, who admit more of mind into their notions of beauty, give the preference to women of thirty. I mean to say that they allow women to be in their most perfect state, when vivacity gives place to reason, and to that majestic seriousness of character, which marks maturity or the resting point. In youth, till twenty, the body shoots out, till thirty, the solids are attaining a degree of density; and the flexible muscles,

---

*Many other names might be added.

**The strength of an affection is, generally, in the same proportion as the character of the species in the object beloved, lost in that of the individual.

growing daily more rigid, give character to the countenance; that is, they trace the operations of the mind with the iron pen of fate, and tell us not only what powers are within, but how they have been employed.

It is proper to observe, that animals who arrive slowly at maturity are the longest lived, and of the noblest species. Men cannot, however, claim any natural superiority from the grandeur of longevity; for in this respect nature has not distinguished the male.

Polygamy is another physical degradation; and a plausible argument for a custom, that blasts every domestic virtue, is drawn from the well-attested fact, that in the countries where it is established, more females are born than males. This appears to be an indication of nature, and to nature, apparently reasonable speculations must yield. A further conclusion obviously presented itself; if polygamy be necessary, woman must be inferior to man, and made for him.

With respect to the formation of the foetus in the womb, we are very ignorant; but it appears to me probable, that an accidental physical cause may account for this phenomenon, and prove it not to be a law of nature. I have met with some pertinent observations on the subject in Foster's *Account of the Isles of the South Sea*,[13] that will explain my meaning. After observing that of the two sexes amongst animals, the most vigorous and hottest constitution always prevails, and produces its kind; he adds,—"If this be applied to the inhabitants of Africa, it is evident that the men there, accustomed to polygamy, are enervated by the use of so many women, and therefore less vigorous; the women, on the contrary, are of a hotter constitution, not only on account of their more irritable nerves, more sensible organization, and more lively fancy; but likewise because they are deprived in their matrimony of that share of physical love which, in a monogamous condition, would be all theirs; and thus, for the above reasons, the generality of the children are born females.

"In the greater part of Europe it has been proved by the most accurate lists of mortality, that the proportion of men to women is nearly equal, or, if any difference takes place, the males born are more numerous, in the proportion of 105 to 100."

The necessity of polygamy, therefore, does not appear; yet when a man seduces a woman, it should, I think, be termed a *left-handed* marriage, and the man should be *legally* obliged to maintain the woman and her children, unless adultery, a natural divorcement, abrogated the law. And this law should remain in force as long as the weakness of women caused the word seduction to be used as an excuse for their frailty and want of principle; nay, while they depend on man for a subsistence, instead of earning it by the exertion of their own hands or heads. But these women should not, in the full meaning of the relationship, be termed wives, or the very purpose of marriage would be subverted, and all those endearing charities that flow from personal fidelity, and give a sanctity to the tie, when neither love nor friendship unites the hearts, would melt into selfishness. The woman who is faithful to the father of her children demands respect, and should not be treated like a prostitute; though I readily grant that if it be necessary for a man and woman to live together in order to bring up their offspring, nature never intended that a man should have more than one wife.

Still, highly as I respect marriage, as the foundation of almost every social virtue, I cannot avoid feeling the most lively compassion for those unfortunate females who are broken off from society, and by one error torn from all those affections and relationships that improve the heart and mind. It does not frequently even deserve the name of error; for many innocent girls become the dupes of a sincere, affectionate heart, and still more are, as it may emphatically be termed, *ruined* before they know the difference between virtue and vice, and thus prepared by their education for infamy, they become infamous. Asylums and Magdalens[14] are not the proper remedies for these abuses. It is justice, not charity, that is wanting in the world!

A woman who has lost her honour imagines that she cannot fall lower, and as for recovering her former station, it is impossible; no exertion can wash this stain away. Losing thus every spur, and having no other means of support, prostitution becomes her only refuge, and the character is quickly depraved by circumstances over which the poor wretch has little power, unless she possesses an uncommon portion of sense and loftiness of spirit. Necessity never makes prostitution the business of men's lives; though numberless are the women who are thus rendered systematically vicious. This, however, arises in a great degree from the state of idleness in which women are educated, who are always taught to look up to man for a maintenance, and to consider their persons as the proper return for his exertions to support them. Meretricious airs, and the whole science of wantonness, have then a more powerful stimulus than either appetite or vanity; and this remark gives force to the prevailing opinion, that with chastity all is lost that is respectable in woman. Her character depends on the observance of one virtue, though the only passion fostered in her heart is love. Nay, the honour of a woman is not made even to depend on her will.

When Richardson* makes Clarissa tell Lovelace[15] that he had robbed her of her honour, he must have had strange notions of honour and virtue. For, miserable beyond all names of misery is the condition of a being, who could be degraded without its own consent! This excess of strictness I have heard vindicated as a salutary error. I shall answer in the words of Leibnitz—"Errors are often useful; but it is commonly to remedy other errors."[16]

Most of the evils of life arise from a desire of present enjoyment that outruns itself. The obedience required of women in the marriage state comes under this description; the mind, naturally weakened by depending on authority, never exerts its own powers, and the obedient wife is thus rendered a weak indolent mother. Or, supposing that this is not always the consequence, a future state of existence is scarcely taken into the reckoning when only negative virtues are cultivated. For, in treating of morals, particularly when women are alluded to, writers have too often considered virtue in a very limited sense, and made the foundation of it *solely* worldly utility; nay, a still more fragile base has been given to this stupendous fabric, and the wayward fluctuating feelings of men have been made the standard of virtue. Yes, virtue as well as religion has been subjected to the decisions of taste.

It would almost provoke a smile of contempt, if the vain absurdities of man did not strike us on all sides, to observe how eager men are to degrade the sex from whom they pretend to receive the chief pleasure of life; and I have frequently with full conviction retorted Pope's sarcasm on them; or, to speak explicitly, it has appeared to me applicable to the whole human race. A love of pleasure or sway seems to divide mankind, and the husband who lords it in his little harem thinks only of his pleasure or his convenience. To such lengths, indeed, does an intemperate love of pleasure carry some prudent men, or worn-out libertines, who marry to have a safe bedfellow, that they seduce their own wives. Hymen[17] banishes modesty, and chaste love takes its flight.

Love, considered as an animal appetite, cannot long feed on itself without expiring. And this extinction in its own flame may be termed the violent death of love. But the wife, who has thus been rendered licentious, will probably endeavour to fill the void left by the loss of her husband's attentions; for she cannot contentedly become merely an upper servant after having been treated like a goddess. She is still

*Dr. Young[18] supports the same opinion, in his plays, when he talks of the misfortune that shunned the light of day.

handsome, and, instead of transferring her fondness to her children, she only dreams of enjoying the sunshine of life. Besides, there are many husbands so devoid of sense and parental affection that, during the first effervescence of voluptuous fondness, they refuse to let their wives suckle their children. They are only to dress and live to please them, and love, even innocent love, soon sinks into lasciviousness when the exercise of a duty is sacrificed to its indulgence.

Personal attachment is a very happy foundation for friendship; yet, when even two virtuous young people marry, it would perhaps be happy if some circumstances checked their passion; if the recollection of some prior attachment, or disappointed affection, made it on one side, at least, rather a match founded on esteem. In that case they would look beyond the present moment, and try to render the whole of life respectable, by forming a plan to regulate a friendship which only death ought to dissolve.

Friendship is a serious affection; the most sublime of all affections, because it is founded on principle, and cemented by time. The very reverse may be said of love. In a great degree, love and friendship cannot subsist in the same bosom; even when inspired by different objects they weaken or destroy each other, and for the same object can only be felt in succession. The vain fears and fond jealousies, the winds which fan the flame of love, when judiciously or artfully tempered, are both incompatible with the tender confidence and sincere respect of friendship.

Love, such as the glowing pen of genius has traced, exists not on earth, or only resides in those exalted, fervid imaginations that have sketched such dangerous pictures. Dangerous, because they not only afford a plausible excuse to the voluptuary, who disguises sheer sensuality under a sentimental veil; but as they spread affectation, and take from the dignity of virtue. Virtue, as the very word imports, should have an appearance of seriousness, if not of austerity; and to endeavour to trick her out in the garb of pleasure, because the epithet has been used as another name for beauty, is to exalt her on a quicksand; a most insidious attempt to hasten her fall by apparent respect. Virtue and pleasure are not, in fact, so nearly allied in this life as some eloquent writers have laboured to prove. Pleasure prepares the fading wreath, and mixes the intoxicating cup; the fruit which virtue gives is the recompense of toil, and, gradually seen as it ripens, only affords calm satisfaction; nay, appearing to be the result of the natural tendency of things, it is scarcely observed. Bread, the common food of

life, seldom thought of as a blessing, supports the constitution and preserves health; still feasts delight the heart of man, though disease and
even death lurk in the cup or dainty that elevates the spirits or tickles
the palate. The lively heated imagination likewise, to apply the comparison, draws the picture of love, as it draws every other picture, with
those glowing colours, which the daring hand will steal from the rain-
bow, that is directed by a mind, condemned in a world like this, to
prove its noble origin by panting after unattainable perfection, ever
pursuing what it acknowledges to be a fleeting dream. An imagination
of this vigorous cast can give existence to insubstantial forms, and stability to the shadowy reveries which the mind naturally falls into when
realities are found vapid. It can then depict love with celestial charms,
and dote on the grand ideal object—it can imagine a degree of mutual
affection that shall refine the soul, and not expire when it has served as
a "scale to heavenly"; and, like devotion, make it absorb every meaner
affection and desire. In each other's arms, as in a temple, with its sum-
mit lost in the clouds, the world is to be shut out, and every thought
and wish that do not nurture pure affection and permanent virtue.
Permanent virtue! alas! Rousseau, respectable visionary! thy paradise
would soon be violated by the entrance of some unexpected guest.
Like Milton's it would only contain angels, or men sunk below the
dignity of rational creatures. Happiness is not material, it cannot be
seen or felt! Yet the eager pursuit of the good, which everyone shapes
to his own fancy, proclaims man the lord of this lower world, and to be
an intelligential creature, who is not to receive but acquire happiness.
They, therefore, who complain of the delusions of passion, do not recollect that they are exclaiming against a strong proof of the immortality of the soul.

But leaving superior minds to correct themselves, and pay dearly
for their experience, it is necessary to observe, that it is not against
strong, persevering passions, but romantic wavering feelings, that I
wish to guard the female heart by exercising the understanding: for
these paradisiacal reveries are oftener the effects of idleness than of a
lively fancy.

Women have seldom sufficient serious employment to silence their
feelings; a round of little cares, or vain pursuits frittering away all
strength of mind and organs, they become naturally only objects of
sense. In short, the whole tenor of female education (the education
of society) tends to render the best disposed romantic and incon-

stant; and the remainder vain and mean. In the present state of society this evil can scarcely be remedied, I am afraid, in the slightest degree; should a more laudable ambition ever gain ground they may be brought nearer to nature and reason, and become more virtuous and useful as they grow more respectable.

But, I will venture to assert that their reason will never acquire sufficient strength to enable it to regulate their conduct, whilst the making an appearance in the world is the first wish of the majority of mankind. To this weak wish the natural affections, and the most useful virtues are sacrificed. Girls marry merely to *better themselves,* to borrow a significant vulgar phrase, and have such perfect power over their hearts as not to permit themselves to *fall in love* till a man with a superior fortune offers. On this subject I mean to enlarge in a future chapter; it is only necessary to drop a hint at present, because women are so often degraded by suffering the selfish prudence of age to chill the ardour of youth.

From the same source flows an opinion that young girls ought to dedicate great part of their time to needlework; yet, this employment contracts their faculties more than any other that could have been chosen for them, by confining their thoughts to their persons. Men order their clothes to be made, and have done with the subject; women make their own clothes, necessary or ornamental, and are continually talking about them; and their thoughts follow their hands. It is not indeed the making of necessaries that weakens the mind; but the frippery of dress. For when a woman in the lower rank of life makes her husband's and children's clothes, she does her duty, this is her part of the family business; but when women work only to dress better than they could otherwise afford, it is worse than sheer loss of time. To render the poor virtuous they must be employed, and women in the middle rank of life, did they not ape the fashions of the nobility, without catching their ease, might employ them, whilst they themselves managed their families, instructed their children, and exercised their own minds. Gardening, experimental philosophy, and literature, would afford them subject to think of and matter for conversation, that in some degree would exercise their understandings. The conversation of Frenchwomen, who are not so rigidly nailed to their chairs to twist lappets, and knot ribands,[19] is frequently superficial; but, I contend, that it is not half so insipid as that of those Englishwomen whose time is spent in making caps, bonnets, and the whole mischief of trimmings, not to mention shopping, bargain-hunting, etc., etc.; and it is the decent, prudent women, who are most degraded by these practices; for their motive is simply vanity. The wanton who exercises her taste to render her passion alluring, has something more in view.

These observations all branch out of a general one, which I have before made, and which cannot be too often insisted upon, for, speaking of men, women, or professions, it will be found that the employment of the thoughts shapes the character both generally and individually. The thoughts of women ever hover round their persons, and is it surprising that their persons are reckoned most valuable? Yet some degree of liberty of mind is necessary even to form the person; and this may be one reason why some gentle wives have so few attractions beside that of sex. Add to this, sedentary employments render the majority of women sickly—and false notions of female excellence make them proud of this delicacy, though it be another fetter, that by calling the attention continually to the body, cramps the activity of the mind.

Women of quality seldom do any of the manual part of their dress, consequently only their taste is exercised, and they acquire, by thinking less of the finery, when the business of their toilet is over, that ease, which seldom appears in the deportment of women, who dress merely for the sake of dressing. In fact, the observation with respect to the middle rank, the one in which talents thrive best, extends not to women; for those of the superior class, by catching, at least, a smattering of literature, and conversing more with men, on general topics, acquire more knowledge than the women who ape their fashions and faults without sharing their advantages. With respect to virtue, to use the word in a comprehensive sense, I have seen most in low life. Many poor women maintain their children by the sweat of their brow, and keep together families that the vices of the fathers would have scattered abroad; but gentlewomen are too indolent to be actively virtuous, and are softened rather than refined by civilization. Indeed, the good sense which I have met with, among the poor women who have had few advantages of education, and yet have acted heroically, strongly confirmed me in the opinion that trifling employments have rendered woman a trifler. Man, taking her* body, the mind is left to rust; so that while physical love enervates man, as being his favourite recreation, he will endeavour to enslave woman:—and, who can tell,

---

*"I take her body," says Ranger.[20]

how many generations may be necessary to give vigour to the virtue and talents of the freed posterity of abject slaves?*

In tracing the causes that, in my opinion, have degraded woman, I have confined my observations to such as universally act upon the morals and manners of the whole sex, and to me it appears clear that they all spring from want of understanding. Whether this arise from a physical or accidental weakness of faculties, time alone can determine; for I shall not lay any great stress on the example of a few women** who, from having received a masculine education, have acquired courage and resolution; I only contend that the men who have been placed in similar situations, have acquired a similar character—I speak of bodies of men, and that men of genius and talents have started out of a class, in which women have never yet been placed.

---

*"Supposing that women are voluntary slaves—slavery of any kind is unfavourable to human happiness and improvement."—KNOX'S *Essays.*[21]

**Sappho, Eloisa, Mrs. Macaulay, the Empress of Russia, Madame d'Eon,[22] etc. These, and many more, may be reckoned exceptions; and, are not all heroes, as well as heroines, exceptions to general rules? I wish to see women neither heroines nor brutes; but reasonable creatures.

# CHAPTER V

## ANIMADVERSIONS ON SOME OF THE WRITERS WHO HAVE RENDERED WOMEN OBJECTS OF PITY, BORDERING ON CONTEMPT

The opinions speciously supported in some modern publications on the female character and education, which have given the tone to most of the observations made, in a more cursory manner, on the sex, remain now to be examined.

### SECTION I

I shall begin with Rousseau, and give a sketch of his character of woman in his own words, interspersing comments and reflections. My comments, it is true, will all spring from a few simple principles, and might have been deduced from what I have already said; but the artificial structure has been raised with so much ingenuity that it seems necessary to attack it in a more circumstantial manner, and make the application myself.

Sophia, says Rousseau,[1] should be as perfect a woman, as Emilius is a man, and to render her so it is necessary to examine the character which nature has given to the sex.

He then proceeds to prove that woman ought to be weak and passive, because she has less bodily strength than man; and hence infers that she was formed to please and to be subject to him, and that it is her duty to render herself *agreeable* to her master—this being the grand end of her existence.* Still, however, to give a little mock dignity to lust, he insists that man should not exert his strength, but depend on the will of the woman, when he seeks for pleasure with her.

"Hence we deduce a third consequence from the different constitutions of the sexes, which is that the strongest should be master in appearance, and be dependent, in fact, on the weakest, and that not from any frivolous practice of gallantry or vanity of protectorship, but from an invariable law of nature, which, furnishing woman with a greater facility to excite desires that she has given man to satisfy them, makes the latter dependent on the good pleasure of the former and compels him to endeavour to please in his turn, in order to obtain her consent that he should be strongest.** On these occasions the most delightful circumstance a man finds in his victory is to doubt whether it was the woman's weakness that yielded to his superior strength, or whether her inclinations spoke in his favour; the females are also generally artful enough to leave this matter in doubt. The understanding of women answers in this respect perfectly to the constitution. So far from being ashamed of their weakness, they glory in it; their tender muscles make no resistance; they affect to be incapable of lifting the smallest burdens, and would blush to be thought robust and strong. To what purpose is all this? Not merely for the sake of appearing delicate, but through an artful precaution. It is thus they provide an excuse beforehand, and a right to be feeble when they think it expedient."

I have quoted this passage lest my readers should suspect that I warped the author's reasoning to support my own arguments. I have already asserted that in educating women these fundamental principles lead to a system of cunning and lasciviousness.

Supposing woman to have been formed only to please, and be subject to man, the conclusion is just. She ought to sacrifice every other consideration to render herself agreeable to him, and let this brutal desire of self-preservation be the grand spring of all her actions, when it is proved to be the iron bed of fate, to fit which her character should be stretched or contracted, regardless of all moral or physical distinctions. But if, as I think, may be demonstrated, the purposes of even this life, viewing the whole, be subverted by practical rules built upon this ignoble base, I may be allowed to doubt whether woman were created

*I have already inserted the passage, p. 32.
**What nonsense!

for man; and though the cry of irreligion, or even atheism, be raised against me, I will simply declare that were an angel from Heaven to tell me that Moses' beautiful poetical cosmogony,[2] and the account of the fall of man, were literally true, I could not believe what my reason told me was derogatory to the character of the Supreme Being; and, having no fear of the devil before mine eyes, I venture to call this a suggestion of reason, instead of resting my weakness on the broad shoulders of the first seducer of my frail sex.

"It being once demonstrated," continues Rousseau, "that man and woman are not, nor ought to be, constituted alike in temperament and character, it follows, of course, that they should not be educated in the same manner. In pursuing the directions of nature, they ought, indeed, to act in concert, but they should not be engaged in the same employments; the end of their pursuits should be the same, but the means they should take to accomplish them, and, of consequence, their tastes and inclinations, should be different.

***

"Whether I consider the peculiar destination of the sex, observe their inclinations, or remark their duties, all things equally concur to point out the peculiar method of education best adapted to them. Woman and man were made for each other, but their mutual dependence is not the same. The men depend on the women only on account of their desires; the women on the men both on account of their desires and their necessities. We could subsist better without them than they without us.

***

"For this reason the education of the women should be always relative to the men. To please, to be useful to us, to make us love and esteem them, to educate us when young, and take care of us when grown up, to advise, to console us, to render our lives easy and agreeable—these are the duties of women at all times, and what they should be taught in their infancy. So long as we fail to recur to this principle, we run wide of the mark, and all the precepts which are given them contribute neither to their happiness nor our own.

"Girls are from their earliest infancy fond of dress. Not content with being pretty, they are desirous of being thought so. We see by all their little airs, that this thought engages their attention; and they are hardly capable of understanding what is said to them, before they are to be governed by talking to them of what people will think of their behaviour. The same motive, however, indiscreetly made use of with boys, has not the same effect. Provided they are let pursue their amusements at pleasure, they care very little what people think of them. Time and pains are necessary to subject boys to this motive.

"Whencesoever girls derive this first lesson, it is a very good one. As the body is born, in a manner, before the soul, our first concern should be to cultivate the former; this order is common to both sexes, but the object of that cultivation is different. In the one sex it is the development of corporeal powers; in the other, that of personal charms. Not that either the quality of strength or beauty ought to be confined exclusively to one sex, but only that the order of cultivation of both is in that respect reversed. Women certainly require as much strength as to enable them to move and act gracefully, and men as much address as to qualify them to act with ease.

———

"Children of both sexes have a great many amusements in common; and so they ought; have they not also many such when they are grown up? Each sex has also its peculiar taste to distinguish in this particular. Boys love sports of noise and activity; to beat the drum, to whip the top, and to drag about their little carts: girls, on the other hand, are fonder of things of show and ornament; such as mirrors, trinkets, and dolls: the doll is the peculiar amusement of the females; from whence we see their taste plainly adapted to their destination. The physical part of the art of pleasing lies in dress; and this is all which children are capacitated to cultivate of that art.

———

"Here then we see a primary propensity firmly established, which you need only to pursue and regulate. The little creature will doubtless be very desirous to know how to dress up her doll, to make its sleeve-knots, its flounces, its head-dress, etc., she is obliged to have so much recourse to the people about her for their assistance in these articles, that it would be much more agreeable for her to owe them all to her own industry. Hence we have a good reason for the first lessons that are usually taught these young females: in which we do not appear to be setting them a task, but obliging them, by instructing them in what is immediately useful to themselves. And, in fact, almost all of them learn with reluctance to read and write; but very readily apply themselves to the use of their needles. They imagine themselves already grown up, and think with pleasure that such qualifications will enable them to decorate themselves."

This is certainly an education of the body; but Rousseau is not the only man who has indirectly said that merely the person of a *young* woman, without any mind, unless animal spirits come under that description, is very pleasing. To render it weak, and what some may call beautiful, the understanding is neglected, and girls forced to sit still, play with dolls and listen to foolish conversations;—the effect of habit is insisted upon as an undoubted indication of nature. I know it was Rousseau's opinion that the first years of youth should be employed to form the body, though in educating Emilius he deviates from this plan; yet, the difference between strengthening the body, on which strength of mind in a great measure depends, and only giving it an easy motion, is very wide.

Rousseau's observations, it is proper to remark, were made in a country where the art of pleasing was refined only to extract grossness of vice. He did not go back to nature, or his ruling appetite disturbed the operations of reason, else he would not have drawn these crude inferences.

In France boys and girls, particularly the latter, are only educated to please, to manage their persons, and regulate the exterior behaviour; and their minds are corrupted, at a very early age, by the worldly and pious cautions they receive to guard them against immodesty. I speak of past times. The very confessions which mere children were obliged to make, and the questions asked by the holy men, I assert these facts on good authority, were sufficient to impress a sexual character; and the education of society was a school of coquetry and art. At the age of ten or eleven; nay, often much sooner, girls began to coquette, and talked, unreproved, of establishing themselves in the world by marriage.

In short, they were treated like women, almost from their very birth, and compliments were listened to instead of instruction. These weakening the mind, Nature was supposed to have acted like a stepmother, when she formed this afterthought of creation.

Not allowing them understanding, however, it was but consistent to subject them to authority, independent of reason; and to prepare them for this subjection, he gives the following advice:

"Girls ought to be active and diligent; nor is that all; they should also be early subjected to restraint. This misfortune, if it really be one, is inseparable from their sex; nor do they ever throw it off but to suffer more cruel evils. They must be subject, all their lives, to the most constant and severe restraint, which is that of decorum: it is, therefore, necessary to accustom them early to such confinement, that it may not afterwards cost them too dear; and to the suppression of their caprices, that they may the more readily submit to the will of others. If, indeed, they be fond of being always at work, they should be sometimes compelled to lay it aside. Dissipation, levity, and inconstancy, are faults that readily spring up from their first propensities, when corrupted or perverted by too much indulgence. To prevent this abuse, we should teach them, above all things, to lay a due restraint on themselves. The life of a modest woman is reduced, by our absurd institutions, to a perpetual conflict with herself: not but it is just that this sex should partake of the sufferings which arise from those evils it hath caused us."

And why is the life of a modest woman a perpetual conflict? I should answer, that this very system of education makes it so. Modesty, temperance, and self-denial, are the sober offspring of reason; but when sensibility is nurtured at the expense of the understanding, such weak beings must be restrained by arbitrary means, and be subjected to continual conflicts; but give their activity of mind a wider range, and nobler passions and motives will govern their appetites and sentiments.

"The common attachment and regard of a mother, nay, mere habit, will make her beloved by her children, if she do nothing to incur their hate. Even the constraint she lays them under, if well directed, will increase their affection, instead of lessening it; because a state of dependence being natural to the sex, they perceive themselves formed for obedience."

This is begging the question; for servitude not only debases the individual, but its effects seem to be transmitted to posterity. Considering the length of time that women have been dependent, is it surprising that some of them hunger in chains, and fawn like the spaniel? "These dogs," observes a naturalist, "at first kept their ears erect; but custom has superseded nature, and a token of fear is become a beauty."

"For the same reason," adds Rousseau, "women have, or ought to have, but little liberty; they are apt to indulge themselves excessively in what is allowed them. Addicted in everything to extremes, they are even more transported at their diversions than boys."

The answer to this is very simple. Slaves and mobs have always indulged themselves in the same excesses, when once they broke loose from authority. The bent bow recoils with violence, when the hand is suddenly relaxed that forcibly held it; and sensibility, the plaything of outward circumstances, must be subjected to authority, or moderated by reason.

"There results," he continues, "from this habitual restraint a tractableness which women have occasion for during their whole lives, as they constantly remain either under subjection to the men, or to the opinions of mankind; and are never permitted to set themselves above those opinions. The first and most important qualification in a woman is good nature or sweetness of temper: formed to obey a being so imperfect as man, often full of vices, and always full of faults, she ought to learn betimes even to suffer injustice, and to bear the insults of a husband without complaint; it is not for his sake, but her own, that she should be of a mild disposition. The perverseness and ill-nature of the women only serve to aggravate their own misfortunes, and the misconduct of their husbands; they might plainly perceive that such are not the arms by which they gain the superiority."

Formed to live with such an imperfect being as man they ought to learn from the exercise of their faculties the necessity of forbearance: but all the sacred rights of humanity are violated by insisting on blind obedience; or, the most sacred rights belong *only* to man.

The being who patiently endures injustice, and silently bears insults, will soon become unjust, or unable to discern right from wrong. Besides, I deny the fact, this is not the true way to form or meliorate the temper; for, as a sex, men have better tempers than women, because they are occupied by pursuits that interest the head as well as the heart; and the steadiness of the head gives a healthy temperature to the heart. People of sensibility have seldom good tempers. The formation of the temper is the cool work of reason, when, as life advances, she mixes with happy art, jarring elements. I never knew a weak or ignorant person who had a good temper, though that constitutional good humour, and that docility, which fear stamps on the behaviour, often obtains the name. I say behaviour, for genuine meekness never reached the heart or mind, unless as the effect of reflection; and that simple restraint produces a number of peccant humours in domestic life, many sensible men will allow, who find some of these gentle irritable creatures, very troublesome companions.

"Each sex," he further argues, "should preserve its peculiar tone and manner; a meek husband may make a wife impertinent; but mildness of disposition on the woman's side will always bring a man back to reason, at least if he be not absolutely a brute, and will sooner or later triumph over him." Perhaps the mildness of reason might sometimes have this effect; but abject fear always inspires contempt; and tears are only eloquent when they flow down fair cheeks.

Of what materials can that heart be composed, which can melt when insulted, and instead of revolting at injustice, kiss the rod? It is unfair to infer that her virtue is built on narrow views and selfishness, who can caress a man, with true feminine softness, the very moment when he treats her tyrannically? Nature never dictated such insincerity; and, though prudence of this sort be termed a virtue, morality becomes vague when any part is supposed to rest on falsehood. These are mere expedients, and expedients are only useful for the moment.

Let the husband beware of trusting too implicitly to this servile obedience; for if his wife can with winning sweetness, caress him when angry, and when she ought to be angry, unless contempt has stifled a natural effervescence, she may do the same after parting with a lover. These are all preparations for adultery; or, should the fear of the world, or of hell, restrain her desire of pleasing other men, when she can no longer please her husband, what substitute can be found by a being who was only formed, by nature and art, to please man? what can make her amends for this privation, or where is she to seek for a fresh employment? where find sufficient strength of mind to determine to begin the search, where her habits are fixed, and vanity has long ruled her chaotic mind?

But this partial moralist recommends cunning systematically and plausibly.

"Daughters should be always submissive; their mothers, however, should not be inexorable. To make a young person tractable, she ought not to be made unhappy; to make her modest she ought not to be rendered stupid. On the contrary, I should not be displeased at her being permitted to use some art, not to elude punishment in case of disobedience, but to exempt herself from the necessity of obeying. It is not necessary to make her dependence burdensome, but only to let her feel it. Subtility is a natural talent to the sex; and, as I am persuaded, all our natural inclinations are right and good in themselves, I am of opinion this should be cultivated as well as the others: it is requisite for us only to prevent its abuse."

"Whatever is, is right," he then proceeds triumphantly to infer. Granted; yet, perhaps, no aphorism ever contained a more paradoxical assertion. It is a solemn truth with respect to God. He, reverentially, I speak, sees the whole at once, and saw its just proportions in the womb of time; but man, who can only inspect disjointed parts, finds many things wrong; and it is a part of the system, and therefore right, that he should endeavour to alter what appears to him to be so, even while he bows to the wisdom of his Creator, and respects the darkness he labours to disperse.

The inference that follows is just, supposing the principle to be sound. "The superiority of address, peculiar to the female sex, is a very equitable indemnification for their inferiority in point of strength: without this, woman would not be the companion of man, but his slave; it is by her superior art and ingenuity that she preserves her equality, and governs him while she affects to obey. Woman has everything against her, as well our faults, as her own timidity and weakness; she has nothing in her favour, but her subtility and her beauty. Is it not very reasonable, therefore, she should cultivate both?" Greatness of mind can never dwell with cunning, or address; for I shall not boggle about words, when their direct signification is insincerity and falsehood, but content myself with observing, that if any class of mankind be so created that it must necessarily be educated by rules not strictly deducible from truth, virtue is an affair of convention. How could Rousseau dare to assert, after giving this advice, that in the grand end of existence the object of both sexes should be the same, when he well knew that the mind, formed by its pursuits, is expanded by great views swallowing up little ones, or that it becomes itself little?

Men have superior strength of body; but were it not for mistaken notions of beauty, women would acquire sufficient to enable them to earn their own subsistence, the true definition of independence; and to bear those bodily inconveniences and exertions that are requisite to strengthen the mind. Let us then, by being allowed to take the same exercise as boys, not only during infancy, but youth, arrive at perfection of body, that we may know how far the natural superiority of man extends. For what reason or virtue can be expected from a creature when the seed-time of life is neglected? None; did not the winds of heaven casually scatter many useful seeds in fallow ground.

"Beauty cannot be acquired by dress, and coquetry is an art not so early and speedily attained. While girls are yet young, however, they are in a capacity to study agreeable gesture, a pleasing modulation of voice, an easy carriage and behaviour; as well as to take the advantage of gracefully adapting their looks and attitudes to time, place and occasion. Their application, therefore, should not be solely confined to the arts of industry and the needle, when they come to display other talents, whose utility is already apparent.

"For my part, I would have a young Englishwoman cultivate her agreeable talents, in order to please her future husband, with as much care and assiduity as a young Circassian[3] cultivates hers, to fit her for the harem of an Eastern bashaw."

To render women completely insignificant, he adds: "The tongues of women are very voluble; they speak earlier, more readily, and more agreeably, than the men; they are accused also of speaking much more: but so it ought to be, and I should be very ready to convert this reproach into a compliment; their lips and eyes have the same activity, and for the same reason. A man speaks of what he knows, a woman of what pleases her; the one requires knowledge, the other taste; the principal object of a man's discourse should be what is useful, that of a woman's what is agreeable. There ought to be nothing in common between their different conversation but truth.

"We ought not, therefore, to restrain the prattle of girls, in the same manner as we should that of boys, with that severe question, *To what purpose are you talking?* but by another, which is no less difficult to answer, *How will your discourse be received?* In infancy, while they are as yet incapable to discern good from evil, they ought to observe it, as a law never to say anything disagreeable to those whom they are speaking to. What will render the practice of this rule also the more difficult is, that it must ever be subordinate to the former, of never speaking falsely or telling an untruth." To govern the tongue in this manner must require great address indeed, and it is too much practised both by men and women. Out of the abundance of the heart how few speak! So few that I, who love simplicity, would gladly give up politeness for a quarter of the virtue that has been sacrificed to an equivocal quality which at best should only be the polish of virtue.

But, to complete the sketch. "It is easy to be conceived, that if male children be not in a capacity to form any true notions of religion, those ideas must be greatly above the conception of the females: it is for this very reason, I would begin to speak to them the earlier on this subject; for if we were to wait till they were in a capacity to discuss methodically such profound questions, we should run a risk of never speaking to them on this subject as long as they lived. Reason in women is a practical reason, capacitating them artfully to discover the means of attaining a known end, but which would never enable them to discover that end itself. The social relations of the sexes are indeed truly admirable: from their union there results a moral person, of which woman may be termed the eyes, and man the hand, with this dependence on each other, that it is from the man that the woman is to learn what she is to see, and it is of the woman that man is to learn what he ought to do. If woman could recur to the first principles of things as well as man, and man was capacitated to enter into their *minutiae* as well as woman, always independent of each other, they would live in perpetual discord, and their union could not subsist. But in the present harmony which naturally subsists between them, their different faculties tend to one common end: it is difficult to say which of them conduces the most to it: each follows the impulse of the other; each is obedient, and both are masters.

"As the conduct of a woman is subservient to the public opinion, her faith in matters of religion should, for that very reason, be subject to authority. *Every daughter ought to be of the same religion as her mother, and every wife to be of the same religion as her husband: for, though such religion should be false, that docility which induces the mother and daughter to submit to the order of nature, takes away, in the sight of God, the criminality of their error.** As they are not in a capacity to judge for themselves, they ought to abide by the decision of their fathers and husbands as confidently as by that of the Church.

"As authority ought to regulate the religion of the women, it is not so needful to explain to them the reasons for their belief, as to lay down precisely the tenets they are to believe: for the creed, which presents only obscure ideas to the mind, is the source of fanaticism; and that which presents absurdities, leads to infidelity."

Absolute, uncontroverted authority, it seems, must subsist somewhere: but is not this a direct and exclusive appropriation of reason? The *rights* of humanity have been thus confined to the male line from Adam downwards.

Rousseau would carry his male aristocracy still further, for he insinuates, that he should not blame those, who contend for leaving woman in a state of the most profound ignorance, if it were not necessary in order to preserve her chastity and justify the man's choice, in the eyes of the world, to give her a little knowledge of men, and the customs produced by human passions; else she might propagate at home without being rendered less voluptuous and innocent by the exercise of her understanding: excepting, indeed, during the first year of

---

*What is to be the consequence, if the mother's and husband's opinion should *chance* not to agree? An ignorant person cannot be reasoned out of an error—and when *persuaded* to give up one prejudice for another the mind is unsettled. Indeed, the husband may not have any religion to teach her, though in such a situation she will be in great want of a support to her virtue, independent of worldly considerations.

marriage, when she might employ it to dress like Sophia. "Her dress is extremely modest in appearance, and yet very coquettish in fact: she does not make a display of her charms, she conceals them; but in concealing them, she knows how to affect your imagination. Everyone who sees her will say, There is a modest and discreet girl; but while you are near her, your eyes and affections wander all over her person, so that you cannot withdraw them; and you would conclude, that every part of her dress, simple as it seems, was only put in its proper order to be taken to pieces by the imagination." Is this modesty? Is this a preparation for immortality? Again, What opinion are we to form of a system of education, when the author says of his heroine, "that with her, doing things well, is but a *secondary* concern; her principal concern is to do them *neatly.*"

Secondary, in fact, are all her virtues and qualities, for, respecting religion, he makes her parents thus address her, accustomed to submission—"Your husband will instruct you in good time."

After thus cramping a woman's mind, if, in order to keep it fair, he have not made it quite a blank, he advises her to reflect, that a reflecting man may not yawn in her company, when he is tired of caressing her. What has she to reflect about who must obey? and would it not be a refinement on cruelty only to open her mind to make the darkness and misery of her fate *visible*? Yet these are his sensible remarks; how consistent with what I have already been obliged to quote, to give a fair view of the subject, the reader may determine.

"They who pass their whole lives in working for their daily bread, have no ideas beyond their business or their interest, and all their understanding seems to lie in their fingers' ends. This ignorance is neither prejudicial to their integrity nor their morals; it is often of service to them. Sometimes, by means of reflection, we are led to compound with our duty, and we conclude by substituting a jargon of words in the room of things. Our own conscience is the most enlightened philosopher. There is no need to be acquainted with Tully's Offices,[4] to make a man of probity; and perhaps the most virtuous woman in the world is the least acquainted with the definition of virtue. But it is no less true, that an improved understanding only can render society agreeable; and it is a melancholy thing for a father of a family, who is fond of home, to be obliged to be always wrapped up in himself, and to have nobody about him to whom he can impart his sentiments.

"Besides, how should a woman void of reflection be capable of educating her children? How should she discern what is proper for them?

How should she incline them to those virtues she is unacquainted with, or to that merit of which she has no idea? She can only soothe or chide them; render them insolent or timid; she will make them formal coxcombs, or ignorant blockheads, but will never make them sensible or amiable." How indeed should she, when her husband is not always at hand to lend her his reason?—when they both together make but one moral being. A blind will, "eyes without hands," would go a very little way; and perchance his abstract reason, that should concentrate the scattered beams of her practical reason, may be employed in judging of the flavour of wine, descanting on the sauces most proper for turtle; or, more profoundly intent at a card-table, he may be generalizing his ideas as he bets away his fortune, leaving all the *minutiæ* of education to his helpmate, or to chance.

But, granting that woman ought to be beautiful, innocent, and silly, to render her a more alluring and indulgent companion;—what is her understanding sacrificed for? And why is all this preparation necessary only, according to Rousseau's own account, to make her the mistress of her husband, a very short time? For no man ever insisted more on the transient nature of love. Thus speaks the philosopher, "Sensual pleasures are transient. The habitual state of the affections always loses by their gratification. The imagination, which decks the object of our desires, is lost in fruition. Excepting the Supreme Being, who is self-existent, there is nothing beautiful but what is ideal."

But he returns to his unintelligible paradoxes again, when he thus addresses Sophia—"Emilius, in becoming your husband, is becoming your master, and claims your obedience. Such is the order of nature. When a man is married, however, to such a wife as Sophia, it is proper he should be directed by her. This is also agreeable to the order of nature. It is, therefore, to give you as much authority over his heart as his sex gives him over your person that I have made you the arbiter of his pleasures. It may cost you, perhaps, some disagreeable self-denial; but you will be certain of maintaining your empire over him, if you can preserve it over yourself. What I have already observed also shows me that this difficult attempt does not surpass your courage.

"Would you have your husband constantly at your feet, keep him at some distance from your person. You will long maintain the authority in love, if you know but how to render your favours rare and valuable. It is thus you may employ even the arts of coquetry in the service of virtue, and those of love in that of reason."

I shall close my extracts with a just description of a comfortable couple: "And yet you must not imagine that even such management will always suffice. Whatever precaution be taken, enjoyment will by degrees take off the edge of passion. But when love hath lasted as long as possible, a pleasing habitude supplies its place, and the attachment of a mutual confidence succeeds to the transports of passion. Children often form a more agreeable and permanent connection between married people than even love itself. When you cease to be the mistress of Emilius, you will continue to be his wife and friend—you will be the mother of his children."*

Children, he truly observes, form a much more permanent connection between married people than love. Beauty, he declares, will not be valued, or even seen, after a couple have lived six months together; artificial graces and coquetry will likewise pall on the senses. Why, then, does he say that a girl should be educated for her husband with the same care as for an Eastern harem?

I now appeal from the reveries of fancy and refined licentiousness to the good sense of mankind, whether, if the object of education be to prepare women to become chaste wives and sensible mothers, the method so plausibly recommended in the foregoing sketch be the one best calculated to produce those ends? Will it be allowed that the surest way to make a wife chaste is to teach her to practise the wanton arts of a mistress, termed virtuous coquetry, by the sensualist who can no longer relish the artless charms of sincerity, or taste the pleasure arising from a tender intimacy, when confidence is unchecked by suspicion, and rendered interesting by sense?

The man who can be contented to live with a pretty, useful companion, without a mind, has lost in voluptuous gratifications a taste for more refined enjoyments; he has never felt the calm satisfaction that refreshes the parched heart like the silent dew of heaven—of being beloved by one who could understand him. In the society of his wife he is still alone, unless when the man is sunk in the brute. "The charm of life," says a grave philosophical reasoner, is "sympathy; nothing pleases us more than to observe in other men a fellow-feeling with all the emotions of our own breast."

But according to the tenor of reasoning by which women are kept from the tree of knowledge, the important years of youth, the usefulness of age, and the rational hopes of futurity, are all to be sacrificed to render women an object of desire for a *short* time. Besides, how could

*Rousseau's *Emilius*.

Rousseau expect them to be virtuous and constant when reason is neither allowed to be the foundation of their virtue, nor truth the object of their inquiries?

But all Rousseau's errors in reasoning arose from sensibility, and sensibility to their charms women are very ready to forgive. When he should have reasoned he became impassioned, and reflection inflamed his imagination instead of enlightening his understanding. Even his virtues also led him farther astray; for, born with a warm constitution and lively fancy, nature carried him toward the other sex with such eager fondness that he soon became lascivious. Had he given way to these desires, the fire would have extinguished itself in a natural manner, but virtue, and a romantic kind of delicacy, made him practise self-denial; yet when fear, delicacy, or virtue restrained him, he debauched his imagination, and reflecting on the sensations to which fancy gave force, he traced them in the most glowing colours, and sunk them deep into his soul.

He then sought for solitude, not to sleep with the man of nature, or calmly investigate the causes of things under the shade where Sir Isaac Newton indulged contemplation,[5] but merely to indulge his feelings. And so warmly has he painted what he forcibly felt, that interesting the heart and inflaming the imagination of his readers, in proportion to the strength of their fancy, they imagine that their understanding is convinced when they only sympathize with a poetic writer, who skilfully exhibits the objects of sense most voluptuously shadowed or gracefully veiled; and thus making us feel whilst dreaming that we reason, erroneous conclusions are left in the mind.

Why was Rousseau's life divided between ecstasy and misery? Can any other answer be given than this, that the effervescence of his imagination produced both; but had his fancy been allowed to cool, it is possible that he might have acquired more strength of mind. Still, if the purpose of life be to educate the intellectual part of man, all with respect to him was right; yet had not death led to a nobler scene of action, it is probable that he would have enjoyed more equal happiness on earth, and have felt the calm sensation of the man of nature, instead of being prepared for another stage of existence by nourishing the passions which agitate the civilized man.

But peace to his manes! I war not with his ashes, but his opinions. I war only with the sensibility that led him to degrade woman by making her the slave of love.

"—Cursed vassalage,
First idolized till love's hot fire be o'er,
Then slaves to those who courted us before."—DRYDEN.[6]

The pernicious tendency of those books, in which the writers insidiously degrade the sex whilst they are prostrate before their personal charms, cannot be too often or too severely exposed.

Let us, my dear contemporaries, arise above such narrow prejudices. If wisdom be desirable on its own account, if virtue, to deserve the name, must be founded on knowledge, let us endeavour to strengthen our minds by reflection till our heads become a balance for our hearts; let us not confine all our thoughts to the petty occurrences of the day, or our knowledge to an acquaintance with our lovers' or husbands' hearts, but let the practice of every duty be subordinate to the grand one of improving our minds, and preparing our affections for a more exalted state.

Beware, then, my friends, of suffering the heart to be moved by every trivial incident; the reed is shaken by a breeze, and annually dies, but the oak stands firm, and for ages braves the storm.

Were we, indeed, only created to flutter our hour out and die—why let us then indulge sensibility, and laugh at the severity of reason. Yet, alas! even then we should want strength of body and mind, and life would be lost in feverish pleasures or wearisome languor.

But the system of Education, which I earnestly wish to see exploded, seems to presuppose what ought to be taken for granted, that virtue shields us from the casualties of life; and that Fortune, slipping off her bandage, will smile on a well-educated female, and bring in her hand an Emilius or a Telemachus. Whilst, on the contrary, the reward which Virtue promises to her votaries is confined, it seems clear, to their own bosoms; and often must they contend with the most vexatious worldly cares, and bear with the vices and humours of relations for whom they can never feel a friendship.

There have been many women in the world who, instead of being supported by the reason and virtue of their fathers and brothers, have strengthened their own minds by struggling with their vices and follies; yet have never met a hero, in the shape of a husband; who, paying the debt that mankind owed them, might chance to bring back their reason to its natural dependent state, and restore the usurped prerogative, of rising above opinion, to man.

## SECTION II

Dr. Fordyce's sermons[7] have long made a part of a young woman's library; nay, girls at school are allowed to read them; but I should instantly dismiss them from my pupil's if I wished to strengthen her understanding, by leading her to form sound principles on a broad basis; or, were I only anxious to cultivate her taste, though they must be allowed to contain many sensible observations.

Dr. Fordyce may have had a very laudable end in view; but these discourses are written in such an affected style, that were it only on that account, and had I nothing to object against his *mellifluous* precepts, I should not allow girls to peruse them, unless I designed to hunt out every spark of nature out of their composition, melting every human quality into female meekness and artificial grace. I say artificial, for true grace arises from some kind of independence of mind.

Children, careless of pleasing, and only anxious to amuse themselves, are often very graceful; and the nobility who have mostly lived with inferiors, and always had the command of money, acquire a graceful ease of deportment which should rather be termed habitual grace of body, than that superior gracefulness which is truly the expression of the mind. This mental grace, not noticed by vulgar eyes, often flashes across a rough countenance, and irradiating every feature, shows simplicity and independence of mind. It is then we read characters of immortality in the eye, and see the soul in every gesture, though when at rest, neither the face nor limbs may have much beauty to recommend them: or the behaviour, anything peculiar to attract universal attention. The mass of mankind, however, look for more *tangible* beauty; yet simplicity is, in general, admired when people do not consider what they admire? and can there be simplicity without sincerity? But, to have done with remarks that are in some measure desultory, though naturally excited by the subject.

In declamatory periods Dr. Fordyce spins out Rousseau's eloquence; and in most sentimental rant, details his opinions respecting the female character, and the behaviour which woman ought to assume to render her lovely.

He shall speak for himself, for thus he makes Nature address man. "Behold these smiling innocents, whom I have graced with my fairest gifts, and committed to your protection; behold them with love and respect; treat them with tenderness and honour. They are timid and want to be defended. They are frail; oh do not take advantage of their weakness! Let their fears and blushes endear them. Let their confidence in you never be abused. But is it possible, that any of you can be such barbarians, so supremely wicked, as to abuse it? Can you find in your hearts* to despoil the gentle, trusting creatures of their treasure, or do anything to strip them of their native robe of virtue? Curst be the impious hand that would dare to violate the unblemished form of chastity! Thou wretch! thou ruffian! forbear; nor venture to provoke Heaven's fiercest vengeance." I know not any comment that can be made seriously on this curious passage, and I could produce many similar ones; and some, so very sentimental, that I have heard rational men use the word indecent, when they mentioned them with disgust.

Throughout there is a display of cold artificial feelings, and that parade of sensibility which boys and girls should be taught to despise as the sure mark of a little vain mind. Florid appeals are made to Heaven, and to the *beauteous innocents,* the fairest images of Heaven here below, whilst sober sense is left far behind. This is not the language of the heart, nor will it ever reach it, though the ear may be tickled.

I shall be told, perhaps, that the public have been pleased with these volumes. True—and Hervey's *Meditations*[8] are still read, though he equally sinned against sense and taste.

I particularly object to the love-like phrases of pumped up passion, which are everywhere interspersed. If women be ever allowed to walk without leading-strings, why must they be cajoled into virtue by artful flattery and sexual compliments? Speak to them the language of truth and soberness, and away with the lullaby strains of condescending endearment! Let them be taught to respect themselves as rational creatures, and not led to have a passion for their own insipid persons. It moves my gall to hear a preacher descanting on dress and needlework; and still more, to hear him address the *British fair, the fairest of the fair,* as if they had only feelings.

Even recommending piety he uses the following argument. "Never, perhaps, does a fine woman strike more deeply, than when, composed into pious recollection, and possessed with the noblest considerations, she assumes, without knowing it, superior dignity and new graces; so that the beauties of holiness seem to radiate about her, and the bystanders are almost induced to fancy her already worshipping amongst her kindred angels!" Why are women to be thus bred up with a desire

*Can you?—Can you? would be the most emphatical comment, were it drawled out in a whining voice.

of conquest? the very word, used in this sense, gives me a sickly qualm! Do religion and virtue offer no stronger motives, no brighter reward? Must they always be debased by being made to consider the sex of their companions? Must they be taught always to be pleasing? And when levelling their small artillery at the heart of man, is it necessary to tell them that a little sense is sufficient to render their attention *incredibly soothing*? "As a small degree of knowledge entertains in a woman, so from a woman, though for a different reason, a small expression of kindness delights, particularly if she have beauty!" I should have supposed for the same reason.

Why are girls to be told that they resemble angels; but to sink them below women? Or, that a gentle innocent female is an object that comes nearer to the idea which we have formed of angels than any other. Yet they are told, at the same time, that they are only like angels when they are young and beautiful; consequently, it is their persons, not their virtues, that procure them this homage.

Idle empty words! What can such delusive flattery lead to, but vanity and folly? The lover, it is true, has a poetical licence to exalt his mistress; his reason is the bubble of his passion, and he does not utter a falsehood when he borrows the language of adoration. His imagination may raise the idol of his heart, unblamed, above humanity; and happy would it be for women, if they were only flattered by the men who loved them; I mean, who love the individual, not the sex; but should a grave preacher interlard his discourses with such fooleries?

In sermons or novels, however, voluptuousness is always true to its text. Men are allowed by moralists to cultivate, as Nature directs, different qualities, and assume the different characters, that the same passions, modified almost to infinity, give to each individual. A virtuous man may have a choleric or a sanguine constitution, be gay or grave, unreproved; be firm till he is almost overbearing, or, weakly submissive, have no will or opinion of his own; but all women are to be levelled, by meekness and docility, into one character of yielding softness and gentle compliance.

I will use the preacher's own words. "Let it be observed, that in your sex manly exercises are never graceful; that in them a tone and figure, as well as an air and depórtment, of the masculine kind, are always forbidding; and that men of sensibility desire in every woman soft features, and a flowing voice, a form, not robust, and demeanour delicate and gentle."

Is not the following portrait—the portrait of a house slave? "I am astonished at the folly of many women, who are still reproaching their husbands for leaving them alone, for preferring this or that company to theirs, for treating them with this and the other mark of disregard or indifference; when, to speak the truth, they have themselves in a great measure to blame. Not that I would justify the men in anything wrong on their part. But had you behaved to them with more *respectful obser-vance,* and a more *equal tenderness; studying their humours, overlooking their mistakes, submitting to their opinions* in matters indifferent, passing by lit-tle instances of unevenness, caprice or passion, giving *soft* answers to hasty words, complaining as seldom as possible, and making it your daily care to relieve their anxieties and prevent their wishes, to enliven the hour of dullness, and call up the ideas of felicity: had you pursued this conduct, I doubt not but you would have maintained and even in-creased their esteem, so far as to have secured every degree of influ-ence that could conduce to their virtue, or your mutual satisfaction; and your house might at this day have been the abode of domestic bliss." Such a woman ought to be an angel—or she is an ass—for I dis-cern not a trace of the human character, neither reason nor passion in this domestic drudge, whose being is absorbed in that of a tyrant's.

Still Dr. Fordyce must have very little acquaintance with the human heart, if he really supposed that such conduct would bring back wan-dering love, instead of exciting contempt. No, beauty, gentleness, etc., etc., may gain a heart; but esteem, the only lasting affection, can alone be obtained by virtue supported by reason. It is respect for the under-standing that keeps alive tenderness for the person.

As these volumes are so frequently put into the hands of young people, I have taken more notice of them than, strictly speaking, they deserve; but as they have contributed to vitiate the taste, and enervate the understanding of many of my fellow-creatures, I could not pass them silently over.

## SECTION III

Such paternal solicitude pervades Dr. Gregory's *Legacy to his Daughters,* that I enter on the task of criticism with affectionate respect; but as this little volume has many attractions to recommend it to the notice of the most respectable part of my sex, I cannot silently pass over ar-guments that so speciously support opinions which, I think, have had the most baneful effect on the morals and manners of the female world.

His easy familiar style is particularly suited to the tenor of his advice, and the melancholy tenderness which his respect for the memory of a beloved wife, diffuses through the whole work, renders it very interesting; yet there is a degree of concise elegance conspicuous in many passages that disturbs this sympathy; and we pop on the author, when we only expected to meet the—father.

Besides, having two objects in view, he seldom adhered steadily to either; for wishing to make his daughters amiable, and fearing lest unhappiness should only be the consequence, of instilling sentiments that might draw them out of the track of common life without enabling them to act with consonant independence and dignity, he checks the natural flow of his thoughts, and neither advises one thing nor the other.

In the preface he tells them a mournful truth, "that they will hear, at least once in their lives, the genuine sentiments of a man who has no interest in deceiving them."

Hapless woman! what can be expected from thee when the beings on whom thou art said naturally to depend for reason and support, have all an interest in deceiving thee! This is the root of the evil that has shed a corroding mildew on all thy virtues; and blighting in the bud thy opening faculties, has rendered thee the weak thing thou art! It is this separate interest—this insidious state of warfare, that undermines morality, and divides mankind!

If love have made some women wretched, how many more has the cold unmeaning intercourse of gallantry rendered vain and useless! yet this heartless attention to the sex is reckoned so manly, so polite that, till society is very differently organized, I fear, this vestige of gothic manners will not be done away by a more reasonable and affectionate mode of conduct. Besides, to strip it of its imaginary dignity, I must observe, that in the most uncivilized European states this lip-service prevails in a very great degree, accompanied with extreme dissoluteness of morals. In Portugal, the country that I particularly allude to, it takes place of the most serious moral obligations! for a man is seldom assassinated when in the company of a woman. The savage hand of rapine is unnerved by this chivalrous spirit; and, if the stroke of vengeance cannot be stayed, the lady is entreated to pardon the rudeness and depart in peace, though sprinkled perhaps, with her husband's or brother's blood.

I shall pass over his strictures on religion, because I mean to discuss that subject in a separate chapter.

The remarks relative to behaviour, though many of them very sensible, I entirely disapprove of, because it appears to me to be beginning, as it were, at the wrong end. A cultivated understanding, and an affectionate heart, will never want starched rules of decorum—something more substantial than seemliness will be the result; and, without understanding the behaviour here recommended, would be rank affectation. Decorum, indeed, is the one thing needful!—decorum is to supplant nature, and banish all simplicity and variety of character out of the female world. Yet what good end can all this superficial counsel produce? It is, however, much easier to point out this or that mode of behaviour, than to set the reason to work; but, when the mind has been stored with useful knowledge, and strengthened by being employed, the regulation of the behaviour may safely be left to its guidance.

Why, for instance, should the following caution be given when art of every kind must contaminate the mind; and why entangle the grand motives of action, which reason and religion equally combine to enforce, with pitiful worldly shifts and sleight-of-hand tricks to gain the applause of gaping tasteless fools? "Be even cautious in displaying your good sense.* It will be thought you assume a superiority over the rest of the company. But if you happen to have any learning, keep it a profound secret, especially from the men, who generally look with a jealous and malignant eye on a woman of great parts, and a cultivated understanding." If men of real merit, as he afterwards observes, be superior to this meanness, where is the necessity that the behaviour of the whole sex should be modulated to please fools, or men, who having little claim to respect as individuals, choose to keep close in their phalanx. Men, indeed, who insist on their common superiority, having only this sexual superiority, are certainly very excusable.

There would be no end to rules for behaviour, if it be proper always to adopt the tone of the company; for thus, for ever varying the key, a *flat* would often pass for a *natural* note.

Surely it would have been wiser to have advised women to improve themselves till they rose above the fumes of vanity; and then to let the public opinion come round—for where are rules of accommodation to stop? The narrow path of truth and virtue inclines neither to the right nor left—it is a straightforward business, and they who are

---

*Let women once acquire good sense—and if it deserve the name, it will teach them; or, of what use will it be? how to employ it.

earnestly pursuing their road, may bound over many decorous prejudices, without leaving modesty behind. Make the heart clean, and give the head employment, and I will venture to predict that there will be nothing offensive in the behaviour.

The air of fashion, which many young people are so eager to attain, always strikes me like the studied attitudes of some modern pictures, copied with tasteless servility after the antiques; the soul is left out, and none of the parts are tied together by what may properly be termed character. This varnish of fashion, which seldom sticks very close to sense, may dazzle the weak; but leave nature to itself, and it will seldom disgust the wise. Besides, when a woman has sufficient sense not to pretend to anything which she does not understand in some degree, there is no need of determining to hide her talents under a bushel. Let things take their natural course, and all will be well.

It is this system of dissimulation, throughout the volume, that I despise. Women are always to *seem* to be this and that—yet virtue might apostrophize them, in the words of Hamlet—Seems! I know not seems! Have that within that passeth show![9]

Still the same tone occurs; for in another place, after recommending, without sufficiently discriminating delicacy, he adds,—"The men will complain of your reserve. They will assure you that a franker behaviour would make you more amiable. But, trust me, they are not sincere when they tell you so. I acknowledge that on some occasions it might render you more agreeable as companions, but it would make you less amiable as women: an important distinction, which many of your sex are not aware of."

This desire of being always women, is the very consciousness that degrades the sex. Excepting with a lover, I must repeat with emphasis, a former observation,—it would be well if they were only agreeable or rational companions. But in this respect his advice is even inconsistent with a passage which I mean to quote with the most marked approbation.

"The sentiment, that a woman may allow all innocent freedoms, provided her virtue is secure, is both grossly indelicate and dangerous, and has proved fatal to many of your sex." With this opinion I perfectly coincide. A man, or a woman, of any feeling, must always wish to convince a beloved object that it is the caresses of the individual, not the sex, that are received and returned with pleasure; and, that the heart, rather than the senses, is moved. Without this natural delicacy, love becomes a selfish personal gratification that soon degrades the character.

I carry this sentiment still further. Affection, when love is out of the question, authorizes many personal endearments, that naturally flowing from an innocent heart, give life to the behaviour; but the personal intercourse of appetite, gallantry, of vanity, is despicable. When a man squeezes the hand of a pretty woman, handing her to a carriage, whom he has never seen before, she will consider such an impertinent freedom in the light of an insult, if she have any true delicacy, instead of being flattered by this unmeaning homage to beauty. These are the privileges of friendship, or the momentary homage which the heart pays to virtue, when it flashes suddenly on the notice—mere animal spirits have no claim to the kindnesses of affection.

Wishing to feed the affections with what is now the food of vanity, I would fain persuade my sex to act from simpler principles. Let them merit love, and they will obtain it, though they may never be told that—"The power of a fine woman over the hearts of men, of men of the finest parts, is even beyond what she conceives."

I have already noticed the narrow cautions with respect to duplicity, female softness, delicacy of constitution; for these are the changes which he rings round without ceasing—in a more decorous manner, it is true, than Rousseau; but it all comes home to the same point, and whoever is at the trouble to analyse these sentiments, will find the first principles not quite so delicate as the superstructure.

The subject of amusements is treated in too cursory a manner; but with the same spirit.

When I treat of friendship, love, and marriage, it will be found that we materially differ in opinion; I shall not then forestall what I have to observe on these important subjects; but confine my remarks to the general tenor of them, to that cautious family prudence to those confined views of partial unenlightened affection, which exclude pleasure and improvement, by vainly wishing to ward off sorrow and error, and by thus guarding the heart and mind, destroy also all their energy. It is far better to be often deceived than never to trust; to be disappointed in love than never to love; to lose a husband's fondness than forfeit his esteem.

Happy would it be for the world, and for individuals, of course, if all this unavailing solicitude to attain worldly happiness, on a confined plan, were turned into an anxious desire to improve the understanding. "Wisdom is the principal thing: *therefore* get wisdom; and with all thy gettings get understanding." "How long, ye simple ones, will ye love simplicity, and hate knowledge?" saith Wisdom to the daughters of men.

## SECTION IV

I do not mean to allude to all the writers who have written on the subject of female manners—it would, in fact, be only beating over the old ground, for they have, in general, written in the same strain; but attacking the boasted prerogative of man—the prerogative that may emphatically be called the iron sceptre of tyranny, the original sin of tyrants, I declare against all power built on prejudices, however hoary.

If the submission demanded be founded on justice—there is no appealing to a higher power—for God is justice itself. Let us then, as children of the same parent, if not bastardized by being the younger born, reason together, and learn to submit to the authority of Reason—when her voice is distinctly heard. But, if it proved, that this throne of prerogative only rests on a chaotic mass of prejudices, that have no inherent principle of order to keep them together, or on an elephant, tortoise, or even the mighty shoulders of a son of the earth, they may escape, who dare to brave the consequence, without any breach of duty, without sinning against the order of things.

Whilst reason raises man above the brutal herd, and death is big with promises, they alone are subject to blind authority who have no reliance on their own strength. They are free—who will be free!*—

The being who can govern itself has nothing to fear in life; but if anything be dearer than its own respect, the price must be paid to the last farthing. Virtue, like everything valuable, must be loved for herself alone; or she will not take up her abode with us. She will not impart that peace, "which passeth understanding," when she is merely made the stilts of reputation; and respected, with pharisaical exactness, because "honesty is the best policy."

That the plan of life which enables us to carry some knowledge and virtue into another world, is the one best calculated to ensure content in this, cannot be denied; yet few people act according to this principle, though it be universally allowed that it admits not of dispute. Present pleasure, or present power, carry before it these sober convictions; and it is for the day, not for life, that man bargains with happi-

---

*"He is the free man, whom the *truth* makes free!"—COWPER.[10]

ness. How few!—how very few! have sufficient foresight, or resolution, to endure a small evil at the moment, to avoid a greater hereafter.

Woman in particular, whose virtue* is built on mutable prejudices, seldom attains to this greatness of mind; so that, becoming the slave of her own feelings, she is easily subjugated by those of others. Thus degraded, her reason, her misty reason! is employed rather to burnish than to snap her chains.

Indignantly have I heard women argue in the same track as men, and adopt the sentiments that brutalize them, with all the pertinacity of ignorance.

I must illustrate my assertion by a few examples. Mrs. Piozzi,[11] who often repeated by rote, what she did not understand, comes forward with Johnsonian periods.

"Seek not for happiness in singularity; and dread a refinement of wisdom as a deviation into folly." Thus she dogmatically addresses a new married man; and to elucidate this pompous exordium, she adds, "I said that the person of your lady would not grow more pleasing to you, but pray let her never suspect that it grows less so: that a woman will pardon an affront to her understanding much sooner than one to her person, is well known; nor will any of us contradict the assertion. All our attainments, all our arts, are employed to gain and keep the heart of man; and what mortification can exceed the disappointment, if the end be not obtained? There is no reproof however pointed, no punishment however severe, that a woman of spirit will not prefer to neglect; and if she can endure it without complaint, it only proves that she means to make herself amends by the attention of others for the slights of her husband!"

These are truly masculine sentiments. "All our *arts* are employed to gain and keep the heart of man":—and what is the inference?—if her person, and was there ever a person, though formed with Medicean[12] symmetry, that was not slighted? be neglected, she will make herself amends by endeavouring to please other men. Noble morality! But this is the understanding of the whole sex affronted, and their virtue deprived of the common basis of virtue. A woman must know, that her person cannot be as pleasing to her husband as it was to her lover, and if she be offended with him for being a human creature, she may as well whine about the loss of his heart as about any other foolish thing. And this very want of discernment or unreasonable anger, proves that

---

*I mean to use a word that comprehends more than chastity, the sexual virtue.

he could not change his fondness for her person into affection for her virtues or respect for her understanding.

Whilst women avow, and act up to such opinions, their understandings, at least, deserve the contempt and obloquy that men, *who never* insult their persons, have pointedly levelled at the female mind. And it is the sentiments of these polite men, who do not wish to be encumbered with mind, that vain women thoughtlessly adopt. Yet they should know, that insulted reason alone can spread that *sacred* reserve about the person, which renders human affections, for human affections have always some base alloy, as permanent as is consistent with the grand end of existence—the attainment of virtue.

The Baroness de Staël[13] speaks the same language as the lady just cited, with more enthusiasm. Her eulogium on Rousseau was accidentally put into my hands, and her sentiments, the sentiments of too many of my sex, may serve as the text for a few comments. "Though Rousseau," she observes, "has endeavoured to prevent women from interfering in public affairs, and acting a brilliant part in the theatre of politics; yet in speaking of them, how much has he done it to their satisfaction! If he wished to deprive them of some rights foreign to their sex, how has he for ever restored to them all those to which it has a claim! And in attempting to diminish their influence over the deliberations of men, how sacredly has he established the empire they have over their happiness! In aiding them to descend from an usurped throne, he has firmly seated them upon that to which they were destined by nature; and though he be full of indignation against them when they endeavour to resemble men, yet when they come before him with all the *charms, weaknesses, virtues,* and *errors* of their sex, his respect for their *persons* amounts almost to adoration." True! For never was there a sensualist who paid more fervent adoration at the shrine of beauty. So devout, indeed, was his respect for the person, that excepting the virtue of chastity, for obvious reasons, he only wished to see it embellished by charms, weaknesses, and errors. He was afraid lest the austerity of reason should disturb the soft playfulness of love. The master wished to have a meretricious slave to fondle, entirely dependent on his reason and bounty; he did not want a companion, whom he should be compelled to esteem, or a friend to whom he could confine the care of his children's education, should death deprive them of their father, before he had fulfilled the sacred task. He denies woman reason, shuts her out from knowledge, and turns her aside from truth; yet his pardon is granted, because "he admits the passion of love." It would require some ingenuity to show why women were to be under such an obligation to him for thus admitting love; when it is clear that he admits it only for the relaxation of men, and to perpetuate the species; but he talked with passion, and that powerful spell worked on the sensibility of a young encomiast. "What signifies it," pursues this rhapsodist, "to women, that his reason disputes with them the empire, when his heart is devotedly theirs." It is not empire,—but equality, that they should contend for. Yet, if they only wished to lengthen out their sway, they should not entirely trust to their persons, for though beauty may gain a heart, it cannot keep it, even while the beauty is in full bloom, unless the mind lend, at least, some graces.

When women are once sufficiently enlightened to discover their real interest, on a grand scale, they will, I am persuaded, be very ready to resign all the prerogatives of love, that are not mutual, speaking of them as lasting prerogatives, for the calm satisfaction of friendship, and the tender confidence of habitual esteem. Before marriage they will not assume any insolent airs, or afterwards abjectly submit; but endeavouring to act like reasonable creatures, in both situations, they will not be tumbled from a throne to a stool.

Madame Genlis[14] has written several entertaining books for children; and her *Letters on Education* afford many useful hints, that sensible parents will certainly avail themselves of; but her views are narrow, and her prejudices as unreasonable as strong.

I shall pass over her vehement argument in favour of the eternity of future punishments, because I blush to think that a human being should ever argue vehemently in such a cause, and only make a few remarks on her absurd manner of making the parental authority supplant reason. For everywhere does she inculcate not only *blind* submission to parents, but to the opinion of the world.*

She tells a story of a young man engaged by his father's express desire to a girl of fortune. Before the marriage could take place she is deprived of her fortune, and thrown friendless on the world. The father practises the most infamous arts to separate his son from her, and when the son detects his villainy, and, following the dictates of honour,

---

*A person is not to act in this or that way, though convinced they are right in so doing, because some equivocal circumstances may lead the world to *suspect* that they acted from different motives. This is sacrificing the substance for a shadow. Let people but watch their own hearts, and act rightly, as far as they can judge, and they may patiently wait till the opinion of the world comes round. It is best to be directed by a simple motive, for justice has too often been sacrificed to propriety—another word for convenience.

marries the girl, nothing but misery ensues, because, forsooth! he married *without* his father's consent. On what ground can religion or morality rest when justice is thus set at defiance? With the same view she represents an accomplished young woman, as ready to marry anybody that her *mamma* pleased to recommend; and, as actually marrying the young man of her own choice, without feeling any emotions of passion, because that a well-educated girl has not time to be in love. Is it possible to have much respect for a system of education that thus insults reason and nature?

Many similar opinions occur in her writings, mixed with sentiments that do honour to her head and heart. Yet so much superstition is mixed with her religion, and so much worldly wisdom with her morality, that I should not let a young person read her works, unless I could afterwards converse on the subjects, and point out the contradictions.

Mrs. Chapone's letters[15] are written with such good sense and unaffected humility, and contain so many useful observations, that I only mention them to pay the worthy writer this tribute of respect. I cannot, it is true, always coincide in opinion with her, but I always respect her.

The very word respect brings Mrs. Macaulay to my remembrance. The woman of the greatest abilities, undoubtedly, that this country has ever produced; and yet this woman has been suffered to die without sufficient respect being paid to her memory.

Posterity, however, will be more just, and remember that Catherine Macaulay was an example of intellectual acquirements supposed to be incompatible with the weakness of her sex. In her style of writing, indeed, no sex appears, for it is like the sense it conveys, strong and clear.

I will not call hers a masculine understanding, because I admit not of such an arrogant assumption of reason; but I contend that it was a sound one, and that her judgement, the matured fruit of profound thinking, was a proof that a woman can acquire judgement in the full extent of the word. Possessing more penetration than sagacity, more understanding than fancy, she writes with sober energy and argumentative closeness; yet sympathy and benevolence give an interest to her sentiments, and that vital heat to arguments, which forces the reader to weigh them.*

---

*Coinciding in opinion with Mrs. Macaulay relative to many branches of education, I refer to her valuable work, instead of quoting her sentiments to support my own.

When I first thought of writing these strictures I anticipated Mrs. Macaulay's approbation, with a little of that sanguine ardour which it has been the business of my life to depress, but soon heard with the sickly qualm of disappointed hope, and the still seriousness of regret—that she was no more!

## SECTION V

Taking a view of the different works which have been written on education, Lord Chesterfield's *Letters* must not be silently passed over. Not that I mean to analyse his unmanly, immoral system, or even to cull any of the useful, shrewd remarks which occur in his epistles. No, I only mean to make a few reflections on the avowed tendency of them, the art of acquiring an early knowledge of the world—an art, I will venture to assert, that preys secretly, like the worm in the bud, on the expanding powers, and turns to poison the generous juices which should mount with vigour into the youthful frame, inspiring warm affections and great resolves.*

For everything, saith the wise man, there is a season; and who would look for the fruits of autumn during the genial months of spring? But this is mere declamation, and I mean to reason with those worldly-wise instructors, who, instead of cultivating the judgement, instil prejudices, and render hard the heart that gradual experience would only have cooled. An early acquaintance with human infirmities; or, what is termed knowledge of the world, is the surest way, in my opinion, to contract the heart and damp the natural youthful ardour which produces not only great talents, but great virtues. For the vain attempt to bring forth the fruit of experience, before the sapling has out thrown its leaves, only exhausts its strength, and prevents its assuming a natural form; just as the form and strength of subsiding metals are injured when the attraction of cohesion is disturbed.

Tell me, ye who have studied the human mind, is it not a strange way to fix principles by showing young people that they are seldom stable? And how can they be fortified by habits when they are proved

---

*That children ought to be constantly guarded against the vices and follies of the world appears to me a very mistaken opinion; for in the course of my experience, and my eyes have looked abroad, I never knew a youth educated in this manner, who had early imbibed these chilling suspicions, and repeated by rote the hesitating *if* of age, that did not prove a selfish character.

to be fallacious by example? Why is the ardour of youth thus to be damped, and the luxuriancy of fancy cut to the quick? This dry caution may, it is true, guard a character from worldly mischances, but will infallibly preclude excellence in either virtue or knowledge.* The stumbling block thrown across every path by suspicion will prevent any vigorous exertions of genius or benevolence, and life will be stripped of its most alluring charm long before its calm evening when man should retire to contemplation for comfort and support.

A young man who has been bred up with domestic friends, and led to store his mind with as much speculative knowledge as can be acquired by reading and the natural reflections which youthful ebullitions of animal spirits and instinctive feelings inspire, will enter the world with warm and erroneous expectations. But this appears to be the course of Nature; and in morals, as well as in works of taste, we should be observant of her sacred indications, and not presume to lead when we ought obsequiously to follow.

In the world few act from principle; present feelings and early habits are the grand springs; but how would the former be deadened, and the latter rendered iron-corroding fetters, if the world were shown to young people just as it is, when no knowledge of mankind or their own hearts, slowly obtained by experience, rendered them forbearing? Their fellow-creatures would not then be viewed as frail beings like themselves, condemned to struggle with human infirmities, and sometimes displaying the light, and sometimes the dark, side of their character; extorting alternate feelings of love and disgust, but guarded against as beasts of prey, till every enlarged social feeling—in a word, humanity—was eradicated.

In life, on the contrary, as we gradually discover the imperfections of our nature, we discover virtues, and various circumstances attach us to our fellow-creatures, when we mix with them and view the same objects, that are never thought of in acquiring a hasty unnatural knowledge of the world. We see a folly swell into a vice, by almost imperceptible degrees, and pity while we blame; but if the hideous monster burst suddenly on our sight, fear and disgust, rendering us more severe than man ought to be, might lead us with blind zeal to usurp the character of omnipotence, and denounce damnation on our fellow-

---

*I have already observed that an early knowledge of the world, obtained in a natural way, by mixing in the world, has the same effect, instancing officers and women.

mortals, forgetting that we cannot read the heart, and that we have seeds of the same vices lurking in our own.

I have already remarked that we expect more from instruction than mere instruction can produce; for instead of preparing young people to encounter the evils of life with dignity, and to acquire wisdom and virtue by the exercise of their own faculties, precepts are heaped upon precepts, and blind obedience required when conviction should be brought home to reason.

Suppose, for instance, that a young person, in the first ardour of friendship, deifies the beloved object, what harm can arise from this mistaken enthusiastic attachment? Perhaps it is necessary for virtue first to appear in a human form to impress youthful hearts; the ideal model, which a more matured and exalted mind looks up to, and shapes for itself, would elude their sight. "He who loves not his brother whom he hath seen, how can he love God?" asked the wisest of men.

It is natural for youth to adorn the first object of its affection with every good quality, and the emulation produced by ignorance, or, to speak with more propriety, by inexperience, brings forward the mind capable of forming such an affection, and when, in the lapse of time, perfection is found not to be within the reach of mortals, virtue, abstractedly, is thought beautiful, and wisdom sublime. Admiration then gives place to friendship, properly so called, because it is cemented by esteem; and the being walks alone only dependent on Heaven for that emulous panting after perfection which ever glows in a noble mind. But this knowledge a man must gain by the exertion of his own faculties; and this is surely the blessed fruit of disappointed hope! for He who delighteth to diffuse happiness and show mercy to the weak creatures, who are learning to know Him, never implanted a good propensity to be a tormenting *ignis fatuus*.[16]

Our trees are now allowed to spread with wild luxuriance, nor do we expect by force to combine the majestic marks of time with youthful graces; but wait patiently till they have struck deep their root, and braved many a storm. Is the mind then, which, in proportion to its dignity, advances more slowly towards perfection, to be treated with less respect? To argue from analogy, everything around us is in a progressive state; and when an unwelcome knowledge of life produces almost a satiety of life, and we discover by the natural course of things that all that is done under the sun is vanity, we are drawing near the awful close of the drama. The days of activity and hope are over, and the opportunities which the first stage of existence has afforded of advancing in the scale of intelligence, must soon be summed up. A knowledge at this period of the futility of life, or earlier, if obtained by experience, is very useful, because it is natural; but when a frail being is shown the follies and vices of man, that he may be taught prudently to guard against the common casualties of life by sacrificing his heart—surely it is not speaking harshly to call it the wisdom of this world, contrasted with the nobler fruit of piety and experience.

I will venture a paradox, and deliver my opinion without reserve; if men were only born to form a circle of life and death, it would be wise to take every step that foresight could suggest to render life happy. Moderation in every pursuit would then be supreme wisdom; and the prudent voluptuary might enjoy a degree of content, though he neither cultivated his understanding nor kept his heart pure. Prudence, supposing we were mortal, would be true wisdom, or, to be more explicit, would procure the greatest portion of happiness, considering the whole of life, but knowledge beyond the conveniences of life would be a curse.

Why should we injure our health by close study? The exalted pleasure which intellectual pursuits afford would scarcely be equivalent to the hours of languour that follow; especially, if it be necessary to take into the reckoning the doubts and disappointments that cloud our researches. Vanity and vexation close every inquiry: for the cause which we particularly wished to discover flies like the horizon before us as we advance. The ignorant, on the contrary, resemble children, and suppose, that if they could walk straight forward they should at last arrive where the earth and clouds meet. Yet, disappointed as we are, in our researches, the mind gains strength by the exercise, sufficient, perhaps, to comprehend the answers which, in another step of existence, it may receive to the anxious questions it asked, when the understanding with feeble wing was fluttering round the visible effects to dive into the hidden cause.

The passions also, the winds of life, would be useless, if not injurious, did the substance which composes our thinking being, after we have thought in vain, only become the support of vegetable life, and invigorate a cabbage, or blush in a rose. The appetites would answer every earthly purpose, and produce more moderate and permanent happiness. But the powers of the soul that are of little use here, and, probably, disturb our animal enjoyments, even while conscious dignity makes us glory in possessing them, prove that life is merely an education, a state of infancy, to which the only hopes worth cherishing should not be sacrificed. I mean, therefore, to infer, that we ought to have a precise idea of what we wish to attain by education, for the immortality of the soul is contradicted by the actions of many people who firmly profess the belief.

If you mean to secure ease and prosperity on earth as the first consideration, and leave futurity to provide for itself; you act prudently in giving your child an early insight into the weaknesses of his nature. You may not, it is true, make an Inkle[17] of him; but do not imagine that he will stick to more than the letter of the law, who has very early imbibed a mean opinion of human nature; nor will he think it necessary to rise much above the common standard. He may avoid gross vices, because honesty is the best policy; but he will never aim at attaining great virtues. The example of writers and artists will illustrate this remark.

I must therefore venture to doubt whether what has been thought an axiom in morals may not have been a dogmatical assertion made by men who have coolly seen mankind through the medium of books, and say, in direct contradiction to them, that the regulation of the passions is not, always, wisdom. On the contrary, it would seem, that one reason why men have superior judgement, and more fortitude than women, is undoubtedly this, that they give a freer scope to the grand passions, and by more frequently going astray enlarge their minds. If then by the exercise of their own* reason they fix on some stable principle, they have probably to thank the force of their passions, nourished by *false* views of life, and permitted to overlap the boundary that secures content. But if, in the dawn of life, we could soberly survey the scenes before as in perspective, and see everything in its true colours, how could the passions gain sufficient strength to unfold the faculties?

Let me now as from an eminence survey the world stripped of all its false delusive charms. The clear atmosphere enables me to see each object in its true point of view, while my heart is still. I am calm as the prospect in a morning when the mists, slowly dispersing, silently unveil the beauties of nature, refreshed by rest.

In what light will the world now appear? I rub my eyes, and think, perchance, that I am just awaking from a lively dream.

I see the sons and daughters of men pursuing shadows, and anxiously wasting their powers to feed passions which have no adequate

---

*"I find that all is but lip-wisdom which wants experience," says Sidney.[18]

object. If the very excess of these blind impulses, pampered by that lying, yet constantly trusted guide, the imagination, did not, by preparing them for some other state, render short-sighted mortals wiser without their own concurrence, or, what comes to the same thing, when they were pursuing some imaginary present good.

After viewing objects in this light, it would not be very fanciful to imagine that this world was a stage on which a pantomime is daily performed for the amusement of superior beings. How would they be diverted to see the ambitious man consuming himself by running after a phantom, and "pursuing the bubble fame in the cannon's mouth" that was to blow him to nothing; for when consciousness is lost, it matters not whether we mount in a whirlpool, or descend in rain. And should they compassionately invigorate his sight, and show him the thorny path which led to eminence, that, like a quicksand, sinks as he ascends, disappointing his hopes when almost within his grasp, would he not leave to others the honour of amusing them, and labour to secure the present moment, though, from the constitution of his nature, he would not find it very easy to catch the flying stream? Such slaves are we to hope and fear!

But vain as the ambitious man's pursuits would be, he is often striving for something more substantial than fame. That, indeed, would be the veriest meteor, the wildest fire that could lure a man to ruin. What! renounce the most trifling gratification to be applauded when he should be no more! Wherefore this struggle, whether man be mortal or immortal, if that noble passion did not really raise the being above his fellows?

And love! What diverting scenes would it produce; pantaloon's tricks[19] must yield to more egregious folly. To see a mortal adorn an object with imaginary charms, and then fall down and worship the idol which he had himself set up—how ridiculous! But what serious consequences ensue to rob man of that portion of happiness which the Deity by calling him into existence has (or on what can His attributes rest?) indubitably promised. Would not all the purposes of life have been much better fulfilled if he had only felt what has been termed physical love? And would not the sight of the object, not seen through the medium of the imagination, soon reduce the passion to an appetite if reflection, the noble distinction of man, did not give it force, and make it an instrument to raise him above this earthly dross, by teaching him to love the centre of all perfection, whose wisdom appears clearer and clearer in the works of nature in proportion as reason is illuminated and exalted by contemplation, and by acquiring that love of order which the struggles of passion produce?

The habit of reflection, and the knowledge attained by fostering any passion, might be shown to be equally useful, though the object be proved equally fallacious; for they would all appear in the same light if they were not magnified by the governing passion implanted in us by the Author of all good to call forth and strengthen the faculties of each individual, and enable it to attain all the experience that an infant can obtain who does certain things, it cannot tell why.

I descend from my height, and mixing with my fellow-creatures feel myself hurried along the common stream. Ambition, love, hope, and fear, exert their wonted power, though we be convinced by reason that their present and most attractive promises are only lying dreams; but had the cold hand of circumspection damped each generous feeling before it had left any permanent character, or fixed some habit, what could be expected but selfish prudence and reason just rising above instinct? Who that has read Dean Swift's disgusting description of the Yahoos, and insipid one of Houyhnhnm[20] with a philosophical eye, can avoid seeing the futility of degrading the passions, or making man rest in contentment?

The youth should *act*, for had he the experience of a grey head he would be fitter for death than life, though his virtues, rather residing in his head than his heart, could produce nothing great, and his understanding, prepared for this world, would not, by its noble flights, prove that it had a title to a better.

Besides, it is not possible to give a young person a just view of life; he must have struggled with his own passions before he can estimate the force of the temptation which betrayed his brother into vice. Those who are entering life, and those who are departing, see the world from such very different points of view that they can seldom think alike, unless the unfledged reason of the former never attempted a solitary flight.

When we hear of some daring crime, it comes full on us in the deepest shade of turpitude, and raises indignation; but the eye that gradually saw the darkness thicken must observe it with more compassionate forbearance. The world cannot be seen by an unmoved spectator; we must mix in the throng and feel as men feel, before we can judge of their feelings. If we mean, in short, to live in the world, to grow wiser and better, and not merely to enjoy the good things of life, we must attain a knowledge of others at the same time that we become acquainted with ourselves. Knowledge acquired any other way only hardens the heart, and perplexes the understanding.

I may be told that the knowledge thus acquired is sometimes purchased at too dear a rate. I can only answer that I very much doubt whether any knowledge can be attained without labour and sorrow; and those who wish to spare their children both should not complain if they are neither wise nor virtuous. They only aimed at making them prudent, and prudence early in life is but the cautious craft of ignorant self-love.

I have observed that young people, to whose education particular attention has been paid, have in general been very superficial and conceited, and far from pleasing in any respect, because they had neither the unsuspecting warmth of youth, nor the cool depth of age. I cannot help imputing this unnatural appearance principally to that hasty premature instruction which leads them presumptuously to repeat all the crude notions they have taken upon trust, so that the careful education which they received, makes them all their lives the slaves of prejudices.

Mental as well as bodily exertion is at first irksome; so much so, that the many would fain let others both work and think for them. An observation which I have often made will illustrate my meaning. When in a circle of strangers or acquaintances a person of moderate abilities asserts an opinion with heat, I will venture to affirm—for I have traced this fact home—very often that it is a prejudice. These echoes have a high respect for the understanding of some relation or friend, and without fully comprehending the opinions which they are so eager to retail, they maintain them with a degree of obstinacy that would surprise even the person who concocted them.

I know that a kind of fashion now prevails of respecting prejudices; and when anyone dares to face them, though actuated by humanity and armed by reason, he is superciliously asked whether his ancestors were fools. No, I should reply. Opinions at first of every description were all probably considered, and therefore were founded on some reason; yet not unfrequently, of course, it was rather a local expedient than a fundamental principle that would be reasonable at all times. But moss-covered opinions assume the disproportioned form of prejudices when they are indolently adopted only because age has given them a venerable aspect, though the reason on which they were built ceases to be a reason, or cannot be traced. Why are we to love prejudices merely because they are prejudices?* A prejudice is a fond obstinate persuasion for which we can give no reason; for the moment a reason can be given for an opinion, it ceases to be a prejudice, though it may be an error in judgement; and are we then advised to cherish opinions only to set reason at defiance? This mode of arguing, if arguing it may be called, reminds me of what is vulgarly termed a woman's reason; for women sometimes declare that they love, or believe certain things, *because* they love or believe them.

It is impossible to converse with people to any purpose who only use affirmatives and negatives. Before you can bring them to a point to start fairly from, you must go back to the simple principles that were antecedent to the prejudices broached by power; and it is ten to one but you are stopped by the philosophical assertion that certain principles are as practically false as they are abstractly true.** Nay, it may be inferred that reason has whispered some doubts, for it generally happens that people assert their opinions with the greatest heat when they begin to waver; striving to drive out their own doubts by convincing their opponent, they grow angry when those gnawing doubts are thrown back to prey on themselves.

The fact is, that men expect from education, what education cannot give. A sagacious parent or tutor may strengthen the body and sharpen the instruments by which the child is to gather knowledge; but the honey must be the reward of the individual's own industry. It is almost as absurd to attempt to make a youth wise by the experience of another, as to expect the body to grow strong by the exercise which is only talked of, or seen.*** Many of those children whose conduct has been most narrowly watched, become the weakest men, because their instructors only instil certain notions into their minds, that have no other foundation than their authority; and if they be loved or respected, the mind is cramped in its exertions and wavering in its advances. The business of education in this case, is only to conduct the shooting tendrils to a proper pole; yet after laying precept upon precept, without allowing a child to acquire judgement itself, parents

---

* *Vide* Mr. Burke.[21]

** "Convince a man against his will,
He's of the same opinion still."[22]

*** "One sees nothing when one is content to contemplate only; it is necessary to act oneself to be able to see how others act."—ROUSSEAU.

expect them to act in the same manner by this borrowed fallacious light, as if they had illuminated it themselves; and be, when they enter life, what their parents are at the close. They do not consider that the tree, and even the human body, does not strengthen its fibres till it has reached its full growth.

There appears to be something analogous in the mind. The senses and the imagination give a form to the character, during childhood and youth; and the understanding, as life advances, gives firmness to the first fair purposes of sensibility, till virtue, arising rather from the clear conviction of reason than the impulse of the heart, morality is made to rest on a rock against which the storms of passion vainly beat.

I hope I shall not be misunderstood when I say, that religion will not have this condensing energy, unless it be founded on reason. If it be merely the refuge of weakness or wild fanaticism, and not a governing principle of conduct, drawn from self-knowledge, and a rational opinion respecting the attributes of God, what can it be expected to produce? The religion which consists in warming the affections, and exalting the imagination, is only the poetical part, and may afford the individual pleasure without rendering it a more moral being. It may be a substitute for worldly pursuits; yet narrow, instead of enlarging the heart; but virtue must be loved as in itself sublime and excellent, and not for the advantages it procures or the evils it averts, if any great degree of excellence be expected. Men will not become moral when they only build airy castles in a future world to compensate for the disappointments which they meet with in this; if they turn their thoughts from relative duties to religious reveries.

Most prospects in life are marred by the shuffling worldly wisdom of men, who, forgetting that they cannot serve God and mammon, endeavour to blend contradictory things. If you wish to make your son rich, pursue one course—if you are only anxious to make him virtuous, you must take another; but do not imagine that you can bound from one road to the other without losing your way.*

*See an excellent essay on this subject by Mrs. Barbauld, in *Miscellaneous Pieces in Prose*.

# CHAPTER VI

# THE EFFECT WHICH AN EARLY ASSOCIATION OF IDEAS HAS UPON THE CHARACTER

Educated in the enervating style recommended by the writers on whom I have been animadverting; and not having a chance, from their subordinate state in society, to recover their lost ground, is it surprising that women everywhere appear a defect in nature? Is it surprising, when we consider what a determinate effect an early association of ideas has on the character, that they neglect their understandings, and turn all their attention to their persons?

The great advantages which naturally result from storing the mind with knowledge, are obvious from the following considerations. The association of our ideas is either habitual or instantaneous; and the latter mode seems rather to depend on the original temperature of the mind than on the will. When the ideas, and matters of fact, are once taken in, they lie by for use, till some fortuitous circumstance makes the information dart into the mind with illustrative force, that has been received at very different periods of our lives. Like the lightning's flash are many recollections; one idea assimilating and explaining another, with astonishing rapidity. I do not now allude to that quick perception of truth, which is so intuitive that it baffles research, and makes us at a loss to determine whether it is reminiscence or ratiocination, lost sight of in its celerity, that opens the dark cloud. Over those instantaneous associations we have little power; for when the mind is once enlarged by excursive flights, or profound reflection, the raw materials will, in some degree, arrange themselves. The understanding, it is true, may keep us from going out of drawing when we group our thoughts, or transcribe from the imagination and warm sketches of fancy; but the animal spirits, the individual character, give the colouring. Over this subtile electric fluid,* how little power do we possess, and over it how little power can reason obtain. These fine intractable spirits appear to be the essence of genius, and beaming in its eagle eye, produce in the most eminent degree the happy energy of associating thoughts that surprise, delight, and instruct. These are the glowing minds that concentrate pictures for their fellow-creatures; forcing them to view with interest the objects reflected from the impassioned imagination, which they passed over in nature.

I must be allowed to explain myself. The generality of people cannot see or feel poetically, they want fancy, and therefore fly from solitude in search of sensible objects; but when an author lends them his eyes they can see as he saw, and be amused by images they could not select, though lying before them.

Education thus only supplies the man of genius with knowledge to give variety and contrast to his associations; but there is an habitual association of ideas, that grows "with our growth," which has a great effect on the moral character of mankind, and by which a turn is given to the mind that commonly remains throughout life. So ductile is the understanding, and yet so stubborn, that the associations which depend on adventitious circumstances, during the period that the body takes to arrive at maturity, can seldom be disentangled by reason. One idea calls up another, its old associate, and memory, faithful to the first impressions, particularly when the intellectual powers are not employed to cool our sensations, retraces them with mechanical exactness.

This habitual slavery, to first impressions, has a more baneful effect on the female than the male character, because business and other dry employments of the understanding, tend to deaden the feelings and break associations that do violence to reason. But females, who are made women of when they are mere children, and brought back to

---

*I have sometimes, when inclined to laugh at materialists, asked whether, as the most powerful effects in nature are apparently produced by fluids, the magnetic, etc., the passions might not be fine volatile fluids that embraced humanity, keeping the more refractory elementary parts together—or whether they were simply a liquid fire that pervaded the more sluggish materials, giving them life and heat?

childhood when they ought to leave the go-cart for ever, have not sufficient strength of mind to efface the superinductions of art that have smothered nature.

Everything that they see or hear serves to fix impressions, call forth emotions, and associate ideas, that give a sexual character to the mind. False notions of beauty and delicacy stop the growth of their limbs and produce a sickly soreness, rather than delicacy of organs; and thus weakened by being employed in unfolding instead of examining the first associations, forced on them by every surrounding object, how can they attain the vigour necessary to enable them to throw off their factitious character?—where find strength to recur to reason and rise superior to a system of oppression, that blasts the fair promises of spring? This cruel association of ideas, which everything conspires to twist into all their habits of thinking, or, to speak with more precision, of feeling, receives new force when they begin to act a little for themselves; for they then perceive that it is only through their address to excite emotions in men, that pleasure and power are to be obtained. Besides, the books professedly written for their instruction, which make the first impression on their minds, all inculcate the same opinions. Educated then in worse than Egyptian bondage, it is unreasonable, as well as cruel, to upbraid them with faults that can scarcely be avoided, unless a degree of native vigour be supposed, that falls to the lot of the very few amongst mankind.

For instance, the severest sarcasms have been levelled against the sex, and they have been ridiculed for repeating "a set of phrases learnt by rote,"[1] when nothing could be more natural, considering the education they receive, and that their "highest praise is to obey, unargued"— the will of man. If they be not allowed to have reason sufficient to govern their own conduct—why, all they learn must be learned by rote! And when all their ingenuity is called forth to adjust their dress, "a passion for a scarlet coat,"[2] is so natural, that it never surprised me; and, allowing Pope's summary of their character to be just, "that every woman is at heart a rake,"[3] why should they be bitterly censured for seeking a congenial mind, and preferring a rake to a man of sense?

Rakes know how to work on their sensibility, whilst the modest merit of reasonable men has, of course, less effect on their feelings, and they cannot reach the heart by the way of understanding, because they have few sentiments in common.

It seems a little absurd to expect women to be more reasonable than men in their *likings*, and still to deny them the uncontrolled use of reason. Why do men *fall in love* with sense? When do they, with their superior powers and advantages, turn from the person to the mind? And how can they then expect women, who are only taught to observe behaviour, and acquire manners rather than morals, to despise what they have been all their lives labouring to attain? Where are they suddenly to find judgement enough to weigh patiently the sense of an awkward virtuous man, when his manners, of which they are made critical judges, are rebuffing, and his conversation cold and dull, because it does not consist of pretty repartees, or well-turned compliments? In order to admire or esteem anything for a continuance, we must, at least, have our curiosity excited by knowing, in some degree, what we admire; for we are unable to estimate the value of qualities and virtues above our comprehension. Such a respect, when it is felt, may be very sublime; and the confused consciousness of humility may render the dependent creature an interesting object, in some points of view; but human love must have grosser ingredients; and the person very naturally will come in for its share—and, an ample share it mostly has!

Love is, in a great degree, an arbitrary passion, and will reign, like some other stalking mischiefs, by its own authority, without deigning to reason; and it may also be easily distinguished from esteem, the foundation of friendship, because it is often excited by evanescent beauties and graces, though, to give an energy to the sentiment, something more solid must deepen their impression and set the imagination to work, to make the most fair—the first good.

Common passions are excited by common qualities. Men look for beauty and the simper of good-humoured docility: women are captivated by easy manners; a gentleman-like man seldom fails to please them, and their thirsty ears eagerly drink the insinuating nothings of politeness, whilst they turn from the unintelligible sounds of the charmer—reason, charm he never so wisely. With respect to superficial accomplishments, the rake certainly has the advantage; and of these females can form an opinion, for it is their own ground. Rendered gay and giddy by the whole tenor of their lives, the very aspect of wisdom, or the severe graces of virtue, must have a lugubrious appearance to them; and produce a kind of restraint from which they and love, sportive child, naturally revolt. Without taste, excepting of the lighter kind, for taste is the offspring of judgement, how can they discover that true beauty and grace must arise from the play of the mind? and how can they be expected to relish in a lover what they do not, or very imperfectly, possess themselves? The sympathy that unites hearts, and invites to confidence, in them is so very faint, that it cannot take fire, and thus mount to passion. No, I repeat it, the love cherished by such minds, must have grosser fuel!

The inference is obvious; till women are led to exercise their understandings, they should not be satirized for their attachment to rakes; or even for being rakes at heart, when it appears to be the inevitable consequence of their education. They who live to please—must find their enjoyments, their happiness, in pleasure! It is a trite, yet true remark, that we never do anything well, unless we love it for its own sake.

Supposing, however, for a moment, that women were, in some future revolution of time, to become, what I sincerely wish them to be, even love would acquire more serious dignity, and be purified in its own fires; and virtue giving true delicacy to their affections, they would turn with disgust from a rake. Reasoning then, as well as feeling, the only province of woman, at present, they might easily guard against exterior graces, and quickly learn to despise the sensibility that had been excited and hackneyed in the ways of women, whose trade was vice; and allurements, wanton airs. They would recollect that the flame, one must use appropriated expressions, which they wished to light up, had been exhausted by lust, and that the sated appetite, losing all relish for pure and simple pleasures, could only be roused by licentious arts or variety. What satisfaction could a woman of delicacy promise herself in a union with such a man, when the very artlessness of her affection might appear insipid? Thus does Dryden describe the situation,

> Where love is duty, on the female side,
> On theirs mere sensual gust, and sought with surly pride.[4]

But one grand truth women have yet to learn, though much it imports them to act accordingly. In the choice of a husband, they should not be led astray by the qualities of a lover—for a lover the husband, even supposing him to be wise and virtuous, cannot long remain.

Were women more rationally educated, could they take a more comprehensive view of things, they would be contented to love but once in their lives; and after marriage calmly let passion subside into friendship—into that tender intimacy, which is the best refuge from care; yet is built on such pure, still affections, that idle jealousies would not be allowed to disturb the discharge of the sober duties of life, or to engross the thoughts that ought to be otherwise employed. This is a state in which many men live; but few, very few, women. And the difference may easily be accounted for, without recurring to a sexual character. Men, for whom we are told women were made, have too much occupied the thoughts of women; and this association has so entangled love with all their motives of action; and, to harp a little on an old string, having been solely employed either to prepare themselves to excite love, or actually putting their lessons in practice, they cannot live without love. But, when a sense of duty, or fear of shame, obliges them to restrain this pampered desire of pleasing beyond certain lengths, too far for delicacy, it is true, though far from criminality, they obstinately determine to love, I speak of the passion, their husbands to the end of the chapter—and then acting the part which they foolishly exacted from their lovers, they become abject wooers and fond slaves.

Men of wit and fancy are often rakes; and fancy is the food of love. Such men will inspire passion. Half the sex, in its present infantile state, would pine for a Lovelace;[5] a man so witty, so graceful, and so valiant; and can they *deserve* blame for acting according to principles so constantly inculcated? They want a lover, and protector; and behold him kneeling before them—bravery prostrate to beauty! The virtues of a husband are thus thrown by love into the background, and gay hopes, or lively emotions, banish reflection till the day of reckoning come; and come it surely will, to turn the sprightly lover into a surly suspicious tyrant, who contemptuously insults the very weakness he fostered. Or, supposing the rake reformed, he cannot quickly get rid of old habits. When a man of abilities is first carried away by his passions, it is necessary that sentiment and taste varnish the enormities of vice, and give a zest to brutal indulgences; but when the gloss of novelty is worn off, and pleasure palls upon the sense, lasciviousness becomes barefaced, and enjoyment only the desperate effort of weakness flying from reflection as from a legion of devils. Oh! virtue, thou art not an empty name! All that life can give—thou givest!

If much comfort cannot be expected from the friendship of a reformed rake of superior abilities, what is the consequence when he lacketh sense, as well as principles? Verily misery, in its most hideous shape. When the habits of weak people are consolidated by time, a reformation is barely possible; and actually makes the beings miserable who have not sufficient mind to be amused by innocent pleasure; like the tradesman who retires from the hurry of business, Nature presents to them only a universal blank; and the restless thoughts prey on the damped spirits.* The reformation, as well as his retirement, actually makes them wretched, because it deprives them of all employment, by quenching the hopes and fears that set in motion their sluggish minds.

If such be the force of habit; if such be the bondage of folly, how carefully ought we to guard the mind from storing up vicious associations; and equally careful should we be to cultivate the understanding, to save the poor wight from the weak dependent state of even harmless ignorance. For it is the right use of reason alone which make us independent of everything—excepting the unclouded reason—"Whose service is perfect freedom."

---

*I have frequently seen this exemplified in women whose beauty could no longer be repaired. They have retired from the noisy scenes of dissipation; but, unless they become Methodists, the solitude of the select society of their family connections or acquaintance, has presented only a fearful void; consequently, nervous complaints, and all the vapourish train of idleness, rendered them quite as useless, and far more unhappy, than when they joined the giddy throng.

# CHAPTER VII

# Modesty—Comprehensively Considered, and Not as a Sexual Virtue

Modesty! sacred offspring of sensibility and reason!—true delicacy of mind!—may I unblamed presume to investigate thy nature, and trace to its covert the mild charm, that mellowing each harsh feature of a character, renders what would otherwise only inspire cold admiration—lovely! Thou that smoothest the wrinkles of wisdom, and softenest the tone of the sublimest virtues till they all melt into humanity; thou that spreadest the ethereal cloud that, surrounding love, heightens every beauty, it half shades, breathing those coy sweets that steal into the heart, and charm the senses—modulate for me the language of persuasive reason, till I rouse my sex from the flowery bed, on which they supinely sleep life away!

In speaking of the association of our ideas, I have noticed two distinct modes; and in defining modesty, it appears to me equally proper to discriminate that purity of mind, which is the effect of chastity, from a simplicity of character that leads us to form a just opinion of ourselves, equally distant from vanity of presumption, though by no means incompatible with a lofty consciousness of our own dignity. Modesty, in the latter signification of the term, is that soberness of mind which teaches a man not to think more highly of himself than he ought to think, and should be distinguished from humility, because humility is a kind of self-abasement.

A modest man often conceives a great plan, and tenaciously adheres to it, conscious of his own strength, till success gives it a sanction that determines its character. Milton was not arrogant when he suffered a suggestion of judgement to escape him that proved a prophecy; nor was General Washington when he accepted of the command of the American forces. The latter has always been characterized as a modest man; but had he been merely humble, he would probably have shrunk back irresolute, afraid of trusting to himself the direction of an enterprise, on which so much depended.

A modest man is steady, an humble man timid, and a vain one presumptuous: this is the judgement, which the observation of many characters, has led me to form. Jesus Christ was modest, Moses was humble, and Peter vain.

Thus, discriminating modesty from humility in one case, I do not mean to confound it with bashfulness in the other. Bashfulness, in fact, is so distinct from modesty, that the most bashful lass or raw country lout, often become the most impudent; for their bashfulness being merely the instinctive timidity of ignorance, custom soon changes into assurance.*

The shameless behaviour of the prostitutes, who infest the streets of this metropolis, raising alternate emotions of pity and disgust, may serve to illustrate this remark. They trample on virgin bashfulness with a sort of bravado, and glorifying in their shame, become more audaciously lewd than men, however depraved, to whom this sexual quality has not been gratuitously granted, ever appear to be. But these poor ignorant wretches never had any modesty to lose, when they consigned themselves to infamy; for modesty is a virtue, not a quality. No, they were only bashful, shamefaced innocents; and losing their innocence, their shamefacedness was rudely brushed off: a virtue would have left some vestiges in the mind, had it been sacrificed to passion, to make us respect the grand ruin.

*"Such is the country maiden's fright,
  When first a redcoat is in sight,
  Behind the door she hides her face;
  Next time at distance eyes the lace;
  She now can all his terrors stand,
  Nor from his squeeze withdraws her hand,
  She plays familiar in his arms,
  And every soldier hath his charms;
  From tent to tent she spreads her flame;
  For custom conquers fear and shame."—GAY.[1]

Purity of mind, or that genuine delicacy, which is the only virtuous support of chastity, is near akin to that refinement of humanity, which never resides in any but cultivated minds. It is something nobler than innocence, it is the delicacy of reflection, and not the coyness of ignorance. The reserve of reason, which, like habitual cleanliness, is seldom seen in any great degree, unless the soul is active, may easily be distinguished from rustic shyness or wanton skittishness; and, so far from being incompatible with knowledge, it is its fairest fruit. What a gross idea of modesty had the writer of the following remark!—"The lady who asked the question whether women may be instructed in the modern system of botany consistently with female delicacy? was accused of ridiculous prudery; nevertheless, if she had proposed the question to me, I should certainly have answered—they cannot." Thus is the fair book of knowledge to be shut with an everlasting seal! On reading similar passages I have reverentially lifted up my eyes and heart to Him who liveth for ever and ever, and said, "O, my Father, hast Thou, by the very constitution of her nature forbid Thy child to seek Thee in the fair forms of truth? And can her soul be sullied by the knowledge that awfully calls her to Thee?"

I have then philosophically pursued these reflections till I inferred that those women who have most improved their reason must have the most modesty, though a dignified sedateness of deportment may have succeeded the playful, bewitching bashfulness of youth.*

And thus have I argued. To render chastity the virtue from which unsophisticated modesty will naturally flow, the attention should be called away from employments which only exercise the sensibility, and the heart made to beat time to humanity rather than to throb with love. The woman who has dedicated a considerable portion of her time to pursuits purely intellectual, and whose affections have been exercised by humane plans of usefulness, must have more purity of mind, as a natural consequence, than the ignorant beings whose time and thoughts have been occupied by gay pleasures, or schemes to conquer hearts.** The regulation of the behaviour is not modesty, though those

---

*Modesty is the graceful calm virtue of maturity; bashfulness the charm of vivacious youth.

**I have conversed, as man with man, with medical men on anatomical subjects, and compared the proportions of the human body with artists, yet such modesty did I meet with, that I was never reminded by word or look of my sex, of the absurd rules which make modesty a Pharisaical cloak of weakness. And I am persuaded that in the pursuit of knowledge women would never be insulted by sensible men, and rarely by men of any description, if who study rules of decorum are in general termed modest women. Make the heart clean; let it expand and feel for all that is human, instead of being narrowed by selfish passions; and let the mind frequently contemplate subjects that exercise the understanding, without heating the imagination, and artless modesty will give the finishing touches to the picture.

She who can discern the dawn of immortality in the streaks that shoot athwart the misty night of ignorance, promising a clearer day, will respect, as a sacred temple, the body that enshrines such an improvable soul. True love likewise spreads this kind of mysterious sanctity round the beloved object, making the lover most modest when in her presence.* So reserved is affection that, receiving or returning personal endearments, it wishes not only to shun the human eye as a kind of profanation, but to diffuse an encircling cloudy obscurity to shut out even the saucy sparkling sunbeams. Yet that affection does not deserve the epithet of chaste which does not receive a sublime gloom of tender melancholy, that allows the mind for a moment to stand still and enjoy the present satisfaction, when a consciousness of the Divine presence is felt—for this must ever be the food of joy.

As I have always been fond of tracing to its source in nature any prevailing custom, I have frequently thought that it was a sentiment of affection for whatever had touched the person of an absent or lost friend, which gave birth to that respect for relics, so much abused by selfish priests. Devotion or love may be allowed to hallow the garments as well as the person, for the lover must want fancy who has not a sort of sacred respect for the glove or slipper of his mistress. He could not confound them with vulgar things of the same kind. This fine sentiment perhaps would not bear to be analysed by the experienced philosopher. But of such stuff is human rapture made up. A shadowy phantom glides before us, obscuring every other object; yet when the soft cloud is grasped, the form melts into common air, leaving a solitary void, or sweet perfume, stolen from the violet, that memory long holds dear. But I have tripped unawares on fairy ground, feeling the balmy gale of spring stealing on me, though November frowns.

---

they did not by mock modesty remind them that they were women—actuated by the same spirit as the Portuguese ladies, who would think their charms insulted if, when left alone with a man, he did not at least attempt to be grossly familiar with their persons. Men are not always men in the company of women, nor would women always remember that they are women, if they were allowed to acquire more understanding.

*Male or female, for the world contains many modest men.

As a sex, women are more chaste than men; and as modesty is the effect of chastity, they may deserve to have this virtue ascribed to them in rather an appropriated sense. Yet I must be allowed to add an hesitating if, for I doubt whether chastity will produce modesty, though it may propriety of conduct, when it is merely a respect for the opinion of the world,* and when coquetry and the lovelorn tales of novelists employ the thoughts. Nay, from experience and reason, I should be led to expect to meet with more modesty amongst men than women, simply because men exercise their understandings more than women.

But with respect to propriety of behaviour, excepting one class of females, women have evidently the advantage. What can be more disgusting than that impudent dross of gallantry thought so manly, which makes many men stare insultingly at every female they meet? Can it be termed respect for the sex? No, this loose behaviour shows such habitual depravity, such weakness of mind, that it is vain to expect much public or private virtue till both men and women grow more modest—till men, curbing a sensual fondness for the sex, or an affectation of manly assurance—more properly speaking, impudence—treat each other with respect, unless appetite or passion give the tone peculiar to it, to their behaviour. I mean every personal respect—the modest respect of humanity and fellow-feeling—not the libidinous mockery of gallantry, nor the insolent condescension of protectorship.

To carry the observation still further, modesty must heartily disclaim, and refuse to dwell with that debauchery of mind, which leads a man coolly to bring forward, without a blush, indecent allusions, or obscene witticisms, in the presence of a fellow-creature; women are now out of the question, for then it is brutality. Respect for man, as man, is the foundation of every noble sentiment. How much more modest is the libertine who obeys the call of appetite or fancy than the lewd joker who sets the table in a roar!

This is one of the many instances in which the sexual distinction respecting modesty has proved fatal to virtue and happiness. It is, however, carried still further, and woman—weak woman—made by her education the slave of sensibility, is required, on the most trying occasions, to resist that sensibility. "Can anything," says Knox, "be more absurd than keeping women in a state of ignorance, and yet so vehemently to insist on their resisting temptation?" Thus when virtue or

---

*The immodest behaviour of many married women, who are nevertheless faithful to their husbands' beds, will illustrate this remark.

honour make it proper to check a passion, the burden is thrown on the weaker shoulders, contrary to reason and true modesty, which at least should render the self-denial mutual, to say nothing of the generosity of bravery, supposed to be a manly virtue.

In the same strain runs Rousseau's and Dr. Gregory's advice respecting modesty, strangely miscalled! for they both desire a wife to leave it in doubt whether sensibility or weakness led her to her husband's arms. The woman is immodest who can let the shadow of such a doubt remain in her husband's mind a moment.

But, to state the subject in a different light, the want of modesty, which I principally deplore as subversive of morality, arises from the state of warfare so strenuously supported by voluptuous men as the very essence of modesty, though, in fact, its bane, because it is a refinement on lust that men fall into who have not sufficient virtue to relish the innocent pleasures of love. A man of delicacy carries his notions of modesty still further, for neither weakness nor sensibility will gratify him—he looks for affection.

Again. Men boast of their triumphs over women. What do they boast of? Truly the creature of sensibility was surprised by her sensibility into folly—into vice*; and the dreadful reckoning falls heavily on her own weak head, when reason wakes. For where art thou to find comfort, forlorn and disconsolate one? He who ought to have directed thy reason, and supported thy weakness, has betrayed thee. In a dream of passion thou consented to wander through flowery lawns, and heedlessly stepping over the precipice to which they guide, instead of guarding, lured thee; thou startest from thy dream only to face a sneering, frowning world, and to find thyself alone in a waste, for he that triumphed in thy weakness is now pursuing new conquests. But for thee there is no redemption on this side the grave! And what resource has thou in an enervated mind to raise a sinking heart?

But if the sexes be really to live in a state of warfare, if Nature have pointed it out, let them act nobly, or let pride whisper to them that the victory is mean when they merely vanquish sensibility. The real conquest is that over affection not taken by surprise, when, like Heloisa,[2] a woman gives up all the world deliberately for love. I do not now consider the wisdom or virtue of such a sacrifice, I only contend that it was a sacrifice to affection, and not merely to sensibility, though she had her share. And I must be allowed to call her a modest woman, before I

---

*The poor moth, fluttering round a candle, burns its wings.

dismiss this part of the subject, by saying, that till men are more chaste, women will be immodest. Where, indeed, could modest women find husbands from whom they would not continually turn with disgust? Modesty must be equally cultivated by both sexes, or it will ever remain a sickly hot-house plant, whilst the affection of it, the fig leaf borrowed by wantonness, may give a zest to voluptuous enjoyments.

Men will probably still insist that woman ought to have more modesty than man; but it is not dispassionate reasoners who will most earnestly oppose my opinion. No, they are the men of fancy, the favourites of the sex, who outwardly respect and inwardly despise the weak creatures whom they thus sport with. They cannot submit to resign the highest sensual gratification, nor even to relish the epicurism of virtue—self-denial.

To take another view of the subject, confining my remarks to women.

The ridiculous falsities* which are told to children, from mistaken notions of modesty, tend very early to inflame their imaginations and set their little minds to work, respecting subjects which Nature never intended they should think of till the body arrived at some degree of maturity; then the passions naturally begin to take the place of the senses, as instruments to unfold the understanding, and form the moral character.

In nurseries and boarding-schools, I fear, girls are first spoiled, particularly in the latter. A number of girls sleep in the same room, and wash together. And though I should be sorry to contaminate an innocent creature's mind by instilling false delicacy, or those indecent prudish notions which early cautions respecting the other sex naturally engender, I should be very anxious to prevent their acquiring nasty or immodest habits; and as many girls have learned very nasty tricks from ignorant servants, the mixing them thus indiscriminately together, is very improper.

---

*Children very early see cats with their kittens, birds with their young ones, etc. Why then are they not to be told that their mothers carry and nourish them in the same way? As there would then be no appearance of mystery, they would never think of the subject more. Truth may always be told to children, if it be told gravely; but it is the modesty of affected modesty that does all the mischief; and this smoke heats the imagination by vainly endeavouring to obscure certain objects. If, indeed, children could be kept entirely from improper company, we should never allude to any such subjects; but as this is impossible, it is best to tell them the truth, especially as such information, not interesting them, will make no impression on their imagination.

To say the truth, women are in general too familiar with each other, which leads to that gross degree of familiarity that so frequently renders the marriage state unhappy. Why in the name of decency are sisters, female intimates, or ladies and their waiting-women, to be so grossly familiar as to forget the respect which one human creature owes to another? That squeamish delicacy which shrinks from the most disgusting offices when affection* or humanity lead us to watch at a sick pillow is despicable. But why women in health should be more familiar with each other than men are, when they boast of their superior delicacy, is a solecism in manners which I could never solve.

In order to preserve health and beauty, I should earnestly recommend frequent ablutions, to dignify my advice that it may not offend the fastidious ear; and by example girls ought to be taught to wash and dress alone, without any distinction of rank; and if custom should make them require some little assistance, let them not require it till that part of the business is over which ought never to be done before a fellow-creature, because it is an insult to the majesty of human nature. Not on the score of modesty, but decency; for the care which some modest women take, making at the same time a display of that care not to let their legs be seen, is as childish as immodest.**

I could proceed still further, till I animadverted on some still more nasty customs, which men never fall into. Secrets are told where silence ought to reign; and that regard to cleanliness, which some religious sects have perhaps carried too far, especially the Essenes,³ amongst the Jews, by making that an insult to God which is only an insult to humanity, is violated in a beastly manner. How can *delicate* women obtrude on notice that part of the animal economy, which is so very disgusting? And is it not very rational to conclude, that the women who have not been taught to respect the human nature of their own sex in these particulars, will not long respect the mere difference of sex in their husbands? After their maidenish bashfulness is once lost, I, in fact, have generally observed that women fall into old habits, and treat their husbands as they did their sisters or female acquaintance.

---

*Affection would rather make one choose to perform these offices, to spare the delicacy of a friend, by still keeping a veil over them, for the personal helplessness, produced by sickness, is of an humbling nature.

**I remember to have met with a sentence, in a book of education that made me smile: "It would be needless to caution you against putting your hand by chance under your neck-handkerchief, for a modest woman never did so!"

Besides, women from necessity, because their minds are not cultivated, have recourse very often to what I familiarly term bodily wit, and their intimacies are of the same kind. In short, with respect to both mind and body, they are too intimate. That decent personal reserve, which is the foundation of dignity of character, must be kept up between woman and woman, or their minds will never gain strength or modesty.

On this account also, I object to many females being shut up together in nurseries, schools, or convents. I cannot recollect, without indignation, the jokes and hoyden tricks which knots of young women indulged themselves in, when in my youth accident threw me, an awkward rustic, in their way. They were almost on a par with the double meanings which shake the convivial table when the glass has circulated freely. But it is vain to attempt to keep the heart pure unless the head is furnished with ideas, and set to work to compare them, in order to acquire judgement, by generalizing simple ones; and modesty, by making the understanding damp the sensibility.

It may be thought that I lay too great a stress on personal reserve, but it is ever the handmaid of modesty; so that were I to name the graces that ought to adorn beauty, I should instantly exclaim, cleanliness, neatness, and personal reserve. It is obvious, I suppose, that the reserve I mean has nothing sexual in it, and that I think it *equally* necessary in both sexes. So necessary, indeed, is that reserve and cleanliness which indolent women too often neglect, that I will venture to affirm that, when two or three women live in the same house, the one will be most respected by the male part of the family who reside with them, leaving love entirely out of the question, who pays this kind of habitual respect to her person.

When domestic friends meet in a morning, there will naturally prevail an affectionate seriousness, especially if each look forward to the discharge of daily duties; and it may be reckoned fanciful, but this sentiment has frequently risen spontaneously to my mind, I have been pleased, after breathing the sweet bracing morning air, to see the same kind of freshness in the countenances I particularly loved; I was glad to see them braced as it were, for the day, and ready to run their course with the sun. The greetings of affection in the morning are by these means more respectful than the familiar tenderness which frequently prolongs the evening talk. Nay, I have often felt hurt, not to say disgusted, when a friend has appeared, whom I parted with full dressed the evening before, with her clothes huddled on, because she chose to indulge herself in bed till the last moment.

Domestic affection can only be kept alive by these neglected attentions; yet if men and women took half as much pains to dress habitually neat, as they do to ornament, or rather to disfigure, their persons, much would be done towards the attainment of purity of mind. But women only dress to gratify men of gallantry; for the lover is always best pleased with the simple garb that fits close to the shape. There is an impertinence in ornaments that rebuffs affection, because love always clings round the idea of home.

As a sex, women are habitually indolent; and everything tends to make them so. I do not forget the spurts of activity which sensibility produces; but as these flights of feelings only increase the evil, they are not to be confounded with the slow, orderly walk of reason. So great in reality is their mental and bodily indolence, that till their body be strengthened and their understanding enlarged by active exertions, there is little reason to expect that modesty will take place of bashfulness. They may find it prudent to assume its semblance; but the fair veil will only be worn on gala days.

Perhaps, there is not a virtue that mixes so kindly with every other as modesty. It is the pale moonbeam that renders more interesting every virtue it softens, giving mild grandeur to the contracted horizon. Nothing can be more beautiful than the poetical fiction, which makes Diana with her silver crescent, the goddess of chastity. I have sometimes thought, that wandering with sedate step in some lonely recess, a modest dame of antiquity must have felt a glow of conscious dignity when, after contemplating the soft shadowy landscape, she has invited with placid fervour the mild reflection of her sister's beams to return to her chaste bosom.

A Christian has still nobler motives to incite her to preserve her chastity and acquire modesty, for her body has been called the temple of the living God; of that God who requires more than modesty of mien. His eye searcheth the heart; and let her remember, that if she hope to find favour in the sight of purity itself, her chastity must be founded on modesty, and not on worldly prudence; or verily a good reputation will be her only reward; for that awful intercourse, that sacred communication, which virtue establishes between man and his Maker, must give rise to the wish of being pure as He is pure!

After the foregoing remarks, it is almost superfluous to add, that I consider all those feminine airs of maturity, which succeed bashfulness, to which truth is sacrificed, to secure the heart of a husband, or rather to force him to be still a lover when Nature would, had she not been interrupted in her operations, have made love give place to friendship, as immodest. The tenderness which a man will feel for the mother of his children is an excellent substitute for the ardour of unsatisfied passion; but to prolong that ardour it is indelicate, not to say immodest, for women to feign an unnatural coldness of constitution. Women as well as men ought to have the common appetites and passions of their nature, they are only brutal when unchecked by reason: but the obligation to check them is the duty of mankind, not a sexual duty. Nature, in these respects, may safely be left to herself; let women only acquire knowledge and humanity, and love will teach them modesty.* There is no need of falsehoods, disgusting as futile, for studied rules of behaviour only impose on shallow observers; a man of sense soon sees through, and despises the affectation.

The behaviour of young people, to each other, as men and women, is the last thing that should be thought of in education. In fact, behaviour in most circumstances is now so much thought of, that simplicity of character is rarely to be seen: yet, if men were only anxious to cultivate each virtue, and let it take root firmly in the mind, the grace resulting from it, its natural exterior mark, would soon strip affectation of its flaunting plumes; because, fallacious as unstable, is the conduct that is not founded upon truth!

Would ye, O my sisters, really possess modesty, ye must remember that the possession of virtue, of any denomination, is incompatible with ignorance and vanity! ye must acquire that soberness of mind, which the exercise of duties, and the pursuit of knowledge, alone inspire, or ye will still remain in a doubtful dependent situation, and only be loved whilst ye are fair! The downcast eye, the rosy blush, the retiring grace, are all proper in their season; but modesty, being the child of reason, cannot long exist with the sensibility that is not tempered by reflection. Besides, when love, even innocent love, is the whole employ of your lives, your hearts will be too soft to afford modesty that tranquil retreat, where she delights to dwell, in close union with humanity.

---

*The behaviour of many newly married women has often disgusted me. They seem anxious never to let their husbands forget the privilege of marriage; and to find no pleasure in his society unless he is acting the lover. Short, indeed, must be the reign of love, when the flame is thus constantly blown up, without its receiving any solid fuel!

# CHAPTER VIII

# MORALITY UNDERMINED BY SEXUAL NOTIONS OF THE IMPORTANCE OF A GOOD REPUTATION

It has long since occurred to me that advice respecting behaviour, and all the various modes of preserving a good reputation, which have been so strenuously inculcated on the female world, were specious poisons, that encrusting morality eat away the substance. And, that this measuring of shadows produced a false calculation, because their length depends so much on the height of the sun, and other adventitious circumstances.

Whence arises the easy fallacious behaviour of a courtier? From his situation, undoubtedly: for standing in need of dependents, he is obliged to learn the art of denying without giving offence, and, of evasively feeding hope with the chameleon's food: thus does politeness sport with truth, and eating away the sincerity and humanity native to man, produce the fine gentleman.

Women likewise acquire from a supposed necessity, an equally artificial mode of behaviour. Yet truth is not with impunity to be sported with, for the practised dissembler, at last become the dupe of his own arts, loses that sagacity, which has been justly termed common sense; namely a quick perception of common truths: which are constantly received as such by the unsophisticated mind, though it might not have had sufficient energy to discover themselves, when obscured by local prejudices. The greater number of people take their opinions on trust to avoid the trouble of exercising their own minds, and these indolent beings naturally adhere to the letter, rather than the spirit of a law, divine or human. "Women," says some author, I cannot recollect who, "mind not what only Heaven sees." Why, indeed, should they? it is the eye of man that they have been taught to dread—and if they can lull their Argus[1] to sleep, they seldom think of Heaven or themselves, because their reputation is safe; and it is reputation, not chastity and all its fair train, that they are employed to keep free from spot, not as a virtue, but to preserve their station in the world.

To prove the truth of this remark, I need not advert to the intrigues of married women, particularly in high life, and in countries where women are suitably married, according to their respective ranks, by their parents. If an innocent girl become a prey to love, she is degraded for ever, though her mind was not polluted by the arts which married women, under the convenient cloak of marriage, practise; nor has she violated any duty—but the duty of respecting herself. The married woman, on the contrary, breaks a most sacred engagement, and becomes a cruel mother when she is a false and faithless wife. If her husband have still an affection for her, the arts which she must practise to deceive him, will render her the most contemptible of human beings; and, at any rate, the contrivances necessary to preserve appearances, will keep her mind in that childish, or vicious, tumult, which destroys all its energy. Besides, in time, like those people who habitually take cordials to raise their spirits, she will want an intrigue to give life to her thoughts, having lost all relish for pleasures that are not highly seasoned by hope or fear.

Sometimes married women act still more audaciously. I will mention an instance.

A woman of quality, notorious for her gallantries, though as she still lived with her husband, nobody chose to place her in the class where she ought to have been placed, made a point of treating with the most insulting contempt a poor timid creature, abashed by a sense of her former weakness, whom a neighbouring gentleman had seduced and afterwards married. The woman had actually confounded virtue with reputation; and, I do believe, valued herself on the propriety of her behaviour before marriage, though when once settled to the satisfaction of her family, she and her lord were equally faithless so that the half-alive heir to an immense estate came from Heaven knows where!

To view this subject in another light.

I have known a number of women who, if they did not love their husbands, loved nobody else, give themselves entirely up to vanity and dissipation, neglecting every domestic duty; nay even squandering away all the money which should have been saved for their helpless younger children, yet have plumed themselves on their unsullied reputation, as if the whole compass of their duty as wives and mothers was only to preserve it. Whilst other indolent women, neglecting every personal duty have thought that they deserved their husband's affection, because, forsooth, they acted in this respect with propriety.

Weak minds are always fond of resting in the ceremonials of duty, but morality offers much simpler motives; and it were to be wished that superficial moralists had said less respecting behaviour, and outward observances, for unless virtue, of any kind, be built on knowledge, it will only produce a kind of insipid decency. Respect for the opinion of the world, has, however, been termed the principal duty of woman in the most express words, for Rousseau declares, "that reputation is no less indispensable than chastity." "A man," adds he, "secure in his own good conduct, depends only on himself, and may brave the public opinion; but a woman, in behaving well, performs but half her duty; as what is thought of her, is as important to her as what she really is. It follows hence, that the system of a woman's education should, in this respect, be directly contrary to that of ours. Opinion is the grave of virtue among the men; but its throne among women."[2] It is strictly logical to infer that the virtue that rests on opinion is merely worldly, and that it is the virtue of a being to whom reason has been denied. But, even with respect to the opinion of the world, I am convinced that this class of reasoners are mistaken.

This regard for reputation, independent of its being one of the natural rewards of virtue, however, took its rise from a cause that I have already deplored as the grand source of female depravity, the impossibility of regaining respectability by a return to virtue, though men preserve theirs during the indulgence of vice. It was natural for women then to endeavour to preserve what once lost—was lost for ever, till this care swallowing up every other care, reputation for chastity, became the one thing needful to the sex. But vain is the scrupulosity of ignorance, for neither religion nor virtue, when they reside in the heart, require such a puerile attention to mere ceremonies, because the behaviour must, upon the whole, be proper, when the motive is pure.

To support my opinion I can produce very respectable authority;

and the authority of a cool reasoner ought to have weight to enforce consideration, though not to establish a sentiment. Speaking of the general laws of morality, Dr. Smith observes,—"That by some very extraordinary and unlucky circumstance, a good man may come to be suspected of a crime of which he was altogether incapable, and upon that account be most unjustly exposed for the remaining part of his life to the horror and aversion of mankind. By an accident of this kind he may be said to lose his all, notwithstanding his integrity and justice, in the same manner as a cautious man, notwithstanding his utmost circumspection, may be ruined by an earthquake or an inundation. Accidents of the first kind, however, are perhaps still more rare, and still more contrary to the common course of things than those of the second; and it still remains true, that the practice of truth, justice, and humanity, is a certain and almost infallible method of acquiring what those virtues chiefly aim at, the confidence and love of those we live with. A person may be easily misrepresented with regard to a particular action; but it is scarce possible that he should be so with regard to the general tenor of his conduct. An innocent man may be believed to have done wrong: this, however, will rarely happen. On the contrary, the established opinion of the innocence of his manners will often lead us to absolve him where he has really been in the fault, notwithstanding very strong presumptions."[3]

I perfectly coincide in opinion with this writer, for I verily believe that few of either sex were ever despised for certain vices without deserving to be despised. I speak not of the calumny of the moment, which hovers over a character, like one of the dense morning fogs of November, over this metropolis, till it gradually subsides before the common light of day, I only contend that the daily conduct of the majority prevails to stamp their character with the impression of truth. Quietly does clear light, shining day after day, refute the ignorant surmise, or malicious tale, which has thrown dirt on a pure character. A false light distorted, for a short time, its shadow—reputation; but it seldom fails to become just when the cloud is dispersed that produced the mistake in vision.

Many people, undoubtedly, in several respects obtain a better reputation than, strictly speaking, they deserve; for unremitting industry will mostly reach its goal in all races. They who only strive for this paltry prize, like the Pharisees,[4] who prayed at the corners of streets, to be seen of men, verily obtain the reward they seek; for the heart of man cannot be read by man! Still the fair fame that is naturally reflected by good actions, when the man is only employed to direct his steps aright, regardless of the lookers-on, is, in general, not only more true, but more sure.

There are, it is true, trials when the good man must appeal to God from the injustice of man; and amidst the whining candour of hissings of envy, erect a pavilion in his own mind to retire to till the rumour be overpast; nay, the darts of undeserved censure may pierce an innocent tender bosom through with many sorrows; but these are all exceptions to general rules. And it is according to common laws that human behaviour ought to be regulated. The eccentric orbit of the comet never influences astronomical calculations respecting the invariable order established in the motion of the principal bodies of the solar system.

I will then venture to affirm, that after a man is arrived at maturity, the general outline of his character in the world is just, allowing for the before-mentioned exceptions to the rule. I do not say that a prudent, worldly-wise man, with only negative virtues and qualities, may not sometimes obtain a smoother reputation than a wiser or a better man. So far from it, that I am apt to conclude from experience, that where the virtue of two people is nearly equal, the most negative character will be liked best by the world at large, whilst the other may have more friends in private life. But the hills and dales, clouds and sunshine, conspicuous in the virtues of great men, set off each other; and though they afford envious weakness a fairer mark to shoot at, the real character will still work its way to light, though bespattered by weak affection, or ingenious malice.*

With respect to that anxiety to preserve a reputation hardly earned, which leads sagacious people to analyse it, I shall not make the obvious comment; but I am afraid that morality is very insidiously undermined, in the female world, by the attention being turned to the show instead of the substance. A simple thing is thus made strangely complicated; nay, sometimes virtue and its shadow are set at variance. We should never, perhaps, have heard of Lucretia,[5] had she died to preserve her chastity, instead of her reputation. If we really deserve our own good opinion we shall commonly be respected in the world; but if we pant after higher improvement and higher attainments, it is not sufficient to view ourselves as we suppose that we are viewed by others,

---

*I allude to various biographical writings, but particularly to Boswell's *Life of Johnson*.[6]

though this has been ingeniously argued, as the foundation of our moral sentiments.* Because each bystander may have his own prejudices, beside the prejudices of his age or country. We should rather endeavour to view ourselves as we suppose that Being views us who seeth each thought ripen into action, and whose judgement never swerves from the eternal rule of right. Righteous are all His judgements—just as merciful!

The humble mind that seeketh to find favour in His sight, and calmly examines its conduct when only His presence is felt, will seldom form a very erroneous opinion of its own virtues. During the still hour of self-collection the angry brow of offended justice will be fearfully deprecated, or the tie which draws man to the Deity will be recognized in the pure sentiment of reverential adoration, that swells the heart without exciting any tumultuous emotions. In these solemn moments man discovers the germ of those vices, which, like the Java tree, shed a pestiferous vapour around—death is in the shade! and he perceives them without abhorrence, because he feels himself drawn by some cord of love to all his fellow-creatures, for whose follies he is anxious to find every extenuation in their nature—in himself. If I, he may thus argue, who exercise my own mind, and have been refined by tribulation, find the serpent's egg in some fold of my heart, and crush it with difficulty, shall I not pity those who have stamped with less vigour, or who have heedlessly nurtured the insidious reptile till it poisoned the vital stream it sucked? Can I, conscious of my secret sins, throw off my fellow-creatures, and calmly see them drop into the chasm of perdition, that yawns to receive them. No, no! The agonised heart will cry with suffocating impatience—I, too, am a man! and have vices, hid perhaps, from human eye, that bend me to the dust before God, and loudly tell me, when all is mute, that we are formed of the same earth, and breathe the same element. Humanity thus rises naturally out of humility, and twists the cords of love that in various convolutions entangle the heart.

This sympathy extends still further, till a man well pleased observes force in arguments that do not carry conviction to his own bosom, and he gladly places in the fairest light, to himself, the shows of reason that have led others astray, rejoiced to find some reason in all the errors of man; though before convinced that He who rules the day, makes His sun to shine on all. Yet, shaking hands thus as it were with corruption,

*Smith. [Adam Smith]

one foot on earth, the other with bold stride mounts to Heaven, and claims kindred with superior natures. Virtues, unobserved by man, drop their balmy fragrance at this cool hour, and the thirsty land, refreshed by the pure streams of comfort, that suddenly gush out, is crowned with smiling verdure; this is the living green on which that eye may look with complacency that is too pure to behold iniquity!

But my spirits flag; and I must silently indulge the reverie these reflections lead to, unable to describe the sentiments, that have calmed my soul, when watching the rising sun, a soft shower drizzling through the leaves of neighbouring trees, seemed to fall on my languid, yet tranquil spirits, to cool the heart that had been heated by the passions which reason laboured to tame.

The leading principles which run through all my disquisitions, would render it unnecessary to enlarge on this subject, if a constant attention to keep the varnish of the character fresh, and in good condition, were not often inculcated as the sum total of female duty; if rules to regulate the behaviour, and to preserve the reputation, did not too frequently supersede moral obligations. But, with respect to reputation, the attention is confined to a single virtue—chastity. If the honour of a woman, as it is absurdly called, be safe, she may neglect every social duty; nay, ruin her family by gaming and extravagance; yet still present a shameless front—for truly she is an honourable woman!

Mrs. Macaulay has just observed, that "there is but one fault which a woman of honour may not commit with impunity."[7] She then justly and humanely adds—"This has given rise to the trite and foolish observation, that the first fault against chastity in woman has a radical power to deprave the character. But no such frail beings come out of the hands of Nature. The human mind is built of nobler materials than to be easily corrupted; and with all their disadvantages of situation and education, women seldom become entirely abandoned till they are thrown into a state of desperation, by the venomous rancour of their own sex."

But, in proportion as this regard for the reputation of chastity is prized by women, it is despised by men: and the two extremes are equally destructive to morality.

Men are certainly more under the influence of their appetites than women; and their appetites are more depraved by unbridled indulgence and the fastidious contrivances of satiety. Luxury has introduced a refinement in eating, that destroys the constitution; and, a degree of gluttony which is so beastly, that a perception of seemliness of behaviour must be worn out before one being could eat immoderately in the presence of another, and afterwards complain of the oppression that his intemperance naturally produced. Some women, particularly French women, have also lost a sense of decency in this respect; for they will talk very calmly of an indigestion. It were to be wished that idleness was not allowed to generate, on the rank soil of wealth, those swarms of summer insects that feed on putrefaction, we should not then be disgusted by the sight of such brutal excesses.

There is one rule relative to behaviour that, I think, ought to regulate every other; and it is simply to cherish such an habitual respect for mankind as may prevent us from disgusting a fellow-creature for the sake of a present indulgence. The shameful indolence of many married women and others a little advanced in life, frequently leads them to sin against delicacy. For, though convinced that the person is the band of union between the sexes, yet, how often do they from sheer indolence, or, to enjoy some trifling indulgence, disgust?

The depravity of the appetite which brings the sexes together, has had a still more fatal effect. Nature must ever be the standard of taste, the gauge of appetite—yet how grossly is nature insulted by the voluptuary. Leaving the refinements of love out of the question; nature, by making the gratification of an appetite, in this respect, as well as every other, a natural and imperious law to preserve the species, exalts the appetite, and mixes a little mind and affection with a sensual gust. The feelings of a parent mingling with an instinct merely animal, give it dignity; and the man and woman often meeting on account of the child, a mutual interest and affection is excited by the exercise of a common sympathy. Women then having some necessary duty to fulfil, more noble than to adorn their persons, would not contentedly be the slaves of casual lust; which is now the situation of a very considerable number who are, literally speaking, standing dishes to which every glutton may have access.

I may be told that great as this enormity is, it only affects a devoted part of the sex—devoted for the salvation of the rest. But, false as every assertion might easily be proved, that recommends the sanctioning a small evil to produce a greater good; the mischief does not stop here, for the moral character, and peace of mind, of the chaster part of the sex, is undermined by the conduct of the very women to whom they allow no refuge from guilt; whom they inexorably consign to the exercise of arts that lure their husbands from them, debauch their sons, and force them, let not modest women start, to assume, in some degree, the same character themselves. For I will venture to assert, that all the causes of female weakness, as well as depravity, which I have already enlarged on, branch out of one grand cause—want of chastity in men.

This intemperance, so prevalent, depraves the appetite to such a degree, that a wanton stimulus is necessary to rouse it; but the parental design of Nature is forgotten, and the mere person, and that for a moment, alone engrosses the thoughts. So voluptuous, indeed, often grows the lustful prowler, that he refines on female softness. Something more soft than women is then sought for; till, in Italy and Portugal, men attend the levees of equivocal beings, to sigh for more than female languor.

To satisfy this genus of men, women are made systematically voluptuous, and though they may not carry their libertinism to the same height, yet this heartless intercourse with the sex, which they allow themselves, depraves both sexes, because the taste of men is vitiated; and women, of all classes, naturally square their behaviour to gratify the taste by which they obtain pleasure and power. Women becoming, consequently, weaker, in mind and body, than they ought to be, were one of the grand ends of their being taken into the account, that of bearing and nursing children, have not sufficient strength to discharge the first duty of a mother; and sacrificing to lasciviousness the parental affection, that ennobles instinct, either destroy the embryo in the womb, or cast it off when born. Nature in everything demands respect, and those who violate her laws seldom violate them with impunity. The weak enervated women who particularly catch the attention of libertines, are unfit to be mothers, though they may conceive; so that the rich sensualist, who has rioted among women, spreading depravity and misery, when he wishes to perpetuate his name, receives from his wife only an half-formed being that inherits both its father's and mother's weakness.

Contrasting the humanity of the present age with the barbarism of antiquity, great stress has been laid on the savage custom of exposing the children whom their parents could not maintain; whilst the man of sensibility, who thus, perhaps, complains, by his promiscuous amours produces a most destructive barrenness and contagious flagitiousness of manners. Surely nature never intended that women, by satisfying an appetite, should frustrate the very purpose for which it was implanted?

I have before observed, that men ought to maintain the women whom they have seduced; this would be one means of reforming female manners, and stopping an abuse that has an equally fatal effect on population and morals. Another, no less obvious, would be to turn the attention of woman to the real virtue of chastity; for to little respect has that woman a claim, on the score of modesty, though her reputation may be white as the driven snow, who smiles on the libertine whilst she spurns the victims of his lawless appetites and their own folly.

Besides, she has a taint of the same folly, pure as she esteems herself, when she studiously adorns her person only to be seen by men, to excite respectful sighs, and all the idle homage of what is called innocent gallantry. Did women really respect virtue for its own sake, they would not seek for a compensation in vanity, for the self-denial which they are obliged to practise to preserve their reputation, nor would they associate with men who set reputation at defiance.

The two sexes mutually corrupt and improve each other. This I believe to be an indisputable truth, extending it to every virtue. Chastity, modesty, public spirit, and all the noble train of virtues, on which social virtue and happiness are built, should be understood and cultivated by all mankind, or they will be cultivated to little effect. And, instead of furnishing the vicious or idle with a pretext for violating some sacred duty, by terming it a sexual one, it would be wiser to show that Nature has not made any difference, for that the unchaste man doubly defeats the purpose of Nature, by rendering women barren, and destroying his own constitution, though he avoids the shame that pursues the crime in the other sex. These are the physical consequences, the moral are still more alarming; for virtue is only a nominal distinction when the duties of citizens, husbands, wives, fathers, mothers, and directors of families, become merely the selfish ties of convenience.

Why then do philosophers look for public spirit? Public spirit must be nurtured by private virtue, or it will resemble the factitious sentiment which makes women careful to preserve their reputation, and men their honour. A sentiment that often exists unsupported by virtue, unsupported by that sublime morality which makes the habitual breach of one duty a breach of the whole moral law.

# CHAPTER IX

# OF THE PERNICIOUS EFFECTS WHICH
## ARISE FROM THE UNNATURAL DISTINCTIONS
### ESTABLISHED IN SOCIETY

From the respect paid to property flow, as from a poisoned fountain, most of the evils and vices which render this world such a dreary scene to the contemplative mind. For it is in the most polished society that noisome reptiles and venomous serpents lurk under the rank herbage; and there is voluptuousness pampered by the still sultry air, which relaxes every good disposition before it ripens into virtue.

One class presses on another, for all are aiming to procure respect on account of their property; and property once gained will procure the respect due only to talents and virtue. Men neglect the duties incumbent on man, yet are treated like demi-gods. Religion is also separated from morality by a ceremonial veil, yet men wonder that the world is almost, literally speaking, a den of sharpers or oppressors.

There is a homely proverb, which speaks a shrewd truth, that whoever the devil finds idle he will employ. And what but habitual idleness can hereditary wealth and title produce? For man is so constituted that he can only attain a proper use of his faculties by exercising them, and will not exercise them unless necessity of some kind first set the wheels in motion. Virtue likewise can only be acquired by the discharge of relative duties; but the importance of these sacred duties will scarcely be felt by the being who is cajoled out of his humanity by the flattery of sycophants. There must be more equality established in society, or morality will never gain ground, and this virtuous equality will not rest firmly even when founded on a rock, if one-half of mankind be chained to its bottom by fate, for they will be continually undermining it through ignorance or pride.

It is vain to expect virtue from women till they are in some degree independent of men; nay, it is vain to expect that strength of natural affection which would make them good wives and mothers. Whilst they are absolutely dependent on their husbands they will be cunning, mean, and selfish; and the men who can be gratified by the fawning fondness of spaniel-like affection have not much delicacy, for love is not to be bought; in any sense of the words, its silken wings are instantly shrivelled up when anything beside a return in kind is sought. Yet whilst wealth enervates men, and women live, as it were, by their personal charms, how can we expect them to discharge those ennobling duties which equally require exertion and self-denial? Hereditary property sophisticates the mind, and the unfortunate victims to it—if I may so express myself—swathed from their birth, seldom exert the locomotive faculty or body of mind, and thus viewing everything through one medium, and that a false one, they are unable to discern in what true merit and happiness consist. False, indeed, must be the light when the drapery of situation hides the man, and makes him stalk in masquerade, dragging from one scene of dissipation to another the nerveless limbs that hang with stupid listlessness, and rolling round the vacant eye, which plainly tells us that there is no mind at home.

I mean therefore to infer that the society is not properly organized which does not compel men and women to discharge their respective duties by making it the only way to acquire that countenance from their fellow-creatures, which every human being wishes some way to attain. The respect consequently which is paid to wealth and mere personal charms is a true north-east blast that blights the tender blossoms of affection and virtue. Nature has wisely attached affections to duties to sweeten toil, and to give that vigour to the exertions of reason which only the heart can give. But the affection which is put on merely because it is the appropriated insignia of a certain character, when its duties are not fulfilled, is one of the empty compliments which vice and folly are obliged to pay to virtue and the real nature of things.

To illustrate my opinion, I need only observe that when a woman is admired for her beauty, and suffers herself to be so far intoxicated by the admiration she receives as to neglect to discharge the indispensable duty of a mother, she sins against herself by neglecting to cultivate an affection that would equally tend to make her useful and happy. True happiness—I mean all the contentment and virtuous satisfaction that can be snatched in this imperfect state—must arise from well-regulated affections, and an affection includes a duty. Men are not aware of the misery they cause, and the vicious weakness they cherish, by only inciting women to render themselves pleasing; they do not consider that they thus make natural and artificial duties clash by sacrificing the comfort and respectability of a woman's life to voluptuous notions of beauty when in nature they all harmonize.

Cold would be the heart of a husband, were he not rendered unnatural by early debauchery, who did not feel more delight at seeing his child suckled by its mother than the most artful wanton tricks could ever raise, yet this natural way of cementing the matrimonial tie, and twisting esteem with fonder recollections, wealth leads women to spurn. To preserve their beauty, and wear the flowery crown of the day, which gives them a kind of right to reign for a short time over the sex, they neglect to stamp impressions on their husbands' hearts that would be remembered with more tenderness when the snow on the head began to chill the bosom than even their virgin charms. The maternal solicitude of a reasonable affectionate woman is very interesting, and the chastened dignity with which a mother returns the caresses that she and her child receive from a father who has been fulfilling the serious duties of his station is not only a respectable, but a beautiful sight. So singular, indeed, are my feelings—and I have endeavoured not to catch factitious ones—that after having been fatigued with the sight of insipid grandeur and the slavish ceremonies that with cumbrous pomp supplied the place of domestic affections, I have turned to some other scene to relieve my eye by resting it on the refreshing green everywhere scattered by Nature. I have then viewed with pleasure a woman nursing her children, and discharging the duties of her station with perhaps merely a servant-maid to take off her hands the servile part of the household business. I have seen her prepare herself and children, with only the luxury of cleanliness, to receive her husband, who, returning weary home in the evening, found smiling babes and a clean hearth. My heart has loitered in the midst of the group, and has even throbbed with sympathetic emotion when the scraping of the well-known foot has raised a pleasing tumult.

Whilst my benevolence has been gratified by contemplating this artless picture, I have thought that a couple of this description, equally necessary and independent of each other, because each fulfilled the respective duties of their station, possessed all that life could give. Raised sufficiently above abject poverty not to be obliged to weigh the consequence of every farthing they spend, and having sufficient to prevent their attending to a frigid system of economy which narrows both heart and mind, I declare, so vulgar are my conceptions, that I know not what is wanted to render this the happiest as well as the most respectable situation in the world, but a taste for literature, to throw a little variety and interest into social converse, and some superfluous money to give to the needy and to buy books. For it is not pleasant when the heart is opened by compassion, and the head active in arranging plans of usefulness, to have a prim urchin continually twitching back the elbow to prevent the hand from drawing out an almost empty purse, whispering at the same time some prudential maxim about the priority of justice.

Destructive, however, as riches and inherited honours are to the human character, women are more debased and cramped, if possible, by them than men, because men may still in some degree unfold their faculties by becoming soldiers and statesmen.

As soldiers, I grant they can now only gather for the most part vainglorious laurels, whilst they adjust to a hair the European balance, taking especial care that no bleak northern nook or sound incline the beam. But the days of true heroism are over, when a citizen fought for his country like a Fabricius or a Washington, and then returned to his farm to let his virtuous fervour run in a more placid, but not a less salutary, stream. No, our British heroes are oftener sent from the gaming-table than from the plough; and their passions have been rather inflamed by hanging with dumb suspense on the turn of a die, than sublimated by panting after the adventurous march of virtue in the historic page.

The statesman, it is true, might with more propriety quit the faro bank,[1] or card-table, to guide the helm, for he has still but to shuffle and trick—the whole system of British politics, if system it may courteously be called, consisting in multiplying dependents and contriving taxes which grind the poor to pamper the rich. Thus a war, or any wild-goose chase, is, as the vulgar use the phrase, a lucky turn-up of patronage for the minister, whose chief merit is the art of keeping himself in place. It is not necessary then that he should have bowels for the poor, so he can secure for his family the odd trick. Or should some show of respect, for what is termed with ignorant ostentation an Englishman's birthright, be expedient to bubble the gruff mastiff that he has to lead by the nose, he can make an empty show, very safely, by giving his single voice, and suffering his light squadron to file off to the other side. And when a question of humanity is agitated, he may dip a sop in the milk of human kindness to silence Cerberus,[2] and talk of the interest which his heart takes in an attempt to make the earth no longer cry for vengeance as it sucks in its children's blood, though his cold hand may at the very moment rivet their chains, by sanctioning the abominable traffic. A minister is no longer a minister, than while he can carry a point, which he is determined to carry. Yet it is not necessary that a minister should feel like a man, when a bold push might shake his seat.

But, to have done with these episodical observations, let me return to the more specious slavery which chains the very soul of woman, keeping her for ever under the bondage of ignorance.

The preposterous distinctions of rank, which render civilization a curse, by dividing the world between voluptuous tyrants and cunning envious dependents, corrupt, almost equally, every class of people, because respectability is not attached to the discharge of the relative duties of life, but to the station, and when the duties are not fulfilled the affections cannot gain sufficient strength to fortify the virtue of which they are the natural reward. Still there are some loopholes out of which a man may creep, and dare to think and act for himself; but for a woman it is an herculean task, because she has difficulties peculiar to her sex to overcome, which require almost superhuman powers.

A truly benevolent legislator always endeavours to make it the interest of each individual to be virtuous; and thus private virtue becoming the cement of public happiness, an orderly whole is consolidated by the tendency of all the parts towards a common centre. But the private or public virtue of woman is very problematical, for Rousseau, and a numerous list of male writers, insist that she should all her life be subjected to a severe restraint, that of propriety. Why subject her to propriety—blind propriety—if she be capable of acting from a nobler spring, if she be an heir of immortality? Is sugar always to be produced by vital blood? Is one half of the human species, like the poor African slaves, to be subjected to prejudices that brutalize them, when principles would be a surer guard, only to sweeten the cup of man? Is not this indirectly to deny woman reason? for a gift is a mockery, if it be unfit for use.

Women are, in common with men, rendered weak and luxurious by the relaxing pleasures which wealth procures; but added to this they are made slaves to their persons, and must render them alluring that man may lend them his reason to guide their tottering steps aright. Or should they be ambitious, they must govern their tyrants by sinister tricks, for without rights there cannot be any incumbent duties. The laws respecting woman, which I mean to discuss in a future part, make an absurd unit of a man and his wife; and then, by the easy transition of only considering him as responsible, she is reduced to a mere cipher.[3]

The being who discharges the duties of its station is independent; and, speaking of women at large, their first duty is to find themselves as rational creatures, and the next, in point of importance, as citizens, is that, which includes so many, of a mother. The rank in life which dispenses with their fulfilling this duty, necessarily degrades them by making them mere dolls. Or should they turn to something more important than merely fitting drapery upon a smooth block, their minds are only occupied by some soft platonic attachment; or the actual management of an intrigue may keep their thoughts in motion; for when they neglect domestic duties, they have it not in their power to take the field, and march and counter-march like soldiers, or wrangle in the senate to keep their faculties from rusting.

I know that, as a proof of the inferiority of the sex, Rousseau has exultingly exclaimed, How can they leave the nursery for the camp! And the camp has by some moralists been proved the school of the most heroic virtues; though I think it would puzzle a keen casuist to prove the reasonableness of the greater number of wars that have dubbed heroes. I do not mean to consider this question critically; because, having frequently viewed these freaks of ambition as the first natural mode of civilization, when the ground must be torn up, and the woods cleared by fire and sword, I do not choose to call them pests; but surely the present system of war has little connection with virtue of any denomination, being rather the school of *finesse* and effeminacy than of fortitude.

Yet, if defensive war, the only justifiable war, in the present advanced state of society, where virtue can show its face and ripen amidst the rigours which purify the air on the mountain's top, were alone to be adopted as just and glorious, the true heroism of antiquity might again animate female bosoms. But fair and softly, gentle reader, male or female, do not alarm thyself, for though I have compared the character of a modern soldier with that of a civilized woman, I am not going to advise them to turn their distaff into a musket, though I sincerely wish to see the bayonet converted into a pruning-hook. I only re-created an imagination, fatigued by contemplating the vices and follies which all proceed from a feculent stream of wealth that has muddied the pure rills of natural affection, by supposing that society will some time or other be so constituted, that man must necessarily fulfil the duties of a citizen, or be despised, and that while he was employed in any of the departments of civil life, his wife, also an active citizen, should be equally intent to manage her family, educate her children, and assist her neighbours.

But to render her really virtuous and useful, she must not, if she discharge her civil duties, want individually the protection of civil laws; she must not be dependent on her husband's bounty for her subsistence during his life, or support after his death; for how can a being be generous who has nothing of its own? or virtuous who is not free? The wife, in the present state of things, who is faithful to her husband, and neither suckles nor educates her children, scarcely deserves the name of a wife, and has no right to that of a citizen. But take away natural rights, and duties become null.

Women then must be considered as only the wanton solace of men, when they become so weak in mind and body that they cannot exert themselves unless to pursue some frothy pleasure, or to invent some frivolous fashion. What can be a more melancholy sight to a thinking mind, than to look into the numerous carriages that drive helter-skelter about this metropolis in a morning full of pale-faced creatures who are flying from themselves! I have often wished, with Dr. Johnson, to place some of them in a little shop with half a dozen children looking up to their languid countenances for support. I am much mistaken, if some latent vigour would not soon give health and spirit to their eyes, and some lines drawn by the exercise of reason on the blank cheeks, which before were only undulated by dimples, might restore lost dignity to the character, or rather enable it to attain the true dignity of its nature. Virtue is not to be acquired even by speculation, much less by the negative supineness that wealth naturally generates.

Besides, when poverty is more disgraceful than even vice, is not morality cut to the quick? Still to avoid misconstruction, though I consider that women in the common walks of life are called to fulfil the duties of wives and mothers, by religion and reason, I cannot help lamenting that women of a superior cast have not a road open by which they can pursue more extensive plans of usefulness and independence. I may excite laughter, by dropping a hint, which I mean to pursue, some future time, for I really think that women ought to have representatives, instead of being arbitrarily governed without having any direct share allowed them in the deliberations of government.

But, as the whole system of representation is now, in this country, only a convenient handle for despotism, they need not complain, for they are as well represented as a numerous class of hard-working mechanics, who pay for the support of royalty when they can scarcely stop their children's mouths with bread. How are they represented whose very sweat supports the splendid stud of an heir-apparent, or varnishes the chariot of some female favourite who looks down on shame? Taxes on the very necessaries of life, enable an endless tribe of idle princes and princesses to pass with stupid pomp before a gaping crowd, who almost worship the very parade which costs them so dear. This is mere gothic grandeur, something like the barbarous useless parade of having sentinels on horseback at Whitehall,[4] which I could never view without a mixture of contempt and indignation.

How strangely must the mind be sophisticated when this sort of state impresses it! But, till these monuments of folly are levelled by virtue, similar follies will leaven the whole mass. For the same character, in some degree, will prevail in the aggregate of society; and the refinements of luxury, or the vicious repinings of envious poverty, will equally banish virtue from society, considered as the characteristic of that society, or only allow it to appear as one of the stripes of the harlequin coat, worn by the civilized man.

In the superior ranks of life, every duty is done by deputies, as if duties could ever be waived, and the vain pleasures which consequent idleness forces the rich to pursue, appear so enticing to the next rank, that the numerous scramblers for wealth sacrifice everything to tread on their heels. The most sacred trusts are then considered as sinecures, because they were procured by interest, and only sought to enable a man to keep *good company.* Women, in particular, all want to be ladies. Which is simply to have nothing to do, but listlessly to go they scarcely care where, for they cannot tell what.

But what have women to do in society? I may be asked, but to loiter with easy grace; surely you would not condemn them all to suckle fools and chronicle small beer! No. Women might certainly study the art of healing and be physicians as well as nurses. And midwifery, decency seems to allot to them though I am afraid the word midwife, in our dictionaries, will soon give place to *accoucheur,* and one proof of the former delicacy of the sex can be effaced from the language.

They might also study politics, and settle their benevolence on the broadest basis; for the reading of history will scarcely be more useful than the perusal of romances, if read as mere biography; if the character of the times, the political improvements, arts, etc., be not observed. In short, if it be not considered as the history of man; and not of particular men, who filled a niche in the temple of fame, and dropped into the black rolling stream of time, that silently sweeps all before it into the shapeless void called—eternity.—For shape, can it be called, "that shape hath none?"

Business of various kinds, they might likewise pursue, if they were educated in a more orderly manner, which might save many from common and legal prostitution. Women would not then marry for a support, as men accept of places under Government, and neglect the implied duties; nor would an attempt to earn their own subsistence, a most laudable one! sink them almost to the level of those poor abandoned creatures who live by prostitution. For are not milliners and mantua-makers[5] reckoned the next class? The few employments open to women, so far, from being liberal, are menial; and when a superior education enables them to take charge of the education of children as governesses, they are not treated like the tutors of sons, though even clerical tutors are not always treated in a manner calculated to render them respectable in the eyes of their pupils, to say nothing of the private comfort of the individual. But as women educated like gentlewomen, are never designed for the humiliating situation which necessity sometimes forces them to fill; these situations are considered in the light of a degradation; and they know little of the human heart, who need to be told, that nothing so painfully sharpens sensibility as such a fall in life.

Some of these women might be restrained from marrying by a proper spirit of delicacy, and others may not have had it in their power to escape in this pitiful way from servitude; is not that Government then very defective, and very unmindful of the happiness of one-half of its members, that does not provide for honest, independent women, by encouraging them to fill respectable stations? But in order to render their private virtue a public benefit, they must have a civil existence in the State, married or single; else we shall continually see some worthy woman, whose sensibility has been rendered painfully acute by undeserved contempt, droop like "the lily broken down by a plowshare."

It is a melancholy truth; yet such is the blessed effect of civilization! the most respectable women are the most oppressed; and, unless they have understandings far superior to the common run of understandings, taking in both sexes, they must, from being treated like contemptible beings, become contemptible. How many women thus waste life away the prey of discontent, who might have practised as physicians, regulated a farm, managed a shop, and stood erect, supported by their own industry, instead of hanging their heads surcharged with the dew of sensibility, that consumes the beauty to which it at first gave lustre; nay, I doubt whether pity and love are so near akin as poets feign, for I have seldom seen much compassion excited by the helplessness of females, unless they were fair; then, perhaps, pity was the soft handmaid of love, or the harbinger of lust.

How much more respectable is the woman who earns her own bread by fulfilling any duty, than the most accomplished beauty!—beauty did I say!—so sensible am I of the beauty of moral loveliness, or the harmonious propriety that attunes the passions of a well-regulated mind, that I blush at making the comparison; yet I sigh to think how few women aim at attaining this respectability by withdrawing from the giddy whirl of pleasure, or the indolent calm that stupefies the good sort of women it sucks in.

Proud of their weakness, however, they must always be protected, guarded from care, and all the rough toils that dignify the mind. If this be the fiat of fate, if they will make themselves insignificant and contemptible, sweetly to waste "life away," let them not expect to be valued when their beauty fades, for it is the fate of the fairest flowers to be admired and pulled to pieces by the careless hand that plucked them. In how many ways do I wish, from the purest benevolence, to impress this truth on my sex; yet I fear that they will not listen to a truth that dear bought experience has brought home to many an agitated bosom, nor willingly resign the privileges of rank and sex for the privileges of humanity, to which those have no claim who do not discharge its duties.

Those writers are particularly useful, in my opinion, who make man feel for man, independent of the station he fills, or the drapery of factitious sentiments. I then would fain convince reasonable men of the importance of some of my remarks; and prevail on them to weigh dispassionately the whole tenor of my observations. I appeal to their understandings; and, as a fellow-creature, claim, in the name of my sex, some interest in their hearts. I entreat them to assist to emancipate their companion, to make her a *helpmeet* for them.

Would men but generously snap our chains, and be content with rational fellowship instead of slavish obedience, they would find us more observant daughters, more affectionate sisters, more faithful wives, more reasonable mothers—in a word, better citizens. We should then love them with true affection, because we should learn to respect ourselves; and the peace of mind of a worthy man would not be interrupted by the idle vanity of his wife, nor the babes sent to nestle in a strange bosom, having never found a home in their mother's.

## CHAPTER X

# PARENTAL AFFECTION

Parental affection is, perhaps, the blindest modification of perverse self-love; for we have not, like the French,* two terms to distinguish the pursuit of a natural and reasonable desire, from the ignorant calculations of weakness. Parents often love their children in the most brutal manner, and sacrifice every relative duty to promote their advancement in the world. To promote, such is the perversity of unprincipled prejudices, the future welfare of the very beings whose present existence they embitter by the most despotic stretch of power. Power, in fact, is ever true to its vital principle, for in every shape it would reign without control of inquiry. Its throne is built across a dark abyss, which no eye must dare to explore, lest the baseless fabric should totter under investigation. Obedience, unconditional obedience, is the catchword of tyrants of every description, and to render "assurance doubly sure," one kind of despotism supports another. Tyrants would have cause to tremble if reason were to become the rule of duty in any of the relations of life, for the light might spread till perfect day appeared. And when it did appear, how would men smile at the sight of the bugbears at which they started during the night of ignorance, or the twilight of timid inquiry.

Parental affection, indeed, in many minds, is but a pretext to tyran-

---

* L'amour propre. L'amour de soi même.[1]

nise where it can be done with impunity, for only good and wise men are content with the respect that will bear discussion. Convinced that they have a right to what they insist on, they do not fear reason, or dread the sifting of subjects that recur to natural justice: because they firmly believe that the more enlightened the human mind becomes the deeper root will just and simple principles take. They do not rest in expedients, or grant that what is metaphysically true can be practically false; but disdaining the shifts of the moment they calmly wait till time, sanctioning innovation, silences the hiss of selfishness or envy.

If the power of reflecting on the past, and darting the keen eye of contemplation into futurity, be the grand privilege of man, it must be granted that some people enjoy this prerogative in a very limited degree. Everything new appears to them wrong; and not able to distinguish the possible from the monstrous, they fear where no fear should find a place, running from the light of reason, as if it were a firebrand; yet the limits of the possible have never been defined to stop the sturdy innovator's hand.

Woman, however, a slave in every situation to prejudice, seldom exerts enlightened maternal affection; for she either neglects her children, or spoils them by improper indulgence. The affection of some women for their children is, as I have before termed it, frequently very brutish: for it eradicates every spark of humanity. Justice, truth, everything is sacrificed by these Rebekahs,[2] and for the sake of their *own* children they violate the most sacred duties, forgetting the common relationship that binds the whole family on earth together. Yet, reason seems to say, that they who suffer one duty, or affection, to swallow up the rest, have not sufficient heart or mind to fulfil that one conscientiously. It then loses the venerable aspect of a duty, and assumes the fantastic form of a whim.

As the care of children in their infancy is one of the grand duties annexed to the female character by nature, this duty would afford many forcible arguments for strengthening the female understanding, if it were properly considered.

The formation of the mind must be begun very early, and the temper, in particular, requires the most judicious attention—an attention which women cannot pay who only love their children because they are their children, and seek no further for the foundation of their duty, than in the feelings of the moment. It is this want of reason in their affections which makes women so often run into extremes, and either be the most fond or most careless and unnatural mothers.

To be a good mother, a woman must have sense, and that independence of mind which few women possess who are taught to depend entirely on their husbands. Meek wives are, in general, foolish mothers; wanting their children to love them best, and take their part, in secret, against the father, who is held up as a scarecrow. When chastisement is necessary, though they have offended the mother, the father must inflict the punishment; he must be the judge in all disputes; but I shall more fully discuss this subject when I treat of private education. I now only mean to insist, that unless the understanding of woman be enlarged, and her character rendered more firm, by being allowed to govern her own conduct, she will never have sufficient sense or command of temper to manage her children properly. Her parental affection, indeed, scarcely deserves the name, when it does not lead her to suckle her children, because the discharge of this duty is equally calculated to inspire maternal and filial affection: and it is the indispensable duty of men and women to fulfil the duties which give birth to affections that are the surest preservatives against vice. Natural affection, as it is termed, I believe to be a very faint tie, affections must grow out of the habitual exercise of a mutual sympathy; and what sympathy does a mother exercise who sends her babe to a nurse, and only takes it from a nurse to send it to a school?

In the exercise of their maternal feelings Providence has furnished women with a natural substitute for love, when the lover becomes only a friend, and mutual confidence takes place of overstrained admiration—a child then gently twists the relaxing cord, and a mutual care produces a new mutual sympathy. But a child, though a pledge of affection, will not enliven it, if both father and mother be content to transfer the charge to hirelings; for they who do their duty by proxy should not murmur if they miss the reward of duty—parental affection produces filial duty.

# CHAPTER XI

# DUTY TO PARENTS

There seems to be an indolent propensity in man to make prescription always take place of reason, and to place every duty on an arbitrary foundation. The rights of kings are deduced in a direct line from King of kings, and that of parents from our first parent.

Why do we thus go back for principles that should always rest on the same base, and have the same weight today that they had a thousand years ago—and not a jot more? If parents discharge their duty they have a strong hold and sacred claim on the gratitude of their children, but few parents are willing to receive the respectful affection of their offspring on such terms. They demand blind obedience, because they do not merit a reasonable service: and to render these demands of weakness and ignorance more binding, a mysterious sanctity is spread round the most arbitrary principle; for what other name can be given to the blind duty of obeying vicious or weak beings merely because they obeyed a powerful instinct?

The simple definition of the reciprocal duty which naturally subsists between parent and child may be given in a few words. The parent who pays proper attention to helpless infancy has a right to require the same attention when the feebleness of age comes upon him. But to subjugate a rational being to the mere will of another, after he is of age to answer to society for his own conduct, is a most cruel and undue stretch of power, and perhaps as injurious to morality as those religious systems which do not allow right and wrong to have any existence, but in the Divine will.

I never knew a parent who had paid more than common attention to his children disregarded.* On the contrary, the early habit of relying almost implicitly on the opinion of a respected parent is not easily shook, even when matured reason convinces the child that his father is not the wisest man in the world. This weakness—for a weakness it is, though the epithet amiable may be tacked to it—a reasonable man must steel himself against; for the absurd duty, too often inculcated, of obeying a parent only on account of his being a parent, shackles the mind, and prepares it for a slavish submission to any power but reason.

I distinguish between the natural and accidental duty due to parents.

The parent who sedulously endeavours to form the heart, and enlarge the understanding of his child, has given that dignity to the discharge of a duty, common to the whole animal world, that only reason can give. This is the parental affection of humanity, and leaves instinctive natural affection far behind. Such a parent acquires all the rights of the most sacred friendship, and his advice, even when his child is advanced in life, demands serious consideration.

With respect to marriage, though after one-and-twenty a parent seems to have no right to withhold his consent on any account, yet twenty years of solicitude call for a return, and the son ought at least to promise not to marry for two or three years, should the object of his choice not entirely meet with the approbation of his first friend.

But respect for parents is, generally speaking, a much more debasing principle; it is only a selfish respect for property. The father who is blindly obeyed is obeyed from sheer weakness, or from motives that degrade the human character.

A great proportion of the misery that wanders in hideous forms around the world is allowed to rise from the negligence of parents; and still these are the people who are most tenacious of what they term a natural right, though it be subversive of the birthright of man, the right of acting according to the direction of his own reason.

I have already very frequently had occasion to observe that vicious or indolent people are always eager to profit by enforcing arbitrary privileges, and generally in the same proportion as they neglect the

*Dr. Johnson makes the same observation.

discharge of the duties which alone render the privileges reasonable. This is at the bottom a dictate of common sense, or the instinct of self-defence, peculiar to ignorant weakness, resembling that instinct which makes a fish muddy the water it swims in to elude its enemy, instead of boldly facing it in the clear stream.

From the clear stream of argument indeed the supporters of prescription of every denomination fly; and taking refuge in the darkness, which, in the language of sublime poetry, has been supposed to surround the throne of Omnipotence, they dare to demand that implicit respect which is only due to His unsearchable ways. But let me not be thought presumptuous; the darkness which hides our God from us only respects speculative truths. It never obscures moral ones; they shine clearly, for God is light, and never, by the constitution of our nature, requires the discharge of a duty, the reasonableness of which does not beam on us when we open our eyes.

The indolent parent of high rank may, it is true, extort a show of respect from his child, and females on the Continent are particularly subject to the views of their families, who never think of consulting their inclination, or providing for the comfort of the poor victims of their pride. The consequence is notorious: these dutiful daughters become adulteresses, and neglect the education of their children, from whom they, in their turn, exact the same kind of obedience.

Females, it is true, in all countries are too much under the dominion of their parents; and few parents think of addressing their children in the following manner, though it is in this reasonable way that Heaven seems to command the whole human race:—It is your interest to obey me till you can judge for yourself; and the Almighty Father of all has implanted an affection in me to serve as a guard to you whilst your reason is unfolding; but when your mind arrives at maturity, you must only obey me, or rather respect my opinions, so far as they coincide with the light that is breaking in on your own mind.

A slavish bondage to parents cramps every faculty of the mind; and Mr. Locke[1] very judiciously observes, that "if the mind be curbed and humbled too much in children; if their spirits be abased and broken much by too strict an hand over them, they lose all their vigour and industry." This strict hand may in some degree account for the weakness of women; for girls, from various causes, are more kept down by their parents, in every sense of the word, than boys. The duty expected from them is, like all the duties arbitrarily imposed on women, more from a sense of propriety, more out of respect for decorum, than reason; and thus taught slavishly to submit to their parents, they are prepared for the slavery of marriage. I may be told that a number of women are not slaves in the marriage state. True, but they then become tyrants; for it is not rational freedom, but a lawless kind of power, resembling the authority exercised by the favourites of absolute monarchs, which they obtain by debasing means. I do not likewise dream of insinuating that either boys or girls are always slaves. I only insist that when they are obliged to submit to authority blindly their faculties are weakened, and their tempers rendered imperious or abject. I also lament that parents, indolently availing themselves of a supposed privilege, damp the first faint glimmerings of reason, rendering at the same time the duty, which they are so anxious to enforce, an empty name; because they will not let it rest on the only basis on which a duty can rest securely; for unless it be founded on knowledge, it cannot gain sufficient strength to resist the squalls of passion, or the silent sapping of self-love. But it is not the parents who have given the surest proof of their affection for their children, or, to speak more properly, who, by fulfilling their duty, have allowed a natural parental affection to take root in their hearts, the child of exercised sympathy and reason, and not the overweening offspring of selfish pride, who most vehemently insist on their children submitting to their will merely because it is their will. On the contrary, the parent who sets a good example, patiently lets that example work, and it seldom fails to produce its natural effect—filial respect.

Children cannot be taught too early to submit to reason—the true definition of that necessity which Rousseau insisted on, without defining it; for to submit to reason is to submit to the nature of things, and to that God who formed them so, to promote our real interest.

Why should the minds of children be warped as they just begin to expand, only to favour the indolence of parents who insist on a privilege without being willing to pay the price fixed by Nature? I have before had occasion to observe that a right always includes a duty, and I think it may likewise fairly be inferred that they forfeit the right who do not fulfil the duty.

It is easier, I grant, to command than reason; but it does not follow from hence that children cannot comprehend the reason why they are made to do certain things habitually: for, from a steady adherence to a few simple principles of conduct flows that salutary power which a judicious parent gradually gains over a child's mind. And this power becomes strong indeed, if tempered by an even display of affection brought home to the child's heart. For, I believe, as a general rule, it must be allowed that the affection which we inspire always resembles that we cultivate; so that natural affections, which have been supposed almost distinct from reason, may be found more nearly connected with judgement than is commonly allowed. Nay, as another proof of the necessity of cultivating the female understanding, it is but just to observe, that the affections seem to have a kind of animal capriciousness when they merely reside in the heart.

It is the irregular exercise of parental authority that first injures the mind, and to these irregularities girls are more subject than boys. The will of those who never allow their will to be disputed, unless they happen to be in a good humour, when they relax proportionally, is almost always unreasonable. To elude this arbitrary authority girls very early learn the lessons which they afterwards practise on their husbands; for I have frequently seen a little sharp-faced miss rule a whole family, excepting that now and then mamma's anger will burst out of some accidental cloud;—either her hair was ill-dressed,* or she had lost more money at cards, the night before, than she was willing to own to her husband; or some such moral cause of anger.

After observing sallies of this kind, I have been led into a melancholy train of reflection respecting females, concluding that when their first affection must lead them astray, or make their duties clash till they rest on mere whims and customs, little can be expected from them as they advance in life. How, indeed, can an instructor remedy this evil? for to teach them virtue on any solid principle is to teach them to despise their parents. Children cannot, ought not, to be taught to make allowance for the faults of their parents, because every such allowance weakens the force of reason in their minds, and makes them still more indulgent to their own. It is one of the most sublime virtues of maturity that leads us to be severe with respect to ourselves, and forbearing to others; but children should only be taught the simple virtues, for if they begin too early to make allowance for human passions and manners, they wear off the fine edge of the criterion by which they should regulate their own, and become unjust in the same proportion as they grow indulgent.

*I myself heard a little girl once say to a servant, "My mamma has been scolding me finely this morning, because her hair was not dressed to please her." Though this remark was pert, it was just. And what respect could a girl acquire for such a parent without doing violence to reason?

The affections of children, and weak people, are always selfish; they love their relatives, because they are beloved by them, and not on account of their virtues. Yet, till esteem and love are blended together in the first affection, and reason made the foundation of the first duty, morality will stumble at the threshold. But, till society is very differently constituted, parents, I fear, will still insist on being obeyed, because they will be obeyed, and constantly endeavour to settle that power on a Divine right which will not bear the investigation of reason.

# CHAPTER XII

# ON NATIONAL EDUCATION

The good effects resulting from attention to private education will ever be very confined, and the parent who really puts his own hand to the plough, will always, in some degree, be disappointed, till education becomes a grand national concern. A man cannot retire into a desert with his child, and if he did he could not bring himself back to childhood, and become the proper friend and playfellow of an infant or youth. And when children are confined to the society of men and women, they very soon acquire that kind of premature manhood which stops the growth of every vigorous power of mind or body. In order to open their faculties they should be excited to think for themselves; and this can only be done by mixing a number of children together, and making them jointly pursue the same objects.

A child very soon contracts a benumbing indolence of mind, which he has seldom sufficient vigour afterwards to shake off, when he only asks a question instead of seeking for information, and then relies implicitly on the answer he receives. With his equals in age this could never be the case, and the subjects of inquiry, though they might be influenced, would not be entirely under the direction of men, who frequently damp, if not destroy, abilities, by bringing them forward too hastily: and too hastily they will infallibly be brought forward, if the child be confined to the society of a man, however sagacious that man may be.

Besides, in youth the seeds of every affection should be sown, and the respectful regard, which is felt for a parent, is very different from the social affections that are to constitute the happiness of life as it advances. Of these equality is the basis, and an intercourse of sentiments unclogged by that observant seriousness which prevents disputation, though it may not enforce submission. Let a child have ever such an affection for his parent, he will always languish to play and prattle with children; and the very respect he feels, for filial esteem always has a dash of fear mixed with it, will, if it do not teach him cunning, at least prevent him from pouring out the little secrets which first open the heart to friendship and confidence, gradually leading to more expansive benevolence. Added to this, he will never acquire that frank ingenuousness of behaviour, which young people can only attain by being frequently in society where they dare to speak what they think; neither afraid of being reproved for their presumption, nor laughed at for their folly.

Forcibly impressed by the reflections which the sight of schools, as they are at present conducted, naturally suggested, I have formerly delivered my opinion rather warmly in favour of a private education; but further experience has led me to view the subject in a different light. I still, however, think schools, as they are now regulated, the hotbeds of vice and folly, and the knowledge of human nature, supposed to be attained there, merely cunning selfishness.

At school boys become gluttons and slovens, and, instead of cultivating domestic affections, very early rush into the libertinism which destroys the constitution before it is formed; hardening the heart as it weakens the understanding.

I should, in fact, be averse to boarding-schools, if it were for no other reason than the unsettled state of mind which the expectation of the vacations produces. On these the children's thoughts are fixed with eager anticipating hopes, for, at least, to speak with moderation, half of the time, and when they arrive they are spent in total dissipation and beastly indulgence.

But, on the contrary, when they are brought up at home, though they may pursue a plan of study in a more orderly manner than can be adopted when near a fourth part of the year is actually spent in idleness, and as much more in regret and anticipation; yet they there acquire too high an opinion of their own importance, from birth, allowed to tyrannise over servants, and from the anxiety expressed by most mothers, on the score of manners, who, eager to teach the accomplishments of a gentleman, stifle, in their birth, the virtues of a man. Thus brought into company when they ought to be seriously employed, and treated like men when they are still boys, they become vain and effeminate.

The only way to avoid two extremes equally injurious to morality, would be to contrive some way of combining a public and private education. Thus to make men citizens two natural steps might be taken, which seem directly to lead to the desired point; for the domestic affections, that first open the heart to the various modifications of humanity, would be cultivated, whilst the children were nevertheless allowed to spend great part of their time, on terms of equality, with other children.

I still recollect, with pleasure, the country day-school: where a boy trudged in the morning, wet or dry, carrying his books, and his dinner, if it were at a considerable distance; a servant did not then lead master by the hand, for, when he had once put on coat and breeches, he was allowed to shift for himself, and return alone in the evening to recount the feats of the day close at the parental knee. His father's house was his home, and was ever after fondly remembered; nay, I appeal to many superior men, who were educated in this manner, whether the recollection of some shady lane where they conned their lesson; or, of some stile, where they sat making a kite, or mending a bat, has not endeared their country to them?

But, what boy ever recollected with pleasure the years he spent in close confinement, at an academy near London? unless, indeed, he should, by chance, remember the poor scarecrow of an usher, whom he tormented; or, the tartman, from whom he caught a cake, to devour it with a cattish appetite of selfishness. At boarding-schools of every description, the relaxation of the junior boys is mischief; and of the senior, vice. Besides, in great schools, what can be more prejudicial to the moral character than the system of tyranny and abject slavery which is established amongst the boys, to say nothing of the slavery to forms, which makes religion worse than a farce? For what good can be expected from the youth who receives the sacrament of the Lord's Supper, to avoid forfeiting half a guinea, which he probably afterwards spends in some sensual manner? Half the employment of the youths is to elude the necessity of attending public worship; and well they may, for such a constant repetition of the same thing must be a very irksome restraint on their natural vivacity. As these ceremonies have the most fatal effect on their morals, and as a ritual performed by the lips, when the heart and mind are far away, is not now stored up by our Church as a bank to draw on for the fees of the poor souls in purgatory, why should they not be abolished?

But the fear of innovation, in this country, extends to everything. This is only a covert fear, the apprehensive timidity of indolent slugs, who guard, by sliming it over, the snug place, which they consider in the light of an hereditary estate; and eat, drink, and enjoy themselves, instead of fulfilling the duties, excepting a few empty forms, for which it was endowed. These are the people who most strenuously insist on the will of the founder being observed, crying out against all reformation, as if it were a violation of justice. I am now alluding particularly to the relics of Popery retained in our colleges, when the Protestant members seem to be such sticklers for the Established Church; but their zeal never makes them lose sight of the spoil of ignorance, which rapacious priests of superstitious memory have scraped together. No, wise in their generation, they venerate the prescriptive right of possession, as a stronghold, and still let the sluggish bell tinkle to prayers, as during the days when the elevation of the host was supposed to atone for the sins of the people, lest one reformation should lead to another, and the spirit kill the letter. These Romish customs have the most baneful effect on the morals of our clergy; for the idle vermin who two or three times a day perform in the most slovenly manner a service which they think useless, but call their duty, soon lose a sense of duty. At college, forced to attend or evade public worship, they acquire an habitual contempt for the very service, the performance of which is to enable them to live in idleness. It is mumbled over as an affair of business, as a stupid boy repeats his talk, and frequently the college cant escapes from the preacher the moment after he has left the pulpit, and even whilst he is eating the dinner which he earned in such a dishonest manner.

Nothing, indeed, can be more irreverent than the cathedral service as it is now performed in this country, neither does it contain a set of weaker men than those who are the slaves of this childish routine. A disgusting skeleton of the former state is still exhibited; but all the solemnity that interested the imagination, if it did not purify the heart, is stripped off. The performance of high mass on the Continent must impress every mind, where a spark of fancy glows, with that awful melancholy, that sublime tenderness, so near akin to devotion. I do not say that these devotional feelings are of more use, in a moral sense, than any other emotion of taste; but I contend that the theatrical pomp which gratifies our senses, is to be preferred to the cold parade that insults the understanding without reaching the heart.

Amongst remarks on national education, such observations cannot be misplaced, especially as the supporters of these establishments, degenerated into puerilities, affect to be the champions of religion. Religion, pure source of comfort in this vale of tears! how has thy clear stream been muddied by the dabblers, who have presumptuously endeavoured to confine in one narrow channel, the living waters that ever flow towards God—the sublime ocean of existence! What would life be without that peace which the love of God, when built on humanity, alone can impart? Every earthly affection turns back, at intervals, to prey upon the heart that feeds it; and the purest effusions of benevolence, often rudely damped by man, must mount as a free-will offering to Him who gave them birth, whose bright image they faintly reflect.

In public schools, however, religion, confounded with irksome ceremonies and unreasonable restraints, assumes the most ungracious aspect: not the sober austere one that commands respect whilst it inspires fear; but a ludicrous cast, that serves to point a pun. For, in fact, most of the good stories and smart things which enliven the spirits that have been concentrated at whist, are manufactured out of the incidents to which the very men labour to give a droll turn who countenance the abuse to live on the spoil.

There is not, perhaps, in the kingdom, a more dogmatical, or luxurious set of men, than the pedantic tyrants who reside in colleges and preside at public schools. The vacations are equally injurious to the morals of the masters and pupils, and the intercourse, which the former keep up with the nobility, introduces the same vanity and extravagance into their families, which banish domestic duties and comforts from the lordly mansion, whose state is awkwardly aped. The boys, who live at a great expense with the masters and assistants, are never domesticated, though placed there for that purpose; for, after a silent dinner, they swallow a hasty glass of wine, and retire to plan some mischievous trick, or to ridicule the person or manners of the very people they have just been cringing to, and whom they ought to consider as the representatives of their parents.

Can it then be a matter of surprise that boys become selfish and vicious who are thus shut out from social converse? or that a mitre often graces the brow of one of these diligent pastors?

The desire of living in the same style, as the rank just above them, infects each individual and every class of people, and meanness is the concomitant of this ignoble ambition; but those professions are most debasing whose ladder is patronage; yet, out of one of these professions the tutors of youth are, in general, chosen. But, can they be expected to inspire independent sentiments, whose conduct must be regulated by the cautious prudence that is ever on the watch for preferment?

So far, however, from thinking of the morals of boys, I have heard several masters of schools argue, that they only undertook to teach Latin and Greek; and that they had fulfilled their duty, by sending some good scholars to college.

A few good scholars, I grant, may have been formed by emulation and discipline; but, to bring forward these clever boys, the health and morals of a number have been sacrificed. The sons of our gentry and wealthy commoners are mostly educated at these seminaries, and will anyone pretend to assert that the majority, making every allowance, come under the description of tolerable scholars?

It is not for the benefit of society that a few brilliant men should be brought forward at the expense of the multitude. It is true, that great men seem to start up, as great revolutions occur, at proper intervals, to restore order, and to blow aside the clouds that thicken over the face of truth; but let more reason and virtue prevail in society, and these strong winds would not be necessary. Public education, of every denomination, should be directed to form citizens; but if you wish to make good citizens, you must first exercise the affections of a son and a brother. This is the only way to expand the heart; for public affections, as well as public virtues, must ever grow out of the private character, or they are merely meteors that shoot athwart a dark sky, and disappear as they are gazed at and admired.

Few, I believe, have had much affection for mankind, who did not first love their parents, their brothers, sisters, and even the domestic brutes, whom they first played with. The exercise of youthful sympathies forms the moral temperature; and it is the recollection of these first affections and pursuits that gives life to those that are afterwards more under the direction of reason. In youth, the fondest friendships are formed, the genial juices mounting at the same time, kindly mix; or, rather the heart, tempered for the reception of friendship, is accustomed to seek for pleasure in something more noble than the churlish gratification of appetite.

In order then to inspire a love of home and domestic pleasures, children ought to be educated at home, for riotous holidays only make them fond of home for their own sakes. Yet, the vacations, which do not foster domestic affections, continually disturb the course of study, and render any plan of improvement abortive, which includes temperance; still, were they abolished, children would be entirely separated from their parents, and I question whether they would become better citizens by sacrificing the preparatory affections, by destroying the force of relationships that render the marriage state as necessary as respectable. But, if a private education produce self-importance, or insulate a man in his family, the evil is only shifted, not remedied.

This train of reasoning brings me back to a subject, on which I mean to dwell, the necessity of establishing proper day-schools.

But, these should be national establishments, for whilst schoolmasters are dependent on the caprice of parents, little exertion can be expected from them, more than is necessary to please ignorant people. Indeed, the necessity of a master's giving the parents some sample of the boy's abilities, which during the vacation is shown to every visitor,* is productive of more mischief than would at first be supposed. For it is seldom done entirely, to speak with moderation, by the child itself; thus the master countenances falsehood, or winds the poor machine up to some extraordinary exertion, that injures the wheels, and stops the progress of gradual improvement. The memory is loaded with unintelligible words, to make a show of, without the understanding's acquiring any distinct ideas: but only that education deserves emphatically to be termed cultivation of mind, which teaches young people how to begin to think. The imagination should not be allowed to debauch the understanding before it gained strength, or vanity will become the forerunner of vice: for every way of exhibiting the acquirements of a child is injurious to its moral character.

How much time is lost in teaching them to recite what they do not understand? whilst, seated on benches, all in their best array, the mammas listen with astonishment to the parrot-like prattle, uttered in solemn cadences, with all the pomp of ignorance and folly. Such exhibitions only serve to strike the spreading fibres of vanity through the whole mind; for they neither teach children to speak fluently, nor behave gracefully. So far from it, that these frivolous pursuits might comprehensively be termed the study of affectation; for we now rarely

---

*I now particularly allude to the numerous academies in and about London, and to the behaviour of the trading part of this great city.

see a simple, bashful boy, though few people of taste were ever disgusted by that awkward sheepishness so natural to the age, which schools and an early introduction into society, have changed into impudence and apish grimace.

Yet, how can these things be remedied whilst schoolmasters depend entirely on parents for a subsistence; and, when so many rival schools hang out their lures, to catch the attention of vain fathers and mothers, whose parental affection only leads them to wish that their children should outshine those of their neighbours?

Without great good luck, a sensible, conscientious man, would starve before he could raise a school, if he disdained to bubble weak parents by practising the secret tricks of the craft.

In the best regulated schools, however, where swarms are not crammed together, many bad habits must be acquired; but, at common schools, the body, heart, and understanding, are equally stunted, for parents are often only in quest of the cheapest school, and the master could not live, if he did not take a much greater number than he could manage himself; nor will the scanty pittance, allowed for each child, permit him to hire ushers sufficient to assist in the discharge of the mechanical part of the business. Besides, whatever appearance the house and garden may make, the children do not enjoy the comfort of either, for they are continually reminded by irksome restrictions that they are not at home, and the staterooms, garden, etc., must be kept in order for the recreation of the parents; who, of a Sunday, visit the school, and are impressed by the very parade that renders the situation of their children uncomfortable.

With what disgust have I heard sensible women, for girls are more restrained and cowed than boys, speak of the wearisome confinement, which they endured at school. Not allowed, perhaps, to step out of one broad walk in a superb garden, and obliged to pace with steady deportment stupidly backwards and forwards, holding up their heads and turning out their toes, with shoulders braced back, instead of bounding, as Nature directs to complete her own design, in the various attitudes so conducive to health.* The pure animal spirits, which make

---

*I remember a circumstance that once came under my own observation, and raised my indignation. I went to visit a little boy at school where young children were prepared for a large one. The master took me into the schoolroom, etc., but whilst I walked down a broad gravel walk, I could not help observing that the grass grew very luxuriantly on each side of me. I immediately asked the child some questions, and found that the poor boys were not allowed to stir off the walk, and that the master sometimes permitted sheep to be turned in to

both mind and body shoot out, and unfold the tender blossoms of hope, are turned sour, and vented in vain wishes or pert repinings, that contract the faculties and spoil the temper; else they mount to the brain, and sharpening the understanding before it gains proportionable strength, produce that pitiful cunning which disgracefully characterizes the female mind—and I fear will ever characterize it whilst women remain the slaves of power!

The little respect paid to chastity in the male world is, I am persuaded, the grand source of many of the physical and moral evils that torment mankind, as well as of the vices and follies that degrade and destroy women; yet, at school, boys infallibly lose that decent bashfulness, which might have ripened into modesty, at home.

And what nasty indecent tricks do they not also learn from each other, when a number of them pig together in the same bedchamber, not to speak of the vices, which render the body weak, whilst they effectively prevent the acquisition of any delicacy of mind. The little attention paid to the cultivation of modesty, amongst men, produces great depravity in all the relationships of society; for, not only love—love that ought to purify the heart, and first call forth all the youthful powers, to prepare the man to discharge the benevolent duties of life, is sacrificed to premature lust; but, all the social affections are deadened by the selfish gratifications, which very early pollute the mind, and dry up the generous juices of the heart. In what an unnatural manner is innocence often violated; and what serious consequences ensue to render private vices a public pest. Besides, an habit of personal order, which has more effect on the moral character, than is, in general, supposed, can only be acquired at home, where that respectable reserve is kept up which checks the familiarity that, sinking into beastliness, undermines the affection it insults.

I have already animadverted on the bad habits which females acquire when they are shut up together; and, I think, that the observation may fairly be extended to the other sex, till the natural inference is drawn which I have had in view throughout—that to improve both sexes they ought, not only in private families, but in public schools, to be educated together. If marriage be the cement of society, mankind

---

crop the untrodden grass. The tyrant of this domain used to sit by a window that overlooked the prison yard, and one nook turning from it, where the unfortunate babes could sport freely, he enclosed, and planted it with potatoes. The wife likewise was equally anxious to keep the children in order, lest they should dirty or tear their clothes.

should all be educated after the same model, or the intercourse of the sexes will never deserve the name of fellowship, nor will women ever fulfil the peculiar duties of their sex, till they become enlightened citizens, till they become free by being enabled to earn their own subsistence, independent of men; in the same manner, I mean, to prevent misconstruction, as one man is independent of another. Nay, marriage will never be held sacred till women, by being brought up with men, are prepared to be their companions rather than their mistresses; for the mean doublings of cunning will ever render them contemptible, whilst oppression renders them timid. So convinced am I of this truth, that I will venture to predict that virtue will never prevail in society till the virtues of both sexes are founded on reason; and, till the affections common to both are allowed to gain their due strength by the discharge of mutual duties.

Were boys and girls permitted to pursue the same studies together, those graceful decencies might early be inculcated which produce modesty without those sexual distinctions that taint the mind. Lessons of politeness, and that formulary of decorum, which treads on the heels of falsehood, would be rendered useless by habitual propriety of behaviour. Not indeed put on for visitors, like the courtly robe of politeness, but the sober effect of cleanliness of mind. Would not this simple elegance of sincerity be a chaste homage paid to domestic affections, far surpassing the meretricious compliments that shine with false lustre in the heartless intercourse of fashionable life? But till more understanding preponderates in society, there will ever be a want of heart and taste, and the harlot's *rouge* will supply the place of that celestial suffusion which only virtuous affections can give to the face. Gallantry, and what is called love, may subsist without simplicity of character; but the main pillars of friendship are respect and confidence—esteem is never founded on it cannot tell what!

A taste for the fine arts requires great cultivation, but not more than a taste for the virtuous affections, and both suppose that enlargement of mind which opens so many sources of mental pleasure. Why do people hurry to noisy scenes and crowded circles? I should answer, because they want activity of mind, because they have not cherished the virtues of the heart. They only therefore see and feel in the gross, and continually pine after variety, finding everything that is simple insipid.

This argument may be carried further than philosophers are aware of, for if nature destined woman, in particular, for the discharge of domestic duties, she made her susceptible of the attached affections in a great degree. Now women are notoriously fond of pleasure, and naturally must be so according to my definition, because they cannot enter into the minutiae of domestic taste, lacking judgement, the foundation of all taste; for the understanding, in spite of sensual cavillers, reserves to itself the privilege of conveying pure joy to the heart.

With what a languid yawn have I seen an admirable poem thrown down that a man of true taste returns to again and again with rapture; and whilst melody has almost suspended respiration, a lady has asked me where I bought my gown. I have seen also an eye glanced coldly over a most exquisite picture rest, sparkling with pleasure, on a caricature rudely sketched; and whilst some terrific feature in nature has spread a sublime stillness through my soul, I have been desired to observe the pretty tricks of a lap-dog that my perverse fate forced me to travel with. Is it surprising that such a tasteless being should rather caress this dog than her children? Or that she should prefer the rant of flattery to the simple accents of sincerity?

To illustrate this remark I must be allowed to observe that men of the first genius and most cultivated minds have appeared to have the highest relish for the simple beauties of nature; and they must have forcibly felt, what they have so well described, the charm which natural affections and unsophisticated feelings spread round the human character. It is this power of looking into the heart, and responsively vibrating with each emotion, that enables the poet to personify each passion, and the painter to sketch with a pencil of fire.

True taste is ever the work of the understanding employed in observing natural effects; and till women have more understanding, it is vain to expect them to possess domestic taste. Their lively senses will ever be at work to harden their hearts, and the emotions struck out of them will continue to be vivid and transitory, unless a proper education store their mind with knowledge.

It is the want of domestic taste, and not the acquirement of knowledge, that takes women out of their families, and tears the smiling babe from the breast that ought to afford it nourishment. Women have been allowed to remain in ignorance and slavish dependence many, very many, years, and still we hear of nothing but their fondness of pleasure and sway, their preference of rakes and soldiers, their childish attachment to toys, and the vanity that makes them value accomplishments more than virtues.

History brings forward a fearful catalogue of the crimes which their cunning has produced, when the weak slaves have had sufficient address to overreach their masters. In France, and in how many other countries, have men been the luxurious despots, and women the crafty ministers? Does this prove that ignorance and dependence domesticate them? Is not their folly the byword of the libertines, who relax in their society? and do not men of sense continually lament that an immoderate fondness for dress and dissipation carries the mother of a family for ever from home? Their hearts have not been debauched by knowledge, or their minds led away by scientific pursuits, yet they do not fulfil the peculiar duties which, as women, they are called upon by Nature to fulfil. On the contrary, the state of warfare which subsists between the sexes makes them employ those wiles that often frustrate the more open designs of force.

When therefore I call women slaves, I mean in a political and civil sense; for indirectly they obtain too much power, and are debased by their exertions to obtain illicit sway.

Let an enlightened nation* then try what effect reason would have to bring them back to nature, and their duty; and allowing them to share the advantages of education and government with man, see whether they will become better, as they grow wiser and become free. They cannot be injured by the experiment, for it is not in the power of man to render them more insignificant than they are at present.

To render this practicable, day-schools for particular ages should be established by Government, in which boys and girls might be educated together. The school for the younger children, from five to nine years of age, ought to be absolutely free and open to all classes.** A sufficient number of masters should also be chosen by a select committee in each parish, to whom any complaints of negligence, etc., might be made, if signed by six of the children's parents.

Ushers would then be unnecessary; for I believe experience will ever prove that this kind of subordinate authority is particularly injurious to the morals of youth. What, indeed, can tend to deprave the character more than outward submission and inward contempt? Yet how can boys be expected to treat an usher with respect, when the master seems to consider him in the light of a servant, and almost to

---

*France.

**Treating this part of the subject, I have borrowed some hints from a very sensible pamphlet, written by the late Bishop of Autun, on "Public Education." [Talleyrand]

countenance the ridicule which becomes the chief amusement of the boys during the play hours?

But nothing of this kind could occur in an elementary day-school, where boys and girls, the rich and poor, should meet together. And to prevent any of the distinctions of vanity, they should be dressed alike, and all obliged to submit to the same discipline, or leave the school. The schoolroom ought to be surrounded by a large piece of ground, in which the children might be usefully exercised, for at this age they should not be confined to any sedentary employment for more than an hour at a time. But these relaxations might all be rendered a part of elementary education, for many things improve and amuse the senses, when introduced as a kind of show, to the principles of which, dryly laid down, children would turn a deaf ear. For instance, botany, mechanics, and astronomy; reading, writing, arithmetic, natural history and some simple experiments in natural philosophy, might fill up the day; but these pursuits should never encroach on gymnastic plays in the open air. The elements of religion, history, the history of man, and politics, might also be taught by conversations in the Socratic form.

After the age of nine, girls and boys, intended for domestic employments, or mechanical trades, ought to be removed to other schools, and receive instruction in some measure appropriated to the destination of each individual, the two sexes being still together in the morning; but in the afternoon the girls should attend a school, where plain work, mantua-making, millinery, etc., would be their employment.

The young people of superior abilities, or fortune, might now be taught, in another school, the dead and living languages, the elements of science, and continue the study of history and politics, on a more extensive scale, which would not exclude polite literature.

Girls and boys still together? I hear some readers ask. Yes. And I should not fear any other consequence than that some early attachment might take place; which, whilst it had the best effect on the moral character of the young people, might not perfectly agree with the views of the parents, for it will be a long time, I fear, before the world will be so far enlightened that parents, only anxious to render their children virtuous, shall allow them to choose companions for life themselves.

Besides, this would be a sure way to promote early marriages, and from early marriages the most salutary physical and moral effects naturally flow. What a different character does a married citizen assume from the selfish coxcomb, who lives but for himself, and who is often afraid to marry lest he should not be able to live in a certain style. Great emergencies excepted, which would rarely occur in a society of which equality was the basis, a man can only be prepared to discharge the duties of public life, by the habitual practice of those inferior ones which form the man.

In this plan of education the constitution of boys would not be ruined by the early debaucheries, which now make men so selfish, or girls rendered weak and vain, by indolence, and frivolous pursuits. But, I presuppose, that such a degree of equality should be established between the sexes as would shut out gallantry and coquetry, yet allow friendship and love to temper the heart for the discharge of higher duties.

These would be schools of morality—and the happiness of man, allowed to flow from the pure springs of duty and affection, what advances might not the human mind make? Society can only be happy and free in proportion as it is virtuous; but the present distinctions, established in society, corrode all private, and blast all public virtue.

I have already inveighed against the custom of confining girls to their needle, and shutting them out from all political and civil employments; for by thus narrowing their minds they are rendered unfit to fulfil the peculiar duties which Nature has assigned them.

Only employed about the little incidents of the day, they necessarily grow up cunning. My very soul has often sickened at observing the sly tricks practised by women to gain some foolish thing on which their silly hearts were set. Not allowed to dispose of money, or call anything their own, they learn to turn the market penny; or, should a husband offend, by staying from home, or give rise to some emotions of jealousy—a new gown, or any pretty bauble, smooths Juno's angry brow.

But these *littlenesses* would not degrade their character, if women were led to respect themselves, if political and moral subjects were opened to them; and, I will venture to affirm, that this is the only way to make them properly attentive to their domestic duties. An active mind embraces the whole circle of its duties, and finds time enough for all. It is not, I assert, a bold attempt to emulate masculine virtues; it is not the enchantment of literary pursuits, or the steady investigation of scientific subjects, that leads women astray from duty. No, it is indolence and vanity—the love of pleasure and the love of sway, that will reign paramount in an empty mind. I say empty emphatically, because the education which women now receive scarcely deserves the name. For the little knowledge that they are led to acquire, during the important years of youth, is merely relative to accomplishments; and accomplishments without a bottom, for unless the understanding be cultivated, superficial and monotonous is every grace. Like the charms of a made-up face, they only strike the senses in a crowd; but at home, wanting mind, they want variety. The consequence is obvious; in gay scenes of dissipation we meet the artificial mind and face, for those who fly from solitude dread, next to solitude, the domestic circle; not having it in their power to amuse or interest, they feel their own insignificance, or find nothing to amuse or interest themselves.

Besides, what can be more indelicate than a girl's *coming out* in the fashionable world? Which, in other words, is to bring to market a marriageable miss, whose person is taken from one public place to another, richly caparisoned. Yet, mixing in the giddy circle under restraint, these butterflies long to flutter at large, for the first affection of their souls is their own persons, to which their attention has been called with the most sedulous care whilst they were preparing for the period that decides their fate for life. Instead of pursuing this idle routine, fighting for tasteless show, and heartless state, with what dignity would the youths of both sexes form attachments in the schools that I have cursorily pointed out; in which, as life advanced, dancing, music, and drawing, might be admitted as relaxations, for at these schools young people of fortune ought to remain, more or less, till they were of age. Those who were designed for particular professions might attend, three or four mornings in the week, the schools appropriated for their immediate instruction.

I only drop these observations at present, as hints; rather, indeed as an outline of the plan I mean, than a digested one; but I must add, that I highly approve of one regulation mentioned in the pamphlet* already alluded to, that of making the children and youths independent of the masters respecting punishments. They should be tried by their peers, which would be an admirable method of fixing sound principles of justice in the mind, and might have the happiest effect on the temper, which is very soured or irritated by tyranny, till it becomes peevishly cunning, or ferociously overbearing.

My imagination darts forward with benevolent fervour to greet these amiable and respectable groups, in spite of the sneering of cold

*The Bishop of Autun's.

hearts, who are at liberty to utter, with frigid self-importance, the damning epithet—romantic; the force of which I shall endeavour to blunt by repeating the words of an eloquent moralist: "I know not whether the allusions of a truly humane heart, whose zeal renders everything easy, be not preferable to that rough and repulsing reason, which always finds an indifference for the public good, the first obstacle to whatever would promote it."

I know that libertines will also exclaim, that woman would be unsexed by acquiring strength of body and mind, and that beauty, soft bewitching beauty! would no longer adorn the daughters of men. I am of a very different opinion, for I think that, on the contrary, we should then see dignified beauty and true grace; to produce which, many powerful physical and moral causes would concur. Not relaxed beauty, it is true, or the graces of helplessness; but such as appears to make us respect the human body as a majestic pile fit to receive a noble inhabitant, in the relics of antiquity.

I do not forget the popular opinion that the Grecian statues were not modelled after nature. I mean, not according to the proportions of a particular man; but that beautiful limbs and features were selected from various bodies to form an harmonious whole. This might, in some degree, be true. The fine ideal picture of an exalted imagination might be superior to the materials which the statuary found in nature, and thus it might with propriety be termed rather the model of mankind than of a man. It was not, however, the mechanical selection of limbs and features; but the ebullition of an heated fancy that burst forth, and the fine senses and enlarged understanding of the artist selected the solid matter, which he drew into this glowing focus.

I observed that it was not mechanical because a whole was produced—a model of that grand simplicity, of those concurring energies, which arrest our attention and command our reverence. For only insipid lifeless beauty is produced by a servile copy of even beautiful nature. Yet, independent of these observations, I believe that the human form must have been far more beautiful than it is at present, because extreme indolence, barbarous ligatures, and many causes, which forcibly act on it, in our luxurious state of society, did not retard its expansion, or render it deformed. Exercise and cleanliness appear to be not only the surest means of preserving health, but of promoting beauty, the physical causes only considered; yet this is not sufficient, moral ones must concur, or beauty will be merely of that rustic kind which blooms on the innocent, wholesome countenances of some country people, whose minds have not been exercised. To render the person perfect, physical and moral beauty ought to be attained at the same time; each lending and receiving force by the combination. Judgement must reside on the brow, affection and fancy beam in the eye, and humanity curve the cheek, or vain is the sparkling of the finest eye or the elegantly turned finish of the fairest features; whilst in every motion that displays the active limbs and well-knit joints, grace and modesty should appear. But this fair assemblage is not to be brought together by chance; it is the reward of exertions calculated to support each other; for judgement can only be acquired by reflection, affection by the discharge of duties, and humanity by the exercise of compassion to every living creature.

Humanity to animals should be particularly inculcated as a part of national education, for it is not at present one of our national virtues. Tenderness for their humble dumb domestics amongst the lower class, is oftener to be found in a savage than a civilized state. For civilization prevents that intercourse which creates affection in the rude hut, or mud hovel, and leads uncultivated minds who are only depraved by the refinements which prevail in the society, where they are trodden under foot by the rich, to domineer over them to revenge the insults that they are obliged to bear from their superiors.

This habitual cruelty is first taught at school, where it is one of the rare sports of the boys to torment the miserable brutes that fall in their way. The transition, as they grow up, from barbarity to brutes to domestic tyranny over wives, children, and servants, is very easy. Justice, or even benevolence, will not be a powerful spring of action unless it extend to the whole creation; nay, I believe that it may be delivered as an axiom, that those who can see pain, unmoved, will soon learn to inflict it.

The vulgar are swayed by present feelings, and the habits which they have accidentally acquired; but on partial feelings much dependence cannot be placed, though they be just; for, when they are not invigorated by reflection, custom weakens them till they are scarcely perceptible. The sympathies of our nature are strengthened by pondering cogitations, and deadened by thoughtless use. Macbeth's heart[1] smote him more for one murder, the first, than for a hundred subsequent ones, which were necessary to back it.

But, when I used the epithet vulgar, I did not mean to confine my remarks to the poor, for partial humanity, founded on present sensations, or whim, is quite as conspicuous, if not more so, amongst the rich.

The lady who sheds tears for the bird starved in a snare, and execrates the devils in the shape of men, who goad to madness the poor ox, or whip the patient ass, tottering under a burden above its strength, will nevertheless keep her coachman and horses whole hours waiting for her, when the sharp frost bites, or the rain beats against the well-closed windows which do not admit a breath of air to tell her how roughly the wind blows without. And she who takes her dogs to bed, and nurses them with a parade of sensibility, when sick, will suffer her babes to grow up crooked in a nursery. This illustration of my argument is drawn from a matter of fact. The woman whom I allude to was handsome, reckoned very handsome, by those who do not miss the mind when the face is plump and fair; but her understanding had not been led from female duties by literature, nor her innocence debauched by knowledge. No, she was quite feminine, according to the masculine acceptation of the word; and, so far from loving these spoiled brutes that filled the place which her children ought to have occupied, she only lisped out a pretty mixture of French and English nonsense, to please the men who flocked around her. The wife, mother, and human creature, were all swallowed up by the factitious character which an improper education and the selfish vanity of beauty had produced.

I do not like to make a distinction without a difference, and I own that I have been as much disgusted by the fine lady who took her lap-dog to her bosom instead of her child; as by the ferocity of a man, who, beating his horse, declared, that he knew as well when he did wrong, as a Christian.

This brood of folly shows how mistaken they are who, if they allow women to leave their harems, do not cultivate their understandings, in order to plant virtues in the hearts. For had they sense, they might acquire that domestic taste which would lead them to love with reasonable subordination their whole family, from their husband to the house dog; nor would they ever insult humanity in the person of the most menial servant by paying more attention to the comfort of a brute, than to that of a fellow-creature.

My observations on national education are obviously hints; but I principally wish to enforce the necessity of educating the sexes together, to perfect both, and of making children sleep at home that they may learn to love home; yet to make private support, instead of smothering, public affections, they should be sent to school to mix with a number of equals, for only by the jostlings of equality can we form a just opinion of ourselves.

To render mankind more virtuous, and happier of course, both sexes must act from the same principle; but how can that be expected when only one is allowed to see the reasonableness of it? To render also the social compact truly equitable, and in order to spread those enlightening principles, which alone can ameliorate the fate of man, women must be allowed to found their virtue on knowledge, which is scarcely possible unless they be educated by the same pursuits as men. For they are now made so inferior by ignorance and low desires, as not to deserve to be ranked with them; or, by the serpentine wrigglings of cunning, they mount the tree of knowledge, and only acquire sufficient to lead men astray.

It is plain from the history of all nations, that women cannot be confined to merely domestic pursuits, for they will not fulfil family duties, unless their minds take a wider range, and whilst they are kept in ignorance they become in the same proportion the slaves of pleasure as they are the slaves of man. Nor can they be shut out of great enterprises, though the narrowness of their minds often make them mar, what they are unable to comprehend.

The libertinism, and even the virtues of superior men, will always give women, of some description, great power over them; and these weak women, under the influence of childish passions and selfish vanity, will throw a false light over the objects which the very men view with their eyes, who ought to enlighten their judgement. Men of fancy, and those sanguine characters who mostly hold the helm of human affairs, in general, relax in the society of women; and surely I need not cite to the most superficial reader of history the numerous examples of vice and oppression which the private intrigues of female favourites have produced; not to dwell on the mischief that naturally arises from the blundering interposition of well-meaning folly. For in the transaction of business it is much better to have to deal with a knave than a fool, because a knave adheres to some plan; and any plan of reason may be seen through much sooner than a sudden flight of folly. The power which vile and foolish women have had over wise men, who possessed sensibility, is notorious; I shall only mention one instance.

Whoever drew a more exalted female character than Rousseau? though in the lump he constantly endeavoured to degrade the sex.

And why was he thus anxious? Truly to justify to himself the affection which weakness and virtue had made him cherish for that fool Theresa.[2] He could not raise her to the common level of her sex; and therefore he laboured to bring woman down to hers. He found her a convenient humble companion, and pride made him determine to find some superior virtues in the being whom he chose to live with; but did not her conduct during his life, and after his death, clearly show how grossly he was mistaken who called her a celestial innocent? Nay, in the bitterness of his heart, he himself laments that when his bodily infirmities made him no longer treat her like a woman, she ceased to have an affection for him. And it was very natural that she should, for having so few sentiments in common, when the sexual tie was broken, what was to hold her? To hold her affection whose sensibility was confined to one sex, nay, to one man, it requires sense to turn sensibility into the broad channel of humanity. Many women have not mind enough to have an affection for a woman, or a friendship for a man. But the sexual weakness that makes woman depend on man for a subsistence, produces a kind of cattish affection, which leads a wife to purr about her husband as she would about any man who fed and caressed her.

Men are, however, often gratified by this kind of fondness, which is confined in a beastly manner to themselves; but should they ever become more virtuous, they will wish to converse at their fireside with a friend after they cease to play with a mistress.

Besides, understanding is necessary to give variety and interest to sensual enjoyments, for low indeed in the intellectual scale is the mind that can continue to love when neither virtue nor sense give a human appearance to an animal appetite. But sense will always preponderate; and if women be not, in general, brought more on a level with men, some superior women like the Greek courtesans, will assemble the men of abilities around them, and draw from their families many citizens, who would have stayed at home had their wives had more sense, or the graces which result from the exercise of the understanding, and fancy, the legitimate parents of taste. A woman of talents, if she be not absolutely ugly, will always obtain great power—raised by the weakness of her sex; and in proportion as men acquire virtue and delicacy, by the exertion of reason, they will look for both in women, but they can only acquire them in the same way that men do.

In France or Italy, have the women confined themselves to domestic life? Though they have not hitherto had a political existence, yet have they not illicitly had great sway, corrupting themselves and the men with whose passions they played? In short, in whatever light I view the subject, reason and experience convince me that the only method of leading women to fulfil their peculiar duties is to free them from all restraint by allowing them to participate in the inherent rights of mankind.

Make them free, and they will quickly become wise and virtuous, as men become more so, for the improvement must be mutual, or the injustice which one-half of the human race are obliged to submit to retorting on their oppressors, the virtue of man will be worm-eaten by the insect whom he keeps under his feet.

Let men take their choice. Man and woman were made for each other, though not to become one being; and if they will not improve women, they will deprave them.

I speak of the improvement and emancipation of the whole sex, for I know that the behaviour of a few women, who, by accident, or following a strong bent of nature, have acquired a portion of knowledge superior to that of the rest of their sex, has often been overbearing; but there have been instances of women who, attaining knowledge, have not discarded modesty, nor have they always pedantically appeared to despise the ignorance which they laboured to disperse in their own minds. The exclamations then which any advice respecting female learning commonly produces, especially from pretty women, often arise from envy. When they chance to see that even the lustre of their eyes, and the flippant sportiveness of refined coquetry, will not always secure them attention during a whole evening, should a woman of a more cultivated understanding endeavour to give a rational turn to the conversation, the common source of consolation is that such women seldom get husbands. What arts have I not seen silly women use to interrupt by *flirtation*—a very significant word to describe such a manoeuvre—a rational conversation, which made the men forget that they were pretty women.

But, allowing what is very natural to man, that the possession of rare abilities is really calculated to excite overweening pride, disgusting in both men and women, in what a state of inferiority must the female faculties have rusted when such a small portion of knowledge as those women attained, who have sneeringly been termed learned women, could be singular?—sufficiently so to puff up the possessor, and excite envy in her contemporaries, and some of the other sex. Nay, has not a little rationality exposed many women to the severest censure? I advert to well-known facts, for I have frequently heard women ridiculed, and every little weakness exposed, only because they adopted the advice of some medical men, and deviated from the beaten track in their mode of treating their infants. I have actually heard this barbarous aversion to innovation carried still further, and a sensible woman stigmatized as an unnatural mother, who has thus been wisely solicitous to preserve the health of her children, when in the midst of her care she has lost one by some of the casualties of infancy, which no prudence can ward off. Her acquaintance have observed that this was the consequence of new-fangled notions—the new-fangled notions of ease and cleanliness. And those who pretending to experience, though they have long adhered to prejudices that have, according to the opinion of the most sagacious physicians, thinned the human race, almost rejoiced at the disaster that gave a kind of sanction to prescription.

Indeed, if it were only on this account, the national education of women is of the utmost consequence, for what a number of human sacrifices are made to that Moloch[3] prejudice! And in how many ways are children destroyed by the lasciviousness of man? The want of natural affection in many women, who are drawn from their duty by the admiration of men, and the ignorance of others, render the infancy of man a much more perilous state than that of brutes; yet men are unwilling to place women in situations proper to enable them to acquire sufficient understanding to know how even to nurse their babes.

So forcibly does this truth strike me that I would rest the whole tendency of my reasoning upon it, for whatever tends to incapacitate the maternal character, takes woman out of her sphere.

But it is vain to expect the present race of weak mothers either to take that reasonable care of a child's body, which is necessary to lay the foundation of a good constitution, supposing that it do not suffer for the sins of its fathers; or to manage its temper so judiciously that the child will not have, as it grows up, to throw off all that its mother, its first instructor, directly or indirectly taught; and unless the mind have uncommon vigour, womanish follies will stick to the character throughout life. The weakness of the mother will be visited on the children. And whilst women are educated to rely on their husbands for judgement, this must ever be the consequence, for there is no improving an understanding by halves, nor can any being act wisely from imitation, because in every circumstance of life there is a kind of individuality, which requires an exertion of judgement to modify general rules. The being who can think justly in one track will soon extend its intellectual empire; and she who has sufficient judgement to manage her children will not submit, right or wrong, to her husband, or patiently to the social laws which make a nonentity of a wife.

In public schools women, to guard against the errors of ignorance, should be taught the elements of anatomy and medicine, not only to enable them to take proper care of their own health, but to make them rational nurses of their infants, parents, and husbands; for the bills of mortality are swelled by the blunders of self-willed old women, who give nostrums of their own without knowing anything of the human frame. It is likewise proper, only in a domestic view, to make women acquainted with the anatomy of the mind, by allowing the sexes to associate together in every pursuit, and by leading them to observe the progress of human understanding in the improvement of the sciences and arts—never forgetting the science of morality, or the study of the political history of mankind.

A man has been termed a microcosm, and every family might also be called a state. States, it is true, have mostly been governed by arts that disgrace the character of man, and the want of a just constitution and equal laws have so perplexed the notions of the worldly wise, that they more than question the reasonableness of contending for the rights of humanity. Thus morality, polluted in the national reservoir, sends off streams of vice to corrupt the constituent parts of the body politic; but should more noble, or rather more just, principles regulate the laws, which ought to be the government of society, and not those who execute them, duty might become the rule of private conduct.

Besides, by the exercise of their bodies and minds women would acquire that mental activity so necessary in the maternal character, united with the fortitude that distinguishes steadiness of conduct from the obstinate perverseness of weakness. For it is dangerous to advise the indolent to be steady, because they instantly become rigorous, and to save themselves trouble punish with severity faults that the patient fortitude of reason might have prevented.

But fortitude presupposes strength of mind, and is strength of mind to be acquired by indolent acquiescence? by asking advice instead of exerting the judgement? by obeying through fear, instead of practising the forbearance which we all stand in need of ourselves? The conclusion which I wish to draw is obvious. Make women rational creatures and free citizens, and they will quickly become good wives and mothers—that is, if men do not neglect the duties of husbands and fathers.

Discussing the advantages which a public and private education combined, as I have sketched, might rationally be expected to produce, I have dwelt most on such as are particularly relative to the female world, because I think the female world oppressed; yet the gangrene, which the vices engendered by oppression have produced, is not confined to the morbid part, but pervades society at large; so that when I wish to see my sex become more like moral agents, my heart bounds with the anticipation of the general diffusion of that sublime contentment which only morality can diffuse.

# CHAPTER XIII

# SOME INSTANCES OF THE FOLLY WHICH THE IGNORANCE OF WOMEN GENERATES;

## WITH CONCLUDING REFLECTIONS ON THE MORAL IMPROVEMENT THAT A REVOLUTION IN FEMALE MANNERS MIGHT NATURALLY BE EXPECTED TO PRODUCE

There are many follies in some degree peculiar to women—sins against reason of commission as well as of omission—but all flowing from ignorance or prejudice. I shall only point out such as appear to be particularly injurious to their moral character. And in animadverting on them, I wish especially to prove that the weakness of mind and body, which men have endeavoured, impelled by various motives, to perpetuate, prevents their discharging the peculiar duty of their sex; for when weakness of body will not permit them to suckle their children, and weakness of mind makes them spoil their tempers, is woman in a natural state?

## SECTION I

One glaring instance of the weakness which proceeds from ignorance first claims attention, and calls for severe reproof.

In this metropolis a number of lurking leeches infamously gain a subsistence by practising on the credulity of women, pretending to cast nativities,[1] to use the technical phrase; and many females who, proud of their rank and fortune, look down on the vulgar with sovereign contempt, show by this credulity that the distinction is arbitrary, and that they have not sufficiently cultivated their minds to rise above vulgar prejudices. Women, because they have not been led to consider the knowledge of their duty as the one thing necessary to know, or to live in the present moment by the discharge of it, are very anxious to peep into futurity to learn what they have to expect to render life interesting, and to break the vacuum of ignorance.

I must be allowed to expostulate seriously with the ladies who follow these idle inventions; for ladies, mistresses of families, are not ashamed to drive in their own carriages to the door of the cunning man.* And if any of them should peruse this work, I entreat them to answer to their own hearts the following questions, not forgetting that they are in the presence of God:

Do you believe that there is but one God, and that He is powerful, wise, and good?

Do you believe that all things were created by Him, and that all beings are dependent on Him?

Do you rely on His wisdom, so conspicuous in His works, and in your own frame, and are you convinced that He has ordered all things which do not come under the cognisance of your senses, in the same perfect harmony, to fulfil His designs?

Do you acknowledge that the power of looking into futurity, and seeing things that are not, as if they were, is an attribute of the Creator? And should He, by an impression on the minds of His creatures, think fit to impart to them some event hid in the shades of time yet unborn, to whom would the secret be revealed by immediate inspiration? The opinion of ages will answer this question—to reverend old men, to people distinguished for eminent piety.

The oracles of old were thus delivered by priests dedicated to the service of the God who was supposed to inspire them. The glare of worldly pomp which surrounded these impostors, and the respect paid to them by artful politicians, who knew how to avail themselves of this useful engine to bend the necks of the strong under the dominion of the cunning, spread a sacred mysterious veil of sanctity over their lies and abominations. Impressed by such solemn devotional parade, a Greek or Roman lady might be excused, if she inquired of the oracle, when she was anxious to pry into futurity, or inquire about some dubious event, and her inquiries, however contrary to reason, could not be

---

*I once lived in the neighbourhood of one of these men, a *handsome* man, and saw with surprise and indignation women, whose appearance and attendance bespoke that rank in which females are supposed to receive a superior education, flock to his door.

reckoned impious. But can the professors of Christianity ward off that imputation? Can a Christian suppose that the favourites of the Most High, the highly favoured, would be obliged to lurk in disguise, and practise the most dishonest tricks to cheat silly women out of the money, which the poor cry for in vain?

Say not that such questions are an insult to common sense, for it is your own conduct, O ye foolish women! which throws an odium on your sex. And these reflections should make you shudder at your thoughtlessness and irrational devotion. For I do not suppose that all of you laid aside your religion, such as it is, when you entered those mysterious dwellings. Yet, as I have throughout supposed myself talking to ignorant women—for ignorant ye are in the most emphatical sense of the word—it would be absurd to reason with you on the egregious folly of desiring to know what the Supreme Wisdom has concealed.

Probably you would not understand me were I to attempt to show you that it would be absolutely inconsistent with the grand purpose of life, that of rendering human creatures wise and virtuous; and that, were it sanctioned by God, it would disturb the order established in creation; and if it be not sanctioned by God, do you expect to hear truth? Can events be foretold, events which have not yet assumed a body to become subject to mortal inspection, can they be foreseen by a vicious worldling, who pampers his appetites by preying on the foolish ones?

Perhaps, however, you devoutly believe in the devil, and imagine, to shift the question, that he may assist his votaries; but, if really respecting the power of such a being, an enemy to goodness and to God, can you go to church after having been under such an obligation to him?

From these delusions to those still more fashionable deceptions, practised by the whole tribe of magnetizers,[2] the transition is very natural. With respect to them, it is equally proper to ask women a few questions.

Do you know anything of the construction of the human frame? if not, it is proper that you should be told what every child ought to know, that when its admirable economy has been disturbed by intemperance or indolence, I speak not of violent disorders, but of chronical diseases, it must be brought into a healthy state again, by slow degrees, and if the functions of life have not been materially injured, regimen, another word for temperance, air, exercise, and a few medicines, prescribed by persons who have studied the human body, are the only human means, yet discovered, of recovering that inestimable blessing health, that will bear investigation.

Do you then believe that these magnetizers, who, by hocus pocus tricks, pretend to work a miracle, are delegated by God, or assisted by the solver of all these kind of difficulties—the devil?

Do they, when they put to flight, as it is said, disorders that have baffled the powers of medicine, work in conformity to the light of reason? or, do they effect these wondrous cures by supernatural aid?

By a communication, an adept may answer, with the world of spirits. A noble privilege, it must be allowed. Some of the ancients mention familiar demons, who guarded them from danger by kindly intimating, we cannot guess in what manner, when any danger was nigh; or, pointed out what they ought to undertake. Yet the men who laid claim to this privilege, out of the order of nature, insisted that it was the reward, or consequence, of superior temperance and piety. But the present workers of wonders are not raised above their fellows by temperance or sanctity. They do not cure for the love of God, but money. These are the priests of quackery, though it is true that they have not the convenient expedient of selling masses for souls in purgatory, or churches where they can display crutches and models of limbs made sound by a touch or a word.

I am not conversant with the technical terms, or initiated into the arcana, therefore I may speak improperly; but it is clear that men who will not conform to the law of reason, and earn a subsistence in an honest way, by degrees, are very fortunate in becoming acquainted with such obliging spirits. We cannot, indeed, give them credit for either great sagacity or goodness, else they would have chosen more noble instruments, when they wished to show themselves the benevolent friends of man.

It is, however, little short of blasphemy to pretend to such powers!

From the whole tenor of the dispensations of Providence, it appears evident to sober reason, that certain vices produce certain effects; and can anyone so grossly insult the wisdom of God, as to suppose that a miracle will be allowed to disturb His general laws, to restore to health the intemperate and vicious, merely to enable them to pursue the same course with impunity? Be whole, and sin no more, said Jesus. And, are greater miracles to be performed by those who do not follow His footsteps, who healed the body to reach the mind?

The mentioning of the name of Christ, after such vile impostors, may displease some of my readers—I respect their warmth; but let them not forget that the followers of these delusions bear His name, and profess to be the disciples of Him, who said, by their works we should know who were the children of God or the servants of sin. I allow that it is easier to touch the body of a saint, or to be magnetized, than to restrain our appetites or govern our passions; but health of body or mind can only be recovered by these means, or we make the Supreme Judge partial and revengeful.

Is He a man that He should change, or punish out of resentment? He—the common father, wounds but to heal says reason, and our irregularities producing certain consequences, we are forcibly shown the nature of vice: that thus learning to know good from evil, by experience, we may hate one and love the other, in proportion to the wisdom which we attain. The poison contains the antidote; and we either reform our evil habits and cease to sin against our own bodies, to use the forcible language of Scripture, or a premature death, the punishment of sin, snaps the thread of life.

Here an awful stop is put to our inquiries. But, why should I conceal my sentiments? Considering the attributes of God, I believe that whatever punishment may follow, will tend, like the anguish of disease, to show the malignity of vice, for the purpose of reformation. Positive punishment appears so contrary to the nature of God, discoverable in all His works, and in our own reason, that I could sooner believe that the Deity paid no attention to the conduct of men, than that He punished without the benevolent design of reforming.

To suppose only that an all-wise and powerful Being, as good as He is great, should create a being foreseeing, that after fifty or sixty years of feverish existence, it would be plunged into never-ending woe—is blasphemy. On what will the worm feed that is never to die? On folly, on ignorance, say ye—I should blush indignantly at drawing the natural conclusion could I insert it, and wish to withdraw myself from the wing of my God! On such a supposition, I speak with reverence, He would be a consuming fire. We would wish, though vainly, to fly from His presence when fear absorbed love, and darkness involved all His counsels!

I know that many devout people boast of submitting to the will of God blindly, as to an arbitrary sceptre or rod, on the same principle as the Indians worship the devil. In other words, like people in the common concerns of life, they do homage to power, and cringe under the foot that can crush them. Rational religion, on the contrary, is a submission to the will of a being so perfectly wise, that all he wills must be directed by the proper motive—must be reasonable.

And, if thus we respect God, can we give credit to the mysterious insinuations, which insult His laws? can we believe, though it should stare us in the face, that He would work a miracle to authorize confusion by sanctioning an error? Yet we must either allow these impious conclusions, or treat with contempt every promise to restore health to a diseased body by supernatural means, or to foretell the incidents that can only be foreseen by God.

## SECTION II

Another instance of that feminine weakness of character, often produced by a confined education, is a romantic twist of the mind, which has been very properly termed *sentimental*.

Women subjected by ignorance to their sensations, and only taught to look for happiness in love, refine on sensual feelings, and adopt metaphysical notions respecting that passion, which lead them shamefully to neglect the duties of life, and frequently in the midst of these sublime refinements they plump into actual vice.

These are the women who are amused by the reveries of the stupid novelists, who, knowing little of human nature, work up stale tales, and describe meretricious scenes, all retained in a sentimental jargon, which equally tend to corrupt the taste, and draw the heart aside from its daily duties. I do not mention the understanding, because never having been exercised, its slumbering energies rest inactive, like the lurking particles of fire which are supposed universally to pervade matter.

Females, in fact, denied all political privileges, and not allowed, as married women, excepting in criminal cases, a civil existence, have their attention naturally drawn from the interest of the whole community to that of the minute parts, though the private duty of any member of society must be very imperfectly performed when not connected with the general good. The mighty business of female life is to please, and restrained from entering into more important concerns by political and civil oppression, sentiments become events, and reflection deepens what it should, and would have effaced, if the understanding had been allowed to take a wider range.

But, confined to trifling employments, they naturally imbibe opinions which the only kind of reading calculated to interest an innocent frivolous mind inspires. Unable to grasp anything great, is it surprising that they find the reading of history a very dry task, and disquisitions addressed to the understanding intolerably tedious, and almost unintelligible? Thus are they necessarily dependent on the novelist for amusement. Yet, when I exclaim against novels, I mean when contrasted with those works which exercise the understanding and regulate the imagination. For any kind of reading, I think better than leaving a blank still blank, because the mind must receive a degree of enlargement and obtain a little strength by a slight exertion of its thinking powers; besides, even the productions that are only addressed to the imagination, raise the reader a little above the gross gratification of appetites, to which the mind has not given a shade of delicacy.

This observation is the result of experience; for I have known several notable women, and one in particular, who was a very good woman—as good as such a narrow mind would allow her to be, who took care that her daughters (three in number) should never see a novel. As she was a woman of fortune and fashion, they had various masters to attend them, and a sort of menial governess to watch their footsteps. From their masters they learned how tables, chairs, etc., were called in French and Italian; but as the few books thrown in their way were far above their capacities, or devotional, they neither acquired ideas nor sentiments, and passed their time, when not compelled to repeat *words*, in dressing, quarrelling with each other, or conversing with their maids by stealth, till they were brought into company as marriageable.

Their mother, a widow, was busy in the meantime in keeping up their connections, as she termed a numerous acquaintance, lest her girls should want a proper introduction into the great world. And these young ladies, with minds vulgar in every sense of the word, and spoiled tempers, entered life puffed up with notions of their own consequence, and looking down with contempt on those who could not vie with them in dress and parade.

With respect to love, Nature, or their Nurses, had taken care to teach them the physical meaning of the word; and, as they had few topics of conversation, and fewer refinements of sentiment, they expressed their gross wishes not in very delicate phrases, when they spoke freely, talking of matrimony.

Could these girls have been injured by the perusal of novels? I almost forgot a shade in the character of one of them; she affected a simplicity bordering on folly, and with a simper would utter the most immodest remarks and questions, the full meaning of which she had learned whilst secluded from the world, and afraid to speak in her mother's presence, who governed, with a high hand; they were all educated, as she prided herself, in a most exemplary manner, and read their chapters before breakfast, never touching a silly novel.

This is only one instance; but I recollect many other women who, not led by degrees to proper studies, and not permitted to choose for themselves, have indeed been overgrown children; or have obtained, by mixing in the world, a little of what is termed common sense; that is, a distinct manner of seeing common occurrences, as they stand detached; but what deserves the name of intellect, the power of gaining general or abstract ideas, or even intermediate ones, was out of the question. Their minds were quiescent, and when they were not roused by sensible objects and employments of that kind, they were lowspirited, would cry, or go to sleep.

When, therefore, I advise my sex not to read such flimsy works, it is to induce them to read something superior; for I coincide in opinion with a sagacious man, who, having a daughter and niece under his care, pursued a very different plan with each.

The niece, who had considerable abilities, had, before she was left to his guardianship, been indulged in desultory reading. Her he endeavoured to lead, and did lead to history and moral essays; but his daughter, whom a fond weak mother had indulged, and who consequently was averse to everything like application, he allowed to read novels; and used to justify his conduct by saying, that if she ever attained a relish for reading them, he would have some foundation to work upon; and that erroneous opinions were better than none at all.

In fact, the female mind has been so totally neglected, that knowledge was only to be acquired from this muddy source, till from reading novels some women of superior talents learned to despise them.

The best method, I believe, that can be adopted to correct a fondness for novels is to ridicule them: not indiscriminately, for then it would have little effect; but, if a judicious person, with some turn for humour, would read several to a young girl, and point out both by tones, and apt comparisons with pathetic incidents and heroic characters in history, how foolishly and ridiculously they caricatured human nature, just opinions might be substituted instead of romantic sentiments.

In one respect, however, the majority of both sexes resemble, and equally show a want of taste and modesty. Ignorant women, forced to be chaste to preserve their reputation, allow their imagination to revel in the unnatural and meretricious scenes sketched by the novel writers of the day, slighting as insipid the sober dignity, and matron graces of history,* whilst men carry the same vitiated taste into life, and fly for amusement to the wanton, from the unsophisticated charms of virtue, and the grave respectability of sense.

Besides, the reading of novels makes women, and particularly ladies of fashion, very fond of using strong expressions and superlatives in conversation; and, though the dissipated artificial life which they lead prevents their cherishing any strong legitimate passion, the language of passion in affected tones slips for ever from their glib tongues, and every trifle produces those phosphoric bursts which only mimic in the dark the flame of passion.

## SECTION III

Ignorance and the mistaken cunning that Nature sharpens in weak heads as a principle of self-preservation, render women very fond of dress, and produce all the vanity which such a fondness may naturally be expected to generate, to the exclusion of emulation and magnanimity.

I agree with Rousseau that the physical part of the art of pleasing consists in ornaments, and for that very reason I should guard girls against the contagious fondness for dress so common to weak women, that they may not rest in the physical part. Yet, weak are the women who imagine that they can long please without the aid of the mind, or, in other words, without the moral art of pleasing. But the moral art, if it be not a profanation to use the word art, when alluding to the grace which is an effect of virtue, and not the motive of action, is never to be found with ignorance; the sportiveness of innocence, so pleasing to re-

---

*I am not now alluding to that superiority of mind which leads to the creation of ideal beauty, when life, surveyed with a penetrating eye, appears a tragi-comedy, in which little can be seen to satisfy the heart without the help of fancy.

fined libertines of both sexes, is widely different in its essence from this superior gracefulness.

A strong inclination for external ornaments ever appears in barbarous states, only the men not the women adorn themselves; for where women are allowed to be so far on a level with men, society has advanced, at least, one step in civilization.

The attention to dress, therefore, which has been thought a sexual propensity, I think natural to mankind. But I ought to express myself with more precision. When the mind is not sufficiently opened to take pleasure in reflection, the body will be adorned with sedulous care; and ambition will appear in tattooing or painting it.

So far is this first inclination carried, that even the hellish yoke of slavery cannot stifle the savage desire of admiration which the black heroes inherit from both their parents, for all the hardly earned savings of a slave are commonly expended in a little tawdry finery. And I have seldom known a good male or female servant that was not particularly fond of dress. Their clothes were their riches; and, I argue from analogy, that the fondness for dress, so extravagant in females, arises from the same cause—want of cultivation of mind. When men meet they converse about business, politics, or literature; but, says Swift, "how naturally do women apply their hands to each other's lappets and ruffles."[3] And very natural is it—for they have not any business to interest them, have not a taste for literature, and they find politics dry, because they have not acquired a love for mankind by turning their thoughts to the grand pursuits that exalt the human race, and promote general happiness.

Besides, various are the paths to power and fame which by accident or choice men pursue, and though they jostle against each other, for men of the same profession are seldom friends, yet there is a much greater number of their fellow-creatures with whom they never clash. But women are very differently situated with respect to each other— for they are all rivals.

Before marriage it is their business to please men; and after, with a few exceptions, they follow the same scene with all the persevering pertinacity of instinct. Even virtuous women never forget their sex in company, for they are for ever trying to make themselves *agreeable*. A female beauty, and a male wit, appear to be equally anxious to draw the attention of the company to themselves; and the animosity of contemporary wits is proverbial.

Is it then surprising that when the sole ambition of woman centres in beauty, and interest gives vanity additional force, perpetual rivalships should ensue? They are all running the same race, and would rise above the virtue of morals, if they did not view each other with a suspicious and even envious eye.

An immoderate fondness for dress, for pleasure, and for sway, are the passions of savages; the passions that occupy those uncivilized beings who have not yet extended the dominion of the mind, or even learned to think with the energy necessary to concatenate that abstract train of thought which produces principles. And that women from their education and the present state of civilized life, are in the same condition, cannot, I think, be controverted. To laugh at them then, or satirize the follies of a being who is never to be allowed to act freely from the light of her own reason, is as absurd as cruel; for, that they who are taught blindly to obey authority, will endeavour cunningly to elude it, is most natural and certain.

Yet let it be proved that they ought to obey man implicitly, and I shall immediately agree that it is woman's duty to cultivate a fondness for dress, in order to please, and a propensity to cunning for her own preservation.

The virtues, however, which are supported by ignorance must ever be wavering—the house built on sand could not endure a storm. It is almost unnecessary to draw the inference. If women are to be made virtuous by authority, which is a contradiction in terms, let them be immured in seraglios and watched with a jealous eye. Fear not that the iron will enter into their souls—for the souls that can bear such treatment are made of yielding materials, just animated enough to give life to the body.

> Matter too soft a lasting mark to bear,
> And best distinguish'd by black, brown, or fair.[4]

The most cruel wounds will of course soon heal, and they may still people the world, and dress to please man—all the purposes which certain celebrated writers have allowed that they were created to fulfil.

## SECTION IV

Women are supposed to possess more sensibility, and even humanity, than men, and their strong attachments and instantaneous emotions of compassion are given as proofs; but the clinging affection of ignorance has seldom anything noble in it, and may mostly be resolved into self-ishness, as well as the affection of children and brutes. I have known many weak women whose sensibility was entirely engrossed by their husbands; and as for the humanity, it was very faint indeed, or rather it was only a transient emotion of compassion. Humanity does not consist "in a squeamish ear," says an eminent orator. "It belongs to the mind as well as the nerves."

But this kind of exclusive affection, though it degrades the individual, should not be brought forward as a proof of the inferiority of the sex, because it is the natural consequence of confined views; for even women of superior sense, having their attention turned to little employments, and private plans, rarely rise to heroism, unless when spurred on by love! and love, as an heroic passion, like genius, appears but once in an age. I therefore agree with the moralist who asserts, "that women have seldom so much generosity as men"; and that their narrow affections, to which justice and humanity are often sacrificed, render the sex apparently inferior, especially, as they are commonly inspired by men; but I contend that the heart would expand as the understanding gained strength, if women were not depressed from their cradles.

I know that a little sensibility, and great weakness, will produce a strong sexual attachment, and that reason must cement friendship; consequently, I allow that more friendship is to be found in the male than the female world, and that men have a higher sense of justice. The exclusive affections of women seem indeed to resemble Cato's[5] most unjust love for his country. He wished to crush Carthage, not to save Rome, but to promote his vain-glory; and, in general, it is to similar principles that humanity is sacrificed, for genuine duties support each other.

Besides, how can women be just or generous, when they are the slaves of injustice?

## SECTION V

As the rearing of children, that is, the laying a foundation of sound health both of body and mind in the rising generation, has justly been insisted on as the peculiar destination of women, the ignorance that incapacitates them must be contrary to the order of things. And I contend that their minds can take in much more, and ought to do so, or they will never become sensible mothers. Many men attend to the breeding of horses, and overlook the management of the stable, who would, strange want of sense and feeling! think themselves degraded by paying any attention to the nursery; yet, how many children are absolutely murdered by the ignorance of women! But when they escape, and are destroyed neither by unnatural negligence nor blind fondness, how few are managed properly with respect to the infant mind! So that to break the spirit, allowed to become vicious at home, a child is sent to school; and the methods taken there, which must be taken to keep a number of children in order, scatter the seeds of almost every vice in the soil thus forcibly torn up.

I have sometimes compared the struggles of these poor children, who ought never to have felt restraint, nor would, had they been always held in with an even hand, to the despairing plunges of a spirited filly, which I have seen breaking on a strand; its feet sinking deeper and deeper in the sand every time it endeavoured to throw its rider, till at last it sullenly submitted.

I have always found horses, animals I am attached to, very tractable when treated with humanity and steadiness, so that I doubt whether the violent methods taken to break them, do not essentially injure them; I am, however, certain that a child should never thus forcibly be tamed after it had injudiciously been allowed to run wild; for every violation of justice and reason, in the treatment of children, weakens their reason. And, so early do they catch a character, that the base of the moral character, experience leads me to infer, is fixed before their seventh year, the period during which women are allowed the sole management of children. Afterwards it too often happens that half the business of education is to correct, and very imperfectly is it done, if done hastily, the faults, which they would never have acquired if their mothers had had more understanding.

One striking instance of the folly of women must not be omitted. The manner in which they treat servants in the presence of children, permitting them to suppose that they ought to wait on them, and bear their humours. A child should always be made to receive assistance from a man or woman as a favour; and, as the first lesson of independence, they should practically be taught, by the example of their mother, not to require that personal attendance, which it is an insult to humanity to require, when in health; and instead of being led to assume airs of consequence, a sense of their own weakness should first make them feel the natural equality of man. Yet, how frequently have

I indignantly heard servants imperiously called to put children to bed, and sent away again and again, because master or miss hung about mamma, to stay a little longer. Thus made slavishly to attend the little idol, all those most disgusting humours were exhibited which characterize a spoiled child.

In short, speaking of the majority of mothers, they leave their children entirely to the care of servants; or, because they are their children, treat them as if they were little demigods, though I have always observed, that the women who thus idolize their children, seldom show common humanity to servants, or feel the least tenderness for any children but their own.

It is, however, these exclusive affections, and an individual manner of seeing things, produced by ignorance, which keep women for ever at a stand, with respect to improvement, and make many of them dedicate their lives to their children only to weaken their bodies and spoil their tempers, frustrating also any plan of education that a more rational father may adopt; for unless a mother concur, the father who restrains will ever be considered as a tyrant.

But, fulfilling the duties of a mother, a woman with a sound constitution, may still keep her person scrupulously neat, and assist to maintain her family, if necessary, or by reading and conversation with both sexes, indiscriminately, improve her mind. For Nature has so wisely ordered things, that did women suckle their children, they would preserve their own health, and there would be such an interval between the birth of each child, that we should seldom see a houseful of babes. And did they pursue a plan of conduct, and not waste their time in following the fashionable vagaries of dress, the management of their household and children need not shut them out from literature, or prevent their attaching themselves to a science, with that steady eye which strengthens the mind, or practising one of the fine arts that cultivate the taste.

But, visiting to display finery, card-playing, and balls, not to mention the idle bustle of morning trifling, draw women from their duty to render them insignificant, to render them pleasing, according to the present acceptation of the word, to every man, but their husband. For a round of pleasures in which the affections are not exercised, cannot be said to improve the understanding, though it be erroneously called seeing the world; yet the heart is rendered cold and averse to duty, by such a senseless intercourse, which becomes necessary from habit even when it has ceased to amuse.

But, we shall not see women affectionate till more equality be established in society, till ranks are confounded and women freed, neither shall we see that dignified domestic happiness, the simple grandeur of which cannot be relished by ignorant or vitiated minds; nor will the important task of education ever be properly begun till the person of a woman is no longer preferred to her mind. For it would be as wise to expect corn from tares, or figs from thistles, as that a foolish ignorant woman should be a good mother.

## SECTION VI

It is not necessary to inform the sagacious reader, now I enter on my concluding reflections, that the discussion of this subject merely consists in opening a few simple principles, and clearing away the rubbish which obscured them. But, as all readers are not sagacious, I must be allowed to add some explanatory remarks to bring the subject home to reason—to that sluggish reason, which supinely takes opinions on trust, and obstinately supports them to spare itself the labour of thinking.

Moralists have unanimously agreed, that unless virtue be nursed by liberty, it will never attain due strength—and what they say of man I extend to mankind, insisting that in all cases morals must be fixed on immutable principles; and, that the being cannot be termed rational or virtuous, who obeys any authority, but that of reason.

To render women truly useful members of society, I argue that they should be led, by having their understandings cultivated on a large scale, to acquire a rational affection for their country, founded on knowledge, because it is obvious that we are little interested about what we do not understand. And to render this general knowledge of due importance, I have endeavoured to show that private duties are never properly fulfilled unless the understanding enlarges the heart; and that public virtue is only an aggregate of private. But, the distinctions established in society undermine both, by beating out the solid gold of virtue, till it becomes only the tinsel-covering of vice; for whilst wealth renders a man more respectable than virtue, wealth will be sought before virtue; and, whilst women's persons are caressed, when a childish simper shows an absence of mind—the mind will lie fallow. Yet, true voluptuousness must proceed from the mind—for what can equal the sensations produced by mutual affection, supported by mutual respect? What are the cold, or feverish caresses of appetite, but sin embracing death, compared with the modest over-flowings of a pure heart and exalted imagination? Yes, let me tell the libertine of fancy when he despises understanding in woman—that the mind, which he disregards, gives life to the enthusiastic affection from which rapture, short-lived as it is, alone can blow! And, that, without virtue, a sexual attachment must expire, like a tallow candle in the socket, creating intolerable disgust. To prove this, I need only observe, that men who have wasted great part of their lives with women, and with whom they have sought for pleasure with eager thirst, entertain the meanest opinion of the sex. Virtue, true refiner of joy!—if foolish men were to fright thee from earth, in order to give loose to all their appetites without a check—some sensual weight of taste would scale the heavens to invite thee back, to give a zest to pleasure!

That women at present are by ignorance rendered foolish or vicious is, I think, not to be disputed; and, that the most salutary effects tending to improve mankind might be expected from a REVOLUTION in female manners, appears, at least, with a face of probability, to rise out of the observation. For as marriage has been termed the parent of those endearing charities which draw man from the brutal herd, the corrupting intercourse that wealth, idleness, and folly, produce between the sexes, is more universally injurious to morality than all the other vices of mankind collectively considered. To adulterous lust the most sacred duties are sacrificed, because before marriage, men, by a promiscuous intimacy with women, learned to consider love as a selfish gratification—learned to separate it not only from esteem, but from the affection merely built on habit, which mixes a little humanity with it. Justice and friendship are also set at defiance, and that purity of taste is vitiated which would naturally lead a man to relish an artless display of affection rather than affected airs. But that noble simplicity of affection, which dares to appear unadorned, has few attractions for the libertine, though it be the charm, which by cementing the matrimonial tie, secures to the pledges of a warmer passion the necessary parental attention; for children will never be properly educated till friendship subsists between parents. Virtue flies from a house divided against itself—and a whole legion of devils take up their residence there.

The affection of husbands and wives cannot be pure when they have so few sentiments in common, and when so little confidence is established at home, as must be the case when their pursuits are so different. That intimacy from which tenderness should flow, will not, cannot subsist between the vicious.

Contending, therefore, that the sexual distinction which men have so warmly insisted upon, is arbitrary, I have dwelt on an observation, that several sensible men, with whom I have conversed on the subject, allowed to be well founded; and it is simply this, that the little chastity to be found amongst men, and consequent disregard of modesty, tend to degrade both sexes; and further, that the modesty of women, characterized as such, will often be only the artful veil of wantonness instead of being the natural reflection of purity, till modesty be universally respected.

From the tyranny of man, I firmly believe, the greater number of female follies proceed; and the cunning, which I allow makes at present a part of their character, I likewise have repeatedly endeavoured to prove, is produced by oppression.

Were not dissenters, for instance, a class of people, with strict truth, characterized as cunning? And may I not lay some stress on this fact to prove, that when any power but reason curbs the free spirit of man, dissimulation is practised, and the various shifts of art are naturally called forth? Great attention to decorum, which was carried to a degree of scrupulosity, and all that puerile bustle about trifles and consequential solemnity, which Butler's caricature of a dissenter[6] brings before the imagination, shaped their persons as well as their minds in the mould of prim littleness. I speak collectively, for I know how many ornaments in human nature have been enrolled amongst sectaries; yet, I assert, that the same narrow prejudice for their sect, which women have for their families, prevailed in the dissenting part of the community, however worthy in other respects; and also that the same timid prudence, or headstrong efforts, often disgraced the exertions of both. Oppression thus formed many of the features of their character perfectly to coincidence with that of the oppressed half of mankind; for is it not notorious that dissenters were, like women, fond of deliberating together, and asking advice of each other, till by a complication of little contrivances, some little end was brought about? A similar attention to preserve their reputation was conspicuous in the dissenting and female world, and was produced by a similar cause.

Asserting the rights which women in common with men ought to contend for, I have not attempted to extenuate their faults; but to prove them to be the natural consequence of their education and station in society. If so, it is reasonable to suppose that they will change their character, and correct their vices and follies, when they are allowed to be free in a physical, moral, and civil sense.*

Let woman share the rights, and she will emulate the virtues of man; for she must grow more perfect when emancipated, or justify the authority that chains such a weak being to her duty. If the latter, it will be expedient to open a fresh trade with Russia for whips: a present which a father should always make to his son-in-law on his wedding day, that a husband may keep his whole family in order by the same means; and without any violation of justice reign, wielding this sceptre, sole master of his house, because he is the only thing in it who has reason:—the divine, indefeasible earthly sovereignty breathed into man by the Master of the universe. Allowing this position, women have not any inherent rights to claim; and, by the same rule, their duties vanish, for rights and duties are inseparable.

Be just then, O ye men of understanding; and mark not more severely what women do amiss than the vicious tricks of the horse or the ass for whom ye provide provender—and allow her the privileges of ignorance, to whom ye deny the rights of reason, or ye will be worse than Egyptian taskmasters, expecting virtue where Nature has not given understanding.

---

*I had further enlarged on the advantages which might reasonably be expected to result from an improvement in female manners, towards the general reformation of society; but it appeared to me that such reflections would more properly close the last volume.

# NOTES

## AUTHOR'S INTRODUCTION

1   *the true style of Mahometanism.* A common eighteenth-century misconception of Muslim doctrine that women have neither souls nor access to the afterlife.

2   *"Sandford and Merton."* Authored by Thomas Day (1748–1789), *The History of Sandford and Merton* was a popular and influential children's book series that provided children with lessons about morality and virtue.

## TO M. TALLEYRAND-PÉRIGORD

1   *M. Talleyrand-Périgord, Late Bishop of Autun.* Charles Maurice de Talleyrand-Périgord (1754–1838), French statesman and diplomat. He was awarded the bishopric of Autun in 1788 by King Louis XVI. In 1790 he adopted the Civil Constitution of the Clergy which reorganized the French church as a democracy, for which he was excommunicated in January 1791.

2   *pamphlet.* Talleyrand's 1791 report on French public education, *Rapport sur l'Instruction Publique, fait au nom de Comté de Constitution.*

3   *"that to see one-half of the human race excluded ... impossible to explain."* From Talleyrand's *Rapport sur l'Instruction Publique.*

4   NEW CONSTITUTION. The French constitution, ratified in 1791, limited the power of both the monarchy and the church and contained a Declaration of the Rights of Man, but did not recognize women as citizens. French women were not enfranchised until 1944.

NOTE

1    *second volume.* Wollstonecraft did not write a second volume; her next published work was *An Historical and Moral View of the Origins and Progress of the French Revolution; and the Effect It Has Produced in Europe.*

CHAPTER I: THE RIGHTS AND INVOLVED DUTIES OF MANKIND CONSIDERED

1    *"must hide its diminished head."* Milton, *Paradise Lost,* Book IV, lines 34–35: "At whose sight all the start/Hide their diminished heads...."

2    *Rousseau.* Jean-Jacques Rousseau (1712–1778), French philosopher and writer, one of whose arguments was that society and civilization are corrupting influences on mankind; the "savage" man, who existed in a state of nature before the development of civilization, was naturally a solitary creature and therefore morally purer.

3    *Fabricius.* Gains Fabricius Luscinus (third century B.C.E.), Roman general and statesman considered a model of Roman virtue. In Rousseau's *A Discourse on the Sciences and the Arts* (1750) he is used as an example of a man who remained honest in the midst of corruption.

4    *Dubois.* Cardinal Guillaume Dubois (1656–1723). French politician and churchman. Tutor of Philippe, duc d'Orléans in 1687 and later his private secretary when the duke was regent, in which position he set the foreign policy of the duke. In 1720 he was named archbishop of Cambrai, in 1722 prime minister.

5    *Dr. Price.* Richard Price (1723–1791), Welsh dissenting minister, moral philosopher, and friend of Wollstonecraft.

6    *purple.* Here meaning monarchy or aristocracy.

CHAPTER II: THE PREVAILING OPINION OF A SEXUAL CHARACTER DISCUSSED

1    *Milton describes our first frail mother.* Eve in *Paradise Lost* (1667)

2    *"Certainly," says Lord Bacon ... "ignoble creature!"* From Sir Francis Bacon's essay XVI, "Of Atheism" (1601). Bacon (1561–1626), an English philosopher, promoted man's pursuit of scientific and empirical knowledge in order to achieve mastery of the natural world.

3    *"To whom thus Eve ... her praise."* *Paradise Lost,* Book IV, lines 634–38. The emphasized words here and in subsequent citations of the poem are Wollstonecraft's.

4    *"Hast thou ... rational delight."* *Paradise Lost,* Book VIII, lines 381–91.

5    *Dr. Gregory.* John Gregory (1724–1773), author of popular eighteenth-century handbook *A Father's Legacy to His Daughters* (1774), detailing what he viewed as proper behavior for young women.

6    *Sophia.* A character in Rousseau's 1762 *Émile,* from Book V, entitled "Sophy, or Woman."

7    *Moses' poetical story.* Genesis, in which Eve is created from Adam's rib.

8    *"Yet ne'er so sure ... all we hate."* From Alexander Pope's *Moral Essays,* Epis-

tle II: Of the Character of Women, lines 51–52. Pope (1688–1744) was a highly influential English poet, satirist, literary scholar, and philosopher.

9   *out-Quixote Cervantes.* Miguel de Cervantes Saavedra (1574–1616), Spanish dramatist, poet, and novelist, whose most famous work, *The Ingenious Gentleman Don Quixote de la Mancha* (1605, 1615), satirizes chivalric romances. Its protagonist, Don Quixote, exhibits a combination of lofty ideals and an overactive imagination.

10   *Rousseau ... love St. Preux.* Rousseau's *La Nouvelle Héloïse* (1761) depicts a scene in which the protagonist ("Eloisa"), as she nears death, reveals her love for the rakish St. Preux.

11   *Swedenborg.* Emanuel Swedenborg (1688–1772), Swedish philosopher, scientist, mystic, and theologian. Wrote interpretations of the Bible that describe mystical visions of otherworldly spirits; he also believed that the marriage bond would transcend death.

12   *"If weak women ... than they."* From Matthew Prior's poem "Hans Carvel," lines 11–12. Prior was an English diplomat and poet (1664–1721).

CHAPTER III: THE SAME SUBJECT CONTINUED

1   *Dr. Priestly.* Joseph Priestly (1733–1804), English Unitarian minister and scientist, credited as the founder of modern chemistry. The work to which Wollstonecraft refers is *A Description of a Chart of Biography* (1765).

2   *bashaws.* Variant of "pasha," Turkish and North African military and civil officers.

3   *Chinese bands.* The Chinese practice of binding women's feet lasted approximately from the tenth century B.C.E. until formally outlawed in 1911.

CHAPTER IV: OBSERVATIONS ON THE STATE OF DEGRADATION TO WHICH WOMAN IS REDUCED BY VARIOUS CAUSES

1   *"Let us eat and drink, for tomorrow we die."* The Greek philosopher Epicurus (342?–270 B.C.E.) maintained that pleasure was the only good.

2   *Lord Monboddo.* James Burnett (1714–1799), Scottish anthropologist whose six-volume work, *Of the Origin and Progress of Language* (1773–1792), presented theories of evolution that anticipated those of Charles Darwin.

3   *Mrs. Barbauld.* Anna Letitia Aikin Barbauld (1743–1825), English poet and abolitionist, and close friend of Dr. and Mrs. Joseph Priestly. Wollstonecraft quotes her poem "To Mrs. P——, with Some Drawings of Birds and Insects," lines 98–99 ("Mrs. P——" is Mrs. Priestly). "To the Lady with Some Painted Flowers" comes from the same collection, *Poems* (1773).

4   *Mr. Hume's.* David Hume (1711–1776), highly influential Scottish philosopher, skeptical of metaphysical theories of being and the reliability of human knowledge. Wollstonecraft cites his 1751 text, *Enquiry Concerning the Principles of Morals.*

5   *"In beauty's empire ... not adored."* Barbauld's "Song V," lines 16–18, from *Poems.*

6   *Lord Chesterfield.* Philip Dormer Stanhope, fourth Earl of Chesterfield (1694–1773), English politician. Wollstonecraft cites his most widely known work, *Letters to His Son* (1774), a collection of almost daily correspondence begun in 1737 to his illegitimate son, Philip Stanhope. In these letters, Chesterfield offers advice about etiquette, conduct, and how to achieve success.

7   *Dr. Smith's Theory of Moral Sentiments.* Adam Smith (1723–1790), Scottish economist, philosopher, and author of *The Wealth of Nations* (1776). *The Theory of Moral Sentiments* (1759) is the source of the long citation Wollstonecraft provides on pages 53–54.

8   *"That what she wills ... on her wait."* Paradise Lost, Book VIII, lines 549–54.

9   *"Fine by defect, and amiably weak!"* A misquote of Pope's *Moral Essays,* Epistle III: Of the Character of Women, line 44, which reads, "Fine by defect, and delicately weak."

10  *Dr. Johnson.* Samuel Johnson (1709–1784), English writer, lexicographer, and critic. Published in 1755 the *Dictionary of the English Language,* the first of its kind.

11  *"He that hath wife and children ... childless men."* From Sir Francis Bacon's essay "Of Marriage and Single Life" (1601).

12  *Cowley.* Abraham Cowley (1618–1667), English metaphysical poet.

13  *Foster's Account of the Isles of the South Sea.* Johann Reinhold Forster, German explorer (1729–1798) who accompanied Captain James Cook. Wollstonecraft is most likely making reference to chapter VI of Forster's 1778 text, *Observations Made During a Voyage Round the World,* "Remarks on the Human Species in the South-Sea Isles."

14  *Magdalens.* Institutions devoted to the reformation of prostitutes.

15  *Richardson makes Clarissa tell Lovelace.* Samuel Richardson (1689–1761), English novelist. *Clarissa; or the History of a Young Lady* (1747–1748) is an epistolary novel that depicts the travails of its Clarissa Harlowe. She leaves home to escape an arranged marriage and falls into the hands of a rake, Lovelace, who tries to seduce her but eventually drugs and rapes her. He then proposes marriage and she refuses, choosing a life of solitude and subsequently dying of shame.

16  *Leibniz.* Gottfried Wilhelm Leibniz (1646–1716), German philosopher and mathematician. Wollstonecraft quotes the preface to Leibniz's *The Theodicy* (1710), concerned with the contradiction of a

world that encompasses both a morally perfect God and arbitrary acts of evil.

17    *Hymen.* Greek god of marriage, depicted as a handsome youth who bears a torch.

18    *Dr. Young.* Edward Young (1683–1765), English poet and playwright, and colleague of Samuel Richardson; his dramatic works criticize subversive thought and defend Christian doctrine.

19    *twist lappets and knot ribands.* Women's practice of modifying or braiding the trim on their hats and dresses.

20    *Ranger.* Rake in Benjamin Hoadly's 1747 play *The Suspicious Husband.* Hoadly (1706–1757) was an English physician.

21    *Knox's Essays.* Vicesimus Knox (1752–1821); Wollstonecraft refers to his *Essays, Moral and Literary* (1778). Known chiefly as an advocate of education reform, Knox was also a literary critic and supporter of the French revolution.

22    *Sappho.* Greek lyric poet (fl. c. 610–580 B.C.E.); only fragments of her poems survive. *Eloisa.* Héloïse (c. 1098–1164), figure of romantic tragedy. She fell in love with and secretly married her tutor, Peter Abelard. When their marriage was discoverd, Abélard was castrated and became a monk; she, a nun. The subsequent publication of their letters made the couple's ordeal famous. In 1817 their bodies were moved to Paris and reburied in a single grave. *Mrs. Macaulay.* Catharine Macaulay (1731–1791), English historian and social critic. Like Wollstonecraft, she denounced women's prescribed social roles and argued for co-education in her *Letters on Education with Observations on Religious and Metaphysical Subjects* (1790). *Empress of Russia.* Catherine II (1729–1796), Catherine the Great. She married Grand Duke Peter, heir to the Russian throne in 1745. In 1762, after Peter had ascended to the throne, she deposed him and became empress. During her reign (1762–1796) she greatly expanded the Russian empire and further established Russia as a world power. *Madame d'Eon.* Born Charles Geneviève Louis Auguste André Timothée d'Eon, Chevalier d'Eon (1728–1810), French secret agent. Under the pseudonym Madame Beaumont, the chevalier was sent by Louis XV as a secret agent to Russia, where he successfully negotiated a treaty with Empress Elizabeth. Wore women's clothing when he returned to London as Madame d'Eon. Claimed to be a woman. His actual sex was not discovered until his death in 1810, well after the publication of *Vindication.*

CHAPTER V: ANIMADVERSIONS OF SOME OF THE WRITERS WHO HAVE REN-
DERED WOMEN OBJECTS OF PITY, BORDERING ON CONTEMPT

1   *Sophia, says Rousseau.* See Chapter II, note 6, above.

2   *Moses' beautiful poetical cosmogony.* The description in Genesis of the creation of the universe.

3   *Circassian.* Women from Circassia, a region in Russia near the Black
Sea, were often sold into prostitution.

4   *Tully's Offices.* Marcus Tullius Cicero (106–43 B.C.E.), Roman orator and
statesman. *De officiis* is one of his treatises on ethics.

5   *shade where Sir Isaac Newton indulged contemplation.* Alludes to the popular
story of Newton's discovery of the law of gravitation, after an apple fell
from a tree and hit his head.

6   *Dryden.* John Dryden (1631–1700), English Restoration poet and playwright. Wollstonecraft quotes *The State of Innocence and Fall of Man: An
Opera Written in Heroic Verse and Dedicated to Her Royal Highness the Duchess*
(1677).

7   *Dr. Fordyce's Sermons.* James Fordyce (1720–1796), Scottish Presbyterian
minister, poet, and author of the popular and highly influential conduct
handbook *Sermons to Young Women* (1765).

8   *Hervey's Meditations.* James Hervey (1714–1758), rector of two par-
ishes in the central English county of Northamptonshire and author of
*Meditations Among the Tombs.*

9   *Seems! ... that passeth show!* From Shakespeare's *Hamlet,* act I, scene 2,
lines 76 and 85–86: "Seems, madam! nay, it is; I know not 'seems.' ... But
I have that within which passes show; These but the trappings and the
suits of woe."

10  *Cowper.* William Cowper (1731–1800), English poet whose poems fo-
cused predominantly on religious subjects; Wollstonecraft quotes from
Book V, "The Winter Morning Walk," of his long poem *The Task*
(1785).

11  *Mrs. Piozzi.* Hester Lynch Salusbury Thrale Piozzi (1741–1821), British
author and biographer of Dr. Johnson. Wollstonecraft quotes from her
"Letter to a Gentleman Newly Married."

12  *Medicean.* Refers to the ancient Greek marble statue of the goddess of
love, Aphrodite, commonly called the Venus de Medici, after its acquisition by the powerful Medici family.

13  *Baroness de Staël.* Anne-Louise-Germaine Necker (1766–1817), wife of
Baron de Staël-Holstein, the Swedish ambassador to France. French
writer who hosted a salon for the intellectuals of the period. She wrote
political tracts criticizing Napoleon's reign. Wollstonecraft quotes from
*Letters sur le caractère et les écrits d. J. J. Rousseau* (1788).

14  *Madame Genlis.* Stéphanie Félicité Du Crest de Saint-Aubin, countess of
Genlis (1746–1830), author of children's and historical literature.

15  *Mrs. Chapone's letters.* Hester Chapone (1727–1801), English essayist and member of the Bluestockings, a women's literary discussion group named after the color of one member's hosiery; *Letters on the Improvement of the Mind, Addressed to a Young Lady* (1772) urges young girls to seek education.

16  *ignis fatuus.* A misleading goal; will o' the wisp. from the Latin "foolish fire."

17  *Inkle.* Thomas Inkle, character in the story of *Inkle and Yarico.* Sailing for Barbados, Inkle, an Englishman, is attacked and wounded by Indians on an island. Yarico, a young native woman, nurses him back to health, and falls in love with him. She becomes pregnant. When a ship rescues him, he brings her along, only to sell her later into slavery. The story became popular throughout Europe in the eighteenth century, and in 1787 was adapted as a comic opera by George Colman from Sir Richard Steele's story in the *Spectator* (1711).

18  *Sidney.* Sir Philip Sidney (1554–1586), English soldier, poet, and politician. Best known for prose pastoral *The Arcadia* (c. 1580), here quoted, and the sonnet sequence *Astrophil and Stella* (1581).

19  *pantaloon's tricks.* Pantalone was a lascivious and foolish Venetian merchant in the *commedia dell'arte.*

20  *Dean Swift ... Houyhnhnm.* Jonathan Swift (1667–1745), churchman and writer. His *Gulliver's Travels* (1726) features the Houyhnhnms, a race of virtuous and highly intelligent horses who rule over the Yahoos, a brutish and degraded race of beings who closely resemble humans.

21  *Mr. Burke.* Edmund Burke (1729–1797), British statesman and philosopher; vehemently opposed to the French Revolution as stated in the text to which Wollstonecraft refers, *Reflections on the French Revolution* (1790).

22  *"Convince a man ... still."* From Samuel Butler's mock-epic poem *Hudibras,* Part III, Canto III, lines 547–48 (1663–1678), satirizing the hypocrisy of the Presbyterians.

CHAPTER VI: THE EFFECT WHICH AN EARLY ASSOCIATION OF IDEAS HAS UPON THE CHARACTER

1  *"a set of phrases learnt by rote."* From Jonathan Swift's "The Furniture of a Woman's World," line 1.

2  *"a passion for a scarlet coat."* From Swift's "The Furniture of a Woman's World," line 2.

3  *"that every woman is at heart a rake."* From Alexander Pope, *Moral Essays,* Epistle II: Of the Character of Women, line 216.

4  *"Where love is duty ... surly pride."* John Dryden, *Palamon and Arcite,* Act III, lines 231–32.

5  *Lovelace.* See Chapter IV, note 15.

CHAPTER VII: MODESTY—COMPREHENSIVELY CONSIDERED, AND NOT AS A
SEXUAL VIRTUE

1  *Gay.* John Gay (1685–1732), English poet, playwright, and satirist. Woll-
    stonecraft quotes Fable XIII, "The Tame Stag," lines 27–36, from Gay's
    last work, *Fables* (1727 and 1738).

2  *Heloisa.* See Chapter IV, note 22.

3  *Essenes.* Members of an ascetic Jewish society located in Palestine from
    200 B.C.E. until 200 C.E.

CHAPTER VIII: MORALITY UNDERMINED BY SEXUAL NOTIONS OF THE IMPOR-
TANCE OF A GOOD REPUTATION

1  *Argus.* In Greek mythology a giant with one hundred eyes set by Hera
    to guard Io, a maiden whom Zeus was pursuing. In response, Zeus sent
    Hermes to lull Argus to sleep and slay him.

2  *"that reputation ... among women."* From Jean-Jacques Rousseau's *Émile*
    (see Chapter I, note 2, and Chapter II, note 6).

3  *"That by some ... very strong presumptions."* From Smith, *Theory of Moral
    Sentiments* (see Chapter IV, note 7).

4  *Pharisees.* Separatist sect that followed strict Jewish orthodoxy; the dis-
    ciple Matthew criticizes them for refusing to believe that Jesus was the
    messiah.

5  *Lucretia.* According to Roman legend, Lucretia, or Lucrece, a virtuous
    matron, was raped by Sextus, son of the king. She begged her husband
    and father to avenge her, and then committed suicide. Her story was
    told in Medieval poems and in Shakespeare's *The Rape of Lucrece,* among
    others.

6  *Boswell's Life of Johnson.* Scottish lawyer James Boswell's famous 1791 bi-
    ography of Dr. Samuel Johnson that shows Johnson to be both brilliant
    and petty.

7  *"there is but one fault ... with impunity."* From Catharine Macaulay's *Letters
    on Education.* (See Chapter IV, note 22.)

CHAPTER IX: OF THE PERNICIOUS EFFECTS WHICH ARISE FROM THE UN-
NATURAL DISTINCTIONS ESTABLISHED IN SOCIETY

1  *faro bank.* In the game of faro, players bet on which card the dealer will
    draw; the faro bank is the money in the "pot" against which they place
    their bets.

2  *Cerberus.* The three-headed guard dog at the entrance of Hades, the
    Greek underworld, who permits none to leave. In Virgil's *Aeneid,* Ae-
    neas journeys to the underworld with the Sibyl, who throws the dog a
    drugged cake to induce sleep; thus, to "dip a sop ... to silence Cerberus"
    means to bribe or placate.

3   *The laws respecting women … a mere cipher.* According to British law, a married couple was a single unit, represented solely by the husband.
4   *Whitehall.* Site of the British government ministries in London.
5   *mantua-makers.* Dressmakers; a mantua was a loose gown.

CHAPTER X: PARENTAL AFFECTION

1   *L'amour propre. L'amour de soi même. L'amour propre* refers to self-centeredness and egoism, and *l'amour de soi-même* refers to self-esteem and self-respect.
2   *Rebekah.* In Genesis, Rebekah is the wife of Isaac and the mother of Esau and Jacob. She helps her younger and favorite son, Jacob, trick the blind Isaac in order to receive the birthright that should have been Esau's.

CHAPTER XI: DUTY TO PARENTS

1   *Mr. Locke.* John Locke (1632–1704), English empiricist philosopher who theorized that the human mind is a tabula rasa (Latin for "blank tablet"), and knowledge is acquired solely through the senses; Wollstonecraft quotes from *Some Thoughts Concerning Education* (1693).

CHAPTER XII: ON NATIONAL EDUCATION

1   *Macbeth's heart.* In Shakespeare's tragedy *Macbeth* (1606), the title character encounters three witches who predict that he will be king of Scotland, but will eventually be overthrown. Macbeth murders King Duncan and assumes the crown. To thwart the second part of the witches' prophecy, he orders the deaths of his colleagues and their families. His assassination attempt on his friend Macduff fails, however, and Macduff slays him.
2   *that fool Theresa.* Rousseau met Thérèse Levasseur, an illiterate hotel servant, in Paris in 1745. She was his lifelong mistress; together they had five children, all of whom Rousseau delivered to the foundling hospital to be reared as orphans.
3   *Moloch.* In Canaanite society, Moloch was a deity who required the sacrifice of children; the name signifies anything that necessitates horrific or excessive sacrifice.

CHAPTER XIII: SOME INSTANCES OF THE FOLLY WHICH THE IGNORANCE OF WOMEN GENERATES; WITH CONCLUDING REFLECTIONS ON THE MORAL IMPROVEMENT THAT A REVOLUTION IN FEMALE MANNERS MIGHT NATURALLY BE EXPECTED TO PRODUCE

1   *cast nativities.* Create astrological charts to forecast the future.
2   *magnetizers.* Hypnotists.

3   *"how naturally do women ... and ruffles."* From Jonathan Swift's "A Letter to a Young Lady on her Marriage" (1727).

4   *"Matter too soft ... or fair."* From Pope's *Moral Essays*, Epistle II: Of the Character of Women, lines 3–4.

5   *Cato.* Marcus Porcius Cato (234–149 B.C.E.), Roman writer and statesman who believed that the destruction of Carthage would reinforce Rome's political and cultural domination.

6   *Butler's caricature of a dissenter.* Hudibras is the eponymous protagonist of Samuel Butler's satirical poem (1663, 1664, 1678). An overweight hunchback, Hudibras is a Puritan on a quest to rid society of all forms of entertainment and amusement.

# MODERN LIBRARY IS ONLINE AT
# WWW.MODERNLIBRARY.COM

---

## MODERN LIBRARY ONLINE IS YOUR GUIDE TO CLASSIC LITERATURE ON THE WEB

## THE MODERN LIBRARY E-NEWSLETTER

Our free e-mail newsletter is sent to subscribers, and features sample chapters, interviews with and essays by our authors, upcoming books, special promotions, announcements, and news.

To subscribe to the Modern Library e-newsletter, send a blank e-mail to: sub_modernlibrary@info.randomhouse.com or visit www.modernlibrary.com

## THE MODERN LIBRARY WEBSITE

Check out the Modern Library website at www.modernlibrary.com for:

- The Modern Library e-newsletter
- A list of our current and upcoming titles and series
- Reading Group Guides and exclusive author spotlights
- Special features with information on the classics and other paperback series
- Excerpts from new releases and other titles
- A list of our e-books and information on where to buy them
- The Modern Library Editorial Board's 100 Best Novels and 100 Best Nonfiction Books of the Twentieth Century written in the English language
- News and announcements

Questions? E-mail us at modernlibrary@randomhouse.com. For questions about examination or desk copies, please visit the Random House Academic Resources site at www.randomhouse.com/academic